Praise for *The World That We Are*

"I found Andrew Furman's *The World That We Are* to be a true delight. Thoreau himself becomes totally alive on the page as a person, not an icon. I was struck time and time again by the tenderness of the portrait, the grace of the writing, and the profound impact past lives can have on present ones. A triumph of research and imagination."

—Peter Orner, author of *The Gossip Columnist's Daughter*

"This exquisite novel follows the lives of one out-of-touch, present-day professor and one ever-relevant thinker of the past (Thoreau!). What results is a generous portrait of friendship, fathership, brothership—and the wild, beautiful effort to save our closest relationships, whatever the cost."

—Leigh Newman, author of *Nobody Gets Out Alive*

"What an intelligent and innovative tribute to Thoreau, the possibilities of love, and the wonder of the natural world. I've long admired Furman's nature writing, and with his new novel, he adeptly carries the reader from vital environmental concerns (never have I cared so much about seaweed!) and into a sumptuous reimagining of American literary history. Throughout these deftly twinned tales, Furman shares inspired, honest meditation on the sometimes confounding, ultimately capacious chambers of the human heart. *The World That We Are* is a beautiful book."

—Emily Nemens, author of *The Cactus League*

"Seldom in recent years have I read a novel that brings pleasure in every sentence, every sound. *The World That We Are* does more than pay homage to Henry David Thoreau. Andrew Furman's carefully researched novel moves flawlessly from past to present, drawing from Thoreau's Journal and other sources to the fictional David Hertzog, a contemporary scholar who—like Thoreau—struggles to anchor his life in love. Hertzog, widowed, estranged from his daughter, lives alone at the outset of the novel. His morning walks through Maine woods and brisk swims across a pond are the closest he comes to joy, or what Thoreau might call gratitude for the 'peculiar intelligence' of the earth. His routines take a sharp turn when his daughter, Ellen, shows up unannounced one morning, and the stories of father and daughter, of a wife and mother lost to tragedy, unfold layer by layer, in perfect prose. *The World That We Are* is a love story with no shred of sentimentality. Thoreau's insight ('How insufficient is all wisdom without love') becomes Hertzog's insight. His life, like Thoreau's, expands from the self to include family, community, a potential lover, and the wide earth which sustains us all."

—James Janko, author of *The Wire-Walker*

"In this ambitious and brilliant literary work, Andrew Furman follows the lives of a retired scholar of Thoreau and young Thoreau himself, both stumbling to identify 'what it means to love at all.' With exquisite language, specific to the nineteenth and twenty-first centuries, *The World That We Are* brings each man to eventually discover what world he is, what love he needs, and his unique place in the cosmos. The natural world abounds, birds call needed messages, and the arc of mountains, trees and ponds enriches the landscape of this impressively researched novel."

—Kathleen Novak, author of *Come Back, I Love You [A Ghost Story]* & other literary novels

"*The World That We Are* intertwines Henry David Thoreau's formative years with the journey of a modern-day scholar navigating personal and familial challenges. Through this dual narrative, Andrew Furman explores self-discovery, community, and the bonds that define us. With prose that echoes Thoreau's reflections, the novel is a luminous meditation on the interplay between individual aspiration and communal responsibility, inviting readers to pause, notice and reconsider where we stand."

—Adrienne Brodeur, bestselling author of *Little Monsters* and *Wild Game*

"In gorgeous pitch-perfect prose, *The World That We Are* connects the existential concerns and joys of Thoreau and his time, with ours. Like twins separated by birth and a couple of centuries, Thoreau and his counterpoint David Hertzog, are both deep thinkers and sensualists, alert to every ruffled feather and fallen leaf, both finding solace from the confusion of human relations in nature and home. Cranky loners unite! Simplify! Thoreau and Hertzog have learned what to discard, and what to keep."

—JoeAnn Hart, author of *Arroyo Circle*

"With lovely and incisive prose and very human characters attuned to the nature around them, Furman's dual timelines make a compelling case that, even in this increasingly fraught and modern world, our desire to love and be loved—and the challenge of that desire—remains unchanged. Thoreau would approve."

—C.B. Bernard, author of *Small Animals Caught in Traps* and *Ordinary Bear*

"'He glimpses in them, or thinks that he glimpses, a perfect reflection of the world that Ellen sees.' So thinks Hertzog, an aging Thoreau scholar, toward the end of Andrew Furman's heartbreakingly beautiful *The World That We Are*, and it's that perfect reflection, the possibility of such, that gives the novel such power. Moving from the present to the past, from Hertzog to a young Henry David, but always deeply animated by the particularities of place, this is a novel about community, about family, and, ultimately—as is all great fiction—a novel about what it means to live a good life. There is a quiet force here, a subtle wind you don't quite feel until you realize it has blown you over."

—Mark Powell, author of *The Late Rebellion*

"Andrew Furman has written in his novel, *The World That We Are*, an extraordinary pair of journeys from two different times: Thoreau's 19th-century America, and David Herzog's 21st-century Maine. The stories are exquisitely interwoven in chapters that intelligently speak to each other while the reader listens in. The author's rich language and lavish detail of the natural world portray David and Henry simultaneously poised on the edges of the sublimely beautiful and the depths of human loss. Furman has given us a book—the most American of books I have read in a long time—that will transport the reader through this finely crafted story of hope and joy and, especially, love. The Thoreau scholarship is impeccable, the sensitivity to father/daughter interplay gorgeous, and the reader is the recipient of the gift of worlds wisely parsed and engaging. Add this book to your shelf of treasured stories to read and reread."

—Michael Strelow, author of *The Moby-Dick Blues*, *John and Julie and Robert*, and other novels

The World That We Are

Andrew Furman

Regal House Publishing

Published by
Regal House Publishing, LLC
Raleigh, NC 27605

ISBN -13 (paperback): 9781646036387
ISBN -13 (epub): 9781646036394
Library of Congress Control Number: 2024951348

Cover images and design by © studiochi.art

Printed in the United States of America

Regal House Publishing, LLC
https://regalhousepublishing.com

For my brother and sister,
Richard Furman and Dana Friedfeld

"Let the daily tide leave some deposit on these pages, as it leaves sand and shells on the shore. So much increase of terra firma. This may be a calender [sic] of the ebbs and flows of the soul; and on these sheets as a beach, the waves may cast up pearls and seaweed."

—Henry David Thoreau, from the Journal (July 6th, 1840)

"Loneliness is solitude with a problem."

—Maggie Nelson, from *Bluets* (2009)

1

November 12th, 1837
I yet lack discernment to distinguish the whole lesson of to-day; but it is not lost—it will come to me at last. My desire to know what *I have lived, that I may know* how *to live henceforth.*

David will live an extraordinary life. Precisely what form such a life will take he is as yet uncertain. He imagines that it might approximate the life of the great man, Mr. E., who held forth at his recent commencement and who challenged him forthwith to keep a journal, as he no doubt advises any number of acolytes and hangers-on.

Yet he finds himself vaguely appalled at the notion, a life resembling that of the sage, notwithstanding the shimmering brilliance of his thoughts recollected in tranquility. The padded quality of the life is what irks him, the propitious first marriage to a darling young girl of both formidable wealth and terminally ill health, affording the great man the luxury of forswearing the pulpit's gainful employment, retreating to the embrace of his orchard and study, all earthly cares now tended by his second wife and truest helpmeet. Such churlish thoughts! D. admonishes himself as he ambles across the packed snow toward the schoolhouse where he labors. His own propitious circumstances, such as they are.

He would fain make directly for the fields and woods were it not for his mother's insistence that he not shirk duty altogether, were it not for his own resolve to maintain peace in the home. A salaried teaching post, any salaried employment, a blessing these dire times. All minds on the economy. Considerable worry over the solvency of the banks, which have proliferated like a pox. *A Panic*, the headlines now read, the price of cotton plummeting on account of the glut, slave-drivers in the south and northern banks having over-speculated on their execrable business. The cold nips at his bared extremities: his prodigious nose, his ears, his handbacks. He gazes down upon the right appendage before him, framed by winter-white, continues his stride along the snow-packed walk, the other hand to-and-fro-ing to maintain his curious bipedal balance. It seems strange to him—this hand—particularly strange as feeling ebbs. So dazzlingly *specific* in form and function. The exquisitely boned and jointed finger. The calloused nail, itself, a marvel.

"Mind your step, young David!" the postman assails him, gripping him by his greatcoat shoulders to set him aright, as his fellows often do. "Lamp-posts make sorry dance partners."

He thanks Mr. Adams and continues on his way. The sturdy shell of numbness now overtakes the ache in his extremities, which makes him wonder: perhaps we ought to meet the spartan elements closer to their own terms, not unlike former inhabitants and certain Hindoos. Shed our woolen layers. Would our bodies not cultivate a fine second skin or cuticle? Thinking such thoughts, he realizes, is one of the reasons his fellows find him strange (save for the lads about, who value his formidable berrying skills summertime). Why they gossip at the bar-rooms, the post office, the dry goods store and bank over his shiftlessness. When they think or speak of him at all.

The Masonic Hall, which is to say the public school. He worries the door knob and enters the cavernous single room stealthy as a thief. His seventy wards (too many souls for a single teacher) disperse from the stove and scurry to their seats the moment they hear the complaint of the latch. He decides to ignore their mischief, as they have grown to expect after mere days of his tenure. He hears chortling from behind as he removes one of the logs from the blaze with his bare hand (it had yet to catch) and sets it back on the pile. "The cord must last us the entire day," he warns, miserable as his students at the prospect. An entire day indoors—the larger part of it, in any wise.

"Let us begin our ciphering. Master Taylor, shall you lead us?" And so the good lad shuffles from his seat in the rear (all the older children sit toward the back, the aisle separating boys from the fewer girls) to the writing slate up front. The boy leads his fellows through their factors. The class chants the 2s along with Robert at a tenor appropriate to the perfunctory nature of the task. Robert wipes the board with the damp sponge before proceeding to the 3s. In this way they learn. Not only ciphering but their grammar and history and Latin, as well—regimentation and rote learning the idee fixe. The schoolmaster, Mr. Thompson, continues to exhort him on the indispensable utility of daily canings, too, while D. continues to ignore such counsel.

The 4s. William and John and Tobias have already nested their heavy heads within the embrace of their elbows, but D. will let this pass. Who knows what coarse labors their fathers had extracted from them in the predawn hours? Poor lads. D. hears the complaint of the door latch, feels the same jolt of panic his students surely felt moments ago upon his own entry, their deviltry at the stove. The overcast outdoors splashes the intruder with indifferent light. D. recognizes him now as none other than Nehemiah Ball, town clerk, trial justice, and secretary of the school committee.

"David, a word, good sir," Mr. Ball commands, scarcely attempting to mask his opprobrium.

"Of course."

D. hears the pine beams creak beneath his feet as he makes his way up the long aisle toward the door, so rapt are his charges by this strange scene. He exits onto the landing with Mr. Ball and awaits instruction. A jay complains from the bare scaffolding of branches across the way. Mr. Ball does not hear the jay, D. discerns by his unflinching eyes, beady pupils inside rheumy whites. Such useless leaves sprouting from either side of Ball's narrow head. Astonishing. They are red, the ears, from the outdoors cold, or maybe from his irritation. Furred at the lobes. Blood pricks his fresh-shaven cheeks in curious archipelagos.

"I apprehend that you have yet to bring the class to heel," Mr. Ball says. Mr. Thompson, no doubt, has reported his recalcitrance to the secretary of the school committee.

The problem of other people!

What he would like to say is that he has no intention of bringing his students to heel, per se, but he cannot quite summon the words. Mr. Ball is a pompous ass (*I apprehend…*), yet twenty years his senior and something of a village figure, a frequent presence at the lyceum, to which D. hopes to contribute his own lectures soon. So D. remains silent—the better of our manifold inclinations—and awaits further instruction.

"You mustn't spare the rod, young man. These urchins have already gleaned the weakness of your resolve. They must tremble before you." Ball, breathing steam perfumed by his breakfast meat, glances down at his time-piece and sighs. A counterfeit, performative gesture. "Razor strop, birch cane, or ferrule. We all have our preference. Now I'll leave you to it."

D. reenters the classroom and shuts the door behind him, quiet as an apology. He knows what he must do.

"Masters Taylor, Williston, Channing, Richardson, Lowell, and Miss Bell"—he will not spare the fairer sex entirely—"to the front."

Save for spanning the ages, seven to eleven, he chooses the six lads and Caroline Bell more or less at random.

"In a line. For your deviltry at the stove. Turn about." He reaches beneath his desk for the leather strop, balances its considerable heft as he handles it now for the first time.

"But—"

"Silence!"

So he conducts his experiment, strikes the poor boys and Caroline on their buttocks through their woolen layers without heat or restraint. The children take their punishment in practiced silence, Miss Bell included. Yet not this youngest child, Michael Taylor, the chandler's son. The lad whimpers upon each blow. After the third strike, as D. pants for breath under his exertions, he looks up at the child's face and sees the tears trailing down a grimy cheek, cleansing the dusky pallor along its river-run. For whatever reason, D. cannot summon a feeling appropriate to the spectacle. What he finds most curious is the absence of any human sympathy he knows he ought to feel for the lad, snorting and snuffling through his third lash, fourth, fifth... Still, D. feels nothing. Nothing.

"Now sit," he instructs Michael and his cohorts, who stand there neither hangdog nor proud. Emptied, rather. Like D. And as he hadn't expected, this being the first time he had discharged this horrid duty deemed essential by the likes of Sirs Ball and Thompson.

He instructs the class to enjoy a moment of silent contemplation while he composes his letter of resignation. He holds the pen inside the seashell of his hand. The pen trembles. Courage, he exhorts himself. His mother, he knows, will be sorely disappointed. The salary he forfeits is outsize, truly. Five hundred dollars a year, an income exceeding that of the new assistant minister. His education at Cambridge (rather uninspiring), plus six weeks of intensive pedagogical training in Canton by the good Reverend Brownson (most profitable, by contrast) has ostensibly prepared him for just such a post. Yet it has taken him only days to discover that the responsibility is utterly beyond his capacities, the expectation that he administer daily canings notwithstanding. And so Mr. Ball has offered him a great good gift, conveying these inexorable expectations of the school committee.

"Leather," he jots with an insouciant hand, "has proven a poor conductor between souls. Unlike the electric wire, it transmits not a single spark of truth or understanding."

The cold outdoors air, mentholated by the pines, verily sweeps clean his lungs and banishes all contagion. He relishes each blessed breath afforded to him. It's something he cannot take for granted, owing to the family disease. Having written his letter of resignation, having discharged his duties this final day, he feels curiously unresigned. Energized, rather. At the beginning rather than at the end of something. A life!

He will adopt a new name. No, he reconsiders. A too-drastic measure. Poor father. He decides, instead, to reverse the order of his given names. He intones his new moniker into the cold air.

Henry.

He will convey his letter directly to Mr. Thompson at the courthouse. But not this very moment. Before taking leave of the village entirely, he glances up the way to spy a fellow citizen scurrying between the comparative warmth of shops. Fare thee well, he offers his silent, and not wholly facetious, benediction, then slips inside the copse of bare-stripped shrub oak, poplar, and alder, the alder dripping hopeful catkins. How short a distance from the school to the woods and the stubble-fields more fertile to his imagination. He ambles toward the pond along this country path in no great hurry. The cold wind crackles firesome through the dead and decaying foliage. Clothed pines gradually displace their rivals (has anyone accounted for such a dispersal of species?), affording a certain slant of light through the canopy, more cordant music through the needle-reeds, and spicier air. Chicadees in their piano-key plumage bicker amongst one another from the fruited trees, sorting out their essential business. A wood-saw calls in the distance at two distinct pitches, as wood-saws do. *Zheep-zhop... zheep-zhop... zheep-zhop.* A truer discourse he has not heard today, certainly not from the likes of Nehemiah Ball.

The frozen pond opens before him like an eyeball through the scaffolding of bare branches and pine foliage. He must crab-claw from the rise of the rocky bank to reach the surface. The slanted earth, mostly snow-bare on account of its curvature, bites his palms with its grit, but he soon reaches the edge, pulls himself erect and wipes his hands clean, summons feeling by clapping them together, making hardly a sound across the flat expanse. He finds it deliciously unnerving, the faintest impression of his hand-claps across creation. He ambles across the blank white toward the center. A softer surface of recently lain snow gives beneath his feet above the ice. He looks up at the slate-grey sky, sniffs the iron air holding the promise of new snow. No longer can he hear the bleating of wintertime birds, but he can still hear the exertions of the woodchopper. *Zheep-zhop…zheep-zhop…zheep-zhop.* The wind, too, whipping across the unimpeded air, vibrates through the curved flutes of his ears. He pivots his head atop his shoulders to effect strange music.

Looking down, he spies small tracks across the otherwise blank canvas and kneels to inspect the precise outlines. Fox! He follows the trail and marvels over its circuitousness. The creature had not simply traversed from one side of the pond to the other. Four steps northeasterly, then a three step jog northwesterly, then eight steps straight north. Had it tracked some unfortunate rabbit or squirrel to this spot? Had they conducted their timeless tête-à-tête mere hours or minutes ago? No. Because the only tracks about are the tracks of a solitary fox. What force of mind impelled the creature to scurry this way, then that? Was it a frolic or some purposeful pursuit? An airborne creature of prey or play? What does this fox know of the world that it might communicate to us were we on better terms, these faint tracks the hieroglyph of the one true mind, perhaps? It would be better to cultivate neighborly relations with these brave creatures, engage them in discourse rather than repulse them with our powder and lead and fearsome curs.

No sooner do these thoughts occur to him than he wonders with whom he might share them. His brother, John, assuredly, and perhaps the great man across the pond on Lexington Road. And perhaps, in due time, a soulmate of the fairer sex. He cannot deny deepest stirrings that seek age-old expression, albeit novel to him. He feels the juices of his organs percolate beneath his woolen layers. In deepest, coldest winter no less. A raven's hoarse call mocks him for his brute instincts from the wooded bank, an inkblot against the ruined choir of branches. It is enough for now to preserve his thoughts for later use. He makes for the rocky bank and woods, steels his mind against forgetting. Homeward. His journal.

2

David Hertzog has negotiated the problem of other people rather successfully by this time. He rises alone and early—both wife and daughter long gone, under different circumstances—increasingly restive well past the age that might reasonably be considered the meaty middle. He sniffs at the air above the quilt, redolent of carbon from the oil-heater that must have kicked in during the mud-season night, wool from the throw-rug his wife purchased years ago, the saccharine lemon of the wood cleanser or polish that Magda, his Slavic housekeeper, applies to the white pine floor, dotted with knots. A sensualist still, Hertzog.

He empties his bladder in dribs and drabs, descends the stair, savors the gurgles and groans of the joinery beneath his modest weight. A fine craftsman a lifetime ago labored over these risers, joists, and landings. He boils water in the Revere-ware saucepan and squints over the percolating oatmeal, the small kitchen sprayed with outdoors light. The sun has already vaulted over the spruce and fir, having swerved from the south, arrogant along its new springtime trajectory. He sets a second saucepan of water over a separate flame for the French press.

His eyes gradually adjust over his meal at the maple table. He eats without relish while the finches and prettier juncos with their black bibs bicker about the shrubbery outside the thin glass, more enthusiastic over their breakfast. He might have added some almonds or dried cranberries to the oatmeal while it cooked, if only to upset the gloopy texture. Oh well. He enjoys the bite of the strong coffee on his tongue, in any case, the premium grounds of Sumatran origin. Quite an indulgence for a man who remembers his mother reserving her wringed purses of tea on a saucer above the sink on their Bronx windowsill for later re-use.

Fueled for the morning, Hertzog dresses in layers for his excursion and stuffs his backpack with the few items he needs. Excepting inclement weather, he daily adheres to his essential routine. Weekend or weekday. It makes no difference, anymore. He tries not to look directly into his wood-paneled study on the way to the stairs' landing. Plenty of time later to brood over the stalled progress of his scholarly research on

Henry David Thoreau. The front door sticks so he must force it closed against the jamb to lock the deadbolt, which he needn't lock. The opioid epidemic and its related smash-and-grab burglaries, a scourge throughout the region, seems scarcely to have impacted Emmenthaler. Small birds scatter at the door's noise from their low perches in his hobblebush hedge toward more distant cover. A few disappear into the dense webbing of one of his neighbor's junipers. The Hinshaws, Stacey and Taylor, are new hires at the college, marine biologists if he recalls, an affable enough married couple about whom Hertzog has yet to form an opinion. Over half of the new hires at Emmenthaler decamp after two or three years, unable to bear the bitter cold and scant light of their long winters or the paucity of choices vis à vis ethnic cuisine, romantic partners, and other entertainments. Mustering the resources to form an opinion one way or the other about the new people from away usually proves pointless.

As he walks the few blocks toward Main, he savors the spiced breath of the woodsy outdoors, tinged with saline from the nearby sea. Come summer days on the east wind, the vegetal aroma of marine plants lolling about the water's surface, buffeting against the granite outcroppings, will sometimes outmuscle the menthol of the conifers. Hertzog's impulses usually lead him inland, toward mountain trails and ponds. Like today. But in certain moods he drives the few miles to the coast, exercises the Subaru's neglected engine to take a meal at the harbor or explore elevated vistas of the jagged coastline, gaze down at the tangled blankets of seaweeds glinting yellow, brown, purple, and green in the sun. Sometimes he'll glimpse the oily dome of a seal.

He walks the better part of the drag to reach the trailhead just beyond the town proper. Hardly a soul about so early, half the restaurants and small shops still shuttered for the off-season. A few service vehicles rumble past, issuing rich exhaust fumes that quickly dissipate. Only the year-round establishments attract his noticing. Guppy's Bar and Grill. First Bank & Trust. Mainely Coffee. Gould's Clothiers. Frank's Barbershop. Downeast Art Gallery and Supplies. The Book Nook. Napoli's Pizzeria. P. Williamson Cobbler and Luggage Repair. Rite Aid Pharmacy (formerly Rexall's Drugs, formerly James Anderson's Drugs and Sundries). Business owners broadcast signage inside their windows advertising lost pets, gas-powered machinery of estimable horse-power for sale, a fundraiser for the cancer-struck Roberson daughter (poor girl), plus competing claims by the Seaweed Council and the Rockweed Coalition. A onetime mill town (lumber and paper), Emmenthaler currently musters the funds necessary to sustain its essential services from the summer people's largesse, the nationally ranked college at a safe remove up on its hill, and their diminishing natural resources, land and sea, managed more carefully these days by the powers-that-be than in the town's heyday. It's a source of considerable controversy and tension among his neighbors, the ever evolving state and federal regulations. The seaweed harvest, of all things, now something over which to argue.

Hertzog stays out of it. He minds his business.

The gauntlet of trees either side of the street have only just started to bud out in their spring clothes. Town elders long before Hertzog's time planted these various deciduous specimens—birch and beech, maple and oak, plus a few horse chestnuts that have managed to evade blight—to upset the conifer rule that still obtains in the neighboring woods. "A good fire all this place needs," he's heard several neighbors opine over the years, alluding to tonier Mount Desert Island not too far away. The island's mid-twentieth century conflagration, devastating as it was to the landscape and the behemoth gilded age "cottages," eventually issued forth a larger proportion of deciduous trees into the new forest mix, along with new tourist dollars to glimpse the sudden fall foliage.

"Good morning, professor," Claire Libby greets him on her beat, the words punctuated by an almost imperceptible nod below her stiff hat. Claire, and half the citizenry of a certain age, still considers Hertzog among the benighted cohort "from away," this despite his thirty-odd years here.

"Good morning, officer," he replies without slowing his gait, surprised to capture the whiff of perfume—or perhaps only Claire's soap—wafting about in the atmosphere, her dirty blond hair darkened by damp from her morning shower and tucked behind her small ears. He listens to the fading *clack* of her stiff-soled shoes against the cement sidewalk. Ever "cunning," Claire Libby, the local parlance for pretty, despite her earnest efforts to disguise her loveliness. It took him only days as a newly hired professor at Emmenthaler to discover that most ladies of Maine eschewed the manifold perfumes, makeup, lotions, and emollients that the other women he'd known in more temperate American climes applied as a matter of course. Their refusal to adorn themselves fairly offended him as a younger man. Good for them, he thinks now.

❧

His right knee aches beneath the denim as he slips inside the spruce canopy and mounts the Randolph Trail up the mountain's south slope. A particularly steep incline, this first stretch, the gradient eased somewhat by risers of pine logs planted up rustic stairs, an Eagle Scout project some years back that the town troop fastidiously maintains upon every spring thaw. The knee loosens up somewhat as he navigates the upslope, enough so that Hertzog can savor the pleasant burn in his quadriceps and calves, the resinous air in his lungs, and the intermittent symphonies of forest birds, fresh arrivals from their winter digs claiming their summer turf. It would be nice to know the birds by ear, like a few summer people he's seen out and about on the trails wearing German binoculars, high socks, beige vests, and copious quantities of noxious bug repellant. Yet beyond the most obvious utterances—the doleful melody of the chickadees (or chicadees, per Thoreau), the fluted notes of the wood thrush, and the repeated refrain of the red-eyed vireo, *here I am! there you are! here I am!*—Hertzog still can't distinguish between most birdsong.

Nonetheless, it cheers him to glimpse the black cap interrupting the yellow on a Wilson's warbler flitting between the conifers ahead, offering the excuse (as if he needs one) to pause between steps and gather his wind. Usually he sees these pretty birds in the feathery willows closer to the pond. He continues on, keeping one eye on the uncertain earth at his feet, lest he twist an ankle on a piece of rock, the other eye peeled for trail markers—the blue blazes above the snow-line on the conifer trunks, the occasional cairn pointing the proper way at pivotal intersections. The five local trails that zigzag across their modest state park land are well marked, Hertzog's immediate environs hardly the "vast and grim and drear" woods that greeted Thoreau. Yet he has veered off-trail on more than one occasion, marveled at the primordial panic seizing his innards. He sometimes wonders whether sensitive amygdalae are the birthright of the Jews, genetically wary of manifold threats even at this late date, even in this place. America.

It's one of Hertzog's favorite times of year, these late mud-season weeks just after classes let out at Emmenthaler and most of the students decamp, just before the summer people descend upon them in waves determined by their weekly rental agreements. He often hikes the entire trail to the pond without seeing a single person. The path levels off after the initial incline and Hertzog follows slow switchbacks the next mile up the mountain. A few strides along this new section and he feels his heart settle more comfortably into the grotto of his chest, the building lactose subside in his hamstrings. The trail here is wider and less rocky. He can gaze up at the mixed canopy of new leaves as he ambles rather than probe the ground for rock and tree-root tripping hazards. The fewer deciduous specimens amid the conifers have partially budded out, each seeking out a glimpse of the sun, but Hertzog can still make out patches of the sky's gray screen through the canopy, the flitting of dark birds at sharp angles too high to identify by sight. He savors the vista at the crest of the hill: the ruffled sheet of the landscape, the mixed lettuce hues, and the distant sea. But only for a few moments. He prefers the up-close earth, not unlike the famous transcendentalist of his scholarly study.

The downhill jog to the pond offers a distinct and unpleasant challenge to his joints and muscles. He must mind the trail more carefully once again to keep himself from tripping and tumbling. This happened to him once last season. He had scratched up his arm against the unforgiving branches of a juniper shrub, scuffed the heel of his palm raw and nearly broken his wrist. The trail was overrun with people foraging for blueberries as it was July. High-season. The stumble must have looked even worse than it was, or maybe he looked even older than his years, because it was all he could do to keep a growing cohort of well-intentioned tourists from plying him with medical attention, bottles of water and, worse, their overblown sympathy. A self-identified Boy Scout from Kentucky rushed over ahead of his parents and seemed disappointed that there wasn't an open wound to which he might apply pressure, a compound fracture he might stabilize with spruce branches.

The pond opens darkly beyond the prison-bar trunks of the spruce and fir, these second-growth specimens having long ago shed the brittle-brush foliage of their lower branches. He still comes here after all these years, despite all that happened. *Because* of all that happened here, rather. It takes only moments for Hertzog to reach the convenient granite ledge of the southern shore. The glacial pond is named for its eighteenth-century surveyor, one M. L. Keith, but locals call it the Bowl, a name he prefers for its simple descriptiveness, the roundish body of water surrounded all sides by rocky lips of the conifer forest, fewer birches and aspen, maple and oak. How did Thoreau describe the waters of his pond?

The expressed juice of the hills and trees whose leaves are annually steeped in it.

He sheds his outer layers quickly, as if pulling off a bandage, crouches in his swim shorts to stuff his clothes into his knapsack and retrieve his goggles, strides the few steps across the sun-warmed ledge and squints against the brighter light of the sudden sky. The overcast morning has given way to the sun and a few cottony clouds tracking west at considerable speed off the coast, tattering the pond with their shadows. He seats himself at the ledge and throws his legs into the cold water, exhales sharply to stiffen his resolve. At least he needn't worry about leeches quite yet. The spindly hairs about his knees above the waterline prick straight and alert, reminding him unflatteringly of the kosher chickens his mother plucked clean before roasting. He can feel the jagged rocks against the muddy bottom but takes care not to place too much weight against his feet, having once sliced his sole. Instead of standing on the bottom, he ungracefully plops his torso into the drink without quite wetting his head, affects a few awkward breaststroke arms to get himself into deeper water, keeping his head above the cold for the moment. A woodpecker giggles from the east bank. The bottom drops off precipitously to a surprising depth he'd rather not contemplate, deep enough that he can drop his head and segue to his more practiced freestyle after only a few yards. The cold water bites his flesh—his ears, especially. It's icy enough that it's not quite a matter of getting used to it. He must force his mind, instead, to ignore the cold, concentrate on his catch, pull, and recovery. He can do this.

It's not the loveliest of strokes, he knows. Stiff. He ought to bend his elbows more. His kick is practically nonexistent. But what Hertzog lacks in form he makes up for in fitness. Even at his advanced age, he clings to a certain vanity over his body, his discernible biceps and pectorals, obliques and abdominals, notwithstanding creeping variables that ought to have inured him to such foolishness: sagging skin over said musculature, thinning pate (once coarsely furred), heavy cheeks spackled with liver-spots, fleshy purses over the corner of his eyelids, nearly obscuring his vision. Yet he persists with these strange, onomastic ablutions to enjoy the work of his near-naked body, which hasn't gone utterly to shit.

Plus, there are those other reasons he swims here still.

He plies the dark water at a constant rhythm, turning to breathe every third stroke, hearing only the quickening of his blood and breath, glimpsing the rock and evergreen shore either side—the pink granite ledges now to his left, where, judging from the detritus they leave behind, teenagers still drink and screw and smoke and leap into the water below. He feels the syrupy water resist and bend to his palm, his forearms, his feet, and feels the thinner air above the water's skin. He can see his hands in the tannic pond upon the catch of each stroke. Once the summer comes on, the water will turn green with sudden plant life, so drenched in algae that he won't be able to see his hands before him. Parties of frogs, tadpoles, turtles, and wading birds will share the pond with him, along with the leeches that tend not to adhere as long as he keeps moving. In only a few weeks, state park lifeguards will man the tower at the manufactured beach at the western shore, the official swimming area at the diagonal toward which he now swims.

Every few strokes, Hertzog lurches his chin above the water and glimpses his trajectory before him to maintain his line. It's less than a thousand yards or so across, an easy swim still for Hertzog at his plodding pace. He need not even rest on his back mid-swim most days. But a twinge now in his right hamstring fires a visceral alarm—those trusty amygdalae!—forces an instinctive roll onto his back to alleviate the strain. He squints against the overhead sun and sucks in a deep draught of air to increase his buoyancy, arms sideward, palms up at the surface like some ludicrous freshwater Christ. He feels the tension abate in his hamstring, the slower rhythm of his breath and blood in his throat. He turns back onto his belly and continues his stroke, favoring his gimpy leg. Before long, he arrives at the beach.

He crawls up on the coarse sand like some instantaneously evolving creature and considers his options. Probably safer for him to walk barefoot along the pond trail quarter-way around the edge back to his starting point at the south end, back to his towel and dry clothes. But hell if he'll be caught by hikers, a sixty-year-old man in swim trunks, bare feet, and goggles limping around the trail like some ignoramus. It's too cold to lie about for long on the pebbly sand mulling over his poor options, so after gathering his breath he launches himself right back into the water for the slow swim back. He'll remain close to the near shore even though it'll extend the yardage, somewhat. Worst case he can flail shoreward on his back and walk the rest of the way.

Thankfully, his hamstring loosens, rather than stiffens, as he plies the tea-stained water with new strokes. He manages to enjoy the exercise, its completion near at hand. Then, upon one of his sightings for shore mid-stroke, Hertzog glimpses the bearded ranger standing on the granite ledge waiting for him. It's rare to see a ranger all the way up at the Bowl so early. He groans bubbles beneath the surface on his next stroke and swallows a peaty gulp of pond water, manages to clear his lungs with a cough above the skin of the surface rather than interrupt his next stroke. After another hundred yards or so, he reaches the sun-warmed ledge and pulls himself out, props his goggles on his forehead. Justin Shetterly, the ranger, backs up a few steps to offer him some space. Hertzog appreciates the gesture, which clarifies certain things, emboldens him despite his near-nakedness. He waits for his former student to initiate their conversation while he bends to retrieve his towel from his backpack.

"Looking good, professor."

"Justin." He wraps the towel about his shoulders and wonders at that ridiculous beard, which the young ranger didn't—or perhaps couldn't—cultivate some eight years ago in class. The copious russet-tinged thicket droops from his chin and creeps all the way up toward his eyeballs. Hertzog wonders if it's something sexual with these young men and their women. Or was it a gay thing? No, he dismisses the thought. Not exclusively a gay thing at any rate. Half the twenty and thirty-something men Downeast would have to be homosexual for this to be true. Thoreau, Hertzog knows, maintained a curious neck-beard to alleviate symptoms of tuberculosis, a ghastly beard even by nineteenth-century standards. *Henry's neck-beard most assuredly deflects all amorous advances to preserve the man's virtue in perpetuity,* the younger Louisa May Alcott, and Thoreau's onetime admiring student, sized up her neighbor's hirsuteness.

He knows that Justin was only breaking the ice with that "looking good" business, so the ranger's next words don't surprise him.

"I know I don't I have to tell you, professor, of all people, that it's against ordinance to swim open-water across the Bowl, that it's dangerous."

"No, Justin." He wraps the towel around his back, wipes it dry. "You're right. You don't have to tell me...of all people."

Hertzog looks straight into Justin's pale eyes until the young ranger averts them, kicks at a nonexistent stone on the ledge with his outsize ranger boots. Everyone knows, Hertzog marvels. Even the young people know, which astonishes him. A woodpecker, perhaps the same woodpecker as before, giggles from the wooded hillside not too far off, joined this time by the laughter of a second bird, a mate or rival. Hertzog fumbles through his backpack for his clothes, the towel still draped over his shoulders for warmth. Out the corner of his eye, he detects the slow bobbing of Justin's beard, measuring the weight of the encounter.

"I won't be the one to cite you, professor. I suppose you know that."

"Appreciate it, Justin."

"But I'd sure enough like to convince you this season to 'least trail a safety buoy."

"I'll think about it, son."

"Oh. Good." The higher notes of Justin's words betray his pleasant surprise. Manipulative on Hertzog's part, the *son* bit, yet not without some sincerity. He always liked Justin. He wasn't the brightest student. But unlike most of Emmenthaler's entitled wards, he read and responded to the material with great earnestness and never hassled him over his grades, and he was a true Mainer (from Bangor, if Hertzog recalls). Why else had he continued as a ranger long after most young recruits figured out that the job pretty much sucked, cleaning up the compost bathrooms and policing yahoo tourists for twelve bucks an hour plus negligible state benefits? A Downeaster for life, his former student.

"I'd like to change now, Justin, if you don't mind."

"Ayuh. Sure professor. Great"—Hertzog watches as the ranger retreats along the shoreside path, calls over his shoulder—"So you'll think on that safety buoy!"

After a last long look at the Bowl, Hertzog walks the Randolph Trail back toward town. He walks at a deliberate unrushed pace, vaguely aware of birdsong, trail, tree, sky, but more fully inhabiting his breath, which is a good feeling to feel. How to describe the chemical calm? It's something about swimming, specifically, that launches him into this space. The liquid immersion radiates placid good feeling about Hertzog's person. He feels like a different animal. Endorphins, he supposes, trigger these mysterious pleasure-centers in his brain. No other form of exercise, no other activity save for sex—as he distantly remembers—moves him in quite this way.

Nothing can touch him now. Until something does pierce his reverie halfway down the series of switchbacks. A voice. The particular voice halts him in his tracks amid other stranger voices. The diphthongs and monophthongs drift across the woodsy breeze. From the Spring Trail, likely. The two trails, Spring and Randolph, veer fairly close to each another somewhere around here. The strange voices edge even closer. He doesn't hear the familiar voice, anymore. Perhaps he had conjured it, the words shared with Justin at the pond stoking his darkest memories, and his imagination. Hertzog gazes up the wooded slope above the sweetfern, blueberry, and bunchberry groundcover toward the sounds, palms the smooth bark of a birch just off the trail for ballast. He can make out distinct syllables now, if not whole words. But he can't quite glimpse the party, can't see much at all through the riot of conifer needles and branches, the sweetfern with its scalloped leaves, the taller sheep laurel, and other understory shrubs. He listens so carefully for the voice that he can hear his own breath in his throat, the beating of his heart. Then—yes!—he hears it once again, the precise pitch and cadence seizing his innards. Those sharpened amygdalae. And now Hertzog glimpses dark shapes through the conifer foliage, higher up the slope—three or four figures—but they disappear against the green as quickly as they emerge. The voices fade. He considers shouting out. *Ellen!* He considers blazing a trail across the understory shrubs and the crunchy carcasses of pine cones and giving chase like a madman. *Ellen!* Then reconsiders. Could it be her? Here? Now? No. Impossible.

3

March 14th, 1838

Let ours be like the meeting of two planets, not hastening to confound their jarring spheres, but drawn together by the influence of a subtile attraction, soon to roll diverse in their respective orbits, from this their perigee, or point of nearest approach.

H. savors the minutes and hours and days returned to him since resigning his teaching post. To maintain peace in the home, he has given over several hours weekly to labor at his father's pencil factory, which is to say the two backyard sheds. Otherwise, he has filled his days with business his betters would deem mere idleness. He saunters about the stubble-fields, woodlots, frozen marshes and ponds, often in the company of his brother, John, or Mr. E., collecting Indian arrowheads and other relics. He meets with the great man certain evenings, as well, for what Mr. E. has taken to calling their "teachers' meetings." H. hopes to deliver a lecture at the lyceum presently touching on the themes of friendship and society. How to maintain the integrity of his individual genius, yet puncture his aloneness?

Writing and reading take up the lion's share of his daylight hours. Goethe has much to teach—his exact and unadorned description of objects and natural phenomena precisely as he sees them. The thing in itself! H.'s own fledgling efforts to express himself in poetry and prose seem impossibly bloated by comparison. He would fain build a garret against the world to sanctify his reading and writing hours. Meanwhile, not a few noblest boys of New England find themselves consigned to actual garrets in the sun-scorched wilds of Georgia and Florida, driving the poor Seminoles to the swampiest redoubts. While H. saunters about and contemplates the manifold impressions of snowfall upon individual trees, the sombre Nobscot fog, the brave notes of year-round birds, the impetuousness of wood ducks in the pond.

Today, he saunters toward Mr. E.'s grand white house so that they might share their well-trod amble. Upon his approach, he spies his mentor outdoors in the orchard, his sleeves rolled, worrying the earth about one of his young peach trees with a shovel. The sweet, strong aroma of animal manure spices the air. H. loves to see the great man so employed, physical labor outdoors the better of our manifold inclinations, as the sage himself has exhorted in a recent address. Mr. E. has taken to calling his home "The Bush," he has planted so many fruiting trees, shrubs, and vines since purchasing the house and its sprawling environs. Even so, it is yet to be determined whether he will prove a capable husbandman. He wears a pair of black leather shoes too dear for the task, better suited for his lectures.

"It looks like you're preparing for a fine harvest," H. utters by way of greeting, which provokes the great man to rise from his labors, the inside of his elbow balancing his weight against the shovel handle, his hand opposite braced at his waist. Was there ever so manly a posture?

"Mr. Wilder of Bolton recommends a greater proportion of lime and ash with the hog manure." Mr. E. launches into pedagogical matters straight away.

"The Irish farmers," H. replies, "favor ample parings of horn and bones from their oxen."

"The Irish," the sage utters neutrally, leaving it to H. to infer the mild insult. However ramshackle their dwellings rising from the pond outside town, these poor railroad workers, it seems to him, have much to teach regarding the practical arts.

H., spitting into his palms, asks his friend whether he might help him with his trench, but the great man demurs.

"I'm nearly done," he says. "Shall we walk?"

"We shall."

"Let me tell Liddie."

Liddie. Lydia her given name, changed to Lidian upon her betrothal to affect finer poetry with her new surname. The utterance of her nickname pricks H.'s insides. Will H. ever enjoy such intimate relations?

H. wonders whether Mr. E. will take advantage of the occasion to exchange his shoes for his stiffer-soled boots of a coarser grain, yet he returns in an instant clad in the same shoes. He considers warning the great man of the wet trail, then reconsiders. They forge a path behind the house on the still winter-burnt grass between the orchard trees—mostly apple, but also peach and plum and berberry and cherry and currant—head down the slope toward Mill Brook and the woods. The unfrozen ground brook-side, as H. feared, is sopped with snowmelt. They must carry on for a quarter-mile or so before the wooden footbridge. They walk single-file, seeking out the untrod earth atop joe-pye weed with its leaf whorls up and down each stem and jewelweed just starting to advertise its blood-orange trumpet blooms beside the trail proper to keep the muck from swallowing them whole. The thawed earth emits a fecal and mushroomy stench H. savors. He listens for frogs and birds, but all he can hear are the distant strokes of a wood-chopper, the great man's labored breath, and the mild brook beside them, licking its ancient pebbles new. The fluted song of the thrush and the chippier notes of smaller yellowthroats with their black-mask and other warblers will soon fill the air, but their fair-weathered birds have yet to arrive. H. slows his pace in deference to his elder.

"I daresay I've worn the wrong shoes for the occasion," Mr. E. says.

"I feared the path would be wet. I might have warned you."

"Oh, we wouldn't want to deprive our dear Liddie of something to chafe against in her husband."

H. laughs to convey his agreement, appreciates the intimacy implied by the "*our* Liddie." He asks the great man after his thoughts over the past few days since they've enjoyed each other's company.

"I've been looking in greater earnestness toward the ancients, convinced evermore by their example that the Whole is in every man, in every age. Don't you agree, H.?"

"I do. And in woman too, yes?"

"Oh yes. Woman too." The sage clears his throat. H. awaits his next words, but they don't come right away. The wood-chopper's notes have also faded. They reach the footbridge and cross into more open land rising from the brook, the rolling stubble-fields of Stratton Farm. They walk side by side now.

"Lucy boasted over the warmth of your sentiments expressed in a recent letter."

"Oh?" H. feels the blood rise to his face. For whatever reason, he didn't anticipate that Lucy would share the contents of his letter with her sister, Lidian.

"Are you sure you are not merely practicing lovemaking on her? She's nearly twenty years your senior."

"They were true sentiments. But I might not have paid close enough attention to how they would be received. Perhaps I have been cruel."

"Oh, Lucy admires your youthful enthusiasms. She's well past the age of pining. Never fear."

He might have more tenderly regarded dear Lucy's emotions. He scans the hillside of mixed woods, can see the earth beneath the mostly winter-bare scaffolding of branches, the tender buds of sumach and maple and grape just beginning to assert themselves. He scans the vista for his fox. He regards the creature in the singular, as if it were the same one he spies traces of hither and thither.

"Are you keeping to your reading and writing?" Mr. E. jolts him from his reverie.

"Oh yes. When I'm not working on Father's pencils."

"And?"

"I still labor toward a form to best express myself. Prose or verse. It hasn't announced itself yet."

"Well, if you're waiting for that…"

The great man lets his words trail off and gathers his breath. H. loves his elder for the mild rebuke. Perhaps this is what defines a true friend. Not so much outward kindness, but sincerity, which might smack of severity from time to time. You must plant your feet even more firmly before your friend than your rival, it occurs to H. Yes. He hopes to retain this thought so that he might preserve it in his journal for possible use at his upcoming lecture at the lyceum. *You must plant your feet firmly before your friend.*

They pass over Hugh Cargill's ditch and enter the drier woodland as willow gradually cedes to poplar, maple and fully-clothed pines and hemlocks—the air tree-spiced now and rich with birdsong on account of the evergreens and their hardy fruits. H. admires the brave stoical essence of their winter chicadees and titmouses.

He considers remarking upon the birdsong to his companion, but Mr. E. surely hears the notes, as well. He savors the intimacy of their human silence shared. His elder soon bursts the silence by asking after his teaching plans, whether he might attempt to open a school with his brother, as mentioned, or seek employment elsewhere for a time to gain experience. He tells Mr. E. about his plans to take a ship from Boston to Maine to explore the possibilities, if only to visit with dear cousins Rebecca and Mary and treat his eyes to new vistas—the sea, the strange towns, the craggy coastline and primeval woods. His elder doesn't respond with words but makes listening noises to convey his approval.

H. can no longer hear the chips and wheezes of the chicadees and tits behind them, busy with their own affairs. But the sight of a nuthatch creeping head-first down a poplar trunk up ahead and just off their trail halts him in his tracks, causing his companion to brush up against him before pausing.

"You see something?"

"The nuthatch. Up ahead." He points just as the bird scurries around the backside of the trunk, but then it thankfully reappears, bobbing its head as it continues its upside-down creep. Then the creature alights on a branch and laughs, as nuthatches do, boastful of its life.

Life! Life! Life!

"Oh yes. Of course."

There's something dismissive in his companion's words. As if to confirm H.'s suspicion, the great man walks on, leading the way now for H. to follow. Mr. E. is not as interested in the nuthatch, or in most of the natural phenomena that occupy H.'s more concerted attention. Their angle of vision outdoors often seems to diverge, the wide open distant views more amenable to his elder's imagination, or simply more soothing to his poor eyes, which plague him.

H. watches the way his mentor clasps his hands behind his back as he walks up ahead. H. keeps his own hands free at his sides, by contrast, ever "on hand," so to speak, to gather what fruits might present themselves.

"Mark the nuthatch of yours," the sage calls behind him without turning his head or slowing his gait, "the unusual trajectory of its amblings."

"Yes, 'tis rather distinctive. Only the creepers and black-and-white warblers move in quite the same manner."

"They follow the path of their genius, you see. Headlong." Mr. E. nearly shouts now to be heard. "They don't hem and haw over prose or verse. They don't wait for the proper path to announce itself or some such nonsense. You must forge ahead. The art is in the doing. What did your bravest Indians do when they exhausted their arrows? Did they retreat? No. They threw *themselves* at the mark."

It was just like the great man. Just as H. doubted his companion's sympathies, his lungs and mouth form these perfect words. When he thinks upon their saunter today, their saunterings most days, what he prizes is the way their thoughts and words tend to circle about the same topics—love, friendship, work, courage—yet follow their strange trajectories, not unlike the strange flight-trajectories distinguishing sapsuckers from swallows. He ponders additional analogues, as the great man has advised, following his elder toward Hubbard's shady swamp, Brister's spring, and the pond.

The planets! Yes. Their minds orbit about the same concerns in their own fashion, drawing close at intervals, not unlike planets or, looking about, not unlike these fir and oak and maple trees whose branches seek their own space and light, yet whose roots surely intermingle beneath the earth's crust. *Planets. Trees. Branches. Roots. Friendship. Love.*

"You're awfully quiet," the great man says as he strides downslope toward the swampland. "Even for you."

H. tells his companion that he was only thinking on his inspired revelations. They pause at the swampy meadow, side by side now, seeking out the driest footpath across the unripe berrying shrubs to the hill. His companion's next words surprise H. yet again.

"I'm certain you'll find a soulmate in due time, dear friend, if a wife is what you seek."

4

Hertzog, his brain fuzzed by the familiar voice in the woods, arrives at his front walk to glimpse Stacey Hinshaw leaning over one of her highbush cranberry shrubs with hand-pruners the other side of their shared hobblebush hedge. He finds it odd. The cranberries with their broad, maple-like leaves hardly need pruning so early in the growing season. He draws too close to his neighbor to ignore her so he wishes her a good morning without any intention of slowing his stride.

"So good to see you, David." She straightens herself and pivots to face him. "I've been meaning to talk with you."

"Oh?" This freezes him on the red bricks as she leans over their hedge, presses her handbacks against her lower spine to affect a feline stretch. Her long-sleeve T-shirt advertises some sort of microbrewery in Oregon.

"Yeah. I just noticed your old book at the Sherman's on campus." Hertzog blanches at the *old,* but Stacey doesn't seem to notice. "So impressive! I couldn't believe it! I just loved *Walden.* I mean, it makes total sense that that was your area of specialization." *Was!* "Where better to teach Thoreau than in the Maine woods?" She waves the red-handled pruner about at their verdant environs, flashing her thin eyebrows, darker than her blond mane. A curious hairstyle, he notices for the first time, an interior section dyed jet-black on one side and trimmed fairly close to the scalp, leaving the long blond shock to drape over at a dramatic angle. He wonders if it signifies something political while he nods at Stacey's words—she's going on about Thoreau—looks for unusual piercings and locates only a tiny gold stud in her right nostril, which might have meant something twenty or thirty years ago. He makes listening noises across the hedge, nonplussed by her enthusiasm more so than by her hairstyle or piercing. He hadn't pegged Stacey as the enthusiastic type. Hadn't pegged her as quite so young as she looks and sounds up close.

"'Why should I feel lonely? is not our planet in the Milky Way?'" she's saying now as Hertzog nods. "I forget which chapter that was from."

"Solitude," he tells her, impressed that she's read and retained a fairly obscure passage from the work, one spared the out-of-context advertisements on book satchels, coffee mugs, greeting cards, and calendars.

"Yeah, 'Solitude.' That was probably my favorite chapter. It really spoke to me in my eco-lit class at Reed. That's where I got my undergrad degree. Guess I was sort of homesick. Never forgot that line. It made me feel better." A strand of her fine hair finds her mouth in the breeze. She tastes it with her tongue, then flicks her head to shed it, exposing more of the close-trimmed portion on the left.

"It's a good part of the book. I'm impressed you've remembered it."

He's missed these rare moments with students, it only now occurs to him, glimpsing the light dance behind their eyes upon discovering a resonant passage of primary text. Yet, something about his new neighbor's words tells Hertzog that this is only the lead-in to something else she wishes to talk about. She wants him, he suspects, to thin his row of cedars to let more light into her home, to split the cost to replace their shared dilapidated wooden fence out back, to reconsider the wattage or directionality of his safety flood lights, or, worse, having discovered his academic specialty, she wants him to guest lecture her Bio 101 class in the fall to introduce her students to Thoreau's scientific advances: the propagation strategies of forest trees, the scientific implications vis à vis climate change of his "Kalendar" data, the spreadsheet of natural phenomena he was tracking in Concord over the ten-year period before his death. People always want something. He braces for the assault.

"Anyway, David, I was thinking, given your scholarly interests, the number of years you've lived here, that you'd be such a valuable voice at our Rockweed Coalition meetings."

He knits his woolly eyebrows. The specific proposal catches him unawares, which isn't lost upon his neighbor. "You know that's what Taylor studies, right? Intertidal zone ecology? Macroalgae, specifically? Seaweed," she clarifies.

"Oh. No. I didn't know. That's, uh, very nice." He hopes this last bit doesn't sound condescending or dismissive—she recalled a passage from Thoreau—but realizes that it probably does, so he leans closer across the hedge and continues. "And what is it, Stacey, that you study?"

She lifts her chin at the question, her face blooming before him. It's the first outright expression of interest in her that he's paid, the first time that he's addressed her by name. Her eyes are brown as his coffee, he notices, when he expected them to be blue. It's not such a little thing, rarer than one might expect and wondrous in its way, squaring one's shoulders and looking another soul straight in the eye, calling him or her by name. They are close enough over the thin hedge that he catches a whiff of her vegetable breath below the spearmint smells of their garden greenery. It pierces him, this mildest of intimacies. Is he simply overwrought by the voice he might have heard mere minutes ago in the woods?

"Oh, I'm working on the same thing as Taylor pretty much," he hears Stacey saying now, her excited syllables tumbling over one another. "We're both phycologists, algae scientists. Exciting, right? But I'm still ABD. Taylor got the position here. He was my prof. Scandalous, I know, but it's not like he's so much older. I'm just adjuncting in the lab, picking up a section or two when they need an instructor while I finish my field work. Not sure if they'll even make a spousal hire once I defend." He wonders if she's angling to see how he feels about grad student relationships with professors (neutral), spousal hires (not a fan), to see if he might volunteer to put the good word in with someone high up the food chain he surely knows (unaware of the ignoble conclusion of his tenure at Emmenthaler). But she's moved on at her enthusiastic timbre. "It doesn't matter for now. This is, like, the perfect place for me to finish my research. We'll just take it from there."

There's something winning about this young woman that he cannot deny. Her youthful enthusiasm. *Nothing great was ever achieved without enthusiasm,* Thoreau's wavering mentor, Emerson, had famously observed. Hertzog had often summoned the remark on enthusiasm by the Sage of Concord to inspire his daughter, though his exhortations typically yielded results opposite his intention.

Part of Hertzog wishes to extricate himself from this conversation before he commits himself to something he'll later regret. Thoughts on Ellen, he fears, have punctured his protections. Yet despite his wariness, part of him doesn't want to let Stacey go. The latter inclination wins out. The attentions of a young woman, however platonic, still mean something to him, apparently. He asks Stacey about the focus of her research, specifically, which prompts her to widen her eyes, showing more of the whites around the coffee irises.

"I'm studying the effects of macroalgae cutting during harvest, comparing the resilience of *Fucus* against *Ascophyllum.* We're concerned that *Fucus* rockweed is already outcompeting *Ascophyllum* on account of global warming and acidification. Overharvesting might be exacerbating matters. Acadian Seaplants has gone on a spree these past five years or so." He bobs his head on his neck in a particular way to suggest understanding as Stacey continues to gloss her research aims and methodology, punching key words and phrases such as *biomass* and *food web* and *frond recruitment* and *maximum sustainable yield.*

Hertzog loses the thread before long. He soon hears only disembodied glottals and fixes his attention, instead, on items in his visual field: the unusual geometries of Stacey's blond-black mane, the juncos and chickadees skittering between the squat jack pines several yards behind her, the enormous cumulus cloud over the sea way back there, the painted slogan of the Oregon microbrewery peeling at the edges from the cotton of Stacey's T-shirt, the red-handled pruners with which she gesticulates. He waits for her to finish, registers the influx and efflux of his breath through his nostrils rather than interrupt her. Before too long, she pauses and awaits his commentary.

"That sounds like important work, Stacey, but listen, I really should get inside. I'm in the middle of some work, myself."

Her aquiline nose, a lovely nose accented by its tiny piercing, twitches rabbit-like at the mention of his work. She hadn't realized her older neighbor still worked. She won't keep him a moment longer, she says. She'll tell him about the next coalition meeting if he's interested in attending. She'll leave some pamphlets in his mailbox. "Get to work," she teases, as only a younger woman might tease a much older man, putting him in his place, snapping her pruners. "Chop-chop."

His work. Hertzog has yet to abandon his efforts. The object of his labors? An authoritative account of Thoreau's cosmology, a work in the offing for over twenty years, once anxiously anticipated by fellow scholars. His contract with Princeton University Press expired years ago, along with the series editor. It might behoove Hertzog to devote the hours of his day toward more tangible pursuits: he might take up woodworking or some other new hobby, pursue volunteer work to promote the civic good like some of the other mossbacks around here, who refuse to decamp to the subtropics or the desert. No one would blame him for jettisoning his scholarly project. The thought brings a bitter smile to his lips as he mounts the oak stairs toward his study. No one cares enough about how a retired white male professor whiles away his days to ascribe praise or blame. He has slipped beyond the screen of local mattering. Hadn't Stacey heard?

An anodyne calm descends upon Hertzog as he plucks Princeton's first Journal volume from his desk and sits in his leather chair, gripping his legal pad of notes, too. Inside this early and underappreciated volume are passages he wishes to return to, hoping to see what he has yet to see. One of Thoreau's key insights, in fact—the limitless scope of the visual field before us, the scant measure we truly behold. *We must look a long time before we can see,* the transcendentalist had jotted several times, and in various permutations. Hertzog gathers his breath in the chair before cracking open the volume. He studies the fine dust suspended in the air by the ray of sunlight, summons in this way the proper contemplative mood while he tries not to think about those hikers up on the Spring Trail and the familiar voice he surely conjured with his imagination. *Ellen.*

To call Hertzog's scholarly career a complete failure would be too harsh. He had published the first monograph in the field to posit the aesthetic primacy of the Journal. It remains de rigeur for scholars to cite his most piquant line from the introduction of *Thoreau Days* (still in print!). "By 1852, Thoreau ceased his practice of writing *in* his journal—which he had heretofore pilfered for his lectures, essays, and his only published books during his lifetime, *A Week on the Concord and Merrimack Rivers* and *Walden*—and began to write *for* his Journal."

Based upon the strength of his monograph, he had been offered the prestigious Norton Chair at Emmenthaler College, a stone's throw from Mt. Katahdin, site of Thoreau's most concerted immersions into the wild, as Stacey seemed to know. Princeton assigned him editor of the third volume of their multi-volume edition of Thoreau's Journals, a monumental project prompted by the burgeoning regard for the Journal in the wake of Hertzog's *Thoreau Days.* (Alfred Kazin, too, commented of Thoreau around this time that "it was not natural for a man to write this well every day.") His ambitions for his second monograph were enormous. He hoped to take in the whole of Thoreau's oeuvre and biography, offer a synthesis of his writings in the context of his felt life to elucidate Thoreau's overarching vision of man's place in the cosmos. Over the first several years at Emmenthaler he compiled hundreds of draft pages, but the work stalled. Colleagues, who initially afforded him their highest respect, began to regard him more coolly at department meetings and in the faculty lounge, across the old corridors and classrooms of Champlain Hall.

The discipline itself began to change. Hertzog's lapsed productivity notwithstanding, devoting one's entire career to the study of a lone dead white male author—the study of primary literary texts of any sort—suddenly seemed out of fashion, if not in poor taste. Hertzog began to behave badly, partly to distract himself from the failed progress of his work. Partly, he can admit now, because he savored the attentions of beautiful young women and what better place to exploit his natural inclinations than a college populated by an ever-replenishing cohort of beautiful young women? Handsome in the Levantine manner, still in his thirties, Hertzog had little difficulty attracting young lovers from the collection of former students. Most wanted nothing more from their former professor than he wanted from them. These young women existed, the same as young men, those who in the bloom of their youth wished only to accumulate varied and vigorous sexual experience. He tried to be discreet, but word traveled after one tryst ended badly, the poor girl morose for weeks after he ended things. Emmenthaler was too small and sleepy a college to overlook scandal of any ilk.

Rebecca had rescued him from such tawdriness. Hertzog had already been at Emmenthaler for almost ten years before she arrived on campus, a new administrative recruit from Yale. The ombudsman position was a big step up for her. Why else would she have left the Ivy League—and proximity to Manhattan—for their frigid backwater? They were both attending a party for Joyce Seltzer, one of Hertzog's English colleagues specializing in what they were just starting to call cultural studies. In those days, there was a small enough cohort of faculty that a party of cocktails and hors d'oeuvres upon the publication of a book was customary in the wood-paneled parlor of President Porterfield's slate-shingled, multi-gabled and chimneyed cottage. Joyce had just published a monograph on the cyborg (whatever the hell that was) with a prestigious academic press.

Hertzog attended these gatherings as a matter of course, because it was the collegial thing to do back when he still cared enough to do the collegial thing. And because sampling Peekytoe crab cakes, gravlax, oysters Rockefeller, steamed fiddleheads on toast points, stuffed mushrooms and what have you, he needn't worry about fixing dinner later for himself. And (mostly) because these events were catered by an outfit staffed almost entirely by a rotating assortment of comely twenty-something women, who weren't Emmenthaler students. Even so, he wasn't on the make the night of Joyce's party. He was bleary-eyed, having pored over facsimiles of Thoreau's Journal pages he was in the midst of editing for Princeton. Addled too from all the high-decibel banter over Joyce's "critical intervention" vis à vis the cyborg. He soon sought refuge at the full bar in the far corner of the room. It was manned by a vaguely Hispanic fellow with a dusty mustache, who worked seasonally, Hertzog soon learned, between In Good Taste Catering and Bean's way down in Freeport. His name was Roger and he favored the heavy pour.

"So the cyborg? This is the sort of thing you English-types are doing these days?"

These were the first words between Hertzog and Rebecca. Her words. He had noticed her earlier in the evening, squired by President Porterfield as he introduced her to various constituencies, smart in her fitted houndstooth suit, the skirt cut well above fine knees, protected from the chill by shimmering hosiery. Hertzog also noted her manicured brows and painted lips, the whole tableau marking her as an administrator rather than a professor, and marking her as "from away." Her remark, and maybe Roger's heavy pour, inspired an uncharacteristically full-throated laugh from Hertzog, who rose from his cushioned stool.

"No," he replied. "Not all of us." He introduced himself. Rebecca's hand was icy and damp from her drink. She raised the molded glass to her mouth, kept her gaze on him. He could hear the mild kiss of her lips against the liquid, the ice glinting against fine teeth. Something caramel, the drink, diluted by the half-melted ice swishing about. Scotch, maybe, which impressed Hertzog, that she wasn't sipping bad chardonnay like most of their colleagues.

"Yes, I know your name," she replied, setting down her glass on the bar. "Everyone's warned me about you."

"Oh?" He gestured for her to take the stool next to his own. They sat.

"Mm-hm."

"Well, don't believe everything you hear."

"I don't. As a matter of course. It's my job not to believe everything I hear, David Hertzog."

They didn't speak for long that first night, which maybe was a good thing as Hertzog was already in his cups. Before long, President Porterfield materialized, smelling of wool and woodsy cologne. He greeted Hertzog perfunctorily and ushered his new hire toward more important constituencies. There was always a trustee or two, one of Rockefeller's heirs or another important donor, attending these events, likely the reason Porterfield hosted them in the first place.

Hertzog called Rebecca's extension the following Monday—she did not feign surprise to hear his voice—and invited her to dinner at one of the fancier restaurants in town, which had just reopened for the season. And so they began to see each other, dating in a manner that David hadn't ventured since college, the years before his parents' illnesses and his deep dive into the transcendental thinkers. There was something sweet about coming to know another person in this deliberate manner. He had forgotten. It was never too late, Thoreau had remarked in one of his final essays, to turn over a new leaf.

Unlike Hertzog, Rebecca was a talker and he learned quite a bit about her only a few weeks into their courtship. She had planned on becoming a neurosurgeon before discovering, a year into medical school at Hahnemann in Philadelphia, that she didn't much care to be around sick people. She enjoyed hiking and swimming and could be awfully competitive, powered through the steepest stretches of the Knife Edge trail up Mt. Katahdin on a day-trip he planned to introduce her to Maine's big woods. She worked hard and prided herself on her ability to intervene constructively between warring constituencies: parents, students, professors, administrators. She enjoyed fine food and wine—lobster thermidor and pecan-encrusted halibut fillets and various meats complemented by Napa Valley cabernets of favorable vintage. She chastised Hertzog for his countervailing asceticism, which she interpreted as weirdly self-indulgent at the core. The first such admonishment she had lobbed over her shoulder as she rubbed lamb chops with garlic and rosemary at the counter in her kitchen, and as he rifled through her pantry (upon her instructions) looking for the olive oil. She had lucked into renting the Queen Anne home on the cheap from a chemistry professor on a Fulbright in Germany. The pantry was loaded with shiny new bottles of cooking liquids he had dimly heard of but would never consider purchasing for his own spartan meals: mirin and truffle oil and balsamic vinegar and Marsala wine. It amused her to introduce Hertzog to the finer things, including her sporty MG, a rear-wheel drive coupe that made no sense in snowy Maine. It wasn't difficult to come around to Rebecca's pleasures, alimentary and otherwise, to come around to the lovely and tough-minded Rebecca, generally.

"Isn't this nice?" she asked him over their rosemaried lamb chops and parsleyed fingerling potatoes, and asked this same, not quite rhetorical, question on manifold occasions their first weeks together. They enjoyed a picnic brunch on the town green, a drive up the rocky coast, a capable production of *West Side Story* at Emmenthaler's John Ford Theater.

Isn't this nice?

When they made love for the first time, it was laced with that brand of unfamiliar awkwardness attendant to actual caring. It was at her home, after the rosemaried lamb and parsleyed potatoes, Hertzog deferring to Rebecca's wishes from the start.

"I sort of thought you'd be better at this," she exclaimed post-coital, teasing him, her chest and neck above the quilt flushed. Excitable moments, he learned, the blood would often rise to Rebecca's flesh forming curious designs on her cheeks, neck, and chest. She slid her dewy arm inside his arm, reached down to lace fingers. She wore a girlish gold ring, he'd noticed earlier, accented by two small sapphire hearts propped sideways, a slightly larger round diamond in the middle. He could feel the ring now pressing against his finger.

Isn't this nice?

They had enjoyed some fine years. Happy years. Blissful, even. And then they had a daughter. And then things weren't so good. And then the bottom fell out, entirely, as even Ranger Justin, his former student, seemed to know, as everyone knew.

This protected him for a while from calls for his ouster at the college on productivity grounds. The faculty and upper administration, however, turned over so frequently that personal tragedies counted for little. He had gone from academic wunderkind to dead weight the administration hoped to shed to maintain its venerable ranking in *U.S. News and World Report.* The college instituted what it artfully designated as the "Sustained Performance Evaluation," a three-year staggered review of all tenured faculty members. Hertzog took his early retirement rather than suffer the indignity of a probationary meeting with the new Dean of Faculty, a humorless onetime geneticist, who, in the first place, couldn't quite fathom the utility of pursuing "unsponsored research."

Hertzog reads now from the early Journal: *As the truest Society approaches always nearer to Solitude—so the most excellent Speech finally falls into Silence.* He increasingly wonders if the key to understanding Thoreau, who wrote so many words, may reside in the elisions, the gaps, the silences between his recorded thoughts. Thoreau, he knows, delivered an early lecture at the Concord lyceum on the topic of Silence, offering Hertzog some textual support for his hunch. Yet how to glimpse an absence? How to give scholarly voice to the unvoiced? He reads on, words he has read with greater and lesser attentiveness countless times over the years, pages he has dog-eared, these lines and full paragraphs he has underscored in pen, or overlooked. He jots new markings as he reads, until the light grows bashful, the sun having vaulted past the steeply graded asphalt shingle roof toward the jagged horizon of mountaintop spruce above the Bowl. The words have long ceased to make an impression. He contemplates the birdsong outside the thin glass, which he hears for the first time this afternoon even though they had likely been gossiping all the while. Juncos and chickadees, he guesses. He'd been thinking of the voice in the woods again—*Ellen!*—weighing options he hadn't contemplated earlier.

He knows something that he might do, someone that he might see, to figure out what's what. Cassidy. One of Ellen's old friends. Her only friend.

5

April 26th, 1838
The bluebird had come from the distant South
To his box in the poplar tree,
And he opened wide his slender mouth,
On purpose to sing to me.

H. enjoys his small downstairs room in the Parkman House, the house shared by his immediate family with Aunt Louisa and Uncle Charles, Aunts Maria and Jane, and with the widow Mrs. Joseph Ward and her daughter Prudence. The downstairs room allows him seamless passage to and from the outdoors at hours the mass of men deem odd. He need not fear the complaint of stairs to take his leave forthwith this purple morn, undetected.

He savors the cold air on the back stoop, which chills his lungs but scarcely cuts inside his sturdy grey trowsers and coat. The crickets still chirp from their hidden perches, loath to cede the day to the birds. The dark outline of the bluebird box built by his brother catches his eye against the poplar's trunk. Beyond the dark silhouette of the leafed-out poplar, H. traces the dizzying trajectories of bats. He takes courage at their silent industry. The pell-mell path might yet find the mark!

He realizes the impertinence of the dawning thought, but these sweet purple mornings invariably persuade H. that he is among the Chosen, like the ancient Hebrews, dealt by superior powers to experience ecstasies deprived his fellows. Such riches to discern while his neighbors abed churn the lambent indoors air through their rusty machinery. H. alone is awake and alive and burning.

Even so, he dons these sturdy clothes this morn to transact business beneath the concerns of crickets and bluebirds and bats. Family business. He walks across the yard and retrieves the cart and shovel from beside the shed, blazes a path through neighboring yards to reach Walden Road. The cart's wheels scarcely make a sound against the earth to interrupt the insects and the occasional gossip of windblown leaves. H. recently lathered the hubs with generous pastings of graphite refuse, in no short supply given the family concern. The business continues to founder, French and German pencils still far superior. Uncle Charles abandoned the venture years ago, leaving H.'s father to carry on for lack of alternative opportunities, and for his wife's insistence that they remain in Concord where her powerful voice might be heard, rather than return to Boston. H. could do worse than model his oracular style after his mother. Co-founder, along with the Ward ladies, of the Women's Anti-Slavery Society, she has made quite the impression about town. Some find her brash. That is to say not everyone likes her, a mark of her strong and noble character, to H.'s mind. For what sort of flaccid idea is *like* anyway?

H.'s thoughts turn once again to his father while he pushes the cart the few miles to the pond, while the morning light begins to fashion distinct branches and leaves from their fuzzy roadside silhouettes and birdsong quiets the crickets. Poor Father's unceasing pecuniary travails. There is something admirable in their persistent poverty, to be sure—his father's refusal to ape the unscrupulousness of Concord's rising business class. Yet there is something H. cannot quite abide in his father, as well, the quiet desperation with which he lives out his days as erstwhile shopkeeper and current pencil-maker. Should he not seize his fate, however low, by the scruff of the neck, deploy a modicum of Yankee shrewdness to the task?

It's been left to H. to seek out improvements to their manufacturing process, which he has done thanks to his library privileges in Cambridge. The *Encyclopedia Perthensis* includes a useful entry on "black lead"—if not on pencil-making, specifically—advising a mixture of plumbago with Bavarian clay. Such clay, which he recently obtained from the New England Glass Company, might solve the problem of their hopelessly gritty, greasy lead. Their first batch was less greasy, but still too gritty. H. has noodled with the proportions of plumbago to clay, but to no avail. The plumbago, itself, he has determined, the final obstacle. And so he has designed and constructed a finishing mill he hopes to employ this morning.

In the meantime, competition from abroad, and even the local concern of the Munroes, threatens their solvency. Which is why H. pushes this empty cart and shovel toward the pond and, more specifically, toward its white-sand shore at its north end. To supplement their modest pencil-making income, they manufacture sandpaper and stove polish, as well. Town elders have yet to decry or tax their harvest of a few yearly cart-loads of finest sand. The citizenry also submits to H. their broken clocks and unsoled shoes, and summons him to their warped or otherwise hobbled furniture.

It takes only moments to fill the cart with enough sand to suit his purpose. He pauses between each scoop to observe a merry pair of wood ducks dabbling at the surface not twenty rods from shore. A devil-may-care insouciance attends their wing-flicks, their bill-nods, their curious stretched-neck calisthenics. Every so often they plunge heels up at precisely the same time, disappearing beneath the water's skin for several seconds, and then bob back to the surface side by side at precisely the same time not far from their descent. H. wonders what silent communication they share to coordinate their efforts.

He courts ducky thoughts the whole walk home, wonders what he might extract, whether he might have incorporated a fowl metaphor into the Society lecture he delivered just last week at the lyceum, already rife with metaphors involving planets and tides, rocks and trees. The great man continues to laud the virtues of metaphor. *We have planted corn and potatoes within speaking distance of one another*, H. argued, *and so formed towns and villages, but we have not associated, only assembled.* He paused after this line to savor the listening noises. He might have done more of this, pause between his sentences rather than stumble headlong over his best lines.

Safely home, H. resists the woodsmoke breakfast odors the house breathes and strides beneath the poplar's canopy to the backyard shed. The metallic *whirring* of gears inside the small shed betray his brother's industry. He deposits the sand-filled cart where he found it and steps inside the low-ceilinged space to find John laboring over the finishing mill, cranking the handle in great revolutions, his elbow akimbo. His brother coughs richly into the darksome graphite-dusted air by way of greeting.

"The dust, John!" H. pulls his brother's woolen shoulders from the mill and assumes his place. "The graphite dust is too fine for your lungs. You must wear your mask." H. works the crank, turns his nose and mouth from the apparatus.

The genius of H.'s mill, indeed, resides precisely in the dust. The plumbago they process at Ebenezer Wood's dam-mill in Acton isn't fine enough to effect a smooth writing point, even substituting clay for their cheaper fillers. So H. constructed this finishing mill before him on the heavy table. The crank works the graphite through a series of mill-stones of ever-finer grit, draughts of air inspired by a spring-wound fan working the finest dust up a narrow, churn-like chamber to the flat box perched just above H.'s head. The coarser graphite sinks to the bottom to be ground over again into a suitable dust to reach the high box upon the next draught of air.

"I can hardly breathe through that mouth-covering of yours," John utters over H.'s shoulder. H. can scarcely hear him above the whirring of the gears, the crunch of the mill-stones, but makes a note to revisit the cloth for the mask he has designed for the mill-shed. Might layers of cheese-cloth accomplish the purpose without constricting the breath?

"Perhaps Helen or Sophia might help with the grinding, their own health providing."

"Perhaps."

H. ceases his labors and stands atop a chair to inspect the box, smiles at the generous drift of grey silt.

"Let's blend a batch," H. proposes, mostly so they might leave the dust-filled chamber and repair to the adjacent shed housing their kiln and finishing equipment. Bracing the tray of graphite against his hip, H. ushers John out the door.

The brothers labor over the family craft for the better part of the day, breaking only for a modest lunch they take outdoors in deference to their mother's housekeeping. In the finishing shed, they mix one part plumbago with three parts clay, knead the dough with their hands, press the loaf into flat sheets, then bake each sheet in the kiln for the better part of an hour. While waiting, they prepare the cedar casements, work the two-man saw to cut slats from the logs.

He minds the way they seamlessly work the saw between them without words, emulating the silent communication of the ducks at the pond. Slats shorn, they hand-plane individual pieces side by side at the long workbench to achieve the proper thickness, trade their planers for awls to carve grooves for the lead into each casement half. H. hopes the wood-dust doesn't exacerbate John's catarrh, the air redolent now of cedar shavings. They exchange few words over their labors, but touch upon teaching prospects in Maine or Virginia, the curious skin inflammation besetting their poor sister, Helen, Sophia's latest linseed oil portrait of their father, the number and variety of melon-seeds they ought to plant out on the hill this season.

They cut and form the finished lead into the grooves before gluing the halves closed. They will wait a day for the casement glue to dry, the lead to fully cure. It's painstaking work, but performed this day with a modicum of pride. Before sealing shut the cedar cases, wiping clean the oozing glue, H. knows that they have produced a finer lead capsule.

"This will change things for Father," John says once they escape the darksome shed, squinting against the white afternoon light. This is how H. knows that his brother, too, discerned the smoother quality of the finished lead against the pads of his fingers as they worked the capsules inside the grooves.

"Yes."

They decide to take an evening walk up Fairhaven Hill, hunt for arrowheads and observe the sunset's paint upon the river. "Here, brother." John brandishes one of yesterday's pencils he must have secreted from the shed. They haven't yet escaped town, proper. Green odors have yet to supplant the horse dung, the smithy's rich smoke, and the butcher's offal. Without breaking stride, John reaches sideways and slides the pencil inside the woolen pocket at H.'s chest. "Oughtn't you to carry a pencil and daybook with you on your saunterings? Then you wouldn't have to tax your brain so upon your return to remember those noble intuitions of yours."

Some facetiousness here, but a thoughtful proposal in the main. John's words and deeds frequently remind H. of the human virtues that reside so naturally within his brother's breast, and which reside somewhat less naturally within his own breast. He must cultivate empathy in greater earnestness if he hopes ever to enjoy the company of a soulmate to complement his solitude.

6

It takes mere minutes on Route 193 for the overpriced lobster pounds and antique shops just outside Emmenthaler proper to give way to dilapidated houses, several landscaped with rusted-out automobiles, unseaworthy boats, and other desiccated machinery. Frowzy service stations, restaurants and bars, meat processing sites, and small stores pockmark the roadside at intervals spaced miles apart. The overtaxed engine of his old Subaru knocks on the inclines. He takes it slow, which offers him the opportunity to scan the homemade wooden signage every so often decrying the Audubon Society. IDENTIFY THIS BIRD! the painted slogan beneath an upraised middle finger.

The paper mill still operates a skeleton crew ten miles farther up the highway from where Hertzog heads—the demand for tissue and toilet paper keeping the outfit afloat—which is the only reason most of these half-lidded establishments haven't shuttered up entirely. That and the state trooper substation he passes now. Who knows if Teddy's still exists? It's been years since he's taken a meal there. It's nearly dark by the time he pulls onto the gravel lot, relieved to see a few cars and a semi parked, folks sitting in booths behind the slats of the window blinds.

He parks and stands inside the glass door by the unmanned register, the chime fading from his entry. His eyes pass over the plastic-wrapped whoopee pies, the fundraising board for a childhood disease he doesn't quite process, festooned with quarters, the bee pollen supplements and associated pamphlets. He scans the linoleum floor for Ellen's old friend but doesn't see her. He only spots an older waitress he doesn't recognize in her waitress frock perched over a far-off booth, chatting it up with a bearded fellow about ten years younger than Hertzog. Driver of the semi outside, likely. The waitress notices him down the aisle and tells him without words, flicking her head, to sit wherever he likes, seems to study him a bit before turning her attention back on her trucker. He slides into a booth equidistant from the few other patrons and scans the laminated menu, figures he'll at least get a turkey club for his troubles, ask after Cassidy.

The waitress keeps him cooling his heels just long enough to peeve

Hertzog. A job to do, you might as well do it right. He's always felt this way—Thoreau's apostasy on this front be damned—a Puritan streak right down the center of Hertzog's Jewish spine. It drove Ellen crazy. The waitress finally strides toward him on her sensible shoes, plops down a small glass of water, the crushed ice lolling about the surface like flotsam.

"Hello, Mr. Hertzog. Been forever, seems like."

"Cassidy?"

"Uh…yeah," she utters, her voice lilting upward, sounding like the young Cassidy he remembers, though hardly looking like that child and young lady. It takes some imagination to reassemble these physical features before him—mousy hair threaded through with gray and pulled back in a ponytail, purse of flesh sagging from beneath her chin—into a viable facsimile. But yes. This is Cassidy, ten years or so down the road. Poor girl. His old colleagues would excoriate him for such thoughts, decry his male gaze. But hell, these are the only eyes Hertzog has; he sees what he sees. Not without sympathy. It's hard living for a young woman out here, enduring the long winters, homebound weeks at a time in the chest-high snow, close-quarters with their surly men also enduring the long winters, tending to their grasping children, half of them conceived during these cold days and nights with scarce alternative distractions, employment or otherwise.

"Sorry, Cassidy, I hardly recognized you." She nods, sniffs out her nostrils, detecting the probable insult. "It's just been so long," he adds, lamely. "Like you said."

"Still at the college?"

"No, not for a while now. What about you? How's Wyatt?" She's surprised he remembers her husband's name. He can tell by the way her lashless eyes widen. It puts her in a different place. She flips over the top sheet of her small order pad and clears her throat.

"We're not together anymore. He's down in Ellsworth."

"Oh. Sorry."

"Don't be. Better ex-husband than husband." It was a practiced line, he could tell. Every syllable she utters she becomes more the Cassidy he remembers, which makes something shift inside him.

"Okay."

"Boys are doing well, anyway."

"Well, that's good," he says. He only has a dim knowledge of Cassidy's children.

While he contemplates asking after the boys' ages, Hertzog notices an elderly female diner, her puff of hair pinked through with dye, lifting her chin toward Cassidy from a few booths down. She wants her coffee warmed or the check, maybe. Cassidy doesn't seem to notice her, or maybe she does, because she cuts to the chase.

"So what can I get for you, Mr. Hertzog?"

He orders his turkey club and decaf, postponing his true business. Probably a mistake, it occurs to him as Cassidy makes her way to the cotton-candy haired diner seated across from a male companion with a high neck. It's not like he'll be able to slip in the query casually after she asks whether he wants a slice of blueberry pie.

He gazes over the crossword he's brought while he waits for his food, the cook's bell sounding brightly now and again to summon Cassidy to a completed order. He can hear, too, the cook's spatula or whatnot *clacking* against the griddle behind the pass-through, the sizzle of frying meat, the window vibrating time to time against the powerful engines hauling their pieces of Maine up and down the highway. He can't concentrate on the puzzle. The unsavory aroma of cruciferous vegetables invades Hertzog's nostrils. Someone's ordered the corned beef and cabbage.

Before long, Cassidy sets down the heavy ironware platter holding his sandwich and too many french fries, a few of which spill onto the Formica tabletop. Cassidy asks whether she can get him anything else right now and Hertzog tells her he's all right. He'll wait until Cassidy checks on him to ask the question he's come here to ask.

He eats the sandwich and some of the fries with gusto, surprised by his hunger. She leaves him to himself longer than he thought she might, or maybe Hertzog just eats faster than he ought to eat. Yes, for when she finally does return to check on him she's surprised to see that he's already done and teases him for it. She asks whether he wants a slice of blueberry pie or a scoop of ice cream, or both, offering him her first smile of the evening. Her sentences skip along now. She seems prettier now, too, and younger, his own eyes joining forces with her voice and smile to restore the Cassidy he remembers. Amazing organs, the eyes, per Thoreau. What they see. What they don't see. He tells her he better pass on dessert. She asks him whether he wants the check, utters the query in a sigh that seems almost an expression of regret over his nearing departure.

"I suppose I was wondering, Cassidy, if you've seen her lately."

"Huh? Seen who?"

"Ellen. Ellen, of course."

The scaffolding of her face stiffens at the mention of her old friend. She flutters her lips to express surprise at Hertzog's inquiry, a gesture he doesn't trust. It restores their ancient calculus, which he had almost forgotten—Hertzog the implacable, impossible father; Cassidy the protective friend.

"Guess I figured from the get-go you didn't drive all this way for the blueberry pie." Hertzog watches as she jots the final sum of his check on her pad, at least partly to give her eyes somewhere else to look.

"No. I suppose not."

The air between them vibrates beneath the fluorescent lighting.

"So? Have you?"

"No. Haven't seen Elle. Or heard from her. Not in years." *Elle!*

"You sure?"

She tells him yes, rips his check from her pad—a tearing sound that physically hurts—and sets it down on the tabletop, then pivots on her foamy shoes. Hertzog's not sure what to make of the exchange, whether or not Cassidy's telling the truth. Clearly, his mention of Ellen has put her out of sorts. She wants him gone.

He leaves cash for the check and the tip on the table rather than face Ellen's old friend at the register. His knees ache from his earlier hike and from sitting so long afterwards: in his study, in the car, in this restaurant booth. The night's cold breath greets him out the glass door. He ought to have worn his fleece. A primordial fear of the moonless dark seizes him as he makes his way across the uncertain gravel to his car, his knees loosening. A security light used to blaze in this lot, didn't it? Constellations, most of which Hertzog can't name, spackle the black screen above the tree-line.

"David!" The voice startles him from behind just as he aims the key toward the Subaru's door lock. It's Cassidy's voice summoning him, he recognizes before turning to face her. He waits while she closes the distance between them, her arms folded against the cold.

"You might check with Jude Winslow about Elle. He's still up the road in Northridge. Bet he'd know if Elle was back."

"Well, all right. Thank you, Cassidy."

He doesn't yet turn away from her, because there's something else she wants to say. He can tell by the way she gazes over his shoulder at the copse of dark woods over the highway. The trees sizzle with insects. She bites her bottom lip, then looks him in the eye again.

"She didn't have much use for me by the end of things. I didn't like Jude much more than you did and told her so. Bet you didn't know that."

"You're right. I didn't."

"But I always liked Elle. I hope she's doing all right now, whether or not she's around. Tell her I said hello if you see her."

"I will."

A semi grumbles past on the highway behind him, silencing the sizzling trees, so Hertzog must wait to continue speaking. He hears the truck's transmission downshifting, the driver preparing for the decline ahead, watches Ellen's childhood friend studying the gravel at her feet.

"She liked you, too, Cassidy, even if she didn't act or speak, accordingly. By the end of things."

7

May 4th, 1838
There is a proper and only right way to enter a city, as well as to make advances to a strange person—neither will allow of the least forwardness nor bustle.

The pencil business thrives now thanks to the improved lead capsule. Their new pencils have attracted favorable notices by the Massachusetts Agricultural Society, the New England Society for the Engineering Arts, and the Acton Guild of Carpenters and Cabinet-Makers. Father now commands twenty cents apiece for their Best-Quality Writing-Pencils. The family concern secure, John has decamped, having gained a teaching position in West Roxbury. What is H. to do?

"You can buckle on your knapsack and roam abroad to seek your fortune." So H's mother advised over supper, releasing him from further obligations. Helen detected her brother's hurt and patted his fresh-shaven cheek with a tender palm. Father glanced their way, then returned to his potatoes.

"Don't listen to Mother," Helen whispered. "Stay with us, dear brother."

But no. Mother has spoken.

❧

And so this seaward journey to Maine, where H. hopes to secure a teaching position in one of the smaller towns. Brunswick, Bath, Gardiner, or perhaps Hallowell. He looks forward to visiting his elder cousins, Rebecca and Mary, in Bangor, as well. He carries letters of support from George Ripley, Harvard's President Josiah Quincy, the Reverend Brownson, and from the great man, himself (who also loaned H. ten dollars for the journey).

The schooner departs from Boston harbor late and sails through the night as close to land as the shoals allow, seeking to avoid the rougher open ocean. Standing amidships, the vessel's turbulence lessened, H. savors the briny atmosphere, gazes starboard out to sea, the moon-bright painting cotton foam against the water far as far can be seen. The endless Atlantic unnerves him. He gazes across the deck toward the meager strip of land, an inky smudge beneath the stars, to gain his bearings. Firelight punctuates the coastline now and again, betraying man's faintest human impression upon the strange shore. Although we know otherwise from our earliest explorers, H. suspects that the mass of men still cling to the illusory belief that the world is continent, not insular. A seaward passage puts us in our place.

No sooner does the insight dawn than the ship rises and descends upon a swell, sending his stomach to his throat. H. tries to contain the chowder recently enjoyed, but it's no use. Neptune will exact his modest tribute. H. expels the codfish and potato contents of his stomach in great heaves utterly foreign to him, his machinery acting upon its own primordial knowledge. He takes care not to sully his woolen coat, but fears the stiff breeze will be his undoing. Some impression he'll make, his clothes reeking of vomit. If only he were blessed with a sturdier constitution. He is sturdier than some, anyway, he reminds himself, savoring the hot breath in his throat, and this will have to suffice.

The captain threads woolly islands come morn to reach Portland's wharf. Inside the harbor, the water calms to glass. Ripe odors of marine life at various states of life, death, and decay overtake the cleaner brine of the open ocean. Seaweeds loll about the surface nearest shore, attracting the interest of seabirds too far off to identify. Brown wrack blankets the damp boulders and ledges just above the tideline. The air grows still and hot. Sandflies buzz beneath the cackle of seabirds. Passengers crowd about with their baggage, anxious to disembark. H. hangs back, wary of the fray. Safely moored, two fishermen's dories dispatched from the dock ferry them ashore, making several trips. When it's his turn for passage, the dories travel side by side for a time at an impressive clip, the lads making a race of it. H. notes the small vessel's lines beside him, bow to stern, bucking under the weight of the passengers and the oarsman's labors, the way the prow slices the smooth dark water, a knife through butter. It would be a fine thing to build a seaworthy boat, even a small one. A black guillemot skitters low, settles amidst the seaweeds and dabbles. H. wonders what sea-fruits the guillemot plucks from the leaves and whether there might be a lesson to extract and preserve in the pages of his journal.

H. and his shipmates fairly overtake the quiet town, the main thoroughfare suddenly awash with fresh-arrived coopers and cobblers, drummers and carpenters and day-laborers, accountants and tailors and lawyers and lumbermen, maidservants and housewives and husbands, teachers and would-be teachers. Amid this frontal assault upon the good people of Portland, H. strides with greater deliberation, senses on high alert in this strange town. He pauses at the roadside, reaches into his knapsack to consult the single book he carries, *Phelps & Squire's Traveller's Guide and Map of the United States.* A few Mainers shuffle to the street-edge with H. to give way to the human throng. He detects introversion in their mien, the curve of their spines, the special way their necks hold their heads, men and women alike. There is a certain way, a better way, to enter a town. You ought to approach a strange town as you would approach a strange person, with a modicum of gentleness.

H. locates the post office and for a modest courtesy secures passage to Bath, via Brunswick, on the mail coach with a Mr. Stark. H. checks his tongue on the bench beside the fellow, the coachman's own words hidden as his mouth beneath the rich foliage of his mustache. The fragrant horses scarcely need encouragement, the route familiar to them, the creatures as single-minded and laconic as their human overseer.

"Have to excuse our roads," Mr. Stark says upon the first bumpy stretch. Is this the first full sentence that he has uttered? H. assures his driver that he much prefers a rough passage on land to the roiling sea, which inspires an assenting nod.

H. feels that he has fully arrived in Maine once farmland supplants the cobblestone streets and shops. No longer green about the gills but bold and sturdy as the pioneers Standish and Church. Dense woods loom behind and between the cleared farmland. From certain vistas along the way, H. can still spy the sea to the east. Or is it south? We carry out our human lives amid the scantest clearings between the forest primeval and the fathomless sea. Yes. H. brandishes one of his excellent pencils from his coat pocket, his daybook from his knapsack at his feet, and labors atop the bucking coach to jot down the kernel, legibly. The rocks and boulders of Maine push through the solid earth with great ambition. Mr. Stark glances his way but makes no inquiries. H. smells rich manure lately lathered across the fields, hears the insistent sentences of vireos in the scrim of woods in between. *Here I am. There you are. Here I am. There you are.* He searches the trees for these fine olive birds, eyes the color of garnets below dark brows, but can't spot one inside the dense forest. There is a certain deciduous tree he spies time to time between the more numerous conifers, neither birch nor beech. He strains his eyes to better discern the leaves, wishes he had brought Father's telescope rather than his flute. An aspen, he would guess, though the leaves seem to boast sharper teeth than the aspens he knows.

"Mr. Stark, do you know what kind of tree that is?" he finally asks above the rattle of the coach, the skidding of wheels, the horses' snorts, aiming a finger roadside.

"Which tree?"

"That one...and *that* one."

Mr. Stark's gaze follows H.'s finger.

"Green kind, I'd venture."

A taciturn lot, these Mainers, which H. ought to admire. Does he not prepare his next lyceum lecture on the virtue of Silence?

"You seem a curious sort," Mr. Stark says, which cheers H. by offering him some grist to grind.

"What else is there to be in this world? You've just betrayed your own curiosity, after all."

"Ayuh, 'bout those trees? Nah."

"No. About me."

8

Days pass. Weeks. Hertzog will not go to Cherryfield Farm in Northridge to seek out the unsavory likes of Jude Winslow. Not yet. He tends to his own business, instead. Mornings, he eats his breakfast, scans the *Bangor Daily News* and sometimes watches the BBC through the internet (stripped of the histrionics of American news alternatives). He keeps up his outdoors exercise amid the increasing trickle of vacationers. Afternoons, he devotes himself to Thoreau's early journal entries, plucking new passages to his consciousness. *We should not endeavor coolly to analyze our thoughts, but keeping the pen even and parallel with the current, make an accurate transcript of them—Impulse is after all the best linguist…* So many impressions faithfully recorded. All the same, so much left unsaid, particularly during the first decade or so of journal-keeping, great chronological gaps between the surviving entries. Next to nothing on the family business (why the allusion to "pen" rather than "pencil"?), the bustle of the family home shared by several relatives and boarders, romantic hopes and rivalries, a dear brother's crisis, the like tragedies of close friends. A scant page or two on his first journey to Maine.

Hertzog sees to a few things before the summer people descend upon his environs in full force. *Newlyweds and nearly-deads*, the local pejorative for the masses arriving by cruise ship. He visits the dentist for his annual checkup, appreciates Dr. Melman's officious mien, the soap-smell of her hands. His ophthalmologist adjusts his prescription, assures him that his vision continues to degrade at a rate acceptably commensurate with a life-span well above average, though he might rest his eyes for longer spells between reading. He schedules a physical with his internist (an impossibly young Indian fellow these past few years since his longtime physician retired to Scottsdale), suffers the indignities of a digital examination to his prostate while Dr. Ramasamay extols the virtues of a vegan diet; the next day, Hertzog appreciates the kinder human touch of his ancient barber. He takes the Subaru into the shop for its oil change, where Brant Jr.—forty-something son of the shop's owner—convinces him to shell out the big bucks for synthetic, plus new rear brakes and an air filter. He ought to drive the car more, as well, longer highway stints now and again. "Cars like to be driven," Brant advises, wiping his dirty hands with a dirtier rag. "Just like people. Gotta keep the oil moving through the old machinery." Brant nudges him with an elbow to make sure the lewd reference isn't lost upon him.

Everyone has advice to proffer to Hertzog these days.

He manages, anyway, to skirt Stacey Hinshaw's advances about her Rockweed Coalition, ignoring a message she left on his phone (she must have looked up his number in the directory online). Moreover, he manages not to think about what he would rather not think about. Ellen. He has always been good at this. Something bloodless in the capacity, he worries, for which Rebecca had admonished him. *You shunt everything and everyone aside! It's like you don't give a shit! It's not normal!* That old chestnut. He wasn't normal. He didn't *feel* enough. This seemed to be the kernel of the complaint. What he might have told his wife was that it was fruitless and counterproductive to vent one's feelings all the time, and that his refusal to do so didn't necessarily connote a deficiency in the feeling arena, per se. It became clear to Hertzog well before their daughter reached school age that raising her would consist primarily of navigating countless emotional and behavioral crises. It was critical to hold something in reserve for the next calamity. And the next.

Hertzog, this morning, like every morning, conducts his morning exercise. Yet, he returns from his hike and swim to a vision on his slate stoop that completes a circuit, sends an electric jolt down his spine. He recognizes her the instant he glimpses the human form sitting there, not by her physical features, per se, so much as the posture, the certain slouch of her vertebrae, which his daughter refused to correct all the years she lived under his roof, despite his hectoring, despite physical therapy, despite the corrective brassiere Ellen refused to wear.

"Hello, Father," she greets him, rising to her feet. Respectful, one would think, the *Father* bit. Yet Hertzog knows better. She has called him Father for as long as he can remember. Not dad. Heaven forbid, dad. In Ellen's *Father*, he hears what he has always heard. Not respect so much as resignation, a concession to terms imposed upon her.

"Ellen," he replies, wondering what she hears in his voice, what she sees in his rigid, bolt upright posture.

"So, I'm back. Just so you know." She's slimmed down since the last time he's seen his daughter, which is good. She wears her hair shorter now, too, but not so short that unruly strands of the curly shock don't fall over her eyes, obscuring them from his full view. He feels the old blood rise to his neck, his cheeks, feels the old words he won't utter rise to his throat. *Wipe your hair off your face!* He never understood why she let her hair fall over her eyes, or, more specifically, why she didn't understand or care about the poor signal it sent to the world.

"Okay. Thank you, Ellen, for letting me know." He doesn't know what he should feel or say now before his daughter. He only knows that he doesn't feel what a father ought to feel (who cares about her fucking hair?), and that he hasn't said what a father ought to say. He utters his next words—"So what are your plans?"—realizes that he's botched these words, too, the moment they leave his lips.

Ellen issues a petulant puff of air from between her lips, a young gesture she ought to have outgrown by now. "Jeez, Father, is that all you care about? My plans? What I plan to do? That it's something constructive or productive or whatever? Fucking rich!" She doesn't quite look him full in the face as she speaks, but aims her gaze (what he can see of it behind the greased curtain of her hair) somewhere over his shoulder. She was never one for direct eye contact.

"All right, Ellen. I'm sorry. I'm just surprised. And concerned. It's been"—he begins to calculate the number of years, then quits trying—"years." He's vaguely aware of the ravens, criticizing each other from the white pine boughs high in the sky, their monotonous vocabulary. He gazes over Ellen's sloped shoulder at the Hinshaw's property over the hobblebush hedge, pleased that neither Stacey nor Taylor seem to be about to observe the domestic rancor.

"Let's go inside, Ellen, and talk for a while. It's silly to stand out here."

His daughter declines with a shake of the head vigorous enough to lash a few stray curls about. The familiar gesture makes her seem like an adolescent again and takes his breath away, quite literally. He must remind himself to inhale and exhale, inhale and exhale. She won't come inside. Memories she'd prefer not to court, he imagines. The dark green tattoo of the spruce inside her left forearm catches his eye. She had gone up to Machias her sophomore year with Cassidy and a fake ID to get this tattoo, which she had managed to conceal from him for months.

"I suppose you're staying out at Jude's place?" he asks, lifting his eyes from the tattoo, reminding himself to breathe.

"Does it really matter, Father?"

Yes, he wants to say. It really matters. But he chooses a separate tack, mostly to avoid further discussion of Jude. He has received his answer, in any case.

"Do you need any money?"

"Oh, you'd just love that, wouldn't you?"

He denies the charge but she doesn't seem to hear.

"Your fuck-up daughter crawling back to beg for your charity. No, I don't need money, Father. That's not why I'm here."

He doesn't know quite what she means by *here.* Here in town, generally, or here now at the old house? "So, anyway, I'll see you around, Father." He doesn't think she means this as a threat. Or maybe she does. Because with that she's off, striding back down the street toward Main, affecting the familiar half-assed slope of her shoulders and neck. She's thinner now, yes. And something else. Something about her stride catches Hertzog's attention, a slight hitch to it, as if a muscle in her leg or foot had fallen asleep while she sat on the stoop too long. The stride improves as she slips from his view—before Hertzog can ask, *Why then? Why are you here?*, ask whether she has a new mobile phone number she might wish to share, or whether she might like to return for a meal or take one out with him if she'd prefer neutral territory, before Hertzog can say how good it is to see her again or thank her for thinking of him and for stopping by, before he can tell her that he's missed her, because he's missed her, terrifically so, he realizes only now. The ravens' cries rise in her wake, criticizing not each other but him.

Caw. Caw. Caw. Caw.

He can hardly concentrate upon his work now. He sets off in the Subaru for the harbor a few miles away, pausing indoors just long enough to relieve his bladder and switch out his sweat-soaked hiking boots for dry socks and sneakers. He'll take a meal at the Dry Dock Café overlooking the marina to think things over, splurge maybe on fried clam bellies, his HDL to LDL ratio holding steady according to the bloodwork ordered by Dr. Ramasamay.

His daughter has returned. Why? For Jude? Impossible.

The road curves between the pine and spruce woods toward the coast, then flirts with the rocky shoreline for a while before reaching the small harbor proper, offering glimpses of the Gulf of Maine for extended stretches at two promontories before curving back toward the woods. A pair of eiders, enormous waterfowl with sloped foreheads, dabble about the rockweed lolling at the surface, gleaning the plants or maybe marine organisms, vertebrate and invertebrate, these tiny creatures going about their own voracious life business amid the indifferent shelter of these tough weeds anchored by their holdfasts to the rocks below.

A waitress he doesn't recognize at the café seats him at a small window booth, her terse words flavored by some Baltic country, if he's not mistaken. He can smell the kitchen fryer mingling with some sort of cleanser they must use to wipe down the tables. Two lobstermen sit at the counter across the aisle, already ashore from tending their traps, suspenders of their rubber clothing looped down either side of their vinyl stools. The waitress returns with his water and introduces herself as Katarina, then in scripted iambs announces that she'll be taking care of him and asks whether he's ready to place his order. He hasn't yet studied the laminated menu, but does so in an instant. He notes the lobster roll price this season (twenty-three dollars!), then orders the fried clam bellies and an iced tea, returns his attention to the lobstermen's backs as Katarina slips away.

The television above the bar segues to a commercial—two lovers on the screen hold hands across the lips of their separate bathtubs perched on a lakeside dock—while Hertzog eavesdrops on the lobstermen. They're native Mainers, he can tell by the way they drop their r's, the string of *ayuhs* punctuating their repartee. The lobsterman doing most of the talking is younger than Hertzog initially gathered, a baby face beneath his ginger beard, maybe the son or nephew of the other fellow as they both sport ginger beards. The lobster season, apparently, hasn't been as gangbusters as Hertzog assumed. The shedders haven't yet come in from the deeper waters. Only lobstermen making money are the "rich fuckas" who can afford to set their traps miles offshore. Things went on like this, the younger fellow complains to his partner, swiveling his stool, pointing a french fry glossed with ketchup over his shoulder out Hertzog's window toward the marina, he'll be trading in half his traps next year for a scallop or seaweed permit. Hertzog knows what his neighbor, Stacey Hinshaw, would think of this idea, fishing "down the chain" to the next resource primed for depletion. He's scanned the pamphlets she's left in his mailbox.

❧

The Robersons enter the café just before Hertzog has the chance to ask for his check. Grace-Ann's Boston Celtics baseball cap, oversize for her head, stands out against the more subdued hues of her jeans and T-shirt. She crosses the threshold first, pushing a walker, the door held open by Will. Cindy pulls up the rear, an oversize purse hanging off one shoulder, a canvas backpack weighing down the other, her countenance fixed in an expression of fierce determination as they pause beside the register and wait for one of the servers to seat them. He didn't know Grace-Ann needed a walker now to get about. A strip of translucent white tape secures an IV port to her arm. Will, scanning the floor for a server, or maybe for an empty booth, spots Hertzog, flashes his eyebrows and walks over to him after guiding his wife and daughter to an empty table not far from the door.

"Good to see you, David." They shake hands. Will Roberson's hand is large and damp, maybe from all his exertions ferrying about his daughter and her walker. Will was Hertzog and Rebecca's financial planner back in the day, championed gold and small-cap stocks, both of which outperformed expectations, Hertzog must admit.

"Good to see you too, Will. How's Grace-Ann?"

"You know"—he gropes for the next words, seems to consider whether or not to offer any—"doctors say it's the chemo making her weak, not the tumor messing up her motor functions. So that's good."

"That *is* good." Hertzog tries to believe him.

"Doing the treatments in town now too. They're sending a new cocktail up from Portland."

"That was a long drive you had to take down there with Grace-Ann."

"Trip to Europe right around the corner, anyway. That's lifted her spirits. Done with this round, doctors say she should get her strength back and we can go."

Grace-Ann wanted to see Rome. The Make-a-Wish Foundation had already funded the trip, but Cindy's sisters had spearheaded a campaign to muster additional resources to make the time abroad extra special, upgrade the hotels and tour-package, maybe buy a few more souvenirs. Hertzog had contributed a sizable donation, anonymously.

Will tells him he better get back to the family and so they shake hands again and that's that, it seems. What else is there to say?

Hertzog flags down his waitress after she finishes her first pass at the Robersons, mimes writing against his upraised palm to ask for the check, an international gesture Katarina seems to understand. While Will studies the menu over there, Cindy seems to be fiddling with some sort of electronic entertainment device in front of their daughter, swiping and tapping at the screen to call up some game for the girl, likely. She must be thirteen or so, Grace-Ann, Will and Cindy having this last child late.

Could die of any number of things, Thoreau's time. A bad fever. A nicked thumb. Things were better now, but not everyone was spared. Upon first learning of Grace-Ann's diagnosis, Hertzog had remembered the scare his wife and he had had with Ellen when she was just three. He remembers now as he tries not to stare at the Robersons, shifts his gaze out the window toward a skiff charging too fast in the idle zone toward the dock, moored boats either side bucking against its foamy wake. During a routine checkup, their pediatrician had felt something on Ellen's neck.

"You haven't noticed this swelling?" Dr. Angelides inquired, brows furrowed while her fingertips massaged both sides of their daughter's neck.

They hadn't noticed.

It turned out to be nothing, but not before a month that included an appointment with a pediatric oncologist in Portland and their frantic waiting for the swelling to go down, or worsen. The swelling went down. They had gotten away with it. That's how it had seemed to him at the time, before he was distracted by the next, lesser crisis, and the crisis after that, and the crisis after that.

The waitress, Katarina, sets down the Roberson's food, then returns to Hertzog's table with the check. He hands her his credit card without inspecting the accuracy of her accounting, notices the giant cruise ship out his window that has just angled into view, emerging from behind Gull Rock. The dredged channel was not nearly deep enough for the behemoth vessel to dock with the lobster boats and fewer recreational sailboats, skiffs, and center consoles. It will moor a ways off in the harbor, its tenders ferrying passengers to shore, buses then taking the newlyweds and nearly-deads back and forth from harbor to town. Hertzog exhales against the onslaught. He's not sure he's prepared to navigate the fast-approaching high season, tourists from practically every state and international locales, too, but most visitors hailing from nearby Massachusetts. Mass-holes.

The Robersons have started in on their food, except for Will who's risen to dissemble the exoskeleton of his daughter's lobster, tending to the task with such urgency you'd think his life depended upon it, slouching over her chair to pierce claws with the metal crackers. Hertzog watches as Will sets large chunks of meat onto her plate, muttering words to his daughter Hertzog can only imagine, discards the mined shells into the metal pail.

He looks back wistfully now at his own days some twenty, thirty years ago, and with wonder, considering the David Hertzog he once was, if only for a brief time, a father who fled the office at a moment's notice to gauge the swollen lymph nodes of a young daughter, a husband who moderated the responses of an excitable wife. Accountable, in a word.

Yes, Rebecca and he had gotten away with it, as he thought about it at the time of Ellen's cancer scare. He still feels this way, despite everything that has transpired in its wake. And so he was accountable still, Hertzog.

9

March 14th, 1838
Hardly a rood of land but can show its fresh wound or indelible scar, in proof that earlier or later man has been there.

H. has arrived in Maine at the wrong time, altogether. The wrong time, in any wise, to secure employment as a schoolteacher. Butcher, baker, or candlestick maker, he might enjoy better luck. Every hamlet he dares enter, carved out from dark woods or raggedly tilled farmland—Brunswick, Bath, Gardiner, Hollowwell—the superintendent of schools chants the same discouragements. Summer positions have been assigned weeks ago. H. receives these rebuffs with equanimity, gathers up his letters of reference from the miserly clutches of his would-be employers, retrieves his *Phelps & Squire's Traveller's Guide and Map of the United States* from his knapsack, and is on his way.

Good day to you too, sir.

By the time he reaches Augusta, however, he senses a sour mood creeping in on cat's feet, not least of all on account of the strange northern meats (moose?) and oleaginous gravies wreaking havoc with the goings on in his digestive tract. He increasingly wonders whether simple fare—rice, bread, peas, and potatoes—might offer nourishment enough to keep soul and body together, and might spare the poor men who mind the privy a measure of malodorous labor.

Today, he sits in a too-short chair before one Jebediah Sibley, other side of an enormous desk. The luminous May daybright renders the sudden interior space of the single-room schoolhouse impossibly dark. For whatever reason, Mr. Sibley, overstuffed and overdressed, refuses to draw the curtains. H. hears the clomping of hooves other side of the timbers, the cawing of crows, the treble notes of a child's ecstatic cries. The man flicks his tongue toadishly to wet his fingers as he shuffles between the letters of reference in his hand, the top corners of the fine cotton stock greased by Sibley's thumb. H. anticipates niggardly words as he waits for him to speak. He tries not to shrink from the fetid odors wafting across the desk in the lambent air. He would hazard to guess that Superintendent Sibley is a great lover of their local meats and ripest cheeses, pocked with fragrant mold.

"Your apprenticeship in Canton hardly suffices as actual experience for a master of schools. Hardly suffices at all, young man." The jowls below Sibley's rubicund cheeks balloon as he challenges young H.'s bona fides.

H. wonders at these strange encounters with Mainers he's sheepishly navigated these past days—wonders, specifically, whether every man, woman, or child set before him might be regarded as a test. Here is this soul before him, this particular force in the world. What of his own force? It seems incumbent upon him now to offer some counterbalance against the superintendent's churlishness.

"I should think the good citizens of Augusta would count themselves blest to secure my services, Mr. Sibley, prepared as I am to teach Latin, Greek, French, German, physics, natural philosophy, natural history, and the various mathematical arts, including geometry. I can scarcely imagine you'll find a more qualified applicant to educate the local youth."

"Pshaw!"

"Though perhaps education is not your principal concern. Perhaps you only wish that the tender souls under your charge be mastered, as you say."

"Sakes alive!" Sibley rises from his chair, taller than H. supposed. His eyes bulge from the sockets. "The temerity! Out! Out this instant! Before I summon the authorities!"

H. wordlessly withdraws, neglecting to retrieve his besmudged letters of referral. He squints against the daybright on the landing, pulls a generous dose of spruced air into his lungs, competing with the not unpleasant horse dung and wood smoke. The great man warned him on a recent amble—or was it during their Hedge Club meeting (as they now call their increasingly popular teachers' meetings in honor of a regular attendee, Frederic Hedge)?—about the sour faces that greet the man who dares to defy local standards of decorum. *For nonconformity, alas, the world will whip you with its displeasure.*

He will start a school of his own in Concord, he decides, despite his lack of experience. He will hew to his own genius rather than follow slavishly the sterner models. To supplement the wisdom of books, they will repair to the outdoors for their natural history lessons and to invigorate the humors. He will enlist his brother, John, lure him back to their hearth from Roxbury to conduct their experiment. But first, he will expand his circumference in this strange state of Maine, this land of late-blooming trees, hardscrabble farmland, and laconic citizens. He can hardly wait to consult the *Phelps & Squire's* guide and be on his way. With any luck, he might secure passage today to visit his Penobscot tribe (as he thinks of his Maine cousins) in Bangor.

Oh, what a cousinly welcome he receives at dear Rebecca's home. Rebecca's husband, George Thatcher, takes H. by train to the last station at the outpost of Oldtown, as George must attend to business matters there pertaining to his logging interest. Upon departing the train, they paste bear fat across a goodly portion of their exposed flesh to discourage the skeeters and strange flies. While George tends to his business at the mill, H. ambles down to the river and encounters a fine Indian sifting through pelts on his pontoon. He wears deer-skin moccasins and pantaloons, his uncut silver and silvering mane tamed from his eyes by a thin leather cord looped round his sloping forehead. H. wonders whether the fate of the red man was sealed the moment most others traded their buffalo and deer-hides for the milled linens of the white man. H. would do well, perhaps, to avoid any enterprise that requires new clothes.

It takes little encouragement to prompt the fellow to share his report of these untrammeled wild lands he sweeps with his gaze. His gregariousness distinguishes him from the mostly silent lot of white Mainers even more so than his sunkiss'd skin and untamed shock of hair. He regales H. with stories of olden days, the moose and bear and deer thick for his family and fewer French trappers, the waters teeming with salmon come to spawn, shad, and alewives. His sons, he explains, have gone off to work for the logging companies.

"Two miles up *Pen*-ob-scot," the Indian says, claiming water rights through his strange pronunciation of the river's name. "Three miles." He sweeps with a single arm the waterscape and distant woods behind the pontoon. "Fine beautiful country."

H. might extend his trip to explore this wild country, but he misses his dear sisters, Helen and Sophia. He misses his brother, John, with whom he must speak about business matters, misses his parents and even their boarders, considerably more skilled in the art of conversation than the lot in Maine. Home. He misses home. He gazes up into the serrated spruceline over the old Indian's shoulder, resolving to return to this wild country while he still retains some semblance of his youthful vigor.

10

Hertzog sets out for Jude Winslow's place in deeper Maine, forgoing his usual morning routine. The Bowl's tannic water won't miss his tired arms thrashing about its surface. He's not sure what he'll do when he gets there. Ellen will be outdoors, with any luck, crouching between rows of nascent leafy greens, pruning the apple trees, pushing a wheel barrow to and fro. He won't have to enter the barn-store or knock on the house door, navigate Jude's truculence or the suspicions of one of Jude's current acolytes. He's not sure what to expect. Who knows what kind of operation Jude still runs out there? Just hippies doing hippie things, the best-case scenario. Yet Jude ever frustrated such a generous appraisal. The college extricated itself from Cherryfield Farm and withdrew their financial support years ago. The farm and its stand had mostly been a front, it seemed, for Jude's more concerted business: growing and selling herbal psychotropics while cultivating a rotating assortment of nubile sexual partners. Parents of Emmenthaler coeds Jude had bedded, granted three-credit internships, had sued the college. There had been a sizeable settlement, even though Jude himself, despite Claire Libby's investigation, couldn't be charged with any criminal wrongdoing, age of consent laws what they were. The illicit substance charge, for reasons Hertzog can't recall, didn't stick, either. This was all before Ellen had even gotten mixed up in Jude. Hertzog hasn't kept tabs on Jude since his creepy business with Robin LaPointe, when Ellen finally got wise and fled, but he's heard rumors about town over the years of Jude's evolving interests to keep up with his taxes on the bucolic property: ostrich farming (or was it llama?), site rental for pony-riding and goat-feeding birthday parties, clothing made from hemp and other natural fibers, dubiously sourced nutritional supplements.

Hertzog must drive some miles beyond Teddy's, where he'd dropped in on Ellen's old friend, Cassidy, to reach the property. The Subaru's engine runs smoothly now, having recovered from Brant's attentions. He drives with the windows rolled down this beautiful June day, the birds' seasonal joy Dopplering through the warmer air, those pretty olive-colored vireos, he thinks. Thrushes too, maybe. A new tree-funk smell infiltrates the car's interior, mingling with the exhaust of vacationers' vehicles and the occasional semi, a familiar, vaguely semen, aroma.

He'd rather think more about the tree, the birds, the lovely June day, but wonders, instead, his grip tightening on the wheel, whether he might be overreacting, seeking out Ellen in this way. No longer a child, it should be up to her to determine what sort of relationship she wishes to cultivate with her father, whether *any* sort of relationship was necessary or advisable. Ellen had indicated her druthers, sure enough, through her silence these past several years. Their most recent encounter suggested further that she wanted little to do with him. Yet here's the thing Hertzog can't quite shake: *She had come to see him.* Ostensibly, she claimed, to offer fair warning. She was back. But this was a flimsy pretext, wasn't it? She had returned. She had made her way to the old house, waited on the stoop for who knows how long to lay eyes upon her father and speak with him. He had flubbed that encounter, to be sure, just as he ever managed to sabotage their most crucial moments. Still, she hadn't returned to their backwater and visited him unannounced just to let him know she was living here again. What she truly wanted was something else, fathering of some ilk. She needed him now, perhaps, more than ever.

He notes the Cherryfield Farm signage well in advance of the actual property. BABY GREENS, an old clapboard advertises in black lettering, the wood peeking through the thin white paint of the backdrop. Jude's half-assedness reveals itself everywhere. Additional rickety clapboard signs spaced at imprecise intervals advertise LOCAL HONEY, T-SHIRTS, PIES, CHEESE, ARTISAN MEATS, SEA VEGETABLES. It's early in the season for produce. Jude might grow the baby lettuces in one of his greenhouses, protected from nighttime frost. Most of the advertised goods he surely purchases from more southerly climes and marks up for the general public. "Sea Vegetables" alone seems strange. Seaweed, does he mean?

He parks the car on a scruffy patch of weed-infested pea rock inside the open gate, modeling the alignment of the two other vehicles, one generously stickered with various progressive slogans. WHAT WOULD WALT WHITMAN DO? WHO'S YOUR FARMER? EVE WAS FRAMED. VISUALIZE WHIRLED PEAS. The property looks pretty much the same: the old barn-store, retrofitted with electric and a concrete floor, the original two-story red farmhouse beyond, which

Jude moved farther off the busy road shortly after purchasing the place, the unpainted barn and larger outbuilding of cheap fiberglass siding he built, which recalls poultry, but where various employees and interns used to live, and likely still live. It somehow passed the building code. Hertzog had checked the town records.

Animal manure and pollen smells outmuscle the weaker green of the forest that looms over the broken fields. An unfamiliar odor invades his nostrils, as well. Something rancid, vegetal. A compost pile, likely. Only mounds he sees are a ways off beyond the barn-shop under blue tarps where a stubble-field meets the spruce-line. The tarps, maybe, to capture heat and spur the decomposition of whatever foul mix of carbon and nitrogen waste lay underneath. He scans the visible acreage for Ellen, but sees only a couple wiry not-Jude white men crouching in the fields, five or six motley goats outside the chicken-wire enclosure gnawing at whatever unfortunate plants had the temerity to advertise a shoot from the rocky soil. A mocha-colored girl, college-age maybe, dreadlocks tamed by some sort of fabric sleeve, sits on a bench closer by just outside the barn-store. She feeds wool into a spindle to make yarn. Is Jude raising sheep now too? Or do these fibers originate in some more exotic animal of his speculation? Alpaca! Yes, *that* was the animal he was mixed up in. Not llamas or ostriches. She works the spindle's pedal with no particular urgency. Hertzog notices the lighter skin-tone of the callus-soled part of her foot beneath her flouncy skirt. She glances up at him as he approaches, flashes bright teeth he hadn't expected. He can't help feeling protective over this young woman, hardly older than a child. He ought to ask her whether she knows Ellen, and where she might be, but demurs—offers a simple hello, instead, which she returns. He'll check inside the store first, see what's what.

CASH ONLY, a sign at the entrance warns. A wide assortment of canned goods and earth-tone clothing take up a good bit of the floor space, shelves and racks upsetting the sloppy pyramids of multicolored potatoes and spring onions and baby lettuces and gnarly-shaped carrots and radishes (white and red). He scans the various jams, candies, honeys, syrups, artisanal salts and hot-sauces, marvels at the outsize wall space afforded to various lotions, salves and unguents, the labels smacking of a rinky-dink, homey operation. Through the misted glass of two refrigerators, he surveys the cheeses and vacuum-packed chicken and pork products—sliced and diced, spatchcocked and sausaged, herb-rubbed and fragrantly oiled. One of the freezers holds ice creams sourced from goat and cow milk, as well as plant-based non-dairy facsimiles.

The "sea vegetables," he finally notices, command space in dedicated produce bins beside the freezer in a sort of out of the way corner of the store. Seaweed, of course. Signage affixed to each bin indicates the specific varieties of dried seaweed, "hand harvested" and packaged in what appear to be zip-locked plastic bags of various size. Alaria. Dulse. Sugar kelp. Laver. Wakame. Ascophyllum/Alaria/Fucus Seasoning Blend. The specimens range in color from blackish green, purple, yellow, and orange and seem to be cut into strips of various size, or, in the case of the seasoning blend, crumbled. Stacey and Taylor Hinshaw must know about Jude's operation. He wonders what they think of it, but Hertzog's not here to scrutinize the ecological integrity of Jude's sea vegetable operation.

Jude, thankfully, doesn't seem to be about. Instead, a young man of indeterminate ethnic origin—chocolate eyes mooned with premature dark beneath—peers over his book toward Hertzog from behind the register. The kid seems to trace him with his eyes as he mills about the store, suspicious or curious or both. Hertzog supposes he doesn't look precisely like their typical customer. Lingering over the gnarly pile of purple carrots, he figures he'll buy a few things to lubricate the encounter, fills a couple (repurposed) paper bags with carrots and potatoes, plus a bag of that rose and purple seaweed called dulse. He brings his purchases to the ancient register, which prompts a weary sigh from the young man, setting his book face down on the scarred wooden counter to save his page. Hertzog scans the cover, expects some sort of leftist political tract, but it seems like a comic book, or "graphic novel," he knows just enough to know.

"Found everything you were looking for?" the kid asks, weighing the purchases on the scale. Strange piercings afflict his ears, wooden circles that stretch the lobes from within, vaguely recalling some primitive African (or maybe South American) tribe.

"Yes. Thank you. I was wondering, though, is Ellen about, Ellen Hertzog?"

"You know Ellen?" The young man's slender fingers dance over the cash register keys. A tattoo of indecipherable lettering rings one of the slender fingers.

"She's my daughter."

"Oh."

Hertzog gauges the tenor of the response, laced only with benign curiosity, it seems. She hadn't mentioned her father, he gathers, at least not to this olive-skinned boy with moons under his eyes and strange piercings.

"She's tending the pigs."

A mordant puff of air escapes Hertzog's lips, which the fellow, raising a dark and strangely manicured eyebrow, seems to detect. There were all sorts of sentences Hertzog might have imagined years ago that someone might utter in reference to his grown daughter. *She's tending the pigs* was not one of these sentences.

"You know where we keep them now?"

He didn't. The young man tells him he'll have to walk back down the road a quarter-mile or so. He points outside the barn-store with his tattooed finger and tells him to look for the green metal fence between the stretches of rock wall. They're not too far inside, under the big apple tree.

"So, anyway, that'll be $15.85."

Hertzog tries not to blanch at the outsize cost of the dulse and a few carrots and potatoes. What a racket.

He slips from the store and squints against the sun, which seems to have just crested the spruce-line of the hill other side of the road. After dropping off his purchases in the passenger seat of the Subaru, he walks down the road on the scruffy berm beside a jagged line of Jude's young fruit trees, mish moshed peach and pear and apple, a random array to (possibly) confuse airborne predators, yet (probably) reflects Jude's catch-as-catch-can predilections. Some of the trees haven't set fruit yet. Dark pollinators loop about the flowers. He walks close to the trees to keep well clear of the fast-moving vehicles, some towing small boats on the way to one of the larger lakes in the area, lashing him with their dust wake. Pebbles carom against his sneakers upon the passage of a semi dispatched from the paper mill.

He glimpses the green fence across the street and crosses. It takes a moment to figure out the rod-and-pin mechanism but he manages to free the latch and enter the parcel of land. He's never seen this section of the property before, a mild downslope canopied by ancient apple and other old orchard trees he doesn't know, planted by the former owners, likely, land that a more ambitious farmer might have grubbed out and replanted years ago. Fewer spruce, white pine, and birch compete for sunlight, as well, their wind-strewn or bird-shat seed finding purchase. Weedy grass of some sort struggles beneath the canopy to paste the rocky red clay. A mowed trail marks the way to the pigs. He sees her, Ellen, stooped over a low fence of wire marked by flags (electrified?), her thatch of hair pony-tailed askance near the back. She doesn't see him yet. He notices the fiberglass pig-sheds inside the low fence, but doesn't see any pigs. The grass is unmown in the middle of the small pasture, a muddy red clay run circling the thicket. He approaches slowly, hoping she might detect his footfalls and glance up at him before he startles her with his presence. A wrench gleams in her fist.

"Ellen," he calls as he nears. A nebulous odor somewhere between mud and shit overtakes the grass smells. He's not ten yards away now. She hears his voice—she must hear him—but won't be distracted from her labors.

"Hello, Father," she says, her eyes still fixed on the mechanism, unflappable before him or putting on a good show of it. It seems to be some sort of water-supply mechanism attached to a hose she's working on. "I figured you might be stopping by soon," she continues, still not looking toward him. Has she once looked him, or anyone else, directly in the eye? She used to complain that direct eye contact was too aggressive, or some such nonsense.

"I just thought I'd check in on you."

She sighs over her labors. "Okay."

Clearly, he'll have to carry this conversation. He might have planned his words more carefully, or at all.

"You startled me the other day. I felt bad about the way I reacted. But I'm glad that you stopped by the house. I shouldn't have hassled you, I suppose I mean."

This seems to amuse her. She rises from the water do-hickey and smiles, displaying the disappointing results of the orthodontia he forced her to endure. She squares her shoulders to him as if to invite his inspection, looks him in the eye for a split-second that nearly blinds him, the brilliant image of Rebecca he suddenly sees in his daughter's face. It puts him in a different place, from which he must return upon a few deep breaths of the mud-shit smells. His daughter is only a few years younger now, it occurs to him, than her mother was when Hertzog first laid eyes upon her at Emmenthaler. He lowers his gaze. Faded jeans hang on Ellen's narrow hips, affirming his initial impressions from the other day. She's more slender than the daughter he remembers, though not quite wiry. Healthful, he'd say. Discernible muscle-cords ride beneath the green spruce tattoo inside her forearm and from both her biceps above, abundantly advertised below the short sleeves of her T-shirt. The antidepressants had plumped her up as an adolescent, her soft belly and love-handles bothering him more than they seemed to bother her. He doubts she takes any medication now, doubts she can afford health insurance. Which may account for the tremor he notices in her hands as he waits for her words and watches her wipe her perspired face with her shirt, reaching inside the fabric to lift it to her forehead, flashing her flat abdomen and the edge of a sports-bra. He feels the gesture as an intestinal hurt. Ellen had lifted her shirt in precisely this way to clean her face straight through her adolescence, jettisoning paper towel, napkin, or moistened wipe from the time she was small. It drove him crazy back then. Now the gesture simply paralyzes him. Ellen, thankfully, takes up the slack.

"It wasn't such a big deal, Father. I shouldn't have gotten so angry at you. I didn't plan on losing my shit. It's just—"

"What?" He hears the pigs now, snorting and snuffing, sees patches of ginger and pink and black within the clumpy grass cover beyond Ellen's shoulder.

"I don't know. I see you, Father, and you start talking, and, well…" She lets the words trail off, leans down to grasp the end of a second hose, maybe to give her trembling hands something to do.

"I know what you mean. I get it, Ellen."

"Good." She opens the spigot and the water streams out the hose inside the weed-choked pasture. Then she makes a sort of loud kissing sound with her cheek. *Where the hell did she learn that?* The pigs hear the sound, or maybe just the hose-water tattering the earth, and emerge suddenly from the thicket, trotting with surprising spry toward them. Five animals. These aren't ordinary pink pigs. These are more handsome creatures, two of them haired over in solid russet, three mottled black and white. Hertzog watches as the creatures lap at the water with their tongues, as Ellen shifts the trajectory now and again to clean their backs and sides. He supposes this is where all that vacuum-packed artisanal pork inside the glassed refrigerator comes from.

"They like being doused by water," Ellen says.

"I can see that, yes."

He wonders if these last bits are performative gestures, her pig cries, the business with the hose. *Look at me, Father. Here I am tending the pigs. This is a thing I do now.*

"So what's wrong with that do-hickey thing attached to the other hose?" he asks. Inspecting it more closely, it seems to be a small reservoir, some sort of spring-loaded device at the lip designed to sense their snouts, maybe, open the water-supply for their at-will consumption.

"Oh, they keep jamming it with their snouts and rear-ends, using it as a scratching post. That's why I have to come out and make sure they have water. I should be able to jury-rig it."

"You were always handy."

This isn't precisely true, unless he were to count Ellen's passing interest in Legos, or the time he found, crammed between her twin mattress and the wall, the bong she crafted out of an aluminum can. Yet it feels good to offer this simple compliment to his daughter and he hopes that Ellen won't press him to cite examples. His daughter was never very politic at navigating verbal encounters, quick to argue with classmates over the most trivial misunderstanding. Never a joiner, she seemed content to spend free time during elementary school alone at her desk rather than trade cards or cloth bracelets—or whatever the wampum of the moment was—not even reading or drawing half the time but just sitting there, brooding. Teachers sent home notes about this, amplified their concern during parent-teacher conferences. *More accord, less discord!* he had taken to warning her at school drop-off outside the chain-link fence, leaving it to Rebecca to kiss their daughter goodbye.

"Thanks," Ellen says now.

"So are you back with him, Ellen? Jude? Is that the deal?"

Hertzog was never very politic at navigating verbal encounters, either. As he waits for her words, he hears the cars zipping past the farm toward the lake on the highway and the high-pitched gossip of birds perched somewhere in the scaffolding of the ancient apple tree's branches, those small gray gnatcatchers, he thinks, or maybe the tinier kinglets with the white eye-rings and wing-bars.

"No. Not in the way that you think, anyway. I'm just living here, working at the farm."

He doesn't say anything, but can't censor his skeptical expression.

"What's the big deal, Father? I mean, what would you have me be? A housewife? An accountant? A lawyer?" The buzz of some armored insect rises to drown out the chatter of the birds.

"No. That's not—"

"I mean, I don't get it. I never have. Never." Just like that it's the old Ellen, nostrils aflare, unkempt hair obscuring her vision. "Isn't Thoreau supposed to be your big hero? Wasn't he all about self-reliance, not following the mob, all that crap?"

"You might be thinking of Emerson, but yes. Yes, I suppose."

"Beware of any job that requires new clothes. Now he's the one who said *that*! Now *that* I know. He'd be totally into the way we live here compared to most."

Hertzog wasn't sure about this. Thoreau had never cottoned to the various communal living experiments of his day, shuddered at George Ripley's invitation to join Brook Farm. *I think I had rather keep batchelor's hall in hell,* he wrote, *than go to board in heaven.* But he doesn't care to refute Ellen's claim outright, impressed as he is that she's remembered her Thoreau.

"Some aspects of life here Thoreau would have approved of, Ellen. You're right. But not all. And what does it matter anyway? *I'm* the one who's concerned. Jude's checkered past. It was good you got away."

One of the russet-colored pigs beyond the field of the hose begins to urinate, a lusty stream that, weirdly, jets almost straight back from its pig-parts. The ammoniac odor invades Hertzog's nostrils, mixing with the mud-shit effluvia.

Ellen has regained her calm, unflared her nostrils, but doesn't say anything.

"I just don't want to see you repeating patterns of error. That's all."

She rolls her eyes at this last bit, which he might have foreseen.

"Patterns of error? Really? I'm not in middle school, anymore, Father."

"I know that, Ellen. I know."

She reaches down to twist off the spigot, prompting the porcine creatures to disperse. One of the black-and-whites bites the rear of one of the russets, who issues an affronted whinny, a sound that Hertzog wouldn't have associated with pigs. "Easy, girls," Ellen says, coiling up the green hose. She's thinking of what to say next, he can tell, something about the deliberate way she coils up the hose, her strong knuckles whiting under the exertion, the hands not trembling anymore while usefully employed. The air between them has grown darker beneath the indifferent canopy, the sun slipping behind a cloud, maybe.

"It kills you, Father, doesn't it, to think that I might just be okay?"

She's standing close enough that he can smell her pleasant clove-smelling breath (some natural toothpaste?) through the mud-shit-urine smells.

"No, that's not it," he says. "That's not it at all." He wonders, however, whether Ellen is right, or partly right. It hasn't even occurred to him that she might be okay.

The gnatcatchers or kinglets wheeze from the apple tree. Ellen gazes over his shoulder, thinking on his words, maybe. But no, that's not why she gazes over his shoulder.

"You all right, buttercup? He's not bothering you?" The voice startles him from behind. (So he still calls her by that infantilizing nickname, buttercup.) She had spotted Jude's approach. Hertzog turns toward the voice and recognizes him in an instant, the chestnut hair slicked back in its ridiculous ponytail, though silvered through now and receding at both temples. Resting a fist on his hip, he juts a new mild paunch out his Bogart undershirt like a muscle he was proud of. Something prissy about the pose. And that ridiculous hair. There was always something effeminate about Jude, which unnerved Hertzog as it weirdly accentuated his unignorable maleness.

"No, Jude. I'm fine. We were just talking."

An ancient feeling seizes Hertzog's gut upon the mere sight of Jude opposite side of Ellen, keeping his fair distance for the moment, a feeling Hertzog hasn't felt for a long time, primal protectiveness for his grown-up child. Jude took one step closer he might strike him with his fist, which Jude intuited, maybe.

"Professor."

"Jude."

It had been a relief when Hertzog didn't have to feel this sensation, anymore, day in and day out, when Ellen flew their backwater's net. Seized once again by this sensation, however, it isn't such a horrible feeling to feel, this significant sensation. Little doubt that Hertzog is awake and alive. He feels his very blood coursing through his veins, his heart thumping in his chest, the wind rising and falling in his throat.

"Can use you at the greenhouse, buttercup, you finish up here." Jude spits something into the weeds, a gratuitous gesture. With that he's gone, not deigning to say goodbye.

Fucking presumptuous shit, Hertzog thinks—*finish up here*—but doesn't say to his daughter. He isn't sure what he ought to say to Ellen concerning the encounter, or about Jude, generally. He's gained a small but certain amount of ground with his daughter today. He doesn't want to put her off once more.

"I'll call you, Father. Okay?"

It was okay. For now. He tells her so and suggests that they walk back together. She nods her head, leans over to fiddle with the spring-loaded device some more, maybe to test it again, or maybe to give Jude ample time to clear out, or both. Hertzog doesn't rush her. He asks if she needs an extra pair of hands (she says no), listens to the outdoor sounds and tries not to wince at the pig-smells while he waits.

Once she's ready to head back, he slows his stride to keep shoulder to shoulder with Ellen on the pebbly berm, taking the outside, forcing the cars to slow and swerve some to pass. She props her hands in the back pockets of her jeans in the way she sometimes affected as an adolescent, palms out so her elbows jut to the side. She strides with an off-beat gait, it seems, but that might just be the sloping berm. It feels almost like one of their compulsory hikes Ellen sometimes enjoyed as a child, despite herself. They share a few words of little consequence concerning the weather, the pigs, Hertzog's daily exercise at the Bowl, which seems to surprise his daughter.

"You still swim there?" she asks. "Still?"

"Yes," he answers. "I do. Still."

To change the subject, he tells her that her old friend Cassidy says hello and that she's still working as a waitress at Teddy's.

"Cassidy," his daughter says, tasting the name in her mouth.

They don't hug goodbye at his car, of course. But she promises again that she'll call. "Soon," she says this time.

Yes, progress of a sort has been made. Not until he's well clear of Cherryfield Farm, easeful with the rpm's, does a less pleasant sensation seize his innards. Why had Jude sought out Ellen when he did? He didn't need her at the greenhouse. That fellow in the barn-store. The one with the strange piercings and dark moons under his eyes. *You know Ellen? She's tending the pigs.* The little shit had sought out Jude after directing Hertzog to the pigs, had maybe noticed him sniffing about the stubble fields and compost piles under the blue tarps before entering the store. Of course. He had gone to warn Jude. Some old dude was here poking around and asking after Ellen, claimed to be her father.

What did it mean? That a warning to Jude was required?

11

Fall of 1839
Then first I conceive of a true friendship, when some rare specimen of manhood presents itself.—It seems the mission of such to commend virtue to mankind, not by any imperfect preaching of her word, but by their own carriage and conduct.—We may then worship moral beauty without the formality of a religion.

They are some fresher wind that blows—some new fragrance that breathes. They make the landscape and sky for us.

H. opens his school in the family home. Why ought not the windows and walls, chairs and tables of the family abode be called upon to perform double-duty? He manages to enroll four lads from Boston, who board with them. Mornings he devotes to Greek, Latin, or mathematics, conveyed in the Socratic manner, then a noontime dinner consisting of his mother's clean ample diet—melons and potatoes and other fruits and vegetables, rolls with butter, nutmeats and cheeses on special occasions, puddings and pies, savory and sweet. He conducts natural philosophy lessons outdoors in the afternoon, partly to facilitate the digestion, leads his boys to Fair Haven Hill, the river, the pond, attentive to the botanical goings on—sporific mushrooms, lichens rainbowed against tree bark (the stained glass of nature's cathedral!), and angiosperms aplenty. You need only look to see, he counsels. Brandishing tweezers, he plucks stamen and stigma from goldenrod, bird's foot violet, sweet rhodora, what have you, inveighs upon his lads to identify the various parts and describe the interdependent functions of pollinators and pollinated. He would leave the living creatures to their kingdom, but cannot resist shooting a slate-colored junco one day with Father's rifle to allow closer inspection—the intricate design of the plumage, the seed-crushing mandible, the fine and flexible reptilian toes. He manipulates the joints with his fingers, allows each boy to handle the fresh-killed specimen to conduct his own inquiries.

Mr. E. and certain influential town elders, Sirs Hoar, Brooks, and Keyes, approve of his progressive methods, not least of all because H. won't spare the youth their Latin and geometry. The dear men initiate a veritable campaign toward his enterprise, bend ears at the lyceum, post office, and church. What's more, the moss-backed headmaster of the Concord Academy propitiously resigns, whereupon the board offers its name, its goodwill, and, of equal importance, their two-story schoolhouse for a modest fee. By the end of the fall quarter, having only initiated his experiment in June, H. enrolls twenty-three students of both sexes. He lures his dear brother from his Roxbury post to join him in shared purpose. Upstairs at the Concord Academy, H. teaches the more arduous college preparation curriculum while John, downstairs, teaches the usual English branches. Few appointments need be mustered toward their aim, the building reasonably outfitted. H., nonetheless, purchases from Mr. Harding's shop a simple pine desk painted green, the top slanted at a most agreeable angle for writing. He anticipates that he will put the small desk to good use over the many years before him, health providing.

Here he sits alone at the desk, recess-time, gazing out the window at John roughhousing with a few of the older boys on the lawn. H. ought to be pleased with recent developments. Yet, since John has joined the enterprise, he feels old patterns reasserting themselves in disconcerting fashion—John, the jovial playmate of their charges, ever lending his back to their younger children for pony-rides, his handbacks to the older lads for their ruffian games, while H. maintains a certain remove, withdrawing somewhere deep inside himself on school grounds. He would attach himself like a bloodsucker to an individual lad or lass of virtuous spirit. H. longs to inspire his charges, or one or two souls.

Along comes eleven-year-old Edmund of Scituate, grandson of mother's beloved boarder, Mrs. Joseph Ward, co-founder of their Women's Anti-Slavery Society. The lad arrives summertime, Concord's flora and fauna bursting. H. takes Edmund sailing on the Concord in the *Musketaquid,* the tidy, tight-planked boat built with John shortly after H.'s return from Maine. He enjoys saunterings with Edmund to the cliffs and pond. To be in this virtuous boy's presence is to be reminded of the one true soul shared by us all, to borrow from the great man's lexicon.

Today, they amble pondward on special lookout for his fox, the air redolent with skunk cabbage, the cloying buttery aroma of berberry, and the more genial kiss of the swamp lilies oranging everywhere. H. recognizes and announces most flowers by their fragrances before catching sight of them, much like he announces the vireo by its call. *Here I am. There you are.* He fears his new student might find him a braggart, identifying this and that plant and bird. Yet Edmund appreciates the instruction.

"What's the name of that flower?" Edmund inquires, kneeling by the riot of small white blossoms partially obscured by its sturdier foliage.

"Trailing arbutus," H. replies. "Note the perfect five-petaled flowers." He crouches beside the child to collect a sample, thankful that he brought his microscope.

"No, don't," the lad interrupts his efforts, placing a moist hand on his bare forearm, which takes him aback. When was the last time another soul touched H., flesh on flesh?

"Don't what, dear Edmund?"

"Don't pluck that poor flower from its host. You'll hurt it."

H. protests that the plant will be fine. There are plenty of flowers on the specimen to perform their flowerly duties, and it's not as if the plant can feel pain.

"How do you know that plants don't smart in their own fashion?"

The question cuts H. to the quick. How *do* we know that plants feel no pain?

You must plant your feet firmly before your friend. H. remembers his earlier intuition shared at his recent lecture at the lyceum. Edmund seems also to have intuited the kernel. He commends the boy for his noble intuitions bravely expressed and rises from the ground. He promises to leave the plant be so that he might reflect more deliberately upon the matter of plants and their feelings.

H. releases the child upon their return to the house. He sits with his daybook on the metal chair beneath the poplar in the backyard and sniffs at the carbon perfume emanating from the pencil shed. He detects virtue, somehow, in the fine particulate atmosphere. Strange. The virtuous qualities he detects in the boy are not so much *in the boy*, it seems to him, as in his own mind that registers such virtue. "I have within the last few days come into contact with a pure uncompromising spirit, that is somewhere wandering in the atmosphere, but settles not positively anywhere," he writes. Virtue suffuses the Kosmos, he infers, resides in all those who retain the poetic faculties. "That virtue we appreciate," he scrawls with a feverish hand, "is as much ours as another's. We see so much only as *we* possess."

So what does it mean to love at all? He ponders the question as if it were an intestinal complaint. What hope is there in ever puncturing his aloneness? Despite the great man's trumpeting of self-trust, the integrity of one's own mind and the like palaver, despite the appeal of such principles amid the rabble of dutifully dull and desperate souls, H. longs for human contact. He wonders if only that concomitant to marriage, sexual congress, facilitates such intimacy with another soul. Truest friendship. He lifts his pencil from the leaf of his journal, lifts his eyes toward the poplar. The squirrels have disappeared. A small brown bird flits across the visual screen, but H. cannot be bothered to trace its trajectory. Do the physical throes between lovers precipitate that exalted friendship that the great man seems to enjoy with his companion and helpmeet, Lidian, and that he surely enjoyed with his younger soulmate before her tragic passing? How does it feel to be joined thusly in shared purpose? There must be something to say for the exercise of coitus for there is no disputing its popularity.

12

Hertzog feels that it would be good to speak with Sheriff Libby. Claire. Tell her Ellen's back in town. Find out what she knows about the goings on lately at Cherryfield Farm. If she might do a little digging for him, his daughter back in the equation. He calls her at the station after checking the listing in the outdated local directory (they stopped printing hard copies years ago), surprised when a receptionist transfers him immediately to her line. He expected he'd have to leave a message.

"Sheriff Libby," she announces.

"Hello, Claire." He assumes a certain intimacy. "It's David. David Hertzog."

"Professor, what can I do for you?" He hears papers shuffling about in the background, imagines the phone braced between her shoulder and ear.

"Hoping I could buy you a cup of coffee. Something I want to talk to you about. Can you meet me at the green later, maybe? Pretty day, looks like." Hertzog gazes out his kitchen window to confirm his suspicions, the needles of the white pines beyond the Hinshaw's property glossed by the strengthening sun. Closer by, small black and white birds—chickadees, likely—trace frenetic vortices within the scaffolding of one of the Hinshaw's squat jack pines over the hobblebush hedge that outsiders mistake for hydrangea.

Claire doesn't reply right away, weighing, Hertzog imagines, whether to press him for additional details, deciding against it in the end.

"Eleven good for you, David?"

He tells her yes and that he'll bring the coffee. They hang up before he thinks to ask her how she likes her coffee. Black, if he recalls.

It's not much of a town green as far as town greens go. No famous battles against the French or Indians or British nearby to commemorate with a monument, no epidemic or plague, no heroic Civil War veteran or gilded age founder to honor. Just a postage stamp of balding lawn, shaded summertimes by carefully spaced sugar-maples and one of the town's few towering horse-chestnuts, zigzagged by asphalt walkways, a swatch of wildflowers maintained by the garden club near the full-sun center, plus the small gazebo, where the volunteer band performs various classical and pop standards twice-weekly during the season, and where mild political rallies sometimes form. He scans the few benches planted here and there on the new grass for Claire, then takes the only open bench nearest the gazebo when he doesn't see her, sets the coffee tray down beside him.

Hertzog doesn't spend much time at the green, typically makes a beeline through to shortcut his way to the town's only bakery. Yet, gazing at the people milling about—a pair of boys tossing a Frisbee, a woman behind a portable card-table seeking signatures for some political cause, her face framed by a halo of curls, two girls chatting conspiratorially beneath the gazebo closer by, clusters of couples and families on blankets snacking on local fare—it occurs to him that he loves their little green. Fewer and fewer of these undeveloped, un-monetized spaces exist anymore for the general public to peaceably assemble. Although not the assembling type, Hertzog appreciates the civic spirit of the space. For others.

One of the boys has flown the Frisbee into the rugosa shrub and struggles to reach it through the bramble. He doesn't recognize the boy, or most of the people here, the better portion of them tourists. He ponders whether it would be appropriate to sample his coffee before Claire's arrival (Hertzog prefers his coffee and soup piping hot) but before he can decide she angles into view. He must shield his eyes from the sun peeking from between the globular leaves of the horse-chestnut to look her in the face.

"How did you *not* notice me, David? I was sitting right there." She swivels her head atop strong shoulders toward a separate bench, opens a palm the same direction for emphasis. "You looked right at me." The corners of her mouth rise as she looks back toward him. She's amused, thankfully, by his blindness. She's taken fewer pains this morning to shroud her cunning looks. Her hair seems blonder, unshadowed by her rigid sheriff's cap and hanging loose below her ears rather than tied back. She seems younger too.

"I guess I expected you to be in uniform."

"Technically, it's my day off. I was just catching up on some paperwork when you called the station."

He can't remember the last time he glimpsed Claire in normal clothes, clean sneakers and jeans (unfaded, unripped, and high-waisted, bucking the current fashion), a white button-down top, embroidered with stitching in a floral design, the dressiest part of the ensemble. Hertzog wears khakis, never quite took to dungarees, even as a child.

Claire sits, then asks him which coffee is hers. He tells her it doesn't matter and holds the tray down while she plucks one of the cups. "Heavens, you brought enough sugar and creamers," she says. "You don't remember I take it black?" She takes a careful sip through the tiny opening in the lid.

"Yes, well, I thought so, but it's been a while. Figured you might take something in it now."

"Who does that?" She takes a bolder sip, the hot coffee chuffing against the lid.

"What?" he asks. "Who does what?"

"Change."

Something sad dances across her face, thinking about this *change* business. Or maybe Claire's remembering the when and the why of their few black coffees together, years ago—Claire to the rescue, helping to negotiate the difficulties between father and daughter around the kitchen table. Best she could, anyway. Ellen seemed to prefer Sheriff Libby to the family therapist his daughter mostly refused to visit after the accident. Hertzog wasn't too proud to call upon Claire a few times when he was at his wit's end. Neighbors called Sheriff Libby, too, a couple times during Ellen's screaming jags. Or maybe Claire's sad expression, those worry lines rising between her eyes, has nothing to do with him. Maybe she's thinking about her grown sons (both out of the state last he'd heard). Or maybe she's thinking on Pete. Claire's had her own troubles, for sure.

Claire's husband, Pete, had been a roofer. A successful one. Several trucks and laborers under his command. Was a time you'd likely see at least one of the Lay-Tite Roofing & Repair trucks out and about if you were on the road for any time in Hancock or Washington counties. Pete replaced Hertzog's steep-pitched asphalt shingle roof twice over the years, convincing him the second time to choose a fancier looking rust color to replace the drab black. Cost was the same. "Live a little," he had said over the quote at the kitchen table, then slurped at his coffee through the baleen of his shaggy gray mustache. He said that a lot, as Hertzog recalls. *Live a little.* Hertzog liked Pete. Everyone did. Hertzog associated his laconic good humor with his upbringing in the highlands region of interior Maine near Baxter State Park and Mt. Katahdin, which he claimed, only after Hertzog pressed him, to have climbed fairly often as a Boy Scout. Few people lived there year-round, or at all, Pete said, the winters so fierce, the summertime mosquitoes even worse. Pete and Hertzog were contemporaries, roughly, which lent something easeful to their business together. Something like intimacy. At any rate, the cancer got Pete about five years back. Hertzog never knew precisely what type of cancer it was, just heard an odd detail about the variation Pete suffered, that it metastasized not through the blood, like an ordinary cancer, but through some sort of toxic mucus creeping from one vital organ to the next.

People kept a certain distance from Claire on account of her being sheriff. Most townspeople didn't quite know how to approach her in her time of need. Hertzog wasn't sure whether Claire had one true friend in the world. Other than Pete. Hertzog, himself, might have offered more solid support during Pete's illness after all Claire did for him.

"So Ellen's back," he says now.

"You don't say."

"She came over to see me. Warn me, more like it."

"Not still mixed up with that Jude Winslow, I hope."

Hertzog nods, which prompts an audible exhale through Claire's lips, strong enough to worry her dirty-blond bangs. She takes another sip of her coffee, crosses her jeaned legs and sort of flexes her upraised sneaker back and forth, agitating upon the news.

"That's not good," she finally says, the horse-chestnut lashing her face with its shadows, the day having breezed up. Her terse words worry Hertzog all the more.

"Ellen claims she's not with him romantically, but I'm not sure whether to believe that."

"Honesty was never her strong suit, was it?"

Something wilts inside Hertzog upon hearing the words. The comment would constitute an overstepping of bounds were this anyone but Claire. She seems to be studying the boys playing Frisbee, her eyes tracing the disc's path back and forth, though he'd bet dollars to donuts she's recalling one of Ellen's episodes. The time, say, Hertzog called Claire out to the house to calm Ellen down after she punched her fist through her window, managing somehow not to cut up her knuckles too badly. Hertzog had finally made good on his threat and dissembled the lock to her bedroom door, knob and all, leaving a softball size peephole, which provoked Ellen's tantrum. Her middle school principal had called earlier that day to report that Ellen hadn't completed any homework in four weeks, even though Ellen had claimed all the while to her father that that's exactly what she'd been doing behind her locked door. Or maybe Claire was remembering the time Hertzog had discovered that his daughter had adopted a secret internet identity to communicate with strange men in dubious chat-rooms, which forced him to commandeer her computer, and which provoked yet another one of her eye-quivering rages and a visit from Claire. Or the time a couple years later when the rangers busted her for smoking marijuana atop the Bowl's pink granite ledge with Cassidy and two scruffy boys, Claire intervening to keep the charges off her record. Or the time just before Ellen ditched town when Claire had to investigate Jude for what happened to Robin LaPointe and kept Ellen's name out of the papers best she could.

"I was wondering about the latest word on Jude? Whether he's been keeping on the up and up far as you know or if there's something specific I should be worrying about."

"So this is why you needed to talk?"

"More or less."

"Glad I didn't wear my fancy underwear, David."

Here she laughs, flashing well-rounded teeth, which makes it okay for Hertzog to laugh. It's an unusual joke from Claire's quarter. He smells something herbal on her breath, or maybe it's her lotion or soap. Wintergreen, he decides.

"Ellen, Ellen, Ellen," she mutters, summoning memories. "You know I always thought she was a good girl. A sweet girl. Just troubled. But a good girl down deep where it counts. Why it was such a shame she couldn't get her act together, mixed up with Jude Winslow and whatnot."

Hertzog agrees.

"Be nice if the two of you could find a way to get along, the both of you adults now."

"Yes," he says, though this isn't his primary concern. He mostly wants to make sure Jude isn't victimizing her in some way, manipulating his impressionable daughter. Of course, any manner of terrible fates might have befallen Ellen in Boston or Washington, DC, or any of the other places from which she has sporadically written to him over the years. Yet it was different now, her being so close. Plus, Hertzog reminds himself, Ellen had sought him out. Yes, this changed things.

"Been through the wringer, the two of you."

"I guess no one gets off scot-free, Claire," Hertzog says, partly to defuse the remark, partly because he'd just been thinking about Pete, while Claire had been thinking about Rebecca.

"There's been some concern about rockweed poaching," she declares. "It's pretty strictly regulated these days."

He tells her yes, that he knows. His new neighbors, the Hinshaws, seem pretty involved in rockweed protection efforts. She bobs her head, but doesn't seem to know the Hinshaws or care enough to inquire about them.

"Not my bailiwick, but I've heard from a marine patrol officer I know that it's like land west of the Pecos, our patch of shoreline. Not enough officers to enforce those new marine resource laws. Anyone owning a skiff can cut up as much seaweed as their boat can float. That big corporation from Canada…uh…"

"Acadian Seaplants." Hertzog fills in the blank.

"Yes."

The faraway sound of Claire's *Yes* betrays her distraction. She seems to be gazing toward the woman with the halo of curls at the card table with her petition, conversing with a fellow Hertzog doesn't know but would peg as a banker, accountant, or lawyer, maybe. Neat creases rise from both sleeves of his blue oxford cloth shirt. The man's straight brown hair is still wet from the shower, or maybe only lacquered with some sort of pomade. Even at this distance, Hertzog can see his sun-pinked scalp at the part. The conversation seems animated, contentious. The woman in her shapeless dress stands before the table, a good head shorter than the fellow with the visible part. She waves an arm unattached to the clipboard to punctuate her points. The man stands, arms crossed, taking it for now.

"What do they use that seaweed for, anyway," he asks, "that it's such a controversy all of a sudden?"

"Lots of things, David, don't you know?"

He thinks about the salves, creams, and unguents on sale in Jude's farm store that he didn't bother to inspect, in addition to the plastic baggies of various seaweeds on sale for eating, the pretty dulse on his kitchen counter he doesn't know what to do with. He thinks about those tarps at Cherryfield Farm and the strange compost smells wafting across the planted ground and stubble fields.

The man with the sun-pinked part in his hair argues now at higher decibels. Hertzog can't make out specific words, but the bass notes of various syllables carry across the lawn. The rancor has summoned the attention of others, as well. The couple picnicking on their blanket a safe distance from the Frisbee-boys stop their snacking to stare over at the combatants. The two girls beneath the gazebo, who'd segued to gymnastic poses, cease their exercise. His eyes drift toward a red squirrel that's scampered off the trunk of the horse-chestnut. The creature takes a few tentative steps on the lawn toward the antagonists—intent on some discarded food item it's sniffed out, likely—then reconsiders and retreats to the fissured bark of the tree.

"My lands," Claire says, slapping her palms against her jeaned thighs to catapult herself off the bench. She walks, doesn't run, toward the scene of the struggle, carries her coffee before her. Hertzog follows. He half-expected that it might be rockweed that the woman was trying to protect, but it seems to be some sort of animal rights cause she's advocating, pamphlets on the table emblazoned with glossy photos of sparsely feathered poultry, sad-looking pigs that look nothing like Ellen's pigs. Claire manages to defuse the argument within seconds of her intervention, allows them each to say their piece for her audience. There's something disarming about her presence, the half-smile painting her face, the nonchalant way she holds her coffee, takes a sip now, then suggests to the fellow (she knows his name, George) that he might as well move along on his way. It's a considerable skill that Claire possesses, and has possessed as long as he's known her, this ability to insinuate herself into the human scene in just the right manner to keep the peace. Hertzog's impacts, vis à vis other people, vis à vis Ellen, ever tended toward the inflammatory.

"Guess I can look into what Jude's been up to. Ask around. See if everything's on the up and up." Claire pauses in her tracks to utter these words halfway back to their bench, causing Hertzog to pause, as well. "Thanks for the coffee, David, but gotta run now, pick up my dry cleaning."

"Dry cleaning?"

"Just a joke, David. You used to have a sense of humor."

13

July 25th, 1839
There is no remedy for love but to love more.

H.'s blood jumps the moment he glimpses her beneath the poplar standing beside Mrs. Joseph Ward, her grandmother. She has just arrived for a summer visit. Slender fingers of both her hands below scalloped sleeves brace the mineralized spirits his mother or the ladies Ward must have provided. He had been in the pencil shed marking the progress of his father's labors when he heard the tinkling notes of female voices outside.

"You'll remember our dearest H." Their boarder marks his sudden appearance on the lawn. Aunts Maria and Jane linger in the backdrop, enjoying the novelty of Ellen's visit.

"Surely dearest *David*, you must mean, Grandmother." Ellen offers her hand, damp from the glass and impossibly soft. The hand lingers in his, though he might only imagine that it lingers, contact with this heroic beauty affecting his very sense of time. Her thick shock of dark hair betrays vivacity, whipped high up on her crown in a bun for her travels. The eyes, electric. Were her irises always rimmed with green?

"You haven't heard? He favors his middle name these days."

"Oh?"

"Gentlemen return from Cambridge with all manner of notions."

"I suppose we are all entitled to our peccadilloes," Ellen says, flashing an unblemished smile, then lifts her gaze toward the trajectory of the returning bluebird, which disappears into John's nest box. Her gaze lingers upward at the box, advertising the Classical contours of her jawline, the proud angle of her nose, a fetching feline crease at the tip. The deep set of those electric eyes betray a like depth of character. "Little brother warns me to prepare for excursions of the most adventuresome sort with his new schoolmaster," she says, returning to him her eyes. H. can hold her gaze just long enough to notice hazel swimming inside the green rims. Sakes alive, he's gobsmacked!

"Perhaps speak a word to Edmund's sister," Mrs. Joseph Ward

advises, "so she needn't report home that her brother is under the tutelage of a mute." Maria and Jane snigger into their palms. A vireo issues its declaratives from somewhere high in the scaffolding of poplar branches, mocking H. for his reticence. *Here I am. There you are. Here I am. There you are.*

"Hello," he says. It's the only word his heavy tongue can shape. The single word inspires open laughter from his aunts, Mrs. Joseph Ward, and her granddaughter. They take it to be a cheeky response, obeying his elder's command to the letter. He smiles. Sometimes, it behooves one to allow a misunderstanding to linger. He will remember this kernel for his journal.

"Oh, H., witty as I remember you. I know we will enjoy merry times these weeks of my visit." He smells Ellen's sweet breath riding the pollinated summer currents as she touches his forearm. The warmth of her touch penetrates the muslin fabric of his old shirt, plumbago-dusted from his brief labors inside the shed.

Hardly the first time H. has laid eyes on Ellen of Scituate. She has visited her Concord relations half a dozen times, he would guess. She must now be—H. counts back from his twenty-two years—seventeen. Yes, seventeen. As youngsters, they had whiled away idle summertime afternoons together, along with John, Helen, and eventually Sophia. If he were to look now under the red bridge he would see the carved initials E S J T D T along with the date, 1830, marking their mischief. So how is it that he sees her now as if for the first time, this exquisite flesh and bone scaffolding for the gentle soul within? We must look a long time, perhaps, before we can truly see. He marvels at the imaginative powers of the eye. This, too, he must remember for his journal.

"And here is John back from his errand," Mrs. Joseph Ward announces, the first to glimpse John's presence. John bounds toward Ellen ahead of their mother and sisters, and Mrs. Joseph Ward's daughter, Prudence. H. knows by his elder brother's very affect that his eyes perform similar work upon Ellen. John bounds toward her as if he were one of the ancient Hebrews glimpsing Canaan at last.

They enjoy a lively supper of puddings and potatoes and beans, a dessert of early-bearing melon from their garden on the hill, the brothers enumerating the activities they hope to enjoy with Ellen, her aunt Prudence acting as chaperone, of course: sailing along the Assabet River in their newly built vessel, the *Musketaquid,* the gardens and groves of various townspeople, the menagerie due to arrive any day from Boston, and walks aplenty to survey the summertime goings on, animal and botanical, in their fairest nook of the world.

"And to church, too, of course," Ellen interjects, half in jest, it seems, yet H. cannot quite be sure.

"Blazes, anywhere but church!" H. replies.

"Your tongue, son," H.'s father reminds him, not bothering to lift his eyes from the surgery he performs on his beans with the cutlery. Aunt Jane coughs mildly into her palm. Ellen's father is a minister. H. wonders whether word of the great man's scandalous address to the divinity school in Cambridge has reached him in Scituate, if H.'s association with the sage will doom certain prospects, vis à vis Ellen, dawning in his mind.

"You forget yourself, brother," Helen observes.

"I'll accompany you to church Sundays," John says, "along with the ladies of the house, of course."

"Of course." Ellen directs a generous gaze toward John, seated beside him.

H. returns his own eyes to his potatoes, shuffles them about the plate, his fork issuing plaintive notes against the porcelain. But then Ellen's shining eyes capture his from across the table once again and she speaks. "I'll rely upon your wise counsel, dearest H., amid the outdoors cathedral."

Throats clear. Glassware bottom *clunks* against wood. Chair legs rumble. Poor John issues a rich cough into his napkin, his lungs embattled these recent days. H.'s mother rises, noting some missing element of the meal she must retrieve, or was it one of young Sophia's recent portraits she wished to display? Her precise words fail to penetrate.

His spirits enlivened, Ellen detained by Sophia and Helen, H. retreats to his tidy first-floor room to commit lines to his journal. He hopes to record the philosophical truths gleaned under the poplar, but the poetic spirit seizes him, instead. He composes iambs in tetrameter, the occasional spondee betraying his ardor, the poet inviting a lover outdoors. H. employs rhyme to complement the strict meter, summons images involving swifts and streamlets, bees and gnats. He thinks of the eye once again, its special sight.

Our rays united to make one Sun,
With fairest summer weather.

Gobsmacked, yes, the only word to describe his strangest condition, John's like ardor (if H. is not mistaken) notwithstanding. He wonders if the great man was affected in a similar manner first sight of his truest, tragic love, the wife before Lidian.

What blithe summer days they enjoy the two weeks of Ellen's visit. H. and John reacquaint her with every hill and dale, forgoing the heavy woods and boggiest swamps in deference to the impossible female fashion that both Ellen and Prudence must uphold in the main, if not in all particulars. July is the month for flowers, grasses, and first fruits. Ellen, not unlike her younger brother, Edmund, delights in the heady blooms on offer and inquires after their names. H. is only too happy to make introductions, although he must rely upon good Prudence's more comprehensive expertise regarding certain flora. There is so much that H. still does not know, despite Phineas Allen's introduction to Concord's plants while H. was a lad at the Academy, Professor Harris's further tutelage at Cambridge, and the current assistance of Bigelow's *Florula Bostoniensis, a Collection of Plants of Boston and Its Vicinity*. Yet this much he knows and relates: Jersey tea snows Brister's hillside with its randy clusters of oval blooms. Blue flag iris enlivens Wheeler meadow and Heywood meadow near the great man's white house. Red clover heads have mostly blacked, but some still sport their luxuriant rosaceous tinge beneath the gnarly apple trees at Baker Farm. (On account of the canopy? Some nutrient of the scattered fruits leeched into the soil?) John, Ellen, Prudence, and H. run a gauntlet of St. John's wort—exuding a peculiar lemony fragrance—either side of Marlborough Road. Wild roses pink the more prodigious alders on the higher embankment and thread through the thickets toward sunbright. H. leans down at the orchard side of Fairhaven Hill to pluck a fistful of clasping harebell's delicate purple blooms that Ellen might press between pages of her herbarium. And more. Concord is abloom with tephrosia and meadowsweet and day-lily and wild mint and Virginia screwstem and loosestrife and goat's-rue and forget-me-not. Even the potatoes and corn at Stratton and Baker Farms boast flowers and tassels, respectively, the nation's tamest vegetables expressing their remnant wild selves!

"Such wonders to gather our attention every step in your learned company," Ellen observes on their walk to Emerson Cliffs. "It's a miracle we cover a single mile on one of our ambles." John and Prudence, distracted by one of the local cats, don't seem to hear the remark. A curious quiet obtains outdoors today, like most recent days. Ellen has arrived at an interregnum for the birds, their voices mostly stoppered as they await the nestlings still percolating within their sturdy encasements. He can hear John's inhalations and exhalations and the occasional susurrus of the bees (honey and bumble), a most pleasant humming in the skies. Finally, a bobolink, its straw-colored nape accenting graphite-black breeding plumage, pipes brave notes in the meadow. H. attempts, somewhat fatuously, to mimic the song with Papa's flute.

"You play so well," Ellen says. He thanks her, but the compliment stops his throat. "Don't stop!" she commands. "Oh, please don't stop." Prudence encourages him, as well, tells Ellen that H.'s sisters clean the brasses at a much faster clip when he offers them his indoors serenade.

A camelopard arrives next day on tour—not a proper menagerie, after all, but a terrific beast, in any wise—an added diversion to Ellen's itinerary. H. escorts Ellen to see the creature straight away before the concern shepherds it off to Roxbury, Fitchburg, or whatever hamlet comes next. The majesty of the animal cannot be denied. The breath from its mighty lungs as it walks sounds above its handlers' wicked oaths and the citizenry's coarse commentary.

"The name does not suit this splendid creature," Ellen finally says as they lope about the square alongside the camelopard and its handlers. "He hardly favors the camel *or* the leopard. The markings are tawny and jigsaw-shaped, nothing like the markings of the leopard at the menagerie we visited in Albany last year." H. watches Ellen's mouth as she speaks, watches as she arches her neck now to gaze up at the camelopard's narrow head and furred horns. "And a horse more closely approximates a camel's shape than this magnificent giant."

"Yes, Ellen, I agree."

"It is very much"—Ellen searches for the truest words—"...very much its own creature." The noblest of sentiments, H. thinks, though he won't be so bold as to express this thought, outright.

"Some call it a giraffe," H. says, instead.

"Giraffe." Ellen tastes the strange word in her mouth, flashes a fetching smile. "Yes, much better. I learn so much every outing with you, dear H. Giraffe. Giraffe. Gir-*affe*!"

Ellen and H. regale the family and their boarders with tales of the giraffe over supper. Sophia and Uncle Charles ask after its size, Helen its deportment, Father and Mrs. Joseph Ward wonder after its much ballyhooed neck, John and Aunts Maria and Louisa its manner of locomotion (Mother more concerned over the neighbors in attendance). Prudence, in obeisance to unwritten rules of the chaperone, mostly holds her tongue while Ellen and H. answer these queries and more. Ellen's powers of observation impress H. as she describes elements he wasn't certain she noticed: its purple prehensile tongue, the unabated working of its jaw as it chewed its cud like other ruminants, the efficacious manner with which it deployed the haired tip of its tail to swat flies. Both H. and Ellen gild the lily somewhat as they describe the giraffe's proportions, exchanging conspiratorial glances over the steamed pouts mother has prepared, these cod-like fish of whitest flesh. He minds how Ellen defers to him upon certain queries with the gentlest slant of her head, a pregnant glance with her deep-set eyes. He calls and responds in kind, putting his prodigious nose to use. How artfully they communicate their essential aims to each other without words. It feels fine, and the least bit scandalous, to join in shared purpose with this eligible young daughter of Scituate.

Mother has a surprise for them in the parlor after supper, at long last having successfully borrowed from the library the volume half the town has been talking about, Franz Joseph Gall's *The Anatomy and Physiology of the Nervous System in General, and of the Brain in Particular, with Observations upon the possibility of ascertaining the several Intellectual and Moral Dispositions of Man and Animal, by the configuration of their Heads*. They take turns thumbing through this already well-thumbed book, the top corners of each page smudged.

"Shall we put Dr. Gall's methods to the test?" young Sophia proposes.

"Oh, let's do!" Ellen says. Already the two seem sisters.

Their mother tells them to consult the chart somewhere near the middle of the volume. H. watches as Sophia flips through the book's leaves—"Here," she declares—arriving finally at the diagram.

"Who's the first patient for our laboratory?" Sophia asks. The elders demur, as does H., but John gamely volunteers, whereupon Helen—in an unusual fit of loquaciousness—instructs him to sit on the Oriental rug so she might ply his scalp with her fingertips from above. He obeys. Their elder sister proceeds to call out the locale of various protrusions while Sophia consults the chart and issues her diagnoses. Apparently, John possesses formidable powers of Calculation, Alimentiveness, Approbativeness, and Suavity, this last announcement from Sophia's quarter eliciting laughter from their whole band, even from their circumspect father, though not from H.

"Suavity." John underscores the diagnosis. "Small wonder, indeed." More laughter.

Ellen rises from the rug, smooths her frock, then surprises H. by turning toward him and insisting that he take a turn. She will perform the experiment. H. obeys, of course, takes his seat on the Oriental rug, sitting in Indian fashion, whereupon Ellen sets to it. Her touch penetrates the ample shock of his hair to make fiery contact in ten discrete locales. He feels the pad of every fingertip as she probes the contours of his cranium. She leans her face close to his head as she conducts her work. He can feel the heat of her breath tickle his ears, smell the plums from her dessert pudding overtake the mustiness of the rug and upholstery, hear the digestive goings as her stomach grumbles. His flesh rises. He must glance downward to ensure he doesn't betray himself. There could be no better advertisement for sturdy trowsers. He wonders what it feels like to Ellen to sit above him thusly, to respire so close to his ears, to sup his breath and other human odors, to plie him with these pets—in short, to realize such contact. Silence permeates the room, save for the minute hand of the great clock, which advances with a singular *thunk*. When will she proffer her diagnosis?

"Well?" Sophia asks, Gall's volume spread like a napkin across her lap.

"Oh, dear," Ellen responds, her fingertips padding more feverishly all about his scalp, mussing his already bothered hair, "your brother possesses a perfectly round skull it would seem. I cannot detect a single protrusion."

Sophia, smiling, flips through the pages, front-ways first, then back-ways, to locate a diagnosis. The book's leaves smack sharply against one another. Ellen's fingers have stopped padding about, but she has not removed them from his thicket of hair. H. remains completely still, savoring this human touch.

"Here it is," Sophia says. "Our dear brother is a genius, apparently..."

Guffaws. Uncle Charles laughs so hard he chokes on his pudding.

"No!" their mother protests.

"Now don't say that, Cynthia," Aunt Jane interjects. "He was always a special child. Why I rememb—"

"Wait," Sophia continues, "a genius, the doctor avers, or a hopeless idiot!"

The clock's glass rattles from their booming laughter. H. laughs, as well, pleased with himself that he can summon his good humor. Ellen finally lifts her fingers from his scalp, disrupting the circuit of their affections, laughs into the seashell of her fist.

"Are you well?" his mother asks, her eyes sweeping his face. "You look flushed, son."

Somewhat bittersweet, Ellen's final days in Concord for H. knows that she fast returns to Scituate by coach. Too, it becomes ever clearer to H. that he competes for her affections. While he assists their father in the pencil-sheds, works the mill to spare John this labor, his elder brother escorts Ellen on a second trip to Clamshell Hill, Prudence in tow, to comb the grasses for Indian relics. They stop at Captain Moore's garden upon their return, according to their report at supper, to inspect the last of the town's blooms. A grasshopper, apparently, gives Ellen quite the fright. Too, John and Ellen chance in town upon the dolt, Robert Keyes, home from his studies in Cambridge, who takes a shine to dear Ellen, judging by the number of times he's loitered about these past days, asking for H.'s advice navigating the mercurial temperament of the college house-master (though he had never previously sought out such counsel), asking if he might borrow their boat (though he's never demonstrated an interest in sailing), and helping H. to mend the roof-shingles on one of the pencil-sheds (hammer and nail clear strangers to his hands and eyes), hoping all the while, no doubt, to secure Ellen's audience.

H. will not be so easily deterred. The day after her departure, he decides to send Ellen the recent collection of poems by Jones Very. What better gesture to demonstrate his generosity of spirit? No sooner does the thought dawn than he spies John preparing a package in the dining room. He knows that the package must be for Ellen by the effervescent manner with which his brother tends to his task, elbows akimbo.

"You're sending Ellen a package I see?"

"Yes, brother." Silence. Then John continues. "She neglected to pack the mementos of our excursion to Clamshell Hill." Vaguely defensive, the explanation. H. watches as John scatters pottery shards, then a slate arrowhead, inside the box. John refuses to meet his glance, his attentions foursquare on his project. He would ask his elder brother after his intentions, if he seeks to court Ellen as a wife or if H. might pursue her affections, outright. But his mouth will not form the words.

"A fine time Ellen seemed to enjoy with us," he says instead.

"Yes, a fine time we all shared," John replies, then pinches his lips about his teeth as he concentrates on his next task, mounting (H. cranes his neck to see) a grasshopper with father's pipe-cleaning wires against the cardboard interior. Strange. Ah, but no. Moore's garden. This mounted insect something of a joke between intimates, he infers. John assuredly expects him to ask after the grasshopper, but H. won't give him the satisfaction. He can hardly send collections of poetry to Scituate now. The younger brother, he must defer. He feels the blood rise to his face. She had touched him. Her lovely hands lingered beneath his shock of hair. The heat of her palms penetrated his scalp. He cannot imagine that she felt nothing, that she feels nothing. The next thought comes unbidden, terrifies him, provoking a bout of hiccups. *If only John were dead.* He shakes his head, banishing murderous thoughts from his mental screen, hiccups again and again. *Hiccup...hiccup...hiccup.* No wonder certain quarters associate these involuntary spasms of the diaphragm with Satan.

"I still need to compose a note to accompany my package." John's words jolt H. from his reverie. "Shall I write to Ellen about our upcoming travels along the Concord and Merrimack on the *Musketaquid*? You still look forward to our journey, yes?" John hears his hiccups, of course, sees his flushed countenance. John knows that something has changed between them—this dear daughter of Scituate, to be precise—or why else ask such a question?

"Of course, dear brother. Yes, of course."

14

Hertzog has yet to hear from Claire. More than a week has passed since they met at the green. He supposes she has bigger fish to fry than lean on her law enforcement cronies in Northridge for the scuttlebutt on Jude Winslow. Hertzog can't remember the precise tenor of the concern he expressed over their coffee. In any case, he won't bother Claire yet. Nor will he drive his Subaru back out to Cherryfield Farm to snoop around or hassle his grown daughter, mostly (it shames him to acknowledge) because he loathes the prospect of negotiating Jude's oleaginous presence.

He keeps to his routine. Eats his spartan breakfasts. Hikes and swims even earlier now to evade the rising heat of summer, the rising population of Mass-holes and others stomping down the sweetfern along the Randolph Trail, upsetting the Bowl's still surface with their thrashing arms and booming cries.

Having completed his exercise this morning, Hertzog wonders whether his life will simply resume as normal, save for the knowledge that his daughter now leads her life nearer by that has little to do with him. He sits at his kitchen table, swallows indifferent bites of his sandwich, the muted din of vehicular bass notes up and down Main seeping through the window screens far side of his home. Just enough days have passed since last seeing Ellen that things seem to have settled. A good thing, perhaps. Yet he cannot deny a certain sadness, as well. A door has opened inside him, leading to warrens of strange feeling, a door he cannot quite seem to shut. Ever since spotting Ellen on his stoop. No, earlier. Ever since his sluggish synapses detonated upon registering those familiar chords filtered through the spruce and birch foliage off Randolph Trail. Ellen's voice.

He ascends the creaking stair toward the study, quickening his rhythm up the steps to counter the lugubrious mood that threatens. He sits down to work. He holds in his mind what he knows of Thoreau's life with the writer's expression of said life in his Journal, watchful of the elisions, the silences, between entries. He's not sure whether it has something to do with Ellen's reemergence, but he finds himself rapt in Thoreau's words in a way he hasn't been rapt for a long time. This passage, for example, he's read countless times, but encounters now as if newly discovered. *I stood by the river considering the forms of the elms reflected in the water. For every oak and birch too, growing on the hill top, as well as for elms and willows, there is a graceful ethereal tree making down from the roots—as it were the original idea of the tree, and sometimes nature in high tides brings her mirror to its foot and makes it visible— Anxious nature sometimes reflects from pools and puddles the objects which our groveling senses may fail to see relieved against the sky, with the pure ether for background.*

To be gifted with such intense sight! Hertzog had long ago gleaned the part of the passage devoted to the elms' reflection against the Concord River, but not the bit about "making down from the roots," as if the special vantage of the canopy against the pure sky (glimpsed indirectly via reflection) set Thoreau's imagination soil-ward toward the source, toward what he could not see with his eyes, the subterranean forest of roots.

Thoreau continued: *It would be well if we saw ourselves as in perspective always—impressed with distinct outline on the sky-side by side with the shrubs on the river's brim. So let our life stand to heaven as some fair sun lit tree against the western horizon, and by sunrise be planted on some eastern hill to glisten in the first rays of the dawn.*

The leap toward the human. Elm as metaphor. The most forceful cohort of contemporary Thoreau scholars—the ecocentrists—don't have much time for these anthropocentric predilections. They much prefer, Hertzog knows, what they see later in Thoreau's life and work as his fixation upon the thing itself, nature itself, stripped of its clunky symbolism—Thoreau's "turn to science," the oft-repeated phrase. There was a time when Hertzog was of like mind with the ecocentrists. Surely Thoreau's close observations of natural phenomena, fiercely documented in his Journal, occupied a greater and greater share of his waking hours. Hertzog had been one of the first scholars to take delight in Thoreau's copious accounts of scampering squirrels, snowmelt trends, the tone of a bullfrog's belch, the alimentary delights of certain local lichens, moonlight, phallic fungi, the wingspan of various moths, the aroma of tree bark and potato blossoms. While he still treasures these passages, Hertzog finds himself wondering now whether he's approached them in the correct spirit. The new Thoreauvians construct a man ever in retreat from a poisoned and poisonous society. Yet this was altogether too reductive a notion, the dichotomy, itself, hopelessly flawed. As if the late great essay, "Wild Apples," was merely a screed against monoculture, "Autumn Leaves" mere paean to fall foliage, whereas both essays—written, purportedly, during Thoreau's most "ecocentric" period—were more truly, or just as truly, the great man's poignant meditation upon his, and our, inescapable mortality. Might it be that Hertzog has misread the man all these years? That he has devoted a lifetime to imagining Thoreau wrong in the most prestigious peer-reviewed academic journals, then imagining him wrong again, then again?

Hertzog fidgets in his reading chair, reconsiders the present metaphor. Such a young man when he transcribed these thoughts, before, though not long before, he was marked by significant losses. Thoreau had studied the reflection of elm leaves and branches in a still river upon a certain slant of light, a certain time of day, yet not to escape the world of other men and women. Not escape, per se, but deepest engagement as he sought to glimpse the world inside all human souls. As he sought to be seen, too, as we all hope that our glistening sunlit leaves might be seen by someone. A separate passage to this effect alights upon his consciousness, also from the early Journal. He flips through the pages of Volume I. Early in 1838, if he recalls. Yes. Hertzog had dog-eared the page, but hadn't found occasion to cite the passage directly all these years. *Man is not at once born into society—hardly into the world—The world that he is hides for a time the world that he inhabits.—*

The world that we are.

Hertzog contemplates afresh the significance of the passage, but a knock at the door interrupts his reverie. Three quick beats, businesslike. A package from the post office, perhaps, though he's not expecting any packages. He waits a moment and listens to the silence to assure himself of the postal worker's departure. Bonnie or Janice, likely. He hears Main Street's distant vehicular groans, the metallic scraping of stiff foliage against his roof gutters. (He may need to thin the cedars, after all.) He will check the stoop for the delivery later. He begins jotting down some notes (*the world that we are!*) on a yellow legal pad. But then there's another rap at the door. Three beats again, though more strident this time.

He descends the stair and opens the front door, glimpses his cross-armed daughter. She'd retreated to the brick walk off the raised porch but hadn't yet given up hope, her hair tied back in a ponytail, tighter and neater than the askew tie that barely contained her unruly strands when he last saw her, tending to her motley crew of porcine creatures.

"Catch you at a bad time, Father?"

He tells her no. That he was only working upstairs. He typically enters a sort of stupor while reading. He tries exercising new muscles around his eyes to rouse himself. It takes a couple sentences to fully regain his voice. He tells her, by way of further explanation, that he thought she'd call before coming, which he immediately realizes sounds standoffish rather than explanatory, so follows up by asking her inside, surprised when she accepts.

"Last minute thing or I would have called," she explains to his back as he leads her into the kitchen. "Some supplies needed picking up in town. Figured I'd volunteer. That way I could stop in on you."

He wishes he hadn't made that asinine comment about her calling first. He asks his daughter to sit while he prepares their coffee. Or would she prefer tea? Or a glass of water?

Coffee would be great, she tells him. He hears the chair's pine spindles complain against Ellen's mild weight as she sits. He tries making small-talk—unpracticed at the exercise—as he measures coffee grounds into the French press. He asks how the crops seem to be doing this season out at the farm (not quite enough rain), asks after the pigs (leading the life of Riley), whether the summer people are driving her crazy yet when she minds the store (Mass-holes, mostly, same as ever), whether she's managed yet to check in on Cassidy (no, not yet, but she will). He pours their coffee and sets the mugs and matching Pfaltzgraff service down on the maple table. He wonders whether she recognizes the simple blue floral design.

Ellen takes a tentative sip, but doesn't seem to notice the old drinkware. "Good coffee," she finally says. He detects that mild tremor in her hand framing the mug, wonders again whether this might be a side effect of whatever medication she's currently on, or not on. It feels strange to have his daughter in their home again, across from him at their kitchen table. Hertzog feels as if the very atmosphere registers her renewed presence, the airborne molecules vibrating between them. His nostrils are drenched with her odors, which he partly recognizes, the musky Ellen-ness radiating from her person. The other part is some strange herbal soap, lotion, or perfume. He sips his own coffee and watches her as she scans the room. He wonders what she sees. Most appointments are the same as when she lived here. The maple table, the off-white tile counters, the wall-mounted GE oven adorned with instructional lettering in cursive that exudes the 1970s, the ghastly amber light fixture hanging above their heads. Ellen seems pretty quiet as she gazes about. Or maybe he simply hasn't given her enough time to speak, filling up the air as he has with his own words. He'll wait now for her.

"It's weird that you're still here," she finally says, her upper lip curling to expose a still-sharp canine.

"Really?"

"Isn't it too big for just one person? I mean, you're not living with someone, are you?"

He laughs off the suggestion. No, he tells her. He's not living with someone.

She looks about more dramatically than before, even under the table at the pine floorboards, as if to verify his claim. He tells her that he likes the house. That he's always liked it. It's not so very big. And how would she have found him had he moved? He doesn't say this last bit, which only now occurs to him as a fully formed thought. Is this why he hasn't moved to a warmer clime, or even to a smaller house in town—so that Ellen would be able to find him?

"I always thought there was something between you and Sheriff Libby," she says, finally adding sugar to her coffee from the Pfaltzgraff jar. The silver spoon trembles in her grip—he hadn't imagined the mild tremor—though not enough to spill the crystals on the table.

"Claire Libby?" Hertzog asks, perhaps affecting too much surprise. "She was married when you knew her, Ellen."

"So."

"She and Pete had two kids in the house."

"So."

"It makes a difference. To some people."

She raises an eyebrow, chuffs air out her nostrils. "I heard Mr. Libby died," she says.

He tells her that she heard correctly. Poor Pete passed away a while back. Cancer.

"Maybe you should get a dog or something."

"Oh yes, that's exactly what I need."

He wonders whether Ellen remembers Everest, the lab-mix puppy they adopted from a rescue organization in Bangor when she was nine. She had expressed vague desires for a "real" pet. Their daughter rarely expressed a desire for anything other than to be left alone, so they welcomed the request. Rebecca and he figured the responsibility of a dog would be good for Ellen, but they returned the poor creature after only a few weeks. Ellen, annoyed by its teething, flat-out refused to walk or even play with her new pet, shut her bedroom door on the whimpering pup as if it were one of her parents. They might have kept Everest, anyway, had it not chewed through all their shoes and riddled practically every item of wooden furniture in the house with its bite-mark impressions, had it not proven impervious to their house-breaking efforts, leaving fragrant piles of its waste in every corner of the home.

But Ellen, now rubbing her fingertips against the maple-grain as if it were a stain she sought to buff clean, doesn't seem to have Everest on her mind.

"This table seemed bigger before," she says.

"It *was* bigger, Ellen. I took out a leaf."

"Oh. That makes sense."

They sit mostly in silence for several moments as they sip at their coffee. Hertzog considers pressing her on the goings on at Cherryfield Farm, the scope of their rockweed concern, specifically. His eyes dart to the clear plastic bag of dulse on the ledge above the sink that he recently purchased at Jude's farm stand, which Ellen hasn't noticed. Is it some rockweed lotion or salve, the herbal aroma she now exudes? He decides not to inquire. It's still Ellen asking the questions.

"So what do you do now? Like, all day? Now that you're retired?"

She knows that he retired. He wonders how she knows, but doesn't ask. Instead, he tells her what he does, more or less, which isn't so different from what he always did, minus the teaching. Something about his explanation surprises her. He watches the way her eyebrows knit together of their own accord. Well, what *should* he be doing? How do most people account for the weeks, days, and hours of their lives?

He peers into Ellen's mug resting inside her weathered hand, which doesn't tremble anymore. The hand looks older than her years—something about the visible veins and bones riding beneath the sun-battered flesh—which pains him. He notices the thumb, perched on the lip, the farm-dirt crescent inside the nail, the nailbed itself oddly squat (only on this right hand, he knows), like her mother's. An odd genetic inheritance. She seems to have mostly finished her coffee. He considers asking whether he might warm it up, then asks a separate question, instead.

"Do you want to see your bedroom, Ellen?"

She seems surprised by the offer, gulps a quick draught of air. Maybe she's surprised he still thinks of it as her room.

"That's okay," she says. "I'm sure it's still there. Let's take a walk or something," she suggests, instead. He feels the corners of his mouth rise at the suggestion.

"What's so funny, Father?" She lifts her fingers to scratch at something behind her ears beneath a loose cord of her curls, feeling his amusement like a pesky itch, maybe.

"You. You're funny, Ellen. You want to go on a walk? With me?"

His memories of their walks together are unpleasant on the whole. She tended toward physical laziness as a child, something neither he nor Rebecca could tolerate, the great outdoors at their doorstep, the inanity of her electronic entertainments. Physical exercise was especially healthful for Ellen's condition, the specialist in Portland claimed, might diminish the need for such strong dosages of the SSRI's and benzodiazepines and lithium they'd been cycling through, hoping to find a drug, or drug combination, that might ameliorate the sadness and rage she pinballed between (as Hertzog saw it), her "oppositional defiance disorder" (according to Dr. Rubin). And so they forced their daughter outdoors to join them on walks—excepting when the snow was knee-high—sometimes in the woods but mostly just around the block, Ellen's lurching shoulders, the pissy way she scuffed her soles against the road cinders, advertising her displeasure. They tried other activities. Cross-country skiing wintertime. Soccer. Basketball. Karate. Swimming, finally.

Swimming was one of the few outdoor activities that Hertzog and his wife could coax Ellen into doing without too much complaint. Her breaststroke was particularly strong. He relished these opportunities to heap praise upon his daughter for this one true thing that she did so well. During the summer, they'd cajole Ellen once or twice a week to hike up to the Bowl with them and swim. She complained less about the walking, the reward of the Bowl dangled before her. She enjoyed capturing the fat tadpoles, these nascent bullfrogs, small fishes, and even leeches in her net. They usually stayed well clear of the public swimming beach, but sometimes children hiking the Bowl's loop with their families would stop and observe Ellen with her net, and sometimes Ellen would even invite the boy or girl to join her in the shallows, hunting for whatever aquatic creatures they might capture. Sometimes Ellen smiled and seemed to enjoy the camaraderie, lent the child her bucket or net for a while, the two of them knee-deep in the lake. These times Hertzog would feel something stir inside him. Rebecca felt the same thing. He knew this, because one time she reached to squeeze his hand as they watched Ellen playing with her new friend from the pink granite ledge. *You see? There's our daughter out in the world, working her way into the human mix. Finding her place.* Which, beyond health, was all a parent truly wanted for a child.

"Sure," he tells Ellen now, rising from the table. Hertzog was always up for a walk, even if he'd already completed his morning exercise.

On the landing, before turning to lock the deadbolt behind him, he spies Stacey Hinshaw standing on her lawn, giving her tabby cat a walk on its pink leash, which he's seen her do a handful of times. He notices the cranberry shrubs framing owner and cat with their pale-green, maple-impostor leaves. The shrubs, thankfully, seem to have recovered some of their foliage since her pruning. The novelty of another human presence emerging from his home has arrested Stacey's attention. She gives him a queer, disapproving look, if he's not mistaken. On account of Hertzog ignoring her messages on the machine? Or could she suspect something untoward? He considers ignoring his neighbor and proceeding down the walk, but she's seen that he sees her.

"Stacey Hinshaw, meet Ellen, my daughter," he calls over the hobblebush hedge, neglecting the deadbolt.

"Oh. Daughter." Guileless Stacey doesn't think to hide her pleasant surprise. She lifts her cat by its belly and strides the few yards over to the property line. The cat seems outsize, suddenly, its backside drooping below Stacey's elbow, the muscle cords of her forearm pulled taut. "David didn't tell us he had a daughter." She reaches over the hobblebush to shake hands, having seamlessly transferred her cat to the other arm. Ellen shakes hands over the hedge, but clearly finds the gesture unnecessary, would have preferred a simple nod of the head or raised palm. The difference between people, Hertzog muses.

"I like your ink," Stacey says, having noticed Ellen's tattoo inside her forearm. "Have to be a true Mainer to get one of those spruce tattoos."

Ellen just nods, sheepishly, as if she were embarrassed about the spruce tattoo she got when she was just sixteen, or maybe she remembers how angry he was upon discovering it and even after all these years doesn't care to have her father reminded of the episode.

"Stacey and her husband teach at Emmenthaler," Hertzog says.

"Cool."

"Visiting for a while?" Stacey asks.

"Something like that," Ellen answers, which elicits a slow nod from Stacey.

It's interesting to see these two young women inhabiting the same space. It hadn't occurred to him to compare, but they're about the same age, Stacey and his child, Ellen a bit older. He wonders what Ellen sees in Stacey, what she infers, if anything, in Stacey's nose-stud, her two-toned hair, the top-layer of blond pulled back today in a ponytail to expose rather dramatically the interior layer of deepest black, plus a gold loop piercing he hadn't noticed before in the cartilaginous upper region of her left ear. A certain left-of-center kinship? Or do the other trappings Ellen's gleaned in an instant counteract these thin bows to fashion. A college job. A husband. A house off Main. An overfed cat on a ridiculous pink leash.

"I've been trying to get your dad involved with the Rockweed Coalition," Stacey's saying. "Not sure if you know what that's all about." Which makes him wonder what Stacey sees in Ellen, her shaggy hair and unadorned features. His daughter never so much as pierced her earlobes.

Ellen nods, noncommittal. Then: "Yeah, I do," having realized that some sort of verbal response was required.

Hertzog senses an opening here, one he hadn't anticipated, but demurs. He doesn't want to involve his next door neighbor in his business with Ellen. He can ask Ellen himself about the goings on at Cherryfield Farm, the extent of her involvement in whatever dubious scheme Jude's been up to, involving or not involving rockweed. Something about that mocha-colored girl with the dreadlocks concerns him, as well. She had been working over a spindle. He fears that Jude might be exploiting her labor, or exploiting her and the other young women in some crueler fashion.

"I've left a couple messages on your machine, David. You got them right?"

He tells his neighbor yes, but that he's been busy.

She arranges her lips over her teeth and shifts her fat cat to the other arm. "Must have been something to grow up with a big-shot professor for a dad."

Is it possible Stacey's heard nothing about him? About his wife? Yes, very possible, he supposes. It was all so long ago, and the Hinshaws have only just arrived.

"Oh, it was…something," Ellen replies.

He tells Stacey that he and Ellen better get going, tells her the cranberry shrubs sure look good since she trimmed them.

"Nice cat," Ellen says by way of goodbye.

He takes care to control his gait alongside his daughter on the road as they walk through town to make their way to the woods. He usually walked well ahead of Ellen, or Rebecca, or the both of them, found himself unable to stride at their laggardly pace. A source of some tension. Ellen seems taller striding beside him. Perhaps she's making an effort not to slouch her neck and shoulders. The town odors of fried food, automotive exhaust, and miscellaneous greenery have overtaken her herbal soap-smells, and his odors, as well, he imagines. He tries not to stare, but finds himself entranced by this human figure cantering beside him in the clear outdoor light, his daughter, her top lip jeweled already with sweat, a tissue of skin flaking from the chapped lip, the ligament cords riding against her olive flesh as she pivots her head to inspect the goings on atop the Miller's roof (a cat he doesn't recognize scrabbles from the asphalt shingle into the dense scaffolding of a cedar to reach the grass below), the mole-crusted birthmark behind her ear that seems to have darkened over the years, the pronounced clavicles out wide to the shoulders testing the thin fabric of her T-shirt like nascent wings. He notices, once again, her lithe athletic build, so unlike the teenage Ellen.

"You can walk faster if you want. I'll keep up." Perhaps his daughter has noticed his noticing. Or perhaps she simply remembers his preferred pace.

He tells her it's okay, that he's slowed down some over these past several years, to which she says, "Good."

Just a half-block past Main, the green smells and intermittent birdsong rise. The automotive roar fades to a hum, though they don't escape mechanized noise, altogether. The bass notes of a lawnmower, or some other motor Hertzog associates with landscaping, grow louder as they walk past colonial, Cape Cod, and fewer Queen Anne homes down the mild slope. He studies the structures as they pass, these properties west of Main more shabbily maintained with their peeling paint, their rotted-out planks of siding, absent shingles here and there calling attention to themselves on asphalt rooftops like missing teeth in a mouth. He wonders how this neighborhood looks to his daughter, so he asks her.

"Pretty much the same," she says. "Never was as nice as our block."

Our block.

They pass outdoor cats on the prowl, poorly supervised local children playing makeshift games, most involving large-caliber plastic weaponry, a metal Lund boat on its trailer in a driveway stripped of its outboard motor and oozing rust-stains, emblazoned with a FOR SALE sign: $500, OR BEST OFFER. They pause to observe goldfinches mobbing a thistle feeder out front of one of the nicer Queen Anne two-stories. Hertzog reminds Ellen how much she used to like these small mustard and black birds and she doesn't contradict him, says "yeah," that she still likes them. Great flocks, she says, mob the heavy sunflower heads at Cherryfield, bowing the thick stems.

It irks him some, her mention of Jude's farm.

The goldfinches scatter from the feeder like so many fireflies once a squirrel manages to leap onto the pronged cylinder from the ground. Hertzog and Ellen move on without words and soon reach the end of the block, where the most ramshackle homes yield to the copse of woods, the human cohort having depleted all energy for further encroachment. For now. "You have time to walk the trail a bit?" Hertzog asks.

"Sure," his daughter replies. This was one of her favorite words, *sure,* which used to drive Hertzog crazy, the grudging half-assed assent he heard in her *sure.* But the word sounds better now in her voice. Or maybe it's only Hertzog's hearing that's changed.

Beneath the mixed canopy they blaze the familiar shortcut to Randolph Trail. The path of dirt and leaves, desiccated pine cones and rock, sweetfern, blueberry, and wintergreen is matted from the regular foot traffic, yet narrow enough between the slender posts of second-growth spruce, birch, beech and fewer maple that they must walk single-file. Hertzog takes the lead.

"So you're all doing quite a bit with rockweed out on the farm, am I right?" Something about having Ellen striding behind him rather than beside him now enables this inquiry. He can hear her footfalls against the forest's crust, her labored exhalations time to time as they begin the mild ascent.

"Yeah. Sure. Not just rockweed. All sorts of seaweeds. We're doing lots of things." She offers these staccato responses to save her breath. Hertzog slows his pace.

He's somewhat surprised by the fast admission, but he supposes that there's nothing illegal about seaweed sourced products, generally, or even rockweed sourced products, specifically. Seaweed, he's learned by now, has been touted as a "greener" source for agricultural fertilizers, pet and human food, and cosmetics than the chemical alternatives. "Organic." "Sustainable." "Macrobiotic." These are the buzz-words in the ether. Jude's line, no doubt—though not Stacey Hinshaw's line, who worries about over-harvesting. It's difficult for Hertzog to place rockweed, to determine how he ought to feel about it.

"It's all on the up and up?"

"Huh?"

"Jude's seaweed concern. There are licenses involved, I understand, new harvesting regulations and whatnot. I just wouldn't want you getting mixed up in any trouble."

"For Christ sake, Father… Really? You're gonna start in with this again?" He can hear her huffing for breath between the word-bursts. He slows his pace so that she might regain her wind. The distant laughter of a pileated woodpecker booms through the forest from the higher elevation before them. He wonders whether Ellen hears the woodpecker, whether she remembers the sounds of these giant birds. It doesn't seem so, for she doesn't remark upon the sound.

"Why do you always have to start something, Father?"

Always. It's been nearly ten years since he's laid eyes on his daughter, ten years since they've exchanged actual words. There *was* no always, anymore, between them, was there? He marvels at the leap Ellen has made between then and now, as if her experience of time has been altogether different than his own.

"I'm sorry," he says. He continues on, slowly, listens for the sound of the woodpecker. He'll remark upon the great bird this time. But the woodpecker has nothing further to say. Instead, he hears the gossip of invisible chickadees, the sky's breath through the reeds of spruce, a squirrel scrabbling up tree bark, the scrape of their shoes against the uncertain earth, the *thump* of his own heart working inside his chest. He sees a dusky-looking creeper walking straight down the trunk of a beech, as creepers do, but it skitters around the blind side of the bark before he can point it out to Ellen. The strengthening sun slips inside the canopy and dances across a cobweb wire.

"Let's just enjoy our walk," Ellen finally suggests, having regained her calm, and her breath. He can't hear her huffing, anymore. He suggests to her that she take a turn walking in the lead so that she might see some birds or other creatures before he scares them off. She leads him longer than he expected up the Randolph Trail, the muscles in her calves bulging with each step, advertising curious veins. Every so often she stumbles a bit, careless with her stride, but quickly regains her balance. He asks whether she wants to hike all the way to the Bowl, but she declines without offering a particular reason. She doesn't need to explain herself. He knows, of course, why she dares not glimpse the Bowl. It's the same reason he can't avoid returning to the glacial pond. He won't press.

"So you really still swim there," his daughter declares more than asks once they turn back.

Yes, he reminds her, he still swims there. He thinks he notices the ligaments back of her neck flexing as she nods, but she doesn't say anything. He asks her if she still swims anywhere, to which she replies, "Hell no."

He's about to say *That's a shame,* or something to that effect, because Ellen was such a good swimmer, and swimming is such good exercise, but leaves well enough alone, listens to the birdsong, most of it inscrutable until he hears a familiar song, *Here I am. There you are. Here I am. There you are.*

"That's one of those red-eyed vireos, right?" Ellen asks.

"Right, Ellen. Yes."

It's a much nicer walk they share today than their walks of old. Hertzog wonders what his daughter remembers of her compulsory walks after Rebecca was gone, when it was just the two of them. It was nearly impossible to coax Ellen out of her room to get some exercise once she hit fifteen or so. She had put on more weight in her thighs, her protuberant belly. Nothing extreme, certainly not by the current standard, and even Hertzog knew enough not to hassle an adolescent girl about her weight. Yet he wouldn't tolerate her sedentary predilections.

"I don't care what you want to do or what you don't want to do," he remembers speaking through her locked bedroom door after she returned from school. (He had reinstalled the door-knob and lock by this time.) "We're going on a walk so put your shoes on, young lady."

"No, I'm not. I'm *not* going!" Through the closed door, he heard the complaint of bed springs, the rattle of the wrought-iron headboard against the wall. His daughter had plopped herself down on her mattress. "I don't have to go," she cried from the bed. "You can't make me."

"Yes, you do. Yes, I can." He didn't shout. He never shouted. To counter Ellen's histrionics, he hewed to a timbre and cadence of adamantine calm. "I'm your father, Ellen, and you're my child, and I'm telling you that we're going. Now put your hiking shoes on—not your flip-flops, the nice L.L. Bean hiking shoes I paid for—and meet me downstairs in five minutes please."

Silence. It was that adamantine calm that so enraged her, which didn't keep him from speaking in this way.

"Ellen?" he had spoken through the door.

"What!"

"Did you hear what I said?"

"I hate you!"

"Yes, Ellen. I know that you hate me. You've told me several times. You've been perfectly clear on that score. But that wasn't my question."

"I fucking hate you!"

"Yes, I know, Ellen. I know. So five minutes then. See you downstairs."

Hertzog sees no reason now to remind his daughter of bitter bygone days. Yet he wonders now whether there was something altogether too bloodless, something not altogether human, in his performances. He wonders if it might have been better to meet the challenge of his daughter during these outbursts closer to her own terms, at least on occasion to yell, *I hate you too, you spoiled little shit!*, to beat down the door, grab a fistful of her mossy hair and drag her out of her room, if only to convey to Ellen that at the time he was also a living, breathing, hurting Hertzog.

The descent takes little time. Ellen, unpracticed at hiking, stumbles and skids on the pebbly trail once, twice, but quickly regains her footing. Once they slip from beneath the bedsheets of the forest canopy into the built town, the June sun bathes their faces in hotter heat than Hertzog expected. "Nice walk!" he says as they approach the intersection at Main. "Sure was a nice surprise this afternoon, Ellen."

"Yeah, it was fun," she replies, her perspired face shaded now by the globular leaves of the towering horse chestnut outside Napoli's Pizzeria. Pedestrians weave around them on the sidewalk, buckled by the horse chestnut's roots. Hertzog becomes enmeshed for a moment in a yippy dog's overlong, retractable leash and strains to keep his patience as its careless, twenty-something owner in spandex leggings labors to untangle him, chuffing through the exercise as if Hertzog were to blame. Ellen seems amused, chuckles at him as he raises one knobby knee, then the other. Once released, he invites Ellen back to the house, if only to drink something and freshen up. Surely she'll want to empty her bladder before the longish drive back to Jude's farm. She declines, which Hertzog doesn't question. Perhaps she'll stop somewhere in town to use the bathroom. He'll leave well enough alone. But he asks whether she wants to give him the number of her mobile phone.

"I don't have a cell phone right now," Ellen says, as if she might have had one yesterday, or plans to have one in the near future. Hertzog wonders whether it's just something she can't afford or whether it has something to do with Jude, worries that he doesn't allow her (or the other, younger girls) a cell phone. She tells him that he can reach her at the farm store's land line. Or leave a message, anyway. They say goodbye. Hertzog watches after her ponytail for a moment before heading up the street for home.

He feels good about the way they leave things, good enough that he exchanges verbose hale and hearties with Tim Miller, fussing with his hydrangeas, tells him about the cat they saw scrabbling off his roof earlier when otherwise he'd likely just wave hello. He feels good enough that he checks his mailbox to see what news of the world might await him, even though Bonnie or Janice rarely deliver his mail before five p.m., good enough that it takes a moment for the musculature in his face to fall after he swings open the front door that he neglected to lock and sees what he sees.

The house. His house. Ransacked.

15

Sept 17th, 1839

Nature never makes haste; her systems revolve at an even pace. The bud swells imperceptibly—without hurry or confusion, as though the short spring days were an eternity. All her operations seem separately for the time, the single object for which all things tarry.—Why then should man hasten as if any thing less than eternity were allotted for the least deed?

H. cannot muster the attention to compose lines in his journal, or even read his Virgil or Kant or Goethe. Tender thoughts on Ellen of Scituate scatter his focus and force. He forgets himself while he sleeps, then prosecutes cold morning baths in the pond. He floats on his back to snatch with his eyes the greatest breadth of sky and traces the peregrinations of clouds. He wishes it were springtime and the pond were colder to more fully settle his humors.

In short, H. does not do much by the current standard. Yet he begins preparations for his river adventure with John, their batchelors' lark, repaints the hull of the *Musketaquid* in the merry colors of green and blue. He musters their provisions. Potatoes, rice, bread, sugar, cocoa, and as many melons from their garden as the deck will allow. Father's buffalo hide for a mattress. The cotton sail will do for a tent, nighttimes. By H.'s calculation—seven miles progress each day aboard their fifteen-foot dory—it should take two weeks, depending upon the winds, to sail down the placid Concord River, then up the Merrimack against the current, bivouacking falls and dams through the assistance of wheels H. outfitted for the hull, relying upon the good services of lock-keepers and more seasoned boatmen ever and anon. Once they reach their terminus at the White Mountains, they will secure their vessel somehow (perhaps a farmer's barn might be put to service) and climb Mount Agiocochook, then float back down to Concord to prepare for the new term at their Academy.

Mother throws their annual melon-party the evening before their departure. All else fails, there is much H. might teach the nation's melon-growers with regard to the aeration of the soil and the virtues of the marigold, a vital companion plant between the rows. H. greets their neighbors amicably enough, deflects Robert Keyes' queries about Ellen Sewall—a black seed pasted to Robert's melon-lathered cheek—but excuses himself from the festivities beneath the poplar so that he might outfit the *Musketaquid.*

The next morn breaks hot, grey, and rainy. John recommends that they postpone their voyage. But the weather clears by afternoon. Enough daylight remains, H. counsels, for them to reach Billerica before setting camp, if not Lowell and the Merrimack. They shove off to a volley of not wholly facetious rifle-shots from their friends, Channing and Brooks and Hoar. Their friends follow them along the bank for almost a mile, making it possible for H. to pluck a few strange hibiscus flowers in bloom at the first bend for them to carry back for Prudence's herbarium. Their friends having departed, H. rows to the deepest center of the river. It feels uncommonly good to be setting off on such a significant, albeit hardly Amazonian, excursion. An impish grin paints John's face, who sets the sail now as H. works the oars. The familiar bulrushes and pickerel weeds of their native riverbed flit strangely in H.'s eye on account of their current voyage, impelling him to reflect upon the relationship between internal and external landscapes. What does John see and feel? Do thoughts of Ellen swim like bream in his brain, as they swim in H.'s mind? He will not inquire, and they will not speak of her for their entire sojourn, it is somehow understood, the agreement sealed by the select few words exchanged during their first stop to snatch restorative bluets at Ball's Hill.

"Berries top of the shrubs sweeter than low fruit," John observes.

"And south-facing fruit sweeter than north-facing fruit, don't you find?"

"I do, brother."

H. trains his senses upon everything, *everything*, these few miles to Billerica, the green heron skittering at the bank snatching fry hither and thither, the mineralized air from the recent rain drenching his nostrils, the alternately green and tannic shade of river water against his oar when he takes his turn, the complex vortices of gnat-clouds, the moss'd stones lying bottom of the shallows having completed their revolutions through air and water and ancient time, the indecipherable bass notes of human voices time to time from inside the scrim of woods. John lies back now at the stern, feet on the cane seat, his head resting on the gunwale. H. will take a longer turn as oarsman in deference to John's embattled lungs.

Their bluet-fueled energies spent, the brothers moor on a sandy bank somewhere near Billerica, anyway. They free the cotton sail from its mast and set up camp, unfurl the buffalo hide inside their makeshift tent. They forage for kindling, kicking the earth about for Indian relics they don't find. Though it's summertime hot, they start a fire to discourage the mosquitoes and heat their cocoa milk, their most perishable provision. They tear spartan portions of bread from one of their loaves, as well, as the flames crackle against their fuel, as dusk overtakes day and the last blackbirds trill from up high in the bulrushes, along with fewer burps of skulking rails down below, these small wading birds he can't see.

"Did Mother bake these raisins into the bread, brother?" John asks above the bird noises.

"No, I did."

"A capital idea."

The rhythmic cries of crickets and frogs overtake the birds as they eat. The bruised sky turns black, save for the stars, the Milky Way gauzed across the horizon. They identify what summer constellations they know. Cygnus. Lyra. Ursa Major. Sagittarius. Then they retire to the tent to snatch as much rest as possible for the journey tomorrow. H. lies on his back and savors the musky aroma of the buffalo hide as if he were an original Indian and listens to the night. The whirring of the frogs and crickets takes on the exalted sound of silence, against which a yelp rises from inside the elevated scrim of woods. The sound lifts gooseflesh on H.'s arms.

"What is that strange yelp, brother? A fyce?"

"No."

"Some other dog?"

"Better. A fox."

"Not better for the farmer," John jokes.

H. considers chasing after this creature of his spirit, but there's little chance he'll stalk it successfully in the dark woods, canopied against the starbright.

❧

H. must have nodded off, because he somehow knows that the rustling he now hears from somewhere proximate their moored boat has woken him. Bandits, he fears, pilfering their scant supplies. Or a runaway slave, perhaps, to whom H. might offer succor. He glances over at John, who slumbers on like a contented husband, a slight wheeze now accenting his inhalations. H. rises slowly, parts the sail's flap and squints his eyes toward the *Musketaquid* grounded on the bank. The starbright blues the landcape, yet he cannot see any human forms lurking above the gunwales. Still, the rustling sound thereabouts continues. He steps into the night and strides quietly on the sturdy soles of his bare feet. He draws within a few rods of their dory when he finally sees the creature well below the gunwale, the red coat and audaciously furred tail of his fox, who likely ceased its yipping the moment it sniffed out their melons. The creature jerks up its head to gaze directly at the human interloper, freezing H. in his tracks. He watches the fox watching him. He is close enough that he sees the gleam of melon-wet against the creature's snout, sees the universe disappear then reappear when the fox blinks.

"Now, fox," H. utters, whereupon the fox plucks up a small melon, then leaps over the gunwales onto the sand, satisfied with the terms of their negotiation. H. watches as the fox trots into the woods with its prize. It may have kits to feed.

Perhaps a muskrat's to blame, John speculates at daybreak as he surveys the modest damage to their melon stores. H. does not set him aright, for whatever reason.

After a most frugal breakfast of bread and water, they shove off and soon reach the first man-made obstruction to the original river, the Middlesex Canal. They must draw the boat along with a cord from the manufactured bank, a few townspeople hurling wicked oaths their way for violating their Sabbath. No matter. They are soon on their way. The only actual words of discord they exchange on their journey concern John's insistence one day upon shooting pigeons for their lunch. No sooner do they set out on the natural river past the locks at Cromwell's Falls than the thin and thinning flock passes overhead. John suggests that they make their way to the sandy bank so that they might secure a feast of fine poultry to roast over a fire, which seems an unnecessary expenditure of time and effort to H., and which he communicates perhaps too mildly to his brother.

"We may not see another flock the entirety of our journey," John counters.

"Our northern forests don't seem to supply them the masts they once favored." Another reason they ought not to harass these birds that once blotted out the sky for hours, even days, during their peregrinations. "We have an ample store of rice and potatoes," he says. A kingfisher rattles from somewhere upriver, as if it were laughing at him.

"Even so," John replies. And this is all that John says. It is somehow understood between them that this is all that the elder brother, their father's namesake, must say to assert his privileges. H. wonders whether their lunchtime meal is truly what they negotiate here and now as tent-mates and brothers.

Ellen!

John's skills as a marksman, in any case, prove wanting. He manages to down only a single bird, whose iridescent plumage the brothers admire for some moments. John sets out into the woods to see if he might secure a squirrel or two to supplement their meal. Meantime, H. cleans their quarry by the riverside. He first plucks the feathers, the shafts making popping sounds freed from flesh, though he might only imagine these sounds. He slices open the belly with his jackknife and scoops out offal from abdomen with the tip of one finger. He rinses clean the blood and frees the remaining viscera in the cool Merrimack, then gauges the weight of their prize in his leather palm. John, of course, has downed the skinniest pigeon on all of creation. The kingfisher, surely the better hunter, giggles again upriver.

John returns to camp with two squirrels just as H. has gathered enough kindling for their fire. They tarry not, though it takes considerable time to clean the squirrels for the flame, unpracticed as they are at such coarse labors. As H. supposed, it has scarcely been worth the trouble to secure these victuals for their lunch.

"I suppose the rice and potatoes will do for supper tonight," John finally allows through his greased mouth, bursting the uncomfortable silence between them. He laughs to punctuate his remark, which prompts laughter from H.'s quarter, as well. John's laughter provokes a coughing fit to clear his lungs, which prompts tender feelings in H. for his tent-mate. Oh, dear brother. They empty their bladders in the bushes and shove off from the bank. What matter if they make it all the way to Bedford by nightfall? It feels uncommonly good to resume their adventure upon such easeful terms. He will put Ellen out of his mind. For now.

The remainder of their journey proceeds in most brotherly fashion. Over their morning meals, H. studies the fog as it drifts across the river. John spots a dragon-backed sturgeon near the river's surface one day while H. rows, yet it slips his net. They enjoy friendly jibes time to time with commercial boatmen and fishermen. They agree to a race against a much larger canal boat to test their mettle, each taking up an oar, and handily defeat the vessel, earning light refreshments from the crew. They toss morsels into the river and watch the fish dimple the surface to secure their prize. They listen to the wind coursing through the pines. They contemplate the travails of migratory fishes—alewives, shad, marsh-bankers, and salmon—as they struggle to bivouac various locks and falls. Depleted by the end of each day, they sleep like stones on the buffalo hide, serenaded by the distinctive melodies of animal citizens and the more boisterous songs of Irish railroad laborers one evening. H. dreams this night near Hooksett of a difference with a friend, but arises to perfectly peaceable humors, the difference having been settled.

In the corn barn of a most generous farmer at the terminus of their river journey, they store the *Musketaquid,* hang their sails and buffalo skin, then take the stage to Plymouth. They hike the fifteen miles up Pemigewasset Valley and secure lodging at James Tilton's Inn in Thornton, where they share the comfort of a large horsehair mattress. Come morn, they hike through Peeling, Lincoln, Franconia—spy the curious Old Man of the Mountain profile in the rock—follow the Amonoosuck River to its source and start up Mount Agiocochook, sampling bluets all the way. H. lingers over the blueberry shrubs longer than necessary in sly deference to John's compromised vitality.

They retrace their hike to retrieve the *Musketaquid* and purchase for ballast (as they have eaten through all their heavy sacks of rice and other provisions) the largest watermelon from the kind farmer, a Mr. Mitchell. They tarry not on the return leg, buffeted along by the downstream current and north wind, carrying with it from Canada the first cool breaths of autumn. They pause only to purchase an apple pie from a farmer's wife, and devour with equal intensity the pie and news of the world from its newspaper wrapping. H. can hardly believe how quickly they cover the many miles to the last canal and the Concord River. He detects the distinctive mud-smells of his native shore before he recognizes its bulrushes and buttonwoods. They row their vessel onto shore across the same keel marks they carved into the mud two weeks ago, then wheel the boat off the bank and tie it against an apple tree. A bittern squawks from the shoreline to welcome them home, or maybe ward them off its hard-earned hunting promontory.

What tender kisses greet them on Sudbury Road before they can even make their way to their Parkman home. Word of their arrival precedes them, apparently. Even the elder Mrs. Ward has joined the welcoming party. Sophia and Helen and Mother assert their privileges to greet them first, clutch them in their embrace, one after the other. It would be good if H. might ever enjoy the primitive life in the midst of such civilization, and enjoy civilization not wholly loosed from the primitive.

H. would regale Helen and Sophia, his aunts and Uncle Charles, his mother and father and the Ward ladies with news of their journey, but before he can broach the subject of their recent adventure John announces his plan, right there middle of the road, to leave for Scituate to visit Ellen. He made no mention of this plan, or mentioned Ellen at all, the past two weeks they slept as tent-mates and shared a horsehair mattress at James Tilton's Inn, or braved the mosquitoes to summit Mount Agiocochook. H. does not know what to say. His parents and sisters also seem dumbstruck by John's announcement. A coachman must shout fair warning for their party to step aside and allow his passage. Thankfully, the elder Ward intercedes.

"Impossible," she cautions, her voice competing against the rhythmic cadence of the horses' hooves. Ellen's parents are away at Niagara Falls, apparently. There is not appropriate chaperonage for such a visit, she insists as the percussive *clippity-clop* notes fade. John will not be deterred. The presence of Edmund and the servants, he avers, will suffice for propriety.

John rides to Scituate by coach the next morn.

16

Ransacked may be too strong a word. No shattered glass or dishware or upended furniture. Only Hertzog's fastidious housekeeping, redoubled by Magda's efforts, betrays what seems to have been a hasty, half-assed burglary. The first items he notices are the upset cabinet drawers and doors in the kitchen, troubled into various degrees of ajar by someone, or two or three someones for all Hertzog knows. Junk mail from the stack he has yet to recycle and a few random worthless objects—a corkscrew, a miniature Phillips-head screwdriver he bought to (unsuccessfully) repair his reading glasses, an oven-mitt—lay strewn across the linoleum.

The sight of the intrusion sends Hertzog bounding the stairs toward his study, fearful that the miscreant or miscreants might have stolen his computer. It's been months since he's printed pages from his work-in-progress, months since he's saved the files on a portable drive. Stomach acids scald his throat the moment before he reaches the open door and spies the computer sitting there inside the leg of his behemoth desk, the clunky monitor undisturbed up above, as well. Not much of a black market for ten-year-old off-brand desktop computers, he supposes, or for the pell-mell jottings of a retired professor. The room seems untouched.

He conducts a quick survey of the remaining upstairs rooms. His bedroom looks strange to his eyes, dust-mites suspended in the still air by the daybright streaming through the half-slanted blinds. He ordinarily doesn't spend much time gazing about his bedroom middle of the day. He opens the mirrored medicine cabinet in the master bath to check on his few prescriptions, the statin for his cholesterol and the Enalapril for his blood pressure. Present. His eyes scan the top shelf for the narrow ochre vial of oxycodone, prescribed years ago by his former general practitioner. Hertzog had wrenched his back dragging too many bags of pine bark mulch from the Subaru to the hobblebush hedge. There the expired prescription sits, which removes a certain type of culprit from suspicion. Or perhaps something startled the intruder and he or she (or they) fled before taking the time to pilfer the upstairs of its scant offerings. Ellen's room, too, appears unmolested. His eyes settle on the objects he has left alone these many years: the defunct ten-gallon terrarium resting atop her pine dresser, the *National Geographic* poster of deep space that Hertzog taped to her wall during middle school to inspire Ellen's inquisitiveness, and which she for some reason let be, the digital clock on her chintzy nightstand that flashed 12:00 in green for months (precipitated by one of their many power outages) before he finally unplugged the device, the few plastic receptacles clustered in a neat circle beside the terrarium holding Ellen's deodorants, lotions, acne creams and whatnot, the jewel-cases stacked vertically across her marble windowsill next to the girlish-looking headboard holding music CDs featuring, no doubt, the joyless variant of rock music his daughter favored as a teen. He strides toward the small closet (which seems fine), then the pine dresser and opens one of the wide drawers. Interesting. His daughter's old T-shirts and dungarees in four separate stacks seem less neatly folded than he had expected—as if they'd been bothered, maybe, then hastily set aright—but when was the last time he had inspected these drawers?

He makes his way back down the stairs, closing Ellen's bedroom door behind him, quiet as an apology. He needs to call Officer Libby, of course. Claire. Before doing so, he scans the open junk drawer beside the phone, where he keeps his weekly cash, not much, in a bank deposit envelope. It didn't occur to him to check the envelope earlier, fearful as he was over his antiquated computer and his more precious Thoreau research. The money, of course, is gone. Two hundred or three hundred dollars, maybe. Only the envelope remains, on the floor, actually, half-hidden beneath the recessed toe-kick of the cabinetry under the GE range.

He doesn't need to consult the outdated directory. He remembers Claire's office phone number, had remembered it, in fact, before consulting the directory to invite Claire for coffee a couple weeks ago. He lifts the phone from its cradle, but hesitates. Ellen. How had it not occurred to him the instant he entered his home and glimpsed the upset cabinet drawers and doors in the kitchen? Or upon inspecting the contents of Ellen's pine dresser, the top layer ruffled some like the surface of an unquiet sea? He cannot ignore the fact that his house had been burglarized (however half-assedly) at the very moment his daughter occupied him with an excursion into the woods. Ellen had been awfully sheepish, too, come to think of it, about not coming inside to use the bathroom after their walk. It had seemed strange to him at the time, yet he had been so pleased to see his grown daughter, happy to spend some time in her presence out from under Jude's watch, and so he dismissed her refusal as her natural wariness to court unpleasant memories. Yet did she know what her father would find once he opened his front door? Was that why she was so anxious to flee the scene of the crime? Had Jude dispatched Ellen on her task so that he might rifle through Hertzog's drawers for money and other valuables? Or did Ellen dispatch Jude to look for something she might have left behind? Perhaps the burglary was all a ruse and the upstairs had, in fact, been discreetly inspected.

Should he summon Claire, she will investigate these possibilities; she will interview Ellen and maybe Jude too. Hertzog doesn't want Claire to bother Ellen, particularly if this line of reasoning is pure paranoia. He can't rule this out. He doesn't quite trust his faculties since Ellen has returned. He won't spook his daughter so soon. What he truly needs to do right now is empty his bladder. And think. Yes, he needs to think before doing anything rash. He notices the bag of that dulse seaweed on the ledge above the kitchen sink and for whatever reason, perhaps only to distract himself, he plucks from it one of the small purple fronds. The dulse feels soft and leathery between his fingers when he had expected it to be brittle. He plops the morsel onto his tongue and winces against the sharp iodine, which slowly melts into more pleasant asparagus notes and a nutty finish as he chews and swallows. Not bad.

Hertzog, next morning, eschews his ordinary routine and follows his impulse oceanward to consult the foamy tide thrashing the pink granite outcroppings where the dulse and other seaweeds grow. To reach his destination, he must drive through the tourist-trammeled stretch beside the harbor, deferring to "cruisers" on foot, oblivious to vehicular traffic, crossing the road on gleaming sneakers and Bermuda shorts between the Dry Dock Café and the few chintzy shops, the shuttle at the public parking lot that will ferry them to and from town, proper. He continues on toward the spot he visits time to time, mostly during high-season as this narrow scrim of woods and bouldered coastline has thus far eluded travel guides and hiking maps. A few miles and minutes and he arrives. The defunct apple orchard opposite side of the road, tree-skeletons poking above advancing shrubbery, tells Hertzog to slow down. There isn't so much as a parking strip on the side of the highway, only a shaggy, cindered berm onto which Hertzog skids to a stop, perturbed by the oversize van parked just ahead. Hertzog usually has these few acres entirely to himself. It's a college vehicle, he recognizes at a glance.

Only a small brown sign marks the narrow trail as a Forest Service access point. It's always been somewhat ambiguous whether the sign is meant to allow or discourage public access. He walks at a deliberate pace, his hands clasped behind him, exercising the joints in his swim-sore shoulders and counterbalancing the weight of his binoculars in front. A scraggly undergrowth of holly, alder, and sumac, and even some grasses Hertzog doesn't know, competes favorably here against thinning woods so close to the shore. Sunken, soggy patches of earth advertise fragrant clusters of skunk cabbage. The few stunted fir and spruce lean away from the invisible ocean, hiding their heads, looking as though they'd rather stand anywhere but here. The sun hides behind an iron sheet of high clouds and the new day shows little evidence of eventual clearing. A squirrel growls at him from its eye-level perch on a sumac, protecting its nut. Hertzog feels a dark mood coming on.

He moves quickly past these blighted acres, pausing only to note the clicks and wheezes of chickadees hidden within a dense stand of cedars. Not far now. Briny seaweed smells overtake the skunk cabbage and pine as he draws closer to the ocean. Low tide, he suspects. The falsetto shrieks of seabirds sound above the wimpier notes of the forest birds behind him. The woods give way to the pink and gray boulders and an expansive view. Low tide, indeed, the funky seaweed stench rich in his nostrils. No foamy tide thrashing the rocky shore, as he had hoped to see. Difficult to discern precisely where, in fact, slick rock gives way to liquid sea. No sign of the party belonging to the college van. Good. He gazes out at the flats and tidal pools beyond the boulders, the granite outcroppings shagged with brownish rockweed here and there. A few terns skitter across his field of view above the mild ocean. A lobster boat chugs toward the harbor, close enough to shore that Hertzog can see the green metal traps stacked at the stern, two figures in bright orange jumpsuits moving about the deck, maybe the fellows Hertzog saw at the Dry Dock Café a few weeks back, hoping that the shedders have finally skittered inshore. Before treading across the boulders to the intertidal zone, he marvels at the forest's final tree beside him, a squat pitch pine, its multi-branched base creeping under the boulders to find purchase.

He re-straps his binoculars cross-wise so they rest just above his hip, minding his every footfall, careful to place a boot only upon the sturdiest-looking boulders. He plans ahead two or three steps at a time to set a circuitous but safe path toward the ledge. He won't even permit his thoughts to wander now toward Ellen and Jude and Claire. *Left foot, right foot, left foot*, is all he thinks. Last thing he needs is to twist an ankle and strand himself out here beyond the service of his cellular phone. Cool air rides across the ocean breeze, chilling the perspiration slicked across his forehead. He might have worn his fleece.

Upon the intertidal zone at last, he strides across the outcropping, riveted with barnacles that scratch against the stiff soles of his boots, weaves between and across the wrack thickets closer to the tide, the funk of dead and undead marine organisms thick in his nostrils, throat, and lungs. He takes special care during stretches where he must tread across the slippery seaweeds. Every few steps he pauses to lift his eyes and look at the sea, receive what wisdom it might offer. A guillemot pair flashes black and white wings low across the sea, so low that their wings seem to skid against the dark water. The rockweed (*fucus* or *ascophyllum*, he hasn't a clue) looks like so much detritus, piled on the dry and drying granite. Yet he knows that the creatures—he thinks of them as creatures now—are alive, that they can withstand almost total desiccation as they await the incoming tide. Even now, they shelter beneath their bladdered blades millions of organisms and microorganisms against predators and the hostile sun.

How timid Hertzog's adventures cast against the daily trials of this matted algae, awaiting high tide to buoy their tendrils from this rocky bed. Hertzog's life, far more sheltered and provincial than Thoreau's life, too, as his daughter had somehow gleaned, chastising him for his hypocrisy just the other day on Jude's farm as she tended to her pigs. *I don't get it. Isn't Thoreau supposed to be your big hero?* Thoreau, who some scholars liked to characterize as a homebody (compared to Emerson's transatlantic cosmopolitanism) was far more adventuresome than commonly supposed. Several trips to Maine, Canada, and Cape Cod, a stint in Staten Island, plus a journey to Minnesota toward the end of his short life to salvage what he could of his lungs. Where had Hertzog ventured, what had he risked, these many years? Ellen was right to find him wanting by his purported hero's example.

Hertzog won't call Claire about the break-in at his house, he decides. His daughter wouldn't forgive him his suspicion of her. This might all be an unfortunate coincidence. Hertzog knows what he needs to do. He will head out to Cherryfield Farm again, have it out with Jude directly. He pauses at the lip of a tidal pool and gazes into the pellucid water. A green crab skitters across the barnacled bottom past a motionless sea star. Or is the sea star moving its thick appendages ever so slightly across the rock?

He lifts his eyes from the pool toward the ocean and takes in a deep draught of sea-air through his mouth and nose. A creature lifts its oiled head from water not thirty yards from Hertzog, close enough that he can see it blink its liquid eyes. He lifts his binoculars to his own eyes. A harbor seal. Does it blink this way to get a better look at the strange primate on shore? As soon as Hertzog wonders this wonder, the creature lowers itself into the sea. Hertzog watches after it for a moment without binoculars to see if and where it might emerge, but soon gives up and continues his walk, breathing deep breaths of briny air into his lungs, perfumed in blows by the vegetal funk of the rockweed and its associates. Yes, he'll pay another visit to the farm before bothering Claire. It feels good to settle things in this way.

He picks up his pace across the outcropping, mostly dry now, the tide still outgoing, he decides. He reaches a bend to a more protected cove and there they are, the party from Emmenthaler, he presumes, congregated about a large mop of rockweed, ten or so young people, a few crouching about the seaweed. They lean their shaggy heads toward their leader, his neighbor. He recognizes Stacey Hinshaw at a glance by her two-toned hair, pulled up in a ponytail, the short black underlayer exposed. A summer class of hers, apparently. She braces a brown clipboard against her jeaned hip with one hand, gesticulates with the other, pointing a pen or pencil here and there. His first instinct is to turn heel and flee the scene, salvage his solitude, maybe walk the other direction for a time past the bouldered point where he entered. Yet something won't let him go. He's too far away to listen in on Stacey's instruction, or for her to recognize him, he's fairly certain. He imagines she's rehearsing the morphology and reproductive goings on of whatever genus and species she looms over: its holdfasts and air bladders, the growth patterns of its fronds, the orchestrated release of its gametes into the spring tides. He finds it affecting, somehow, beyond earshot, only Stacey's animated choreography and the attentive postures of her students betraying the pedagogical goings on. There's something beautiful about this sight of a teacher teaching, especially out in the great wide world. He always considered himself a good, if not great, teacher, though he might have been bolder with his pedagogy, taken more field trips, or some, follow Thoreau's practical teaching model, like Stacey. Even on brilliant spring days he chafed against student requests to hold class on the quad's silky lawn. He feared the outdoors would prove too distracting. Eventually, the students stopped asking.

Having seen enough, he decides it's silly to upset his walk on account of Stacey's class. He straps his binoculars cross-wise again to walk past the group, charting a path farther inland to do so as unobtrusively as possible. Unless he wants to traverse boulders once again, however, he must draw somewhat closer to the lesson, and does so, close enough that he can now hear the unintelligible glottals of the students, his neighbor's strangely familiar bass and treble notes in between.

"Hey there! David! Dr. Hertzog!" Stacey calls before he can scuttle past. "Come on over and say hi to my superstars."

Well, what can he say to that? He nods and makes his way oceanward the twenty yards or so to the group. The students turn their attention toward him, shifting shoulders and gazes, a few rising from knees.

"I *thought* that was you over there."

"Yes, well, I didn't want to bother you."

"Class, this is Professor Hertzog, a former professor of environmental literature at the college."

Environmental literature. This was never how Hertzog saw his specialization, per se, but he lets it pass, waves lamely to the students, who seem impossibly young up close, younger than he remembers.

"I was just introducing the class to the intertidal zone." She opens a palm to the granite ledge, as if she were showcasing a new car. The gold stud in her nostril winks against the daybright as she turns toward him. Her nostrils seem rimmed with wet from the chilly morning or allergies, maybe, which Hertzog finds winsome, somehow.

"I see."

She lifts the sleeve of her sweatshirt—embroidered with a likeness of their college's mascot, a fighting puffin—to wipe the nose dry. She explains to Hertzog that they're almost done with their lesson and that he should "hang out" for a few minutes so they can talk.

"Rachel Carson, troops, described the intertidal zone as an 'underwater forest,' capturing the unique complexity of this ecosystem."

"You mean the DDT Rachel Carson?" one of the students inquires.

"Yes, *that* Rachel Carson. She wrote mostly about the sea, actually, wrote beautifully about the sea."

Stacey continues to gloss the complex web of interactions in the diverse rockweed community, rockweed's role as critical habitat for over 150 species, from the microscopic spat of bivalves and periwinkles to estuarine birds and fish, such as cod, pollock, eiders, and buffleheads. He wonders if she only called him over to educate her crusty old neighbor along with her students, enlist an ally for the Rockweed Coalition?

Up close to this particular cluster of rockweed, Hertzog notices that it looks different than the other clusters he walked past before the bend, paler maybe. But that's not all. The bladders are more pronounced. And it's webbed through with browner tendrils. He wonders whether this is *fucus* or *ascophyllum* but won't interrupt the lesson to ask. A student chimes in, however, to ask about the browner tendrils.

"Great, Ross," Stacey replies. "That's actually a separate species associated with *ascophyllum nodosum*, and that we talked about in class. Remember, everybody?"—her voice rises to summon a response. "It's an epiphyte?" she continues.

"Tubed weed," a student finally answers, her voice inflected by the dialect of a Caribbean island, unless he's mistaken.

"Good job, Simone." The student smiles, flashing overcrowded teeth.

Stacey has established a strong rapport with her students. He misses teaching, it occurs to him. He misses his students.

The symbiotic relationship between *ascophyllum* and tubed weed, Herzog learns, appears to be "commensal" in nature. The tubed weed, that is, does not harm its rockweed host, but doesn't do much for it, either.

"Oh God, my boyfriend's a tubed weed!" a female student jokes—her dirty blond hair dreadlocked, a wrist festooned with multi-colored cloth and leather bracelets—inspiring a chorus of laughter from her peers.

The lesson concluded, Stacey instructs her class to explore the intertidal zone a bit on their own and make their way back to the van no later than noon, warns them not to take any live periwinkles or other creatures. She lifts a wrist toward them and taps a nonexistent watch.

"Let's walk this way for a bit," she proposes once her students disperse.

"You're a good teacher," Hertzog says, shoulder to shoulder with his young neighbor, a bit shorter than he thought.

"Thanks," she answers.

"I didn't know you were teaching a summer class."

"Can't pass up the money. Taylor and I are trying now…you know, to start a family and all that."

"Oh," he replies, flummoxed by the confidence. "That's good," he says, unsure what else he ought to say. He breathes in the briny air to seek its counsel and gazes toward the sea. A party of gulls at the lip of the granite fight over some prize, crying their cacophonous cries, the lot of them harassing one with a dark creature in its yellow mandible, a crab maybe. It's enough of a spectacle that Hertzog and Stacey both hold up on the rock to watch until the harassed gull takes to the wing, the rest of the flock rising in pursuit, riding the brisk current down the shore.

"So it was nice meeting your daughter," Stacey says, their saunter resumed.

"Oh. Thanks."

So this might have been why Stacey called him over to her rockweed lesson moments ago, to inquire further about Ellen, whom she had only briefly met yesterday. For all Hertzog knows, she had made inquiries with some of her Emmenthaler colleagues during the night, got the scoop on her solitary neighbor who turned out to have a grown daughter.

"You have a complicated relationship with her, don't you?"

Hertzog feels the fine particulate wet against his face. He can't tell whether it's the lightest rain or sea spray, or maybe only the salt breeze licking the perspiration on his nose and cheeks.

"I suppose so. Yes."

"I could tell."

Stacey seems to wait for Hertzog's next words, realizing, perhaps, that she ought not to pry further on the subject of Hertzog's relationship with Ellen, and that she ought not to share what seems likely to have been her unflattering first impressions of his daughter. He considers asking his neighbor whether they've had any trouble with break-ins next door, or if they've heard of other recent break-ins in town. The words rise from his throat to his lips, but he swallows them before speaking. It seems too odd a segue and will only inspire further questions he'd rather not answer.

Stacey, glancing back toward her students scrabbling this way and that across the granite outcroppings, suggests that they cut into the woods here, enjoy the longer trail through the battered spruce and fir to the highway. He tells her sure and follows along, treads across the barnacled flats, then atop the boulders somewhat faster than before to not seem like such an old man in Stacey's company.

The atmosphere beneath the torn canopy seems wholly different—the pressure reduced, somehow, as if punctured by the coniferous needles. A new order of quiet obtains, which Hertzog only perceives given its contrast to the rocky, windblown coast. After taking only a few strides inside the copse of low trees, Stacey does a funny thing, laces her sweat-shirted elbow inside his own elbow, to offer or receive ballast he hasn't a clue.

"It's good, maybe, that you have any sort of relationship at all with your daughter, David. It's more than some people can say."

"That's true," he replies, glad that he resisted his initial impulse to shrink from Stacey's platonic clutch. The age difference between them emboldened her to perform this gesture. Hertzog's not sure how he should feel about this, so clearly aged-out of the sex game with young women that his neighbor can reach out to him in this way without fretting that she might unintentionally signal romantic intent. He ought to feel very old. Yet it mostly feels nice to have his young neighbor's arm wrapped inside his own. She had dressed more appropriately for the chill, her heat radiating against his ribs. Riding below the woodsy smells of the spruce and fir and the lingering brine of the ocean, he can smell her wheaty breath competing against the floral notes of her soap or moisturizer. The chatter of chickadees rises as they draw closer to the thicket of cedars.

"Tell me about Ellen's mother," she says. "I'm curious."

"You mean you haven't asked about Rebecca at school? You haven't asked about me?"

"Rebecca? That's her name? No. I haven't asked anyone. Why would I? You live right next door. I'm asking you, David."

He contemplates what he might tell his neighbor about his wife. He wants to tell her something. Remarkable, how Stacey's simple human touch has disarmed him.

They had only been seeing each other for six weeks or so when Hertzog called Rebecca at home to cancel their Friday night dinner date, which had almost, but not quite yet, segued into a mutually assumed happening. He was feeling ill. Nothing serious. Indigestion. "Curse of our tribe," he joked of their Jewishness, the line salty with static. She said okay, told him to feel better, and hung up the phone. Somewhat terse for Rebecca, which he didn't think much about at the time. He had no appetite, but forced himself to down half a bowl of oatmeal and tried (unsuccessfully) to make some headway on a stack of student papers before turning in. He slept fitfully, arose feeling more nauseated to the bickering of juncos. He showered and shaved to revive himself, padded downstairs to the dark kitchen, his small rented home shaded mornings by two enormous white pines. He drank a half-glass of water from the tap fizzed with Alka-Seltzer. He tried convincing himself that he felt better as he retrieved the *Bangor Daily News* from the brick stoop and scanned the headlines.

The phone rang while he was still in the kitchen deciding whether he felt well enough to get some air. The antique clock above the sink caught his eye upon hearing Rebecca's voice other end of the line. It was precisely nine o'clock. He found it poignant somehow that she had waited for this time (distracted herself, maybe, with laundry or some other errands) before checking in on him.

"A bit better," he assured her. "No, not well enough to get together later I'm afraid. I wouldn't want to get you sick—"

"Oh, David, let's not play games. If you're seeing someone else, you can just—"

"I'm not seeing someone else. Is that what you think, Rebecca?"

He heard what he thought was her exhalation through her nostrils. His abdomen twinged with pain. It didn't occur to him that she might have suspected that he was seeing someone else, that she thought he might be shacked up with one of his former students or someone from the catering company even now. It might have peeved him, the accusation—she was pretty much calling him a liar—but it only made him feel more rotten than he already felt. Rebecca suspected that he might still be playing the field between their hikes and dinner dates and lovemaking.

She was awfully cool about it, too, which prompted a separate thought.

"Are *you* seeing someone else, Rebecca?" It surprised him how much it bothered him, the thought blooming in his mind, Rebecca entangled with another lover.

"No, David. Of course I'm not."

She insisted on coming over to check on him. She didn't like the way his voice sounded, not like himself at all, which was the only reason she suspected something untoward, she insisted. What could he do but relent?

His pallor alarmed her the moment she crossed the threshold, wearing a smart zippered sweatsuit, her shock of curly black hair tamed in a tight, high ponytail. "You look green," she said. He imagined she planned on going for a run after checking on him. She reached for his forehead in the foyer. Her hand was cold from the still chilly spring morning. "You're warm," she said, her forehead creased with concern. "Definitely feverish."

"Now now," he replied, careful to keep his distance lest he get Rebecca sick. "Just a cold, I bet. Flu at the worst."

He ushered her out the door and told her to enjoy her Saturday exercise. She told him she'd check in on him again in the afternoon.

The abdominal pain increased over the morning. An odd brain-fuzz too. Strange virus, indeed. He tried doing a bit of yard work to get some air—his landlord gave him a break on the rent for his light landscaping—spread some compost from his backyard heap about the still-sleeping spirea, bunchberry, rugosa, and hobblebush shrubs. The perspiration rose too fast to his forehead. He felt both cold and hot. Clearly he was ill. But Hertzog wasn't truly concerned until the impulse to vomit seized him while pushing the wheelbarrow between plantings. He was more nonplussed than pained by the spasms, by these strange sounds emanating from his throat as he emptied the malodorous oatmeal and acids from his gut onto the lawn. He couldn't remember the last time he had vomited. When Rebecca returned, he told her that maybe it wouldn't be a bad idea if she dropped him at the ER.

A CT scan confirmed what the young emergency room doctor suspected. Hertzog's appendix was badly infected and needed to be removed tout suite. That's the expression she used, tout suite, which seemed sort of cavalier under the circumstances, Hertzog laid out on the gurney, his head propped by pillows. A lab tech refused to make eye contact, fiddled with the machinery in the background. The young doctor was surprised, gesturing toward inscrutable monochromatic images on the film, that he wasn't feeling more discomfort. She kept clicking her pen. He *was* feeling discomfort, Rebecca told her. She asked the doctor whether she could give him something for the pain. The doctor explained that this wasn't possible just before surgery. It was a routine operation, she assured him directly, evading Rebecca. The surgeon had been called and was already scrubbing up, the hospital's best general surgeon. Dr. Marvin Gelb. An orderly would be by any moment to take him to prep. She directed Rebecca to the surgical waiting room, but Rebecca said she would wait with her friend until the orderly came. The doctor, maybe a few years younger than Rebecca and Hertzog, seemed to think about this for a moment behind a frozen expression. She clicked her pen, again. Then, perhaps taking Rebecca's measure, she turned her attention back to Hertzog. She wished him good luck, touching his shoulder, and departed.

"Bitch," Rebecca said, mostly to leaven the mood with humor, it seemed. It hurt to laugh.

A male orderly arrived within minutes, mustached and muscled. Rebecca kissed Hertzog on the forehead and told him through clipped and breezy syllables that she would see him soon. Hertzog squeezed her hand before she could go, thanked her for coming over to his house and driving him to the hospital, and for staying with him. The orderly wheeled him on his gurney to prep, pasted his hirsute belly with shaving foam and shaved it close with a cheap Bic single-blade razor. A nurse ran a line to administer antibiotics, poked him a few times before locating the vein. The last time he could remember needing anesthesia was when he had his wisdom teeth removed as a teenager. The harsh florescent lighting, which seemed to pulsate, unnerved him. He was frightened, it occurred to him, and glad that Rebecca was spared this scene of his silly fright over a routine procedure.

Next thing he knew he was awake and looking into Rebecca's eyes, hazel swimming inside the green rims, which he hadn't noticed before, the precise patterning. He wondered how long she had been standing there, shading him from the outdoors light that leaked from the edges of the window blind.

"There you are," she said.

"Yes. Here I am."

His mouth was dry and his tongue tasted of copper.

"Looks like you're going to live, David Hertzog."

"Looks like."

She handed him a flimsy plastic mug, the paper insert half-filled with water. He drank.

A nurse entered the room, her soles squeaking against the hard floor. She flicked on the fluorescents. "Rise and shine, Dr. Hertzog." She was much older than the nurse who had pricked him earlier hunting for a vein, even wore one of those stiff frocks and hosiery (rather than scrubs) that Hertzog associated with nurse-hood, and which he found strangely comforting. She introduced herself as Dorothy as she checked the pouches of antibiotics and other fluids, adjusted the drip, and inspected his fresh wound. "Dr. Gelb always does such a tidy job," she said. She asked him to rate his pain on a scale of one to ten and when he answered (he felt no pain), she declared, "Well, that number will go up," her eyes shining, as if she were amused by his impending discomfort. She asked whether he had any questions, but he couldn't think of any just then. Rebecca, in his stead, lodged various queries regarding the prospective discharge date, wound care, activity guidelines, and dietary prohibitions, which Dorothy answered gamely enough, assuring her that they'd include instructional materials on all such matters in his discharge papers, as well. Hertzog would be able to leave sometime tomorrow, once he could get himself to the commode on his own and pass a stool. Dorothy departed toward her other duties, her shoes squeaking once again against the linoleum.

Then Rebecca did something that surprised Hertzog. She lowered the safety rail (as if she were familiar with the mechanism) and propped herself up above the stiff sheets, careful not to upset the IV tubes on the other side. "Scoot over, David, you big baby, would you?" She was still wearing her smart exercise clothes, hadn't left the hospital during the operation. Her running shoes with their thick cushioned soles dangled off the side. Above the starchy aroma of the hospital linens, he could smell her Rebecca smells rising from her pores as she lay back against the inclined headrest, her hands folded at her waist. She sighed. They didn't speak for a time. Hertzog listened to the hum of the climate control. The forced air rattled time to time against the small vent near the ceiling—a loose screw, maybe—then quieted as the system paused. He could hear Rebecca's inhalations and exhalations, feel her side brush up against his arm as her lungs filled with breath.

He noticed the graceful way she folded her lovely hands, these being the days when he noticed pretty much everything about Rebecca.

He glimpsed her girlish sapphire and diamond ring, the jewels aslant. The ring was slightly oversize for her finger and he often caught her adjusting it instinctively with the thumb of her same finger, though she sometimes neglected to do so.

Lying there in shared silence, Hertzog had never felt so—what was the word?—partnered. Here was the whole deal with being partnered, it occurred to him, beyond the sexual access, the financial advantages, the societal approbation and what have you. Partnered, there was another being in the world to witness the ordinary and extraordinary, but mostly ordinary, contours of your existence. This separate soul watched your life on this middle-aged planet hurtling through space, knew that you had just survived a rather routine operation, that you harbored strange desires, boasted certain talents, realized certain wishes, wronged certain people, and did better by others. Your partner knew simply that you existed in the world, and in a certain way, if only for an infinitesimally brief time. Hertzog, thinking these thoughts in his hospital gown, realized that he had been lonely—not solitary in the numinous Thoreauvian sense, but lonely—and that Rebecca, breathing beside him, had punctured his loneliness.

Hertzog shares these recollections, or most of them, or some, with his young neighbor, then waits for her next question, the obvious question, while a flycatcher buzzes from the copse of cedars. *Zheep zheep zheep.* But Stacey doesn't ask the obvious question about Rebecca. She doesn't say anything at all. The dogged past tense of his recollections, perhaps, or maybe something rueful in Hertzog's voice, puts Stacey on notice. Hertzog hears the grasses brush against their jeans as they step along the rarely trod trail. She has yet to release his arm. He hears Stacey's stomach grumble, or is it his own stomach? The flycatcher *zheeps* again behind them, tending to its own essential business.

Whatever happened to Rebecca's girlish sapphire and diamond ring, Hertzog has no idea. He can't even remember when she stopped wearing it, as she simply switched it to her other hand once Hertzog asked her to marry him with a square-cut diamond ring set in platinum.

"She sounds like quite a woman," Stacey finally says, "your wife." Hertzog almost loves his neighbor for these simple and true and carefully measured words.

"Yes. She was."

17

June 19th, 1840
The other day I rowed in my boat a free—even lovely young lady—and as I plied the oars she sat in the stern—and there was nothing but she between me and the sky. So might all our lives be picturesque if they were free enough—but mean relations and prejudices intervene to shut out the sky, and we never see a man as simple and distinct as the man-weathercock on a steeple...

John returns from Scituate with a sermon from the minister Sewall to mollify Mrs. Joseph Ward. No news of nuptials proposed or accepted, yet John's peppered gait, the starbright in his eyes, cannot be denied. The next weeks, as the maples and oak, birch and beech finally blush against the autumn chill, H. commits lugubrious lines to his journal on rain drops and regret, on men braver than he. Prometheus. Mercury. Aeschylus. Linnaeus. He administers daily doses of Latin and Greek and French to his students at the Academy without enthusiasm, watches on from the second-floor window as John provokes their monkeyshines on the blond lawn of the yard. On Hedge Club evenings at the great man's home, he suffers Alcott's inanities on certain grains he favors for the digestion, the movement of his bowels, and suffers a lecture on Minerva from Richard Fuller's smarter sister, Margaret. He nearly chips a tooth on the brittle biscuits served by dear Lidian, likely prepared by one of her Irish servants. He suffers a cold he fears might settle in his lungs. Christmas holiday, his bodily health restored, Prudence invites H. and John to accompany her on a visit to her relations in Scituate.

It affects him powerfully to see Ellen amid the colder, coastal clime, her brave features (that Roman nose, the promontory of her brow, the deep-set, soulful eyes) peeking from the woolen layers as they march to the Scituate Light looming over the bouldered beach. H. cannot secure an audience with Ellen alone the few days of their visit, but then neither can John. No sooner do they arrive back in Concord than Ellen's letter to Prudence awaits, regaling her aunt (who reads apposite portions of the missive at the supper table) on how good it was to once again be in their tender and wise company, remarking upon John's lively humor,

H.'s fine fluting and ornithological expertise. H. will not be so importunate as to seek Ellen's heart outright, considering John's like ardor, yet he will not remove himself entirely from the field of play. He finally sends that volume of poems by Jones Very to Ellen, raising by a most subtle degree the temperature of his avowed affection.

John will not be outdone. He sends Ellen a collection of opals from South America for her commonplace book, and to Edmund (for appearances) sends Samuel Johnson's *A Journey to the Western Islands of Scotland*. Prudence receives a letter from Ellen relating how much the family enjoyed the collection of poems recently sent by H. and asking her aunt to relay their gratitude. She likely sends a similar letter for Prudence to share with John.

In any case, his muse has returned. The next months, as the ice forms and then slowly breaks across the pond, he writes a series of original verses and sends them to Ellen. *Up this pleasant stream let's row...*

In a brief letter accompanying the poems, he warns her of the importance of restful slumber and springtime air, the dangers of excessive tea and coffee consumption. Weeks pass without a response. He fears that his pedantry, his fuddy-duddy-ness, have gotten the better of him. Oh, why carry on so about salutary and corrosive influences, alimentary and otherwise? No sooner do these thoughts consume him than he recognizes Ellen's hand against her familiar ivory stationery top of the mail stacked on the silver dish in the foyer. He does not say anything to Prudence all through supper, waits for her to convey the news from Scituate. Sophia, instead, occupies their boarder's attentions, lodges queries over her mashed peas about Masaccio and chiaroscuro and perspective.

Prudence finally alludes to Ellen's missive over their dessert pudding, as if she had been saving her words regarding sweet Ellen for this sweetest portion of their meal. Ellen, Prudence relates, apologizes profusely for neglecting to send her appreciation to H. for sharing his lines of original poetry. And more. She plans a June visit, just weeks away. The brothers lock eyes upon the report, then lower their gazes to the plums swimming in Mother's pudding. John coughs into his fist, which seems mostly a performative gesture.

How instantly H.'s eyes charge affection soulward upon glimpsing Ellen. She arrives earlier this summer than summer last, the Concord earth offering a fresh face to this daughter of Scituate. The brothers, accompanied by Prudence, introduce Ellen to entirely new hill, cliff, meadow, swamp, and dale, painted now with lady's slipper pinking the air with perfume, small snapdragon, yellow Bethlehem star—which ought to be called yellow-eyed grass, H. declares—heal-all, bastard toadflax, lousewort, and the ever-splendid purple rhodora! The clover's rosaceous blooms Ellen missed last season carpet the fields now, which vibrate with the industry of bees. John, alas, attaches himself like a bloodsucker to Ellen's side on their ambles, provokes her easy laughter, leaving it to H. and to Prudence to scour the trail-sides for their botanical entertainments. He minds the increased vigilance with which John plies cheek and chin with the razor, morningtimes. He would fain ask after John's intentions, but fears what he might hear in reply and cannot coax his tongue and lips to shape the words. He waits for the occasion he might secure Ellen's audience sans filial company.

The occasion arrives the morn H. proposes over their breakfast rolls a sail on the river and John demurs, citing the still air. Ellen surprises H., and surely surprises John, by leaping at the proposal, putting John in a most untenable position. His brother cannot artfully reverse course now, can only exhale audibly to express his disapprobation.

John was correct, of course, about the lambent air. Their sailing morn fast becomes a rowing excursion. No matter. The doldrums offer H. the opportunity to showcase his manly skills as an oarsman, thankful for having designed a narrow beam for the *Musketaquid*. Ellen faces him from the stern only arm's length away, Prudence beside her on the cane seat. Prudence gazes shoreward, but Ellen studies him rather unabashedly, the coordinated effort of his hands, elbows, back, and shoulders as he works the oars in their locks. Her bold mien encourages H. to look Ellen straight in the eye, as well, between sightings over his shoulder to check their course. Perspiration pearls her upper lip. The pronounced dewy cleft between her lip and nasal septum moves him, powerfully. To kiss those lips with his own lips, to achieve such flesh on flesh contact with this precious feminine soul! A cold sweat rises to his forehead. H. rows with great care, lest he splash the ladies or interrupt the quiet noises all about—the intermittent sizzle of insects crossing their sphere, the kerplunk of a fish hawk seeking its reward, the monotonic chuff of a woodchopper's ax, the loopy interrogatives of a scarlet tanager, a chanticleer's cry, a dog's bark. He does not speak, and Ellen does not speak. He recalls the poem he wrote and sent to Ellen in anticipation of this splendid day. *Up this pleasant stream let's row/ For the livelong summer's day,/ Sprinkling foam where'er we go/ In wreaths as white as driven snow—/Ply the oars, away! away!...*

H. raises the dripping oars once they reach the hidden bank pinked last August with saucers of hibiscus John and he plucked for Prudence's herbarium the start of their river expedition. No blooms now, alas. Yet the aroma of hidden flowers somewhere overtakes the copper and fish smells rising from the placid river. He discerns from the dilation of Ellen's nostrils that she enjoys the earth's odors, as well, discerns from her protracted silence that she too listens to the outdoors orchestra. A rare soul, who refrains from cluttering up creation with human noise. He could be no more certain of Ellen than he is now, savoring this moment of shared solitude and silence, nothing between them but the limitless sky. And Aunt Prudence, of course. And the specter of his brother's intentions, vis à vis Ellen. Oh, were it not for mean relations and prejudices, Ellen and he might live united and free. The poisonous thought of last season invades his skull once more as the woodchopper's ax chuffs and chuffs and chuffs.

If only John were dead.

"You look troubled," Ellen says, her brow rising. She asks if he feels unwell. He offers a spate of fraudulent sentences to allay her anxiety, but tells her they better turn back for home now, lest the family worry. Her hazel-flecked eyes shine with wet.

"Thank you for rowing Aunt Prudence and me on your vessel. I have so missed such adventuresome days with you these long months I've been home." Her voice sounds different, the familiar brightness tinged by plaintive notes. Prudence clears her throat.

"You are most welcome, dearest Ellen," he tells her, making careful orbits with the right oar to turn the boat about. The syrupy water sounds pleasant kisses against the wood. So this is what it feels like, he thinks. To be in love, romantic love, with a soulmate. So distinct from love in its other variants he has supped. There is something ferocious in love of this ilk, something he doesn't fully trust.

H. wonders whether they have reached an understanding. He doesn't know enough—or anything—about such matters and cannot gauge the severity of Ellen's feelings. He might seek the great man's counsel, but hesitates. The complication of John renders the predicament unspeakable. Ellen departs for Scituate on their familiar, friendly terms.

Yet John must sense a perilous shift in the atmosphere, for he seems determined to force the moment to a crisis. Just days before the Ward ladies' planned visit to Scituate a month hence, Prudence secures H.'s audience in his bedroom while he composes an essay on the Roman satirist Aulus Persius Flaccus for the transcendental journal that Mr. E. has decided to publish.

"Might I interrupt your studies for a moment, dear H?" He didn't recognize the knock. It is most unusual for Prudence to summon him from behind his closed bedroom door.

"Of course." He swings open his shoulder, inviting Prudence inside the open threshold. Something is afoot concerning Ellen, he somehow knows. He keeps one of his mother's old dining room chairs in his bedroom for the rare visitor he entertains indoors. Prudence sits. H. descends into his seat, as well, shifting it about from the desk so that he might face their boarder. A jay barks out the open window in the interim between Prudence gathering her breath and speaking her first words.

"John has asked to join Mother and me on our visit to the Sewalls next week."

"Oh. I see." He receives the news as an intestinal complaint. That his brother seeks a visit to Ellen's home so hard upon Ellen's own recent visit to Concord can mean only one thing, as Prudence, too, has gleaned.

"Are you certain you shouldn't accompany us, as well?" The sugar maple out the window lashes Prudence's face with its shadows. The jay barks once more. He will not speak false words.

"No. I am not certain. Yet…"

He lets the words hang in the dust-moted atmosphere between them as he ponders the circumstances. The thin glass shifts within the panes and complains against their wood encasements. An afternoon storm brews, he knows from the quality of wind and heat through the screen, the iron air in his nostrils, though he spies not a cloud in the sky from his current vantage.

"…yet my higher instincts compel me to remain," he finally continues.

What demon possesses H. that he behaves so well?

He watches as Prudence clutches a great draught of air through her nostrils. The set of her shoulders suggests that she considers imploring H. to reconsider, but then her shoulders fall and she exhales audibly.

"John, to be sure, could not possess a more loving brother."

❧

H. tends to his own business. In work there is life. Though what constitutes one's fruitful labors? He studies the trajectory of the sun. He dispatches his duties as curator of the lyceum, engaging the fiery abolitionist, Wendell Phillips (to the consternation of some), who promises to impart dire forebodings on the annexation of Texas. He calls upon and schedules Ephraim Bull, the horticulturalist who developed the Concord grape (to the consternation of no one). He bathes in the town's overheated ponds. He loses himself in the woods in deepest night, touches with his palm the familiar chests of individual trees to gain his bearings, parses distinctions among cricket melodies at various locales and wonders as to the significance. He works the plumbago mill daily to spare his father and sisters this most tedious and dusty labor. He dresses and sits for an interminable session in the parlor so that dear Sophia might paint his portrait. Upon inspection, he can only hope that the painting does not survive him, though he spares his younger sister his appraisal. He redrafts his essay on Aulus Persius Flaccus, as Margaret Fuller, the editor of their fledgling magazine, has scribbled furious notes in the margins and between his cursive lines. He assists the great man in his orchard, constructs scaffolding of wood and string for his cherries and apples, and offers preliminary instruction on grafting scion to stock. Through great force of mind, he cultivates tend'rest thoughts toward his silent brother.

"I greet thee, my elder brother," he writes in his journal, "who with thy touch ennobles all things."

To spend no mean hours. This shall be his work. To appreciate every precious breath granted to him and accept what fruits life brings, as the sea-waves cast up its pearls and seaweed. These lines, too, he commits to his journal.

John returns home by coach in advance of the ladies Ward. His silent presence beneath the poplar gives H. a start upon opening the shed door and stepping out into the daybright, coughing to expel the mill-dust from his lungs. H. knows not how to read his brother's overly prompt arrival, or his immovable presence beneath the bluebird nest box, unemployed this season.

"I heard you, brother," John greets him, "working the mill inside the shed."

"Yes," H. says. "Welcome home, dear brother." He would embrace

John, exchange manly kisses on John's pallid cheek, but something keeps him, keeps the both of them, from expressing their affections. H. waits for his brother to speak. A vireo's strident sentences seem to mock their reticence. *Here I am. There you are. Here I am.*

"I suppose I must beseech you not to commit to your journal what I wish now to tell you."

"Certainly." The news, H. knows, must pertain to Ellen of Scituate.

"The field is clear for you, dear brother, regarding the object of your affections."

Poor John. The next days and weeks, as summer yields to fall, H. labors to cultivate lachrymose sentiments on behalf of his brother, spurned by Ellen, rather than revel in his renewed prospects for winning her hand. He broods upon the systole and diastole of the heart, the circulation of the blood to the extremities. He listens to the din of crows massing in the sky, the final flutings of the wood thrush at bog and creek as it prepares for its southerly departure. He traces clouds touring creation. He follows the scant progress of a worm burrowing between moldering layers of leaf and soil. Nighttimes, he studies the waning symphonies of crickets and frogs.

Yet Nature conspires against his fraternal sorrow, refuses its sympathies. He reads enthusiasm in the earth's most doleful sights and sounds, enthusiasm above all. *Life! Life! Ever more life!* The very eye, the beveled edges of lid before lash, prevent brotherly tears from overbrimming onto his fresh-shaven cheeks. He commits these lines to his journal.

The first issue of their transcendental magazine is printed and contains his long essay on the Roman satirist and the poem he wrote a year ago for Ellen's brother. *Lately alas I knew a gentle boy …*

Freshest stars spangle the night sky and he cannot look away.

He must not call upon Ellen too soon. Instead, he continues his work on his heroism essay, long and mosaical in form, inspired. He feels certain that Margaret will snatch it up for the second issue of their magazine. He observes a fevered rally for the Whig party's horrid pro-slavery presidential candidate, William Henry Harrison, replete with a gargantuan red-white-and-blue slogan-ball, worries that modern politicking whips up the worst beast within. He offers a second grafting lesson to the great man and introduces him to manifold methods. Splice. Tongue. Whip.

Cleft. Saddle. Too late in the season to apply their efforts—the sap now stilled within the tree veins—yet as good a time as any to learn new skills. He gathers the proper portions of horse dung, horse hair, and clay and mixes the grafting-paste outside the shed before the master's watchful eyes. The distraction of such concerted tactile employment, his hands lathered with fragrant dung and clay, offers H. the occasion to broach the subject of his ardor for the daughter of Scituate.

"I have lately considered asking for the hand of a lovely young lady."

"Mrs. Joseph Ward's granddaughter, I take it. Ellen."

"How did you know?" He turns from his labors to look the sage in the eye, smells the not unpleasant dung and clay smells wafting in the crisp autumn air between them.

"Dear H., the entire town has witnessed the circuit of affections between the fetching Sewall girl and the brothers T. these past many months."

He turns his eyes back toward the bucket of dung and clay and hair, kneads the dough with force as he feels his dander rise. He doesn't like that he and John have been the subject of the town's petty gossip at church, the post office, the lyceum, the public house, private gardens and parlors.

"It's important that you don't add too much horse hair, no more than the proportion you see here," H. changes the subject, "or the mixture won't adhere properly at the union."

"Bullocks to the graft, what is your plan, dear lad?" Mr. E. will not be so easily distracted. "You will set out to Scituate with one of the Ward ladies soon, I hope, before the first snow," he states more than asks.

"I was contemplating writing her a letter, instead. I feel I might express my sentiments more clearly in written form."

The great man guffaws. "I urge you to reconsider. A matter of such gravitas, you ought to press your case in person, allow your future wife to look you in the eye to gauge the sincerity and depth of your ardor."

"Yes, well—"

"The precise words you choose will scarcely matter. Words are mere signs of natural facts, the natural fact being *you* in this instance." A titmouse flock chitters and chatters from the stand of evergreens beside the grove trees. He glimpses a grey crest. "I hardly know how the girl might deny the force of your character were you to stand up for yourself. Although it would be wise," E. scrunches up his nose, "to wash your hands before setting off."

18

The day breaks wet and cold. Yet Hertzog will not deprive himself his morning exercise if only to delay his visit to Cherryfield Farm, his confrontation with Jude, and to preserve the comfortable dailiness of the life that he knows. He mounts the Randolph Trail headlong, stomping the scattered pinecones and the sweetfern, the hardy little crowberry and blueberry shrubs, to shortcut stretches here and there.

He huffs at the clean air on the rocky ledge, lip of the Bowl. The aggressive hike has heated him through. Drizzle blurs the water's tannic surface with its soft blows, the Bowl skewing toward a peaty brown lately rather than green, for whatever reason. He sets down his backpack and sheds his outer layers right there in the wide open—who's to see?—pauses briefly to contemplate his groin, the pale phallus, the flesh veined and corrugated, the pendulous testicles, the still-shaggy fur. If thinning. If graying. Enough of that. He pulls on his jammers, seats himself at the ledge and launches his legs into the water, which doesn't feel quite as cold as he expected. The muddy moss-rocked bottom feels warmer than the water above, having retained yesterday's hotter heat. Fry of some sort (bluegills?) nip at his feet and calves, startling him before he recognizes the familiar aquatic kisses for what they are, tiny fishes seeking the nourishment of his flaked skin, the detritus clinging to the few dark hairs.

Ordinarily, he launches into his stroke to escape these creatures once they discover him, but a thought seizes him, freezing the placid expression on his face—Ellen's red-faced terror upon her introduction to the gently-nipping fry in the Bowl. She must have been only four. Maybe five. Hertzog was already thigh-deep in the water waiting for Ellen while Rebecca shed her clothes on the ledge. The summer had been warm and so the water was warm too, bean-green with plant life.

"Come to me, Ellen," he said, opening his palm. "We'll try swimming from here."

She made it about halfway to him, shuffling her feet across the gravely bottom, before pausing, waving both her arms back and forth strangely, a sort of clapping motion arrested just before the actual clap might occur.

"Something's biting me!" she screeched, rushing from the water back onto the ledge and the safety of Rebecca. By this time, his wife was standing in her one-piece, the modest black racing suit with bright red piping that she wore across several seasons. They tried to reassure her in soothing tones that the tiny fish were harmless, that they wouldn't even bother her anymore once she started swimming, but Ellen—incomparably, insufferably, ineluctably Ellen—would not be mollified.

Hertzog found her reaction, like most of his daughter's reactions, outsize and unacceptable. After a bit more verbal coaxing, he gripped her biceps—"We can't baby her like this, Rebecca!"—and dragged her from his wife toward the water, Ellen screeching all the while.

"Stop, David! She's frightened!"

He stopped, partly on account of Rebecca's words, mostly on account of Ellen's unceasing cries, which he hadn't quite anticipated, though he ought to have anticipated them.

He was dimly aware of the hush of the few other hikers and bathers about taking in the scene, the suddenly still human forms on the trail in the backdrop half-hidden by foliage, bathing at various depths closer by in the lake, wondering whether they ought to intervene, deciding against it for the moment. A dog's staccato bark echoed across the Bowl from the other side, then stopped. He released Ellen's arm. His daughter scurried back to the safety of her mother's embrace. Rebecca glowered at him, her lips pursed.

"What's the matter with you?" Rebecca scolded him as their fellow citizens returned to their leisure. The dog continued its staccato song. It might have been two dogs. "For God's sake, what's the matter with you, David?"

What *was* the matter with him? Hertzog wonders now, easing into his stroke, then rolling onto his back, spreading his arms and legs, clutching great gulps of spruced air into his lungs to lift his torso high on the surface. Raindrops tatter his torso with cold blows. He opens his mouth to receive the mild rain. Thoughts on his final swim with Ellen and Rebecca burrow into his skull as he tastes the iron drops, colder in his mouth than the peaty pond water. What on earth was the matter with him?

❧

An entirely new day greets Hertzog by the time he showers and exits the house to drive all the way up to Northridge and Jude's farm, the cool sun having pierced the cloud cover. Only the iron smell and stained asphalt and the water pearling still on the new grass remind him that it had just rained. Taylor Hinshaw, Stacey's bearded husband, waves hello to him from the other side of the hobblebush hedge while Hertzog double-locks the front door. He lifts his hand and says hello. Taylor's turn to walk their tabby cat, apparently. They typically exchange neighborly courtesies, but Taylor's expression today seems different, reminding Hertzog of a shiny penny, freezing him in his tracks. Stacey, the affable expression reveals, has spoken to her husband about her recent encounters with their crusty older neighbor, who wasn't quite so crusty, after all.

"I wanted a dog," Taylor jokes, realizing how ridiculous he looks standing there holding a thin pink leash attached to their fat cat, the creature pouncing now on a moth or some other bug hidden between blades of grass.

"Dogs are more work," Hertzog replies. Taylor nods inside his dark beard. He tells Hertzog to have a good one, releasing him.

Once safely past the food smells and automotive exhaust of town, the heady aromas of angiosperms going about their randy summertime business infiltrate the Subaru's interior. He averts his eyes from the road every so often to gaze inside the canopied woods and spies the silhouettes of birds looping about, looking carefree yet likely fighting pitched battles amongst themselves. He wonders, passing Teddy's some twenty minutes into his drive, blinds closed against the mid-day sun, whether Cassidy is inside working a shift, and whether Ellen has called her old friend. He hopes so, though doubts it.

His insides blanch as he draws closer to Jude's farm and notices the half-assed clapboard signage along the roadside. BABY GREENS. LOCAL HONEY. T-SHIRTS. PIES. CHEESE. ARTISAN MEATS. SEA VEGETABLES. A couple new signs, too, he hadn't recognized last time. FLOWERS. LOCAL POTATOES. HEMP PRODUCTS. COSMETICS.

Hertzog isn't sure what he'll do, exactly, once he reaches Cherryfield. He's sort of hoping he'll spot Jude somewhere out and about the property and that he won't see Ellen. But what will he do if he does see her first or if she sees him? How will he explain his presence to Ellen without alienating her, utterly? Even if things go precisely as he hopes, he might still anger his daughter, but he cannot leave things alone. He must confront Jude about the break-in at his house, though mostly about his intentions with Ellen, generally, put him on notice at the very least. Ellen still has a father looking after her best interests. He can't wait on Claire, who likely won't be able to lean on Jude, anyway. He passes the line of miscellaneous orchard trees and pulls into the scruffy parking lot, which is mostly full and which is good—enough distractions about that his own presence won't call too much attention to itself. He angles his car beside an ancient mustard-colored Volvo station wagon and exits. A few customers mill about nearby, wearing sunglasses and fanny packs.

Hertzog scans the property, pollinators and small birds working the few wild trees that shade the ground here and there between the tilled fields and outbuildings. His eyes wash over the two greenhouses, the windows clouded, the unpainted barn, the red farmhouse, and just beyond the farmhouse the living quarters of cheap siding better suited for poultry than people. Farther off, he sees those blue-tarped mounds bordering the scrim of woods. What stews beneath those tarps? Misbegotten seaweeds? he wonders, mostly on account of his new friend, Stacey. He doesn't smell the fetid marine aromas from last visit, the air, instead, spiced with dirt and manure and perfumery from the farm's manifold upstart plants encouraged by these longer, hotter days. He spies a few young men and women here and there crouched between rows, tending the various stalks and leaves, flowers and fruit. The spindle rests on the redwood picnic table closer by, but no girl today feeding it wool to make yarn. Dusky birds, sparrows likely, hop about the unmown grass beneath the blighted table foraging on the wild seeds or whatever crumbs the farmworkers or tourists might have left behind.

Rather than head inside the store, where Ellen might be, he walks past the few loitering tourists and out to the fields, hoping he might spy Jude overseeing his acolytes. He walks a diagonal toward the barn and those fields beyond, his olive hiking pants thwacking against unmown grasses, the earth's red pebbly crust—damp from the recent rain—sinking somewhat beneath his boots. He rounds the old barn and spots strange fruit dripping from several clotheslines, arranged strategically, it appears, to catch the wind. Seaweeds, it takes him only a moment to discern. This must be where Jude dries his harvest. Two girls sit close to the operation as if to guard the bounty. They seem to notice him the split-second after he sees them, the both of them lifting their gaze from their labors. They sit on low stools, the stools mostly hidden by their flouncy skirts and some sort of table shrouded by a bone-white cloth. They each wear bandanas to tame their hair and wield some sort of tool (knives?) in their narrow fists, a five-gallon paint bucket between them. It's impossible to stride past without acknowledging them in some way.

"Can we help you, sir?" the darker girl finally bursts the silence. He recognizes her now. It's the mocha-colored girl with whom he exchanged hellos the last time he visited, the one who had been working the spindle, her voice, unless he's mistaken, accented by England or some commonwealth. He hadn't noticed the dialect before, but they had only exchanged a word or two a few weeks ago.

"I'm wondering if Jude's about," he replies. They seem to be picking through the dried leaves of seaweed spread before them on the white-sheeted table, culling tagalong crusty detritus—animal or vegetable—from the foliage, depositing the clean leaves in the plastic bucket.

"Jude?" the other girl asks, her pale face pock-marked with pimples. Hertzog nods. Her blue bandana tames dirty-blond hair. The poor child ought to be wearing a proper hat instead of that bandana, Hertzog thinks, to protect her from the strengthening sun. "He's out with the goats, I think," she says, lifting her implement (yes, it's a knife) and pointing off in the general direction Hertzog was walking. The blade glints against the sunbright. She speaks with an accent, as well, but Hertzog can't quite place it. The girls seem open and unsuspicious. They seem okay. They might *be* okay, he considers, just as his daughter might be okay. Or maybe not.

"So where are you both from?" he asks.

"I'm from the Netherlands," the blond girl answers, smiling now to advertise her glossy teeth.

"And I'm from Australia," the mocha-colored girl says. They seem happy to talk with him, happy for this diversion from what looks like tedious labor. He asks them how they found themselves here of all places, working at Cherryfield Farm for Jude Winslow.

"We're woofers!" the mocha-colored girl declares, delighted with this phrase she must be used to uttering. Her forehead and cheeks shine beneath the sun and her rising sweat. She looks more well-fed than her blond friend, a healthful layer of subcutaneous fat riding beneath the skin on her arms.

"Woofers?"

"Working-On-Organic-Farms," she continues. "They bring most of our lot here. Send folk all about the world, actually."

"Oh, isn't that nice." *Nice for Jude,* he thinks, but doesn't say.

"Those seaweeds you're working on?"

"Uh-huh," the mocha colored girl answers, seemingly unperturbed by the query. "Dulse and kombu today. Isn't the dulse pretty?" She waves her knife toward the purplish leaves clipped to the clotheslines behind her.

Hertzog nods.

"Customers don't fancy dried periwinkles and other shell-bits with their sea vegetables," she continues. "Or the holdfasts. Good for the compost pile though."

"I'm sure." Hertzog wonders who harvests all these seaweeds (Jude?), and from where, precisely, and whether some of the varietals are the protected rockweeds that Jude oughtn't to be harvesting at all. From Stacey's pamphlets, he knows that ripping the holdfasts straight off the rocks is illegal now, that the new regulations stipulate that fronds must be cut at least twelve inches from the holdfasts to ensure regeneration. Or was it sixteen inches? Seaweeds, in any case, and Jude's possible poaching, aren't Hertzog's primary concern today. He thanks the girls for the information and heads off to find him.

It doesn't take long. A hundred yards or so and Hertzog spots his ridiculous ponytail silvering about as he crouches before a low wooden fence, struggling over a furred creature half-hidden by Jude's legs. He can't quite make it out at this distance but he assumes the animal must be a goat. A newish-looking wooden shelter with a single-pitched asphalt roof, a ramp leading inside, borders the oval fence-line. This is where Jude keeps the animals. Yes, it's definitely a goat, he sees now. More goats, seven or eight, mill about inside the pen, nosing the muddy ground, bucking at each other. The smell of their excrement rises above the dirt and pollen smells. It's more pleasant than the ammoniac aroma of the pigs, anyway.

"Jude!" he calls as he draws near. "Hello there!"

His voice startles Jude, who flinches and swivels his head toward the sound, then turns back toward the black goat, affecting nonchalance.

"Professor," he says, still bent over his task. The poor goat seems to have trapped its curved horns in the wooden slats bottom of the fence. It emits whiny bleats as Jude attempts to free it, handling the creature's head and neck more roughly than seems warranted. Something about the goat's eyes seem strange, otherworldly. Its pupils, Hertzog realizes. The black slashes—rather than circles, per se—bisect the yellow irises on the horizontal. Hertzog can't claim any particular affection for livestock, yet the sight of the bowed creature with these strange eyes, the sound of its pathetic bleats, move him.

"Let me help," he says, lurching toward the scene of the struggle.

"I have it, professor! For Christ's sake!"

Hertzog leans back, props his hands on his hips as Jude continues to wrestle with the whining goat, horns scraping against the wood. The veins bulge in Jude's wiry and weirdly hairless forearms. "This fucking goat! Every goddamn fucking day he does this!" Hertzog fears that Jude will break the goat's neck, that his own presence has only agitated Jude, making matters worse for the distressed creature.

"Take your time," he urges just as Jude manages to free the animal. It scurries from the fence-line so fast that it plows recklessly into one of its fellows, who chuffs out its nostrils at the insult, bucks at the air with both hind legs.

"Ellen know you were coming?" Jude asks, rising from the fence, his face flushed and wet, his voice sharp if not quite angry. He wears gray sweatpants below his V-neck undershirt, the knees stained with farm dirt, a white double-stripe up the sides. There's something vaguely European about them, vaguely effeminate, or maybe it's only the ponytail and his wiry physique that makes everything else about Jude seem vaguely effeminate. A strange get-up for a farmer, in any case, which only bolsters Hertzog's impressions that Jude mostly leaves the actual work to others. Any self-respecting farmer, it seems to Hertzog, ought to wear sturdy jeans or work pants with complicated pockets, riveted fabric loops for holding tools.

He tells Jude no, that he didn't tell Ellen he was coming.

Jude lifts the front of his undershirt to wipe the sweat from his face, flashing surprising abdominal muscles across his mild paunch and a fur trail below his navel, which makes it impossible for Hertzog not to notice his protruding groin testing the thin gray pant fabric.

"It's not so easy for her to see you, professor," Jude says. "Maybe you don't fully appreciate that, but you should."

They are close enough that Hertzog can smell coffee on Jude's breath mingling with the goat smells, spruce smells, and the rich pollen smells of manifold plants riding the warm currents between them. The words make Hertzog wonder what Ellen has told Jude about her impossible father, whether Jude speaks now upon new confidences or ancient ones.

"I'm not here to see Ellen. I came to see you."

This gains Jude's more concerted attention. His eyes widen, flashing his clear whites all the way around the blue middles.

"Okay. What do you want?"

"You know why I'm here, Jude. You practically called me. The funny business at my house a couple days ago. You're really going to stand there and tell me you know nothing about it?" The goats bleat and snort behind Jude in the pen, a motley cluster bucking at one another with their horns.

"I have no *idea* what you're talking about." Hertzog studies his adversary as Jude shifts his weight on his crusty running shoes, as puzzled creases rise across his perspired brow, as he lifts his fingers to tame silvered strands that had escaped his ridiculous ponytail while he labored to free his goat. He doesn't seem in any obvious way to be lying—seems more annoyed than anything else—but this doesn't give Hertzog much to go on. Jude was a practiced liar. There were people like this in the world, Hertzog was reminded time to time, who lied through their teeth as naturally as they spoke the truth. Ellen, to her credit, was never quite in this camp, even though she lied plenty.

"The break in," Hertzog continues. "You had nothing to do with that?"

"Why would I want to break into your house? Think I was running low on liniment?" *Liniment.* An odd word. He was educated, Jude, as Hertzog recalls. Graduate degree in one of the agricultural sciences from some Big Ten university. Director of operations of the organic farm at Williams—or was it Bates?—before purchasing the Cherryfield property so that he might enact his vision with greater autonomy. That was his line, anyway. Who knew what scandals Jude had escaped by descending upon their backwater?

"To intimidate me," Hertzog says, refusing to let Jude's age-baiting distract him. "To put me on notice now that Ellen's back and I've been poking about again."

"And why would I have to put you on notice?" Hertzog glimpses the green worm of a vein throbbing at Jude's hairline. "What would I have to worry about from you regarding Ellen?"

"It's not just Ellen. My interest again in whatever it is you've got going on out here. Something fishy, that's for sure." He surveys the grounds with a sweep of his eyes, the young men and women in the fields working between the rows of leafy vegetables. "Quite an operation, Jude. These young people doing all your work, earning peanuts for themselves if you're paying them at all beyond their room and board. And how many of these vulnerable young girls are you screwing over there in that crappy outbuilding? Even while Ellen's living under your roof again in the main house, I bet." The goats' bleats and snorts have grown more exercised. A mob of them, Hertzog notices, seem to be picking on one goat, in particular, the goat that Jude had just freed. It fends off the mob, then lopes away, but its tormentors pursue the creature and he, or she (do female goats have horns?) must turn about and defend itself once again.

"Oh, so there we have it. That's fucking rich, professor. *You*, lecturing *me* on how to treat young women. Like you weren't chasing every plaid skirt around the quad back in the day."

"You don't know what you're talking about, Jude."

"Oh, don't I? Everyone knows. Everyone knows who you really are, professor."

Bile rises in Hertzog's throat. He chokes down the acid, tasting some peaty Bowl water, too, from his earlier swim. Jude carries on as if he's meant to speak these words to Hertzog for years, and what can Hertzog do but listen as the goats snort and squabble over the fence, as their piquant odors invade Hertzog's nostrils along with Jude's acrid coffee breath, as vehicular traffic from the highway rumbles in and out of earshot?

"Town's just treated you with kid gloves all these years. Because of what happened. The accident. Poor pitiful Professor Hertzog. Then saddled all by his lonesome with a slutty teenage delinquent, a bad girl, Ellen Hertzog. What a cross to bear! Well, the college finally wised up and sacked your ass, what I hear. 'Cause you've milked that whole thing long enough, don't you think, professor? Don't you think?"

Because of what happened. The accident. Poor pitiful Hertzog...

It was a beautiful summer day was the thing of it. A day you'd only expect good things to happen. Ellen, fourteen, hadn't even complained about their plan to hike up to the Bowl for their swim. They'd leave her alone for the rest of the day, Rebecca promised, if she'd leave her room and join them for some morning exercise. Hertzog still remembers how Rebecca couched the incentive. *Your father and I will leave you alone for the rest of the day.* That was Ellen's greatest wish those adolescent days. Not for the latest electronic gizmo, or designer jeans, or makeup, or ski vacations to Sugarloaf, like most of her classmates. Ellen, by contrast, only wished to be left alone. It was a request beyond the capacities of either Hertzog or Rebecca to honor.

The hike up the mountain had been uneventful. Ellen dogged it, but she always dogged it. No big deal. Hertzog slowed his pace and didn't hassle her. He listened as Rebecca, some paces back with Ellen, peppered their daughter with questions about what she might especially care to do before school started up again, whether she might appreciate a weekend trip to Boston, just the girls. Catch a show, or maybe the Fine Arts Museum. She liked it last time, Rebecca reminded her, the Monets especially. Ellen often needed to be reminded of her mild enthusiasms. *There is this thing in the world that you like to do. Remember?* He couldn't hear Ellen's response, only her labored breathing behind him. She likely shrugged her shoulders, saving her breath. Hertzog paused and gazed up inside the canopy of a giant birch, as if he had spotted a bird or some other creature worthy of inspection, but he only meant to give Ellen a brief rest. He lifted his binoculars and gazed blankly above, heard Ellen skid to a stop beside him.

"Whadya see?" she asked, huffing between her words.

"Nothing. It flew off."

There were no other people swimming or sauntering about the Bowl when they arrived, as Hertzog expected and hoped. Only the lightest breeze blurred the water's surface. A kingfisher's rattle announced its presence down the shore, a common enough sound that it didn't merit mention. Hertzog watched the pretty bird with the blue collar and crest as it hawked its wings above the surface, plunged for its prey, then returned to its perch in an overhanging spruce, a small prize flashing in its mouth. They wore their bathing suits beneath their clothes and stripped down to them on the rock ledge. Rebecca wore an all-black Speedo one-piece. He would think about this later.

"Oh, Ellen, the water's so warm," his wife said, having already slipped off the ledge, submerging herself to her shoulders, treading water rather than touching the moss-rocked bottom with her feet. She had tamed her raven hair in a complicated ponytail, but wouldn't wear a cap. Ellen's one-piece was too small for her (Hertzog noticed, but knew enough not to mention) as she refused to shop for a new suit with her mother, even online, and as she had gained more weight lately than was healthful. Puberty had arrived early for their daughter—cruelly so, he thought—the trip-wired hormones precipitating changes Ellen wasn't remotely prepared to navigate.

"Okay, let's get this over with so I can get back," Ellen said, splashing into the water less artfully than her mother.

Or she might have said, "Okay, I'll beat you over to the other side and back."

Or she might have said, "Okay, soon as we get this over with I want a snack."

Hertzog could barely hear as he had retreated to the trail to hide their backpacks in the foliage. The kingfisher continued its rattle.

Rebecca and Ellen had already gotten a headstart by the time he entered the water, both breaststroking. They looked quite similar from behind, the angle at which their head and neck connected to their shoulder, their like coordination stroking their strokes, their daughter a bit larger and a shade paler on account of her general aversion toward outdoors exercise, or exercise of any sort. It was colder than he expected given Rebecca's announcement, but not cold, the surface colder than the currents below. Even with his goggles, he couldn't see much past his own hands in the bean-green water, plant-life muscling inside every molecule. Swimming freestyle, it took him only moments to catch up. They treaded water beside one another to regroup. The water tasted vaguely of asparagus on his lips.

"Grody, Dad, you got a bat in the cave," Ellen complained. He said something jokey while he wiped at his nose, while Ellen skittered away toward her mother—"super-gross," she continued—while Rebecca smiled and told Ellen to give her poor father a break. It pleased him, this bit of snot in his nose, as it offered something at least for Ellen to react against and draw her toward Rebecca. Anything that drew his distant daughter closer to one of them pleased him those days.

It was their custom to skirt the perimeter of the Bowl in a shallow C to remain close to shore at all times, and for Hertzog and Rebecca to swim either side of Ellen so that they could both keep an eye on her. They were careful in this way. He took the inside, the deepest end, as they stroked loose and easy freestyle strokes. They kept their distance from one another to avoid thwacking arms, but he could just glimpse his daughter's right arm parting the bean-green water, could see the pale bubble vortices in her stroke's wake. Ellen, despite herself, was a fine swimmer. One of the reasons she agreed to join them on these excursions, he suspected, was so she could enjoy this estimable skill she possessed that not so many people her age possessed, though she would never admit to such a shameful thing. Every so often when he turned his head to breathe, he could hear Ellen's practiced intake of air. He couldn't see Rebecca on the other side, but figured she was there. He couldn't hear much as he stroked, but time to time he heard one of Ellen's hands slice into the water on her catch, time to time he heard snippets of the kingfisher's persistent rattle. Although this was technically an open-water swim, he didn't worry so much about Ellen. She was such a strong swimmer, and they weren't so very far from shore, and if she ever got tired all she had to do was roll over on her back. He had taught her this.

Their plan was to stop together roughly halfway to the other side once they glimpsed the pink granite outcropping. There, they would tread water or float a bit to catch their breath, or maybe head to the outcropping to rest or leap into the water from its modest height before the teenagers arrived. So it surprised Hertzog when Ellen held up about fifteen minutes into their swim, which caused him to drop his feet and hold up, as well.

"Where's Mom?" she asked, the slightest tinge of worry in her voice, freezing Hertzog's expression on his face. Ellen coughed to clear the water from her throat. Where *was* Rebecca? He could see no trace of her beside or behind Ellen, or anywhere on the nearby shore. He yanked his clear goggles up on his forehead, treaded water in quick jerky strokes as he spun his torso 360 degrees, gazing all about for his wife. The kingfisher continued its rattle, but Hertzog didn't hear.

"When's the last time you noticed her?" he asked.

"I don't know!" Ellen cried. "Like way back there!" His eyes darted toward Ellen just long enough to follow her finger's trajectory. He swam toward the spot some fifty yards away in choppy freestyle strokes, his eyes down into the green all the while searching for the billowing tress of his wife's ponytail, a pale hand or shoulder, her black swimsuit. Anything! The sun had grown stronger since they'd arrived at the Bowl, spearing the water with shafts of light, but it was mostly just a brighter bean-green that Hertzog gazed down at just beyond his outstretched hands, then dark the deeper he dove from the sun. He dove aimlessly, groped every which way across the colder currents some ten feet down, the pressure smarting his ears, resurfaced to gulp great clutches of air between dives.

"Mom! Mooommm!" Ellen cried at the surface, flailing her arms about as if Rebecca were within arm's reach.

"Ellen!" he grasped the knobs of his daughter's shoulders and looked into her eyes. "Swim to shore!" He squared her shoulders toward the Bowl's rim, absorbed the blow of one of her heels against his thigh. "You need to swim to shore now!" he shouted into her ear, close enough that his lips brushed the stiff cartilage. "You hear me? Swim to the shore right there right now and wait for me!"

She obeyed. Hertzog watched after her just long enough to make sure she obeyed. Then he returned to his frenzied dives, calling for Rebecca on the surface between huffs of breath. He tried to fan about each dive to cover different patches of water but it was difficult to gauge his position. He swallowed water, hacked out great green gulps, foaming the surface with his mucous. Soon, he could only dive a few shallow feet, taking longer and longer pauses at the surface between dives. Ellen emitted wolf-like yelps he barely heard from the nearby shore between his lame plunges and groping about in the green. He tired quickly. So quickly! He still marveled at this, that he had tired so soon groping for his wife in the water, that he had so little strength to offer. Hertzog was not a particularly large or powerful man, but he was strong enough and fit, especially those days. He ought to have been able to summon inexhaustible physical resources upon such an occasion, but this was not the case at all. Not at all.

Ellen's wolf-yelps and maybe his own thrashing about attracted the attention of the nearest hikers, two of whom plunged in after Hertzog, joined him in diving after Rebecca, though without terrific urgency, an air of bafflement attending their every dive. There was something obligatory about their efforts from the start. They seemed to know that it was hopeless, yet also knew that you couldn't just let someone disappear beneath the water's skin without expending every reasonable effort to save that person. This was the human deal. Hertzog, spent, mostly gasped for breath atop the surface. A woman on shore crouched beside

Ellen on her boulder, he noticed through his goggles, wrapped her arms and a towel about her. A third man with red trunks swam to them from the rocky shore, a red foam buoy trailing on a cord behind him.

"Sir, come with me now!" he commanded. "Your face is blue! You hear! You need to swim to shore with me now! Now!" The bearded lifeguard gasped for air between his words. He had sprinted about the Bowl's circumference to the scene along the trail from the public beach, Hertzog would later learn, where he had been setting up the flags and buoys and few chairs and chaise lounges. Hertzog obeyed the bearded lifeguard, but wouldn't grasp the buoy. He thwacked his way to shore.

More people had arrived at the scene by this point, two of whom shed their clothes to their boxers and plunged into the water, stiffly, as Hertzog hacked up more Bowl water onto the rocks and pointed toward where they ought to try. Someone threw a towel around his shoulders as he hacked and urged him to sit on the boulder beside Ellen, silent and rocking now inside her towel, head hidden within her nest of elbows, cords of her hair flecked with algae, the stranger's arm still wrapped around her shoulders. Hertzog's eyes darted between his daughter and the water where the would-be rescuers dove and surfaced, dove and surfaced. The stranger cooed words or maybe just sounds into Ellen's ear. He tried wrapping his own arm about his daughter from the other side but she was having none of it, blaming him from the start, because who else was there to blame? He rose to his feet. Couldn't sit. Another someone, a woman, asked about his wife's bathing suit or cap and he told her she wasn't wearing a cap, that her suit was black. That's when he wondered whether Rebecca's old suit with the bright red piping might have made all the difference, whether he might have just caught enough of a glimpse to see her descend in those first moments, whether he might have been mere inches from brushing up against her hair or fingers or toes in the murky green.

He watched the good Samaritans out on the water with singular intent as they dove and surfaced. His eyes throbbed from staring so hard. Then something in his brain clicked, because he picked up the kingfisher's frequency, still rattling above the water farther down the lake. It plunged for prey, rose and plunged, rose and plunged, and finally settled upon its spruce perch. Their human business barely brushed up against this bird's sphere. This fucking kingfisher! Someone placed a plastic water bottle in his hand, used both his hands to wrap Hertzog's own hand about the bottle, instructed him to drink. "Drink," the person said. A ranger arrived, signaling for help on her walkie-talkie before exchanging any words with him. She asked several questions, which he answered. Then Claire Libby arrived, surprising him. How did she get there so fast? Perhaps it wasn't fast at all. How long had it been since Rebecca slipped below the surface? Claire wrapped a wool blanket around Ellen, then wrapped a second blanket about him even though he wasn't cold.

"Take her," he told Claire. "Please."

"Yes, that's what I was just going to do, David."

Hertzog crouched beside the boulder to lift up his daughter, told her she had to go with Officer Libby now, that Officer Libby would take care of her, as Ellen rose to her feet but resisted—"Noooo!" she cried—as the stranger beside her withdrew, as Claire placed a palm on Ellen's woolen shoulder.

Maybe he ought to have let his daughter remain with him, maybe this was her daughterly right, he would later wonder, as Claire's deputy and the rangers cleared bystanders from the Bowl's perimeter, as the sun strengthened in the summering sky, as the professional rescue divers paddled out in the small aluminum boat the lifeguards kept on the public beach, their flippered feet disappearing beneath the surface, as the fucking kingfisher continued to ply the surface for fish and frogs, as Hertzog traced the efforts of the divers by their bubbled breath, percolating at the surface, as they retrieved Rebecca's lifeless body from the depths within an hour of anchoring, struggling to lift her human heft over the tilting gunwale.

But Hertzog hadn't let his daughter stay and wait with him, even though she resisted Officer Libby's encouragements and bucked from his embrace.

"Let me go!" she cried.

"Shh," he cooed.

"Just let me *go-ooo!*"

"Let my daughter go!" Hertzog cries now at Jude.

"You're raving, professor. Ellen's not a baby anymore. She's a grown woman. She can come and go as she pleases." The goats had settled down, but jays skreighed from the edge of the woods. *Skreigh! skreigh! skreigh!*

"That's what you say, Jude. Of course that's what you say."

"It's light years ago, whatever troubles we had."

Hertzog seethes at the blithe way he refers to the matter. *Whatever troubles we had.* As if Ellen were somehow party to Jude's scurrilous behavior years ago, as if Hertzog didn't know exactly what these problems were. Jude's philandering. Poor Robin LaPointe. She had been the wife of Warren LaPointe from up near Machias, who Jude contracted to build that cheap dormitory not too far from the barn, where these young "woofers," apparently, still lived. Somehow, she had let herself get tangled up in Jude. That's how most of the locals referenced the whole sordid affair after all was said and done, attributing the lion's share of the blame to Robin herself, a married woman, an older woman to boot. She had swallowed a fistful of pills and ended her life in the middle of one of their coldest winters on record, months after she had traveled all the way to Portland for an abortion, weeks after Jude had broken things off, and just after (Hertzog supposed) she had lost all hope in whatever future she saw in Jude. The only reason anyone knew any of this was that she had kept a detailed diary and a sister insisted on talking to the local news to prevent future suicides through erasing the stigma of bipolar disorder. The sister soft-pedaled the incident of the affair and kept Jude's name out of it, but she probably knew that this wasn't the sort of thing that could be kept a secret. It wasn't long after the scandal broke that Ellen picked up and left for parts unknown. Hertzog would call Jude out on all of this, but Jude is still speaking.

"Where do you get off, anyway, with this holier than thou crap? You *want* her alone and unhappy is the truth of the matter. Like you've been alone and miserable all these years. That's what you've always wanted, blaming her the way you do. You think that's what she deserves, your shitty solitary life!"

"You don't know what—"

"All you've managed to do all these years, far as I can see, is shut yourself up in that prison of yours you call a home. And now it's too late to get back in the game, your cock soft, your balls all dried up."

The words ought to enrage Hertzog, but they stun him, instead. He stands there on the fragrant earth, slack-jawed and speechless. He scarcely hears the goats snorting and pawing the pebbly earth in the pen, the jays skreighing from the scrim of woods. Jude has never spoken to him quite this way before—has hardly spoken to him at all before—and he isn't finished yet.

"You think it was easy for her even before what happened to her mother, living with the two of you Emmenthaler snobs, Mr. and Mrs. Perfect?" His voice is calmer now, yet all the more troubling for it. "It's no wonder she came running to me. But don't take it so hard. It wasn't even you she complained about most. Bet you didn't know that." Hertzog tries to mask his expression, but knows by Jude's rising smile that his face betrays his surprise. "It's her mother she really couldn't stand."

"I'm warning you, Jude. Not another word about—"

"Should make you feel better. Didn't blame you hardly at all for being such a douche of a father. The ice queen's the one she mostly complained about when she talked about you two back then."

"Enough, Jude!"

"No, not ice queen, there was another name she called her"—Jude's pale eyes rise to the sky as if the name were scrawled across the cumulous clouds—"what was it?"

"Don't!"

"Bitch-queen! Yes, that's how she—"

And just like that Hertzog is upon him, battering Jude with clumsy blows.

"What the fu—?" Jude feints from the assault, raises his elbows to his face to protect himself, but not punching back. Then he does a strange thing, begins laughing maniacally as Hertzog continues to fling unpracticed blows, the strange high-pitched peals only rising upon the rare blow striking home, which further enrages Hertzog, that his fists inspire not fear or anger, but this maniacal, pig-squeal laughter. Hertzog hasn't struck someone in years, not since he was a Bronx schoolboy. The awkwardness of his efforts soon displace his rage. It isn't a natural thing at all, to curl fingers into a fist and strike another person all about to inflict harm. He tires quickly from this strange exercise, even before he makes rare contact and feels the pain shoot through his left fist, before he feels himself being pulled from his adversary by younger, stronger men, and one girl—"Call the cops!" someone shouts—as Jude continues to laugh his strange laugh, as the goats continue their goat business, as he spots Ellen now amid the few onlookers, her mouth forming an astonished O.

19

Friday Dec. 4th, 1840
Methinks I have experienced a joy sometimes like that with which yonder tree for so long, has budded and blossomed—and reflected the green rays…I love to look aslant up the tree tops from some dell, and finally rest myself in the blueish mistiness of the white pines.

Many's the pine I know—that's greybeard and wears a cocked hat.

Mr. E.'s advice notwithstanding, H. cannot bring himself to travel to Scituate. He fears the spectacle he would make of himself, setting out by coach, the townspeople sniggering into their palms. He fears injuring his brother unnecessarily should Ellen turn him away, though fears wounding him more gravely should she accept. He fears Ellen's father, if he were to be honest, the stern Unitarian minister. He wishes that the whole of society might roar away so that he and Ellen might enjoy a partnership on pure and silent terms. He puts it thusly in a long letter to his beloved, wishing that the sun of their love might rise as noiselessly as the sun from the sea. Ah, silence. He includes a poem, inspired by the seasons—recalls the red clover's springtime blooms lathered with pollen, the tender young petals yielding to the industry of the honeybee—the symbolism of which cannot escape Ellen. He alludes to their rowing adventures on the river, their merry ambles in the countryside, their inspection of the camelopard, their walk to the Light in frosty Scituate, her most tender inspection of his scalp, per Dr. Gall's phrenological methods. He follows his genius this way and that, but by the end of the six-page letter he issues his proposal outright, seals the missive and walks up Main to dispatch it, penny-post.

While he awaits Ellen's response, H. delivers careful instruction to their wards, taking pains to treat Edmund no more tenderly than their other charges. He will not make of the innocent child Cupid's go-between. One of Alcott's daughters, Louisa, has recently enrolled and H. delights in her fierce intelligence, her independent spirit. Oddly, he feels not the least bit anxious. Rather, he revels in this interregnum between his proposal and Ellen's response, the pregnant possibility that resides in the silence. He courts the most reverent and attentive posture toward the actual world. His sensate mind has never felt so receptive. His ears drink the pattering of raindrops on the sill as he retires early to sleep. He wonders whether such a life of careful observation and thought might rival the adventures of Crusoe or Marco Polo. Within the compass of his ribs, there is space enough for a lifetime of adventure. He earns fifty cents Saturday repairing the frame of Mr. Gibson's harrow and seventy-five cents shoveling his farm beasts' waste. He contemplates the proportion of hay that constitutes the diet of these ruminants, troubling clods with the tine of his pitchfork. With the largesse, he purchases a circumferentor and levelling instrument with which he measures the height of Lee's Cliff above the river at various points. He jots the measurements in his daybook and journal. If H. were not a schoolteacher, he might greatly enjoy the serenity and pure science of the surveyor's life. Crows mass silently in the sky.

Not a fortnight passes before he receives a letter in Ellen's hand. It is the first communication he has received from her, directly. He repairs to his bedroom and rips opens the seal posthaste.

> November 16, 1840
> Master H. D. T.,
>
> I am in receipt of your recent letter professing, quite circuitously, yet in the end, quite clearly and importunately, your intentions that we join as man and wife. Whereas my feelings for you have ever remained within the sphere of sisterly affection (nor can I imagine how you might have inferred otherwise), and whereas it is altogether unclear that you have secured a position steady enough to support a wife, and whereas the views you have articulated—political, philosophical, religious, spiritual—veer dangerously afield from the standards of polite society, I must respectfully decline this proposal.
>
> Yours,
> Ellen S.

H. gleans the minister's malevolent influence in the gaseous prose, the very diction (polite society?) and syntax (...and whereas...and whereas...) recalling Sewall's stultifying, spiritless sermons. His tender Ellen could never express such callous sentiments. He carries on with his teaching duties, saunters across the fall-beaten blond fields for extended hours after dismissing his charges, stalks his sly fox and, more successfully, minds the brave industry of the squirrel and chicadee. He wonders what, if anything, he ought to do, vis à vis Ellen. He considers the trials of Odysseus, the obstacle of Minister Sewall a mere trifle, comparatively. It may not be too late to follow the great man's advice and take action, bring the whole of his human force to bear upon the minister, and upon Ellen.

Before he can formulate a concrete plan of action, a second letter arrives addressed to him in Ellen's unmistakable hand. He turns the ivory envelope about, inspecting both sides, gauging the ample weight of the contents, the quality of the cardstock, with the calloused pads of his fingers. Might she have changed her mind? Does she propose a means by which he might liberate her from beneath her father's stern hand? Or did the cruel minister only impel her to add more brass to the blow? He cannot bring himself to break the seal just now, having retreated to his quarters. It calms him to sit on his batchelor's bed, the letter on his trowsered lap, dwelling in possibility as the living earth carries on outside. A bird flits darkly across the sky's grey screen. A horse whinnies. Finally, though, he must face his future. Three leaves, twice-folded, painted by Ellen's careful cursive.

> November 19, 1840
> Dearest Henry,
>
> I must inveigh upon you in strongest terms to burn this letter forthwith upon reading. I trust that you have already received my earlier communication declining your most heartfelt and generous proposal. It caused me most grievous pain to imagine the hurt that my words surely provoked. Yet I took comfort in the knowledge that you must readily have ascertained that these were not truly my words, nor my sentiments. My imperious father commanded that I issue a response that was brief, explicit, and cold. Moreover, he insisted upon reviewing my reply before it was sealed so that there would be no danger of a misunderstanding, given what he described pejoratively as your poetical sensibilities. You assuredly gleaned father's influence from the moment your eyes glimpsed the first fraudulent line, yes?
>
> Even so, I find that I cannot let matters stand but must more properly explain myself. I feel it behooves me to confess at the outset that the net effect of my honest thoughts and feelings I

now express could not, and cannot, diverge from Father's wishes. Though redoubtable on matters of my betrothal, he has proven himself a most dutiful and loving father, and though I betray him even now, I cannot dishonour him in grander fashion. I hope you can understand that it would be impossible for me, knowing me as you do. There is the matter of your brother's feelings, as well. In the face of these deleterious influences, I would have to be a person of titanic size, or perhaps a very small person, to proceed in the manner you propose. I find, alas, that I am only a young woman of average proportions.

Which is not to say that I do not share your sentiments in the main. I might have been your most faithful wife and helpmeet had circumstances conspired more favorably for our union. In your letter, you recount the manifold merry occasions that we enjoyed together these past months. I would recall a separate moment when I glimpsed your tender soul. We were walking en route to visit the camelopard. There was a tabby kitten that wandered perilously middle of the avenue, its progress frozen, head between its shoulders. It might have been trammeled by coach or horse at any moment. A half-dozen souls ahead surely spied the poor kitty but could not be bothered to delay their progress toward the grander animal attraction up the way. You, however, were upon the babe in an instant. Moreover, you knew to handle it by the scruff, which quite magically calmed the creature as you shepherded it to a neighbor's house (the Blandings?). You explained, as it issued plaintive mewls, how such a tactile strategy, though it looked frightful, reminded the creature of its mother's touch. You secured a saucer of milk for the babe from the Blanding's Irish girl and stroked the kitten tenderly while it drank. I shall never forget the manly look in your eyes as you petted the poor creature. Your eyes betray you, dear H., as they betray us all. I wonder, verily, whether you jot such happenings in the journal you speak of. I think not, as we made no mention of the kitten to our relations that evening. Yet this may have been the most heroic exploit in all of Massachusetts this day in July!

I would implore you to treat my brother as tenderly while he remains in your charge, though I know such exhortations are unnecessary. Time shall prove, I feel certain, that you, unlike me, are one of those titanic souls among us, who cannot and will not truck the mean prejudices and expectations of our supposed betters. You are a most peculiar man, dearest Henry. I hope that this storm between us soon passes and that we shall enjoy once again free and easy intercourse.

Most affectionately and regrettably yours,
Ellen

Tears overbrim the beveled borders of his lids and blur his vision before he even reads Ellen's last words. There is no denying her genius now. He lies back on his pillow and tastes the saline seeped into his mouth. He lifts his elbow to shield his wet eyes from the world. Mother will call him for supper shortly. He must gather his humours, locate a place within where he might quarantine his emotions. He will not make a spectacle of himself. Instead of wallowing in grief, he knows what he must do.

He repairs to the finishing shed with the letter and envelope, secreted between his breastbone and shirt, strikes a match and burns the whole of it above the workbench, holding the fiery mass in his hand before the conflagration grows too brightly hot and he must fling it onto the table. The flames lick the ceiling, frightening H., but the fire soon exhausts itself. What to do with the charred remains? A spontaneous impression seizes him and he must obey. He wipes the refuse from the tabletop into his palm and deposits the char onto the high shelf of the mill along with the finest plumbago dust to be baked into their next batch of pencils. Why he does this he is not certain. Perhaps he cannot bear to banish Ellen entirely to the void. It offers strange comfort that words from her hand might live on in the transcribed thoughts of manifold, mysterious others. He wipes his eyes, which still smart from their salt, and enters the home to tend to his ablutions before supper.

He receives a letter from Margaret Fuller the very next day in which she quite peremptorily rejects his experimental poem and his essay on heroism, "The Service," for publication in their transcendental magazine. While both pieces suggest a rich and lively mind, the manly thoughts expressed, she argues, exist so outside any natural order of elocution as to cause great pain to the reader. "There is a want of fluent music," according to the redoubtable she! Poor John suffers a nosebleed so severe while teaching elementary mathematics downstairs in their schoolhouse that he faints, leaving brave Louisa to tend to him while Edmund dashes upstairs to secure H.'s attention. John's cough grows worse, too, and H. must assume all teaching duties while his brother convalesces under their mother and sisters' care. H. wonders if his brother is not heartbroken, but he can scarcely talk about the matter of Ellen with John.

Moribund over his own dimming prospects as husband, writer, teacher, and pressed as he is at the school, H. can scarcely read or jot a word in his journal. He can scarcely abide the day. He suffers a bout of bronchitis. He takes long walks at night, nuzzling against the trunks of beloved trees for ballast time to time, supping the frosty air into his clotted chest. He listens in vain for the yipping bark of his fox and gazes at the moonbright until its glare forces him to avert his eyes. He refuses to run for a new term as lyceum curator. He refuses George Ripley's invitation to join his utopian community of Brook Farm in West Roxbury. Regarding all such communities, he would rather keep batchelor's hall in hell than go to board in their heaven. He refuses to pay the tax levied annually by the First Parish Church, as he no longer considers himself a member. He considers life as a farmer, even purchases a farm on the Sudbury River, but in the end the landholder refuses to complete the sale, whereupon H. refuses the prospect of farming altogether, fearing the loss to his freedom as farmer and landholder.

He finds he is quite good at refusing things.

Once winter overtakes fall, he finds it easier to meet the day on its own terms. Most of the village retreats indoors, ceding the landscape to his concerted inspection. He likes to stand beneath the largest white pine he knows and look up into its blueish mist. Greybeard, he calls his forest friend. It wears a cocked hat. Curious fungi populate the oak understory beside the pond. H. contemplates their sporules, uncrushable beneath his heel, as indefatigable as truth. In these indomitable mushrooms, he begins to glimpse his recovery. A lone fisherman cuts holes in the ice to catch pickerel in Walden Pond and lifts his gloved hands to greet him.

"Good day, young man!"

"Good day!"

Pine saplings sprout heroic and futile from the fallow cornfields.

20

Hertzog contemplates bravery from the backseat of the police cruiser, redolent of someone's pungent odors. The pain still shines in his fist beneath a chemical cold-pack, no longer cold. Bravery was a favorite topic of Thoreau while he labored to locate his place in the Cosmos. How might he best gather and distribute his force rather than squander all his power? He looked toward the examples of various predecessors, mythical and actual—Prometheus, Aeschylus, Sir Walter Raleigh—to weigh action against restraint, speech against silence. He considered what passed for bravery in his benighted nation, shopkeepers minding their stores, soldiers scattering the Indian tribes to boggiest Florida. He sought intelligence with the earth, listened to the varied cries of Concord birds—veery and tanager, field-sparrow and phoebe—to gauge the heroic or base content of their character. He gazed upward into the foliage of Concord's tallest tree citizens.

What would Thoreau think of Hertzog's half-assed show of violence back at Cherryfield Farm? Not much. Pure folly, flailing his fists to enact the formalities of some hackneyed chivalry. Excepting the most desperate and noble cause—John Brown taking up arms against the scourge of slavery—Thoreau championed silence, patience, thoughtfulness, and restraint. A line from Thoreau's early journal rises to his consciousness. *Bravery deals not so much in resolute action, as in healthy and assured rest.* Sure, Henry, Hertzog thinks now, the roadside spruce and fir whizzing past, noble thoughts while you pine, meekly, after your true love. Hertzog's hero, he knows, had his own self-justifying reasons for touting patience and rest. Had Thoreau not sat back and allowed his older brother to confuse matters by proposing to Ellen first, had he professed his love early and outright to the beautiful young lady of Scituate, he might have won her hand.

"That Jude Winslow sure has a face I'd like to punch, I'll give you that," the officer driving the car utters through the perforated plastic shield separating front and back seats. His partner smiles beside him while he scrolls through text on the laptop attached to the center console. They wear matching crew-cuts atop pallid razor-burnt faces, which makes Hertzog wonder whether they might be brothers. The driver already told him that he doesn't see the assistant district attorney making a federal case out of the incident, considering he has no priors (his partner entered his driver's license number on the laptop), considering Jude's verbal provocation, considering Jude. The officers are both too young to know the whole backstory on Jude, but they seem to know something.

"Everyone knows that guy's a weasel," the officer in the passenger seat says. "Or worse."

"Yeah, everyone knows," the driver declares. "Fucking dirtball."

Hertzog doesn't know quite how to read the officers' suspicions of Jude, whether it betrays Jude's actual malfeasance or only their small-minded prejudice against anyone associated with so dubious an enterprise as organic husbandry, or against any man wearing a ponytail. In any case, Hertzog will not punish himself for diverging from Thoreau's example. He cannot deny how good it felt to express himself so directly and without subterfuge, on purely physical terms beyond the confusion of words. He cannot wholly censure himself, despite his broken hand, despite this disposable zip-tie that apparently passes for handcuffs these days binding his wrists—and which the officer in the passenger seat felt bad about having to secure, uttering "protocol" like an apology—despite the outsize civil charges that Jude may pursue, and despite the fallout with Ellen.

Yet here's the curious thing about that. His daughter now drives his Subaru—he swivels his shoulders to glance out the back window at its daytime beams—trailing the police cruiser en route to the hospital. While the two Northridge officers questioned him separately from Jude, he couldn't help looking over their shoulders at his daughter and Jude standing beside the goat fence, the angle of Ellen's elbows, the slant of Jude's head and the bemused smirk on his face, suggesting that she was trying to explain something to him. It was only after Ellen asked him for his keys, as the officers led him to their two-toned brown car parked beside the farm store, its blue lights still flashing silently, that Hertzog realized what she had been explaining to Jude. She would drive his car back to town for her father, if only to get it off the farm, find her way back to Cherryfield tonight. He was her father, after all, her responsibility. Or something to that effect, Hertzog imagined. All she had told him before they lowered his head into their car was that she was driving his

Subaru back to the house for him. *The* house. That's the phrase she had used, which wasn't quite the same thing as saying *your* house, and which buoyed Hertzog's spirits out of all proportion to the utterance.

The officer driving the car—Officer Kirby, he remembers upon glimpsing his nameplate—snips off the zip-tie restraints in the hospital parking lot, sparing Hertzog the further indignity. His partner will wait in the cruiser, apparently. The spruced air, food smells riding beneath, smells a heck of a lot better than the back seat of the police car. Two ambulances sit rear-end to the red brick building in their reserved spots, anxiously awaiting their summons. Crows criticize one another from the old white pines framing the pebbly asphalt. Treble notes of vacationing children sound above the intermittent growls of vehicular traffic along Main, just a few blocks off. It seems like a different town, having entered it escorted upon such terms. There was a closer hospital to the farm outside Northridge so Hertzog isn't sure why they decided to take him all the way back to Mercy in Emmenthaler. But he doesn't inquire. Ellen must have peeled off blocks ago to park the Subaru at the house. He isn't sure what she plans on doing from there, or where she will leave his keys, even.

The glass doors at the entrance don't open right away, which doesn't seem to surprise Officer Kirby, who sighs as they wait. Hertzog notices the camera above the doors, which finally part to allow them entry. The ammoniac odor of industrial cleanser commingled with the smell of cheap upholstery assaults Hertzog's senses along with the harsh fluorescent lighting, launching him to a different time he resists by focusing upon the security guard kiosk that he doesn't recognize manned by a Black officer with a feathery mustache. It must have been installed fairly recently. The security guard nods fraternally at Officer Kirby and buzzes them into a separate interior warren of the building past heavy double doors. Perhaps the opioid epidemic has been worse around here than Hertzog has realized, precipitating these new security measures, hospital drug closets and pharmacies a prime target.

"This way to triage," Kirby says. The officer leads the way down the linoleum hall past art works selected to uphold a color scheme more so than for any of their individual virtues. Hertzog notices, cannot help but notice, the elevator leading down to the morgue, where he had asked to visit his wife one last time. The coroner (whom Hertzog didn't know), had brushed Rebecca's hair straight back to expose her face, neck, and shoulders fully above the starched sheet. He could still see the tracks from what must have been a broad-toothed comb, straightening out her curls. Some algae still flecked the edges where the hairline met her sloping forehead, her flesh, particularly her lips, blued below her algaed hair.

"Likely a heart attack," she said as they both stared for a while at Rebecca's face. "That's why the divers didn't find her all the way at the bottom."

The coroner had thought that the authorities already told him where they located his wife's body in the pond, still drifting and descending ever so slowly toward the Bowl's deep bottom.

"Be interesting to see how much fluid's in her paranasal sinuses and lungs."

"Yes. Interesting." It was more chilling, somehow, to imagine poor Rebecca, not resting at the bottom of the Bowl, but tossing and tumbling in its amniotic depths like an overgrown fetus.

Sudden cardiac death, the autopsy confirmed some days later. Ventricular fibrillation. Faulty electrical impulses from the ventricles. Just bad luck Rebecca's arrhythmia hadn't been diagnosed earlier, bad luck the "massive cardiac event" (another phrase from the report) had occurred while she was swimming without a safety buoy in the middle of a deep glacial lake, although his wife might have dropped dead anywhere, anytime—while composing a carefully worded email at her desk at the college, while sleeping, while folding laundry, while walking aside the hobblebush hedge to the curb for the mail, while making love, although they hadn't been doing much of that at the time. "It's not like we have so many defibrillators stationed up and down Main." The coroner sought to console him over the phone, as she had sought to console him in person, initially, when she speculated that a heart attack, not drowning, was the primary cause of death. Life could slip away in an instant. For some people. Or all people, truly. Even now, Hertzog thinks, in this late age of man.

"David, is that you?"

"Huh."

"What the hell are you doing here?" The man rises from his vinyl seat in the waiting room, his eyes ricocheting between the police officer and Hertzog, his balding scalp sunburned beneath the fluorescents.

"Um...well...I had a little dust-up. Hurt my hand."

Will Roberson, Grace-Ann's father. He still clutches the magazine he'd been reading, *Field & Stream.* Hertzog doesn't have to ask his onetime financial planner why he's here. The treatments Grace-Ann receives in town now rather than all the way down in Portland—at least that's what Hertzog hopes, that it's only a routine appointment for her chemotherapy cocktail.

"Dust-up? You mean fight? Christ, David, is there anything I can do? Anyone I can call?" Will's eyes dart toward Officer Kirby. "You need a lawyer? Who do you use?"

He doesn't use anyone, certainly not on a routine basis, he thinks but doesn't say. "Hal," he says instead, because Hal Shepherdson handled the terms of his early departure from Emmenthaler and was sort of a jack-of-all-trades, as any local attorney needed to be to muster a vigorous enough business. "Hal, I suppose."

"Wouldn't hurt to give him a heads-up," Officer Kirby interjects, "just to make sure the assistant DA's office doesn't close up for the afternoon. Sheriff Libby is going to process you. Should be on her way."

"Oh?" This comes as a surprise.

"She picked up the call over the radio. We've turned this over to the sheriff as a courtesy."

"I'm calling Hal right now, David," Will says, brandishing his cell phone from thin air. "I'm sure he'll be right over."

Only a few other souls sit in the waiting room chairs, none of whom seem to be in any obvious distress and none of whom Hertzog recognizes. Summer people, probably. They all gaze toward their conference for lack of better entertainments. The television attached high on the corner wall emits no sound. "Better take the call outside," Will says, as if he had just noticed the other people looking their way.

He tells Will okay and thanks him as Officer Kirby directs him toward the intake receptionist to check in. Hertzog hands the woman his driver's license and his insurance card. She also takes the warm cold-pack and tosses it in the small trash bin behind her.

"Nice guy," Kirby says.

"Yeah. Nice guy."

The triage nurse calls him back after only a few moments. The mousy middle-age fellow sports an indifferent shave and exchanges few pleasantries with Hertzog during his brief exam, perhaps because the police officer looms above them. Or perhaps he's only a native Mainer and native Mainers aren't exactly a gregarious lot. He studies Hertzog's handback on a Formica table he wheeled before Hertzog's vinyl seat, the grotesquely swollen middle knuckle, which has just begun to purple. He smells vaguely of cigarette tobacco. He jots a note in his file, then flips the hand over briefly as if to make sure there's another side. Flipping it back, he asks Hertzog to wiggle his fingers (which he does), to make a fist (which he can't), asks him to rank his pain on a scale of one to ten, which seems like the first thing he ought to have asked. Five, Hertzog says, then downgrades it to a four after the nurse gives him the fisheye. Will pokes his head into the triage station to tell him Hal's on the way and that he advised him not to say anything more to the police than he's already said. "No offense," Will says to Officer Kirby, who raises his palm to indicate that no offense was taken. The nurse escorts Officer Kirby and him to a separate, not quite private station deeper in the bowels of the ER. They pass a child framed by parents, who seems to be receiving a breathing treatment through a nebulizer, a stout middle-age fellow receiving stitches in his leg from a dark woman in a white coat wearing some sort of magnifying headlamp. The doctor will see him soon, the nurse says, after his X-rays.

Claire, in uniform and carrying a backpack, doesn't pull open the curtain to his examination space in the ER (he won't be afforded a dedicated room) until after he returns from radiology, while the diminutive Dr. Jaffrey (the same woman who had been stitching up the leg of the stout fellow) describes the significant damage to his third metacarpal, his trapezoid and capitate carpals, the hairline fracture in his wrist, pointing toward the mashed bones illuminated against the screen. "Hands aren't made for hitting," she utters, as if she were speaking to a toddler. She must have children, it occurs to him. Claire doesn't interrupt the doctor, but Officer Kirby does.

"Okay, so bye, Claire," he says, taking a swig of the coffee one of the nurses handed to him.

"Thanks, Fred," Claire replies.

He wishes Hertzog good luck and is gone. Dr. Jaffrey, flicking off the X-ray screen, tells him they don't need to set the bones, but the hand and wrist must be immobilized. A lab tech will be in soon to fit him for his cast. Jaffrey wishes him good luck, as well, just before flicking the curtain closed behind her. Everyone is wishing Hertzog good luck these days. Suddenly, he is alone with Claire, or semi-alone in the moderately busy ER theater, the squeak of gurney wheels and voices sounding amid the weirdly vibrating fluorescent light.

"Heaven's sake, David, next time you want to see me you can just call again. You don't have to go through all this trouble." Claire utters these words at a different timbre than the timbre she deployed with her younger colleague, a voice that betrays a certain intimacy that pierces him. She wears no hat, he takes note as she sets her backpack down on a vinyl chair. Youthful silver barrettes hold her hair back on both sides above her small ears.

"Haven't been able to find anything out about Jude if this is your idea of a follow-up. Been minding his p's and q's far as anyone knows."

"Okay."

"So what's this that John outside tells me about a break-in at your house?" John, Hertzog presumes, is Officer Kirby's partner. "That's why you charged over to Jude's farm your hair on fire?"

Technically, he shouldn't be talking to Claire and she probably oughtn't to be asking him any questions. But he doesn't care. He tells her about the break-in and his suspicions, which sound paranoid in his own ears as he gives utterance to the thoughts. She tells him rather neutrally that there's been a spate of break-ins in town. Public record. Hasn't he been reading the paper? Probably bored local kids who couldn't get summer jobs in town. Or sternmen laid off from their lobster boats, season piss-poor as it's been. The shedders haven't come in from the deep water for some reason. Or junkies, most likely. Car windows have been shattered for purses visible in front seats, even for mere change glittering from their wells. She wishes he would have spoken with her about it before flying off the handle. He agrees it would have been a good idea, lifting his injured hand for rhetorical effect.

"Still, it's interesting," Claire says.

"What? What's interesting?" Hertzog asks.

"The burglary at your house, ayuh? The timing. The timing's interesting. I'll give you that."

He's not sure what to do with this information. He was sort of hoping, he realizes only now, that she would just call him nuts, thereby quashing his inconvenient suspicions of his daughter.

"I saw Will out there in the waiting room." Claire switches the topic.

"Yeah. Me too."

Someone, a man, moans from a nearby station, an old-sounding, plaintive, pain-induced moan, which they both decide to ignore for the moment.

"Says he called Hal for you. On his way, apparently."

"Yeah. I'm not supposed to be talking to you." He smiles, which makes Claire smile.

The moaning continues, but Hertzog now hears, as well, the unintelligible glottals of a nurse or maybe the doctor speaking with the distressed patient, the tenor suggesting stern sympathy.

"They say Grace-Ann should pull through is the latest."

"Oh?"

"Been responding well to that new experimental cocktail."

"Well, that's really good."

He means this, of course, despite the ancient business with his former financial planner.

It happened well before Grace-Ann had been born, while Will and Cindy seemed fully occupied keeping up with the four children they already had, twin boys and two older girls, who they had ushered into the world in quick succession. Will was thick-coiffed in those days and reeked of cologne, his temples often beaded with perspiration from his lunchtime exercise at the Y, the shower that never quite took. He outfitted his second-story office above Gould's Clothiers with exorbitantly cushioned leather upholstery and panoramic landscape photographs of incongruous desert scenes, a western artist prominent enough (apparently) that each installation merited dedicated lighting. His work station consisted of a walnut desk and credenza large enough to support three computer screens so that he could keep abreast of the latest worldwide financial developments, a gaudy display of technology in their little hamlet, especially those days. Most of the credenza was taken up by ever-updated photographs of the children within gleaming silver and gold frames, as if to verify his family-man bona fides, advertising the various sports the children pursued with gusto, the progress of their orthodontia. Hertzog noticed the photographs right away every time he and Rebecca visited Will's office. He envied the healthful life-stage progress of Will and Cindy's progeny. He imagined that Rebecca noticed the tableau, as well, envied Will and Cindy's efforts domestic, too, and just had a different way of rising to its challenge.

Will and Rebecca had been lovers, briefly, which was why Hertzog sought financial counsel elsewhere. He couldn't really blame Rebecca at the time for straying—or didn't blame her much—as their own home fires had all but petered out. If you were a certain type of person, if you were Hertzog, say, you responded in a certain way when you shared a home with a daughter who failed to thrive, as one of her pediatricians in Portland put it, refused the breast, refused to sleep at reasonable intervals, refused to hold her fork properly at the table, refused to defecate upon her body's repeated signals to do so (which resulted in an impacted colon), refused potty training altogether, refused to learn how to ride a bicycle, refused to conduct the most basic exercises in hygiene, refused to sit through a meal at a restaurant without screaming bloody murder over some small hurt, real or imagined, refused to pronounce, or learn to pronounce, her r's properly ("languages shouldn't have r's, she complained, "they're too much of a hassle, mouthwise"), refused to respect elders—doctors, dentists, teachers, police officers—refused to put forth the most minimal effort required to make or sustain friendships, refused to cultivate anything that might be regarded as a constructive interest, much less a passion; who sometimes simply refused.

You responded in a certain way as your daughter's problems intensified with age, as problems do. Over a period of several days, Ellen cut up the inside of both her arms six ways from Sunday with the bent-open end of a paper clip for no good reason that she or any of her formidably credentialed health-care providers could explain. Her physical education teacher at school had noticed the wounds at various stages of healing upon growing suspicious of Ellen's long sleeves. After a week-long inpatient stay at Portland General, Ellen mostly managed to stop the self-harm yet still clawed the inside of her arms with her dirty fingernails during occasions of acute stress and scratched up the constellations of acne on her forehead until she bled, compelling Rebecca to buy an assortment of hair bands to cover the scars and curb Ellen's impulses. Ellen wouldn't develop anything that approximated a normal crush on an actual flesh-and-blood peer, but as a thirteen-year-old girl suffering from deep-seated anomie, she adopted a separate internet identity and visited chat-rooms populated (as Claire later informed them) by mostly middle-aged white male sexual predators searching for thirteen-year-old girls suffering from deep-seated anomie. She cultivated an intense relationship with some creep, who had been grooming her for an eventual meet-up before Rebecca (alerted by the inexplicable uptick in their daughter's mood) unlocked her computer while Ellen was at school and figured out what was what. Ellen grew morose when they cut off her internet access, broke into the liquor cabinet middle of the night and drank the better part of a two liter bottle of Ketel One Vodka. They needed to have her stomach pumped in this very ER. He still recalls the precise pitch and cadence of her gastric throes as she was compelled to regurgitate, the putrid olfactory notes of her vomit that overtook the entire room. The episode occasioned a two-month stay at Portland General this time and their rental of a one-bedroom apartment, where either Rebecca or Hertzog (but mostly Rebecca) stayed so that one of them could visit their daughter each day. Ellen was only discharged once she could satisfactorily convince her doctors that she had developed various constructive modes of negotiating her "cheese," a metaphor that Hertzog never fully understood.

In any case, if you were a person like Herzog confronted by such circumstances, you withdrew somewhere deep within yourself, mustered your emotional reserves to weather each day, remembered to breathe as you conducted only the most essential of your affairs. The simple affection concomitant with lovemaking was something you couldn't fathom expressing under your roof, or anywhere, toward anyone. There was a shameful thought you thought from time to time. *If only she were dead.* You wondered what small pleasures you might still extract from this one wild life of yours. *If only Ellen were simply dead.*

But let us say you were a different sort of person, a person like Rebecca—in short, a more hopeful, life-affirming sort of person. If you were this sort of person you didn't entertain ghastly fantasies of your daughter's demise. You took life as it came to you. You snatched some shred of happiness where you could find it, not in the touch of your spouse, who had long since stopped touching you with the simple affection concomitant with lovemaking, but in the embrace of someone younger and well-coiffed, someone sweet-smelling and new.

Claire, fiddling for something now inside her backpack, explains to him why it took so long for her to get here, that she's already talked with Kirby's partner and had been on the horn with the assistant DA, Erica Greenberg, up in Machias, someone Claire knows pretty well. Given all the circumstances—that he has no priors, Jude's more colorful track record—Erica is willing to chalk it up as simple assault, class D, which means it's only a misdemeanor. "You plead nolo contendere," Claire says, "she'll only seek the state minimum three hundred dollar fine, no jail time, of course. I'm pretty certain Hal'll approve, but you'll talk it over with him."

He tells her thanks, that he'll have Hal call Greenberg's office soon as he gets here. She approaches him at the examination table, sets down beside him the materials she retrieved from the backpack, the paperwork she needs to fill out with him, plus the materials she needs to take his fingerprint. She plans to process him here, spare him the further inconvenience.

"My oh my, this fluorescent light's not doing you any favors, David," she says, gazing slightly upward to meet his eyes. Cunning Claire. She lifts a hand as if she were about to reach toward him, maybe trace with her fine fingers the wrinkles sun-bursting from the corners of his eyes back toward his temples, tame a stray lock of his thinning hair; but she merely opens the ink-pad beside him and asks in a more officious voice for his thumb from his good hand.

She grasps his good hand with both of hers. Her hands feel small and dry. She blots the pad of his thumb against the ink, broadcasting the neat part in her blond hair threaded through with gray. He breathes in her no-nonsense soap-smelling shampoo. Her eyes dart toward his injured paw. "Sure seems like you got a few good licks in, anyway," she says. "Gracious."

He nods his head while he thinks of something to say. But then Claire says something else as she presses his inked thumb against the paper. "I wonder why Ellen came back here."

"For Jude," Hertzog says, even though he knows there must be some other reason. He mostly says this to hear Claire dismiss it, which she does.

"But why else?"

The lab tech arrives toting a metal cart behind him, a young fellow whose shaved head gleams beneath the florescent light. Claire withdraws to a chair. Donning purple latex gloves, the fellow rather expertly applies the cast over his hand and arm. Richard, as he introduces himself, rolls a separate stockinette over his thumb to form what he calls a Gumby, wraps a web-roll over the larger stockinette from fist to elbow, then wraps the wet fiberglass over the web-roll, asking first whether he prefers blue, pink, or forest green (Hertzog picks green). The fellow's deportment hews to workmanlike rather than tender, per se, but Hertzog, who isn't used to receiving care of any sort, finds himself curiously moved by the young fellow's ministrations—as he was moved when Stacey slipped her arm inside his own arm recently beneath the copse of seaside woods—the practiced coordination as he whirls the fiberglass wrap about his arm to effect the appropriate tension, the expert pressure he applies to particular locales at the palm and inside forearm to mold the cast for maximum efficacy and comfort, the way he passes his latex fingertips lightly over the cast surface to check for snags.

"Used to be able to sign those casts, the way they were before," Claire says, maybe just to say something.

"Yeah," Richard says. "Before my time but I know what you're talking about. The white ones."

"Mmhm."

Hal strolls in wearing khakis and a polo shirt once Richard is almost through and exchanges pleasantries with the room. He seems determined to keep things light, chides Hertzog for keeping him from the striped bass he was planning on harassing in the bay from his center console. Claire clears the room once the lab tech is finished without having to be asked so Hal can speak with him, confidentially. After Hertzog tells him what happened—Hal interrupting with a series of "ayuh" listening noises and a "that little fucker" twice—Hal advises (as Hertzog suspected) that they take the deal the assistant DA has offered. Part of Hertzog resists the suggestion, as it reminds him of the simple expediency that ever seemed to motivate Hal's lawyerly advice. But in the end he agrees. "Civil case will be the fun part," Hal says to punctuate their conference. He calls Claire in and that's that. But not quite.

A final visitor approaches as they wait on Dr. Jaffrey to return and inspect Richard's handiwork. Hertzog registers in his spine the familiar notes of her voice above the squeaking wheels of a cart or gurney against the linoleum, asking after his whereabouts, the strangely familiar tenor of the conversation his daughter shares with a nurse or orderly, as if she knew the fellow. Perhaps she does, having grown up here. The curtain parts and there she is.

"Ellen Hertzog, as I live and breathe," Claire says.

"Hi, Officer Libby." His daughter's lips part in a mild smile to reveal her overcrowded, yet white, teeth. He hadn't noticed how white they were. Yet the unfortunate florescent lighting also raises new fissures about her eyes and forehead. The bronzed skin about her neck and fine clavicles, too, scallops loosely over the scaffolding of bone and muscle, perhaps on account of her weight loss or overexposure to the sun since she's been back.

Hertzog watches as both Ellen and Claire lean in to share a brief hug. Now how did they both know to do something like that? He wonders what the gesture communicates. Simple affection? Or maybe something else, it occurs to him, an affinity rooted in the shared struggle of the moment. *Here we are, the two of us, looking after David Hertzog.* When was the last time he and Ellen had hugged? When was the last time he had touched his daughter with a modicum of fatherly affection, cupped the back of her slender neck, jostled her shoulder, palmed her forehead to check her temperature? He can't recall. When did fathers, under the best of circumstances, stop touching their daughters?

"I think you can call me Claire now," Claire says, leaning away from Ellen to gain a clearer vantage.

"She looks good, David. So tan and lean. But muscular too." She reaches to squeeze his daughter's biceps, the tanned flesh goose-pimpled beneath the hospital's climate control. "You didn't tell me how good she looked." Hertzog's first impressions of Ellen were the same as Claire's, mostly on account of his daughter's leaner physique. But he wonders now. Does she look good? She's tidied up the ponytail holding back her raven curls, at any rate, revealing her thick-lashed eyes, brown like his rather than green and hazel-flecked like Rebecca's. Lovely, all the same.

"Yes, I should have mentioned that." Hertzog can't imagine talking with Ellen now about his dust-up with Jude at Cherryfield Farm, deciding on the fly what details he ought to censor. He can't imagine that his daughter has anything nice to say to him. "You came to drop off the keys, Ellen?" he asks, tamping down his expectations.

"No, Father. I'm here to see how you're doing. I'm here to take you home."

21

March 13th, 1841
How alone must our life be lived—We dwell on the sea-shore and none between us and the sea—Men are my merry companions—my fellow pilgrims—who beguile the way, but leave me at the first turn in the road—for none are travelling one *road so far as myself.*

Where shall he call home? Here is the pressing question deep into winter. He can no longer board at the family home. This much is clear. Relations with dear John, in Ellen's wake, will not be restored to their former amity. A shadow falls between them, having finally shuttered the windows and doors of their school on account of John's clotted lungs. They see too much of each other, the intervals between very short. Each glance they share in the parlor, the dining room, the pencil sheds and yard seems laced with recrimination beneath fraudulent gestures of cordiality. *How goes it today, dear brother? Well as can be expected, dear brother. And how goes it with you?* The titmouse overhead all the while lisps truer words from the poplar's bare choir of branches. H. would find a way to better serve his brother if he only knew how.

His life has grown slovenly, he fears. He finds he must exercise constant vigilance over his soul to beat back drowsiness, both spiritual and physical. Instead of reading, sauntering, or writing some afternoons (Fuller has assigned him an essay-review of four Reports on the Zoological and Botanical Survey of Massachusetts, published by order of the State Commissioners), he sleeps in his overheated bedroom, cooked a la mode beneath a bedsheet crust by the stove Mother insists upon stoking. He spends only a few hours a week assisting Father in the pencil sheds, earning his keep. His mother cannot countenance his malaise. Innuendos of disapprobation ride beneath even her pleasantest utterance, her strident jabs with the poker against the oak corpses in his stove, her insufferable exhales. On occasion, she hectors him outright over his plans, the prodigal son they sent to Harvard. To quiet her, he applies for a teaching position at the Perkins' Institute for the Blind in Boston, from which he is most thankfully turned away. Perhaps he was too hasty in spurning Ripley's offer to join his community, where a Mr. Hawthorne (about whom Mr. E. speaks approvingly) now shovels manure mornings before eating his own breakfast oats.

He evermore feels he ought to build a small house on the southern slope of a hill or beside a pond or stream and take there the life the gods send his way. He saunters about Fair Haven Hill today in search of a suitable locale, having already been denied Sandy Pond's most promising shore by the curmudgeonly Mr. Flint, and having determined the weird dell too wet and shady for husbandry. He cherishes the noisome silence of the woods. The winter breeze sings through the sturdy pine foliage as through a reed, harmonizing with the complementary notes of the chicadee. Each species of tree sings its own distinctive song against the breeze. H. knows them by their voices alone. Red pine and white. Cedar and spruce. Quaking aspen, poplar, ash, and chestnut. Does such peculiar intelligence with the earth matter? He believes that it does. Tromping onward through the snow, he reaches the orchard side of the hill facing the low sun. He pivots about to take in the circumference that would be his home. Fair Haven Pond and Hill and orchard, open and shadowed sky, all close at hand. A few spotted apples, sampled by woodpeckers and flickers, still cling to their boughs. The village only a modest amble northward. Yet here is the precise locale where he plucked clasping harebell's delicate purple blooms for dear Ellen's herbarium. He still longs for the lovely girl, arises nighttimes asweat, besieged by fuzzy images of her downy flesh athwart his hips, his nightclothes damp with seminal wet, though he dare not transcribe such bestial lines in his journal.

He makes his way to the center of the frozen water to gather his wind and gain a new angle of vision on the possible site of his enterprise and upon the horizon, unimpeded by tree boughs. He wipes his wet eyes with cold-numbed handbacks. While the great man would have him look up and away, where lofty thoughts reside, he cannot help but inspect the crusty snow beneath his feet, scored with the impressions of his fox. Even the fox, he reflects, digs its own burrow. Oh, what this fox might tell him of the actual earth! How meek his civilized life compared to the daily travails of this small animal.

He still wishes to live a brave life.

Perhaps this winter walk had been a fool's errand, for H. rises two days hence gasping for air in his dark room. He diagnoses the illness seizing his lungs instantly, no stranger to bronchitis. St. Valentine's Day, no less. Poor Mother and Sophia must now deliver broth and fresh cords of wood to both brothers, quarantined stove-side in their rooms. The only unimpeded sky he will see the many days of his recovery is the square patch through the chimney. H. must combat the dark mood that rides the coattails of his ailment. If he is not healthier than most, he reminds himself—as he so often does—he is healthier than some, including poor John, swaddled infant-like beneath woolen blankets in the parlor when he musters the will to leave his bed, mesmerized by the dancing flames in the hearth. Dear Helen, too, appears to have contracted the family illness and so now the three of them struggle over each breath.

He resolves to apply all his wit and wisdom to the repair of his body, as if it were any other mechanical problem, the poor grind of plumbago for pencil-making, say. As February yields to March, H.'s condition improves. Helen and John recover, as well, albeit more slowly. The faint, flitting notes of the goldfinch announce the turning point of the year. Owing to his precarious health and inexperience in housebuilding, he will not be digging his own burrow, fox-like, any time soon. What is he to do? He puts the question somewhat importunately to the great man on their first amble of the season, their feet sopped by spring mud on the trail to Mill Brook, whereupon his elder issues his proposal: "Come live with me, dear H.! Bullocks to Brook Farm! We shall conduct our own experiment. I shall provide room and board for one year and you shall continue to teach your hapless companion how to graft his trees." H., fairly gobsmacked, keeps his eyes on the muddy earth as he considers his response. Nary a weed has sprung from the still-cold ground, neither Joe-pye nor jewelweed, nor willow-herb. To fill the silence, Mr. E. tells him that he has attempted an even bolder experiment by inviting the Alcotts to join them, as well, yet Abigail will have none of it. He has asked the Irish servants to join them mealtimes in the dining room rather than eat by themselves in the kitchen or retreat to their mattresses in the attic. Their young maid, Annabelle, has proven game enough, yet the cook continues to take her meals amid the smoke and foodsmells. "You're my last hope, dear H.!" he utters, somewhat facetiously, the muddy earth kissing his shoes upon each stride. A downy woodpecker laughs and drums, while a woodchopper farther off holds to a more lugubrious melody.

The next day he packs up his knapsack and walks the scant mile to the great man's estate, The Bush, taking a room on the first floor beside the library. Five-year-old Waldo seems positively smitten by the novelty of his presence, bounding upon his narrow bed while he unpacks his few items of clothes, his daybook and journal, his father's flute. He has brought two boxes of their finest pencils as a gift for the sage, a loaf of bread he has prepared with water-plump'd raisins for Lidian, which she mistakes for vermin, gasping at the loaf, before he sets her aright. Two-year-old Ellen (it seems H. cannot escape reminders of unrequited love) seems wary, lingers at the threshold, minded by the young maid, though H. feels confident he can bring her around.

What merry days H. enjoys at the great man's house serving as his handyman, Lidian's sometime confidante, and playmate to Waldo. There is another woman boarding with them, as well, Mary Russell. She conducts something of a school out of the house. Upon Lidian's outsize avowals of H.'s botanical expertise, Mary seeks his assistance in updating her natural history curricula. The great man would have him continue his grafting lessons straight away, yet H. puts him off for these first weeks. Winter has yet to release its grip, he explains. The sap must run more freely within the cambium, else the graft will not take. Cherry and plum the first scion and stock of the season. Pear and apple, some weeks later. All of which is true.

But it is equally true that he finds himself cultivating more intimate relations with the ladies and the children. While Mr. E. busies himself with lectures in Boston, New York, Philadelphia and elsewhere—neglecting poor Lidian—H. sets up shop in the barn. Upon his approach to the workshop each morn, he cannot help but notice the bluebird box nailed slightly aslant above the broad doors, John's house-warming gift to the family. First, H. builds a small sliding drawer for Lidian's Sunday gloves, which he attaches to the underside of her dining room chair.

"Oh, dearest H.," she exclaims, clapping lovely fingers below her chin, "how very thoughtful of you."

He builds from remnant lumber in the barn a facsimile of Noah's Ark for Waldo, teaches the lad to whittle with a dull jack-knife and chisel. They carve a horse, a cow, and, of course, a fox. He builds a hobby-horse for Ellen, who, indeed, has come around to reciprocate his affections, often seeking his knee suppertimes. He builds a dollhouse for her, as well, carving out a cross-section of an old chest of drawers the great man designated for the scrap heap. Lidian complains about her scratching chickens, so he secures leather remnants from Mr. Stone, the cobbler, and sews rather serviceable booties for the pesky creatures, who seem not to appreciate their fancy shoes one jot. Perplexed by the encumbrances, they issue strange bleats and pursue all manner of calisthenics to flick them off their feet. One poor hen cannot bring herself to a proper amble at all, tilts sideward upon the ground like a felled tree each time the children set her aright, which sets them to whooping and wailing, and which sets Mary and Lidian to laughter as well. To observe such hearty belly-laughs of the babes makes all the hours he spent with needle and thread worth the while.

He reads the Reports on Fishes, Reptiles, Insects, and Invertebrate Animals of Massachusetts, more copiously researched than the other Reports Fuller has sent his way. He ought to begin writing his essay-review—considers what lines of natural philosophy he might filch from his journal—yet he cannot deny the pleasure he gleans in loco parentis while the sage is off on his lecture tour. He delights in making a new treat for the children and ladies to enjoy, popping corn, which he prepares in the cast-iron spider over an outdoors fire beside the barn. Serenaded by the applause of crickets and the crunching of teeth, the constellations winking above, H. contemplates the perfect white flower of the popped corn, declaring its alliance with its vegetable relatives. He wonders whether a soul might flower so instantaneously given the proper element of conduction, commits lines to this effect in his journal.

On such familiar terms with Lidian and the children, H. can verily imagine himself as man of the manor. He can't deny the kernel of resentment against Mr. E. that grows inside, to be bless'd with such riches, this family, yet be lured from the hearth so many days, weeks, and months on end. A man must make a living, true—and what H. would do to secure any sort of audience for his writing?—yet it seems vainglorious to chase after fame so.

Lidian seems to read his thoughts, at least partly, for she seeks him out one evening in the barn after supper, where H. often labors into the night repairing an item of household furniture. This evening he works with chisel and the foot-wheel lathe to build a yo-yo for the younger Waldo.

"Waldo told me about your disappointment with that silly girl from Scituate."

There is no shilly-shally about dear Lidian. Her appeal to the great man, H. believes, resides largely in her eschewal of feminine equivocation.

"I may have been the silly one, dear Lidian." He feels the blood in his face. He holds his gaze on the spinning lathe, the chisel, the block of ash, to spare them both his eyes. "In any case, the season of forlornness is long past."

"Is it? You seem different these days and weeks since your arrival. Kinder, but—"

"But what?" Now he stops pedaling the wheel and lifts his eyes to face Lidian. Shadows cast by the two whale-oil lamps deepen the ever-present furrows across her thoughtful brow. She clasps her hands before her waist, a pose that betrays her steely determination to speak her piece.

"A lingering sadness seems to ride beneath your most tender gestures, I fear. You ought not to brood over that Sewall girl an instant longer."

"It was a long winter. I suffered two bouts of bronchitis. My lungs have yet to regain their full function. Perhaps my lingering infirmity is what you more truly detect."

A strong gust rattles the cedar shingles atop the barn, the very earth admonishing him for his fraudulence.

"Perhaps. Yet I worry you'll squander your remaining opportunities making love to old women, instead."

"You don't mean your sister Lucy? I already explained to—"

"Not only Lucy. To me, as well, now. That's why I pursued you here in the barn rather than the house. So that we might speak frankly."

"Of course." His face scarlets once more. She alludes, he knows, to the poem he had composed and shared with her in sweetest friendship.

"You must stop writing poems to old ladies."

"You're not old, Lidian," he replies, in earnest, which makes her lower her eyes to the earthen floor, bite her lower lip as she considers her next words.

"I wonder if you don't express such tender affection to ineligible ladies, because you need not fear where it might lead."

"We *are* speaking frankly, I see."

What shall he tell Lidian in the same spirit? That he *does* fear, suddenly, where this all might lead? That he truly doesn't pine, anymore, for that silly girl from Scituate, as Lidian referred to her. That when he closes his eyes in his garret beside the stairs, the maid and cook and children safely abed, the great man lecturing Philadelphians on self-reliance, his thoughts alight only upon Lidian now, that he wonders what chivalric demon possesses him that he does not mount the stairs and enter the bedroom, nuzzle up beside her and enjoy connubial delights. He feels primordial stirrings in his breast even now, and lower, despite the cold night inside the barn, despite the fecal stench of bat droppings radiating from the corners.

"Young Waldo loves you so." Lidian lowers her eyes. "Ellen too."

He wonders what would happen if he were to force the matter to a crisis, if he were to say, like Marlow, *Live with* me, *dear Lidian, and be* my *love, and we shall all the pleasures prove!* If he were to take Lidian in his arms now and plant passionate kisses all about her neck, goose-fleshed, he sees, from the cold.

"I feel most tender thoughts toward the dear children, as well," he says instead, returning his attention to chisel and lathe. Its whirring under his command tamps down the electricity in the atmosphere between them. He tells her that he ought to return to his labors and that she ought to return to the warmth of the house before she catches her death. She ought not to worry about him.

The sage finally returns from his lectures. The presence of his formidable intelligence, for the time being, clarifies the hegemony. They set to grafting his trees in earnest while goldfinches mob the first grasses between, their trifling weight testing the rigidity of the stalks, their thinly sweet phrases silencing all but the most imperative communications between the men. He teaches the great man a new technique he has learned from the French, whip tongue-grafting—a variation of two methods he earlier introduced to Mr. E.—to join scion to stock more firmly. From the same French source, H. has also learned a new recipe for the grafting wax, consisting of equal parts tallow, beeswax, and resin, which they melt in a cast-iron pan over an outdoors fire.

The weeks and months pass thusly, more or less amicably, at the great man's abode. H. is hardly expected to keep shopkeeper's hours. He spends some days back at the family home making pencils, experiments with a more sturdy one-piece cylindrical cedar case but cannot quite mold the lead capsule for proper insertion. He entertains Waldo and Ellen with new wooden toys now and again. He tutors Margaret's excellent brother Richard in Greek to prepare him for his studies in Cambridge. He enjoys near daily saunters with the great man to the pond and takes him sailing on the river, entertains him with the flute. He begins writing his essay-review, "Natural History of Massachusetts." Upon reading a draft, Margaret reproves him for his baffling circuitousness and the trifling attention he pays to the actual Reports under review, though she admires his manly thoughts on nature. He contemplates the qualities of a well-built sentence while he repairs apron, stile, and spindle of Lidian's dining room chairs in the barn. He reflects upon Merrimack nights with dear John, before all their trouble ensued, wonders if there might be a book in their adventure, which seems so long ago. He visits Sampson Wilder at his Bolton orchard and studies his methods for setting out peach trees. He rereads Homer and wonders darkly at his prospects for contributing anything nearly so great, then next morn thinks he might write a poem called Concord, and for argument—jettisoning the conventional demigods and demons—he will deploy the river and woods, swamps and meadows, streets, buildings, and villagers. Oh, and the seasons!

The sage certainly makes the most of his home stint, as Lidian delivers to Mr. E. a third child in November, a girl they name Edith. H. observes the passing of spring, summer, and fall with terrific care throughout Lidian's confinement and convalescence, the subtle changes, animal and vegetable, as the days grow short. He visits Charles Miles' swamp and wonders how art might ever approximate nature's sylvan luxury. He does seem to enjoy kith and kin in the bogs and woods more so than in dining rooms and parlors. A peculiarly wild nature possesses him. But how insufficient life seems without human love on this green orb hurtling through the Kosmos. How meekly he had supped love with dear Ellen of Scituate, or with Lidian, gifting her Sunday glove-drawers and poultry-booties, sturdy chairs and tightly upholstered sofas. He has scarcely nibbled about the edges of love's feast. How and where and when might H. realize his utmost self, entire? He has not given up his plans on building his own burrow. Yet he cannot deny his fierce longing for Lidian, nor his suspicion—even as she tends to the great man's babe—that she feels the same ache in her breast.

22

"So I'll stay tonight if that's okay with you," Ellen says after turning off the ignition in the driveway. She sets the parking brake with oomph as if to settle matters.

"It's not necessary," Hertzog replies. "I can fend for myself with one arm."

Now why did he go and say a thing like that? He wants Ellen to stay, doesn't he? She breathes audibly out her nostrils, contemplating her next words. His hand aches anew. "But it would be good if you stayed, Ellen. Really. I'd appreciate it."

She retrieves from the back seat a worn leather satchel or purse-looking thing that he doesn't recognize (holding a change of clothes, he imagines, perhaps some toiletries) and they make their way to the front door, scattering dusky birds from the hobblebush hedge. The sky has turned leaden, thick with gnats he flicks away with his good hand. He gazes toward the invisible sun probably somewhere below the spruce line already. It's that time of day when it's difficult to determine what accounts for the darkness, the late hour or the gray sheet scrolled over the sky. He's glad that Stacey and Taylor must be inside or away from home. He knows he'll have to explain his green fiberglass cast to Stacey at some point, but would just as soon put that off for a while. His throbbing hand must show on his face as Ellen, inserting the house key into the deadbolt of the side door, tells him that he can probably take a Vicodin soon. They enter the mudroom and remove their shoes, Hertzog managing to shed both sneakers with his feet. "I'll pick up the script from the Rite-Aid," she says, "once I put my stuff down."

He tells her he's okay, that ibuprofen will do just fine. He has no idea what his daughter has been up to lately, but her track record with drugs and alcohol isn't so great. It seems imprudent to involve her with his prescription for narcotics. He doesn't trust her, he realizes now that she's inside the house. Not fully. He hates that he feels this way.

"You don't get extra points for suffering, Father," she says as they enter the dark kitchen, where she does a curious thing, reaches reflexively for the switch low on the inside wall beneath the cupboard to flick on the lights. It's always been an odd place for the switch. Hertzog marvels at her muscle memory. Then he thinks, *You don't get extra points for suffering, Father.* Where did she pick up a line like that? He can't recall her ever having deployed it, but he can see why it would appeal to her. Hertzog and Rebecca were of an American generation not so convinced that suffering didn't earn you extra points. Some of this might have come from the Jewish side too. It was one of the things that drove Ellen crazy about them, that her parents made her do things in the world that amounted to suffering by her lights.

He watches as she sets her leather satchel down on the maple table (wishing she would have placed the germ-ridden thing on a chair, instead), and continues to watch as she opens the mostly barren Formica cupboards above the white tile counters, appraising the meager cache of food. "Jeez, Father, what's the deal? You live on just oatmeal, almonds, and dried apricots?"

She's missed the leopard-stained bananas on the table, he protests mildly, aiming for a laugh, the few boxes of dried spaghetti in the cupboard above the cutlery drawer, the wire-handled pan of Jiffy Pop.

Her shoulders offer the gesture of a chuckle, anyway. He wonders if she'll say something about the dulse sitting up there on the ledge above the sink. But no. "Well, I guess Mom was always the foodie," she says, opening and shutting new cupboards.

Something about this innocuous mention of Rebecca stuns him. Is this the first time since Ellen has been back that she's uttered such a direct reference to her mother? He releases a great gulp of air as if from a distended balloon. "Yes," he tells her. "Your mother was quite the cook."

It feels good to speak about his wife.

Ellen moves on to the refrigerator, saying, "We have to start thinking about supper," as if to explain all her snooping about. He watches the way the light from the appliance raises those crow's feet at the corner of her eye and deeper wrinkles across her brow he first noticed at the hospital. He remembers how his daughter used to twist up her face into so many anxious and angry expressions as a child and wonders now whether such long-ago duress left its mark in this way, not unlike seismic traumas the earth suffers leave indelible imprints over epochs in the sediment and soil.

Hertzog hands her cash from the envelope he has replenished in the junk drawer, which she accepts without protest, so she can retrieve some groceries from Hannaford. Meanwhile, he takes a shower, the goat-smells and his ripe body odors rich in his nostrils now that he's inside the house. Showering proves more difficult with one arm than he anticipated, dispensing the shampoo and working up a lather with the bar of soap, all the while holding his left arm outside the curtain, shower water spattering the tile floor he'll have to mop up later. He urinates right there in the stall, directing the gold thread straight down the drain. Wiping his ass on the toilet, something he usually does with his left hand, will be a real adventure, it occurs to him.

The fingers on his cast hand are mostly free, so dressing isn't difficult. Ordinarily, he would wear pajama-bottoms and a Bogart T, but he chooses sweatpants instead, Ellen returning to cook their supper. *Ellen*, he marvels as he pads down the stairs. He scans the newspaper absently at the maple table and tries not to think about his aching hand while he awaits his daughter, gone just long enough for him to wonder, fleetingly, whether she plans on returning at all, as if she has gone through all this trouble to take off with his petty cash and ancient Subaru. He hears light rain begin to fall, leaving its fingerprints all about the asphalt shingle roof Claire's husband installed years ago.

The sounds announcing his daughter's arrival—the car door slamming shut on the drive, the metallic complaint of the mudroom's door latch twisting open, the jostling of plastic grocery bags—lifts goose pimples on his flesh. He helps her unpack the groceries in the kitchen best he can with one arm, performing a loose survey. *Wheat bread. Eggs. Orange juice. Canned tomatoes.* He can smell the metallic outdoors on her sopped, scoop-necked T-shirt and on her hair, dark and flat from the wet.

"You're soaked through, Ellen," he says, setting the large can of tomatoes on the counter beside the stove. "Maybe you should dry off upstairs and change so you don't catch cold."

Romaine lettuce. Lemons. Garlic bulb.

She shrugs off the suggestion and he doesn't insist.

Parmesan cheese. Chianti. The bottle of wine surprises him enough that he announces the purchase. She tells him he could use the drink after the day's excitement. So can she. "Good idea," he says. He asks her whether she'd prefer the wine chilled and she says yes.

He wonders when she plans on inspecting the upstairs, her room, specifically, which she might find creepy given how unaltered it remains since her departure.

Italian parsley. Almond milk. Skim milk.

"I wasn't sure if you still drank milk," she says as she observes him filing away the gallon in the fridge next to the wine.

"I do," he replies, which seems to disappoint her.

"We're the only animals that drink another creature's milk," she says, which prompts him to ask whether she observes a vegan diet.

"No, just vegetarian. Milk just doesn't agree with me."

Shredded wheat. Kosher salt. Dehydrated blueberries. Onions. Bananas.

It's silly, and stupid, but he's tempted to call bullshit on her milk commentary. She had never been lactose intolerant. And who cares what other animals do or don't do regarding another creature's milk? "Impressive," he says, instead. "To stick with something like that. Takes a lot of discipline, I'm sure, to be a vegetarian."

"Not really. You get used to it." The tenor of his daughter's response is familiar. The rare words of praise he extended to her when she was growing up tended to ricochet, like pebbles off armor.

Extra virgin olive oil. French bread. Bavarian pretzels.

"Bavarian Pretzels?" he asks, sliding them next to the spaghetti boxes in the cupboard.

"You used to love those," Ellen replies, rooting below the counter now next to the stove for a pot or pan, he imagines. "It used to drive me ape-shit crazy the sound you made crunching down on them." Certain sentences she sounds just like the Ellen he remembers, yet he detects a curious withholding too, her voice like the tide advancing and retreating, advancing and retreating.

"I remember," he says, which is true. He remembers Ellen screaming at him before one of her TV shows to chew more quietly, Hertzog hollering at her for screaming at him, Rebecca playing referee. She has found the aluminum pot and fills it with a fizzy stream of water at the sink, smiling at the memory of his mouth's unfortunate acoustics. What does it say about them that this constitutes a fond memory? She tells him as she washes her hands that they'll eat spaghetti and a salad with garlic bread, though shrugs off his help. He can just relax in the family room or upstairs if he wants (he doesn't). Did he take his Advil? Was he in much pain? Yes, he took the Advil, he reports from his chair at the maple table now. And no, he wasn't in much pain. He watches in silence as she prepares their meal, fairly dazzled by her take-charge efficiency—totally alien from the Ellen he knows—preheating the oven for the bread, sowing salt crystals like seeds across the pot of water she sets to boil, drizzling olive oil into the yellow enameled cast-iron pot she surely remembers, slicing garlic with graceful strokes of a chef's knife from the block, scraping them into the sizzling oil with a flourish, adjusting the heat, twisting open the tomato cans, macerating the limp fruits between her clenched fists above the garlic and oil. The corded muscles in her forearms ripple with each step. She goes about her business with such practiced coordination that he wonders whether she consciously performs for him—even the expert way she blows a strand of her damp hair out of her eyes while her hands are occupied—doubtful that she cares enough about what he might think of her to put on this show. She only makes one misstep as she reaches for the colander in the low cupboard, descending to a knee somewhat oddly to peer inside the space as if she had lost her balance.

"You've turned into quite the cook," he says upon her rapid recovery, to which she says thanks as she deposits the colander in the sink. She continues her bustling about to drop the spaghetti into the boiling water, chop the parsley and a fresh bulb of garlic for their bread, which she pastes with garlicked and parsleyed oil then slides into the oven.

The aroma of all that garlic and olive oil overtakes the metallic outside smells of Ellen as she moves on to the lettuce, chopping broad cross-sections of the curly leaves before setting them into the colander to rinse. Does she cook the meals for Jude and the other residents of Cherryfield Farm? Is this one of her duties along with caring for the pigs? Or did she work at a diner or restaurant these many years she has been away? As she doesn't volunteer this information he doesn't ask. She does a strange thing once the sauce cooks for a while, deposits a halved onion directly into the pot.

The mealtime conversation might best be defined by what they don't talk about in between twirling strands of spaghetti onto their spoons, stabbing lettuce leaves with their forks, and sipping their wine. They don't talk about the burglary at the house. They don't talk about Hertzog's visit to Jude's farm, what he and Jude were arguing about, or why Hertzog attacked him. They don't talk about what Ellen thinks Jude plans on doing now, from a legal standpoint. They don't talk about Claire and how good it was of her to intercede to the extent that she could. They don't talk about which room Ellen plans on sleeping in tonight, or whether she plans on staying for more than just one night. Mostly, they don't talk at all. It feels good for the short duration of the meal his daughter has prepared to sit in silence with her as they both chew and taste their food, as they listen to the pleasant outdoor sounds fairly unimpeded by the porous wood-frame house and ancient windows: the rain tattering the roof and siding with light blows and leaking now from one of the downspouts, a squirrel scrabbling across the shingles, the bright tweets of a cardinal from the shrubbery, last of the local birds to relinquish the day, the crickets sawing from the treetops (at what time did they begin singing?), and the more distant hum of high-season traffic on Main. He knows, of course, Thoreau's several meditations upon the virtues of silence. *As the truest Society approaches always nearer to Solitude—so the most excellent Speech finally falls into Silence.* And later, lines Thoreau had included in his ill-fated marriage proposal to his own dear Ellen: *I thought that the sun of our love should have risen as noiselessly as the sun out of the sea…* Hertzog knows by heart these lines and many others extolling the virtues of silent society. Yet he inhabits these truths more fully now.

"The tomato sauce tastes good," he utters, softly. She had discarded the halved onion after it had flavored the sauce.

"Thanks," she says. "I just got it from a recipe."

Hertzog watches as his daughter takes another sip of her wine, swishing it around in her mouth as if to jog free a thought. A faraway look seizes her and he somehow knows where her mind has traveled, that she's about to broach the subject of her mother once again.

"It feels weird being here without Mom," she says, twirling spaghetti strands onto her spoon, twirling and twirling even after the loose threads had been gathered into a tight knot. Here is Ellen, sounding like Ellen, the tide of her voice rising on the shore. She had made this same comment, more or less, the last time she had visited him at the house.

"We were here without her for several years," Hertzog replies now.

Ellen nods as she chews, contemplating the remark. He listens to the workings of her mouth, waits for her to swallow and speak fresh words. He doesn't feel the ache in his fist. He doesn't hear the rain outside. Or the whining crickets. Finally, Ellen swallows, which he does hear.

"Yes," she says, "it felt weird then too."

Silence.

❧

After half-assedly helping his daughter with the dishes he announces that he's turning in, because he ought not to crowd Ellen, and because he's not used to drinking alcohol anymore and the wine has fogged his brain. He lies flat on his back above his sheets but doesn't fall asleep right away. Rather, he listens. The house seems so different, his daughter once again living and breathing within its thin walls—ascending and descending the creaking stairs, flushing the toilet, opening and closing shower pipes, sending torrents of water to slap the tile now and again, snapping drawers open and closed (is she searching for something?), testing the bedsprings as she tosses and turns. She decided to sleep in her own room, after all, issued only an understated "Wow" upon crossing its threshold with her satchel.

Ellen home now makes him think about the whole business of house and home. What it means to be homed. Thoreau spent a lifetime in search of a home, very much in the literal sense. *At a certain season of our life we are accustomed to consider every spot as the possible site of a house.* Thoreau, throughout his short life, transitioned between several houses featuring varied domestic circumstances. The old Minot house as an infant before the Chelmsford house, a brief move to Boston, then the brick house on Main and Walden Streets back in Concord, two additional homes on Main before he even left for Cambridge, the large and noisy Parkman home upon his return from school, replete with boarders, then two years at Emerson's bustling home, where he worked as a handyman, playmate and sometime tutor to Emerson's first son, Waldo, a brief and unhappy stint at Emerson's brother's house on Staten Island, where he tutored Emerson's nephew, then upon his return to Concord a new family house on Texas Street, which doubled as his father's pencil shop, the foundation and cellar of which Thoreau helped the carpenter to build, monitoring his work closely enough to convince himself that he could surely construct his own modest house just up the north shore of Walden Pond, which he set about doing, presently, only to return two years later to his family's new yellow house back on Main Street. Hertzog wants to believe, but can't be sure, that Thoreau ultimately found his home in the world.

Is this what Ellen has been doing too these past ten years, her peregrinations here and there? And what does it mean that Hertzog has stayed put all this time in the same house, on the same block, in the same town, this old house he once shared with his family? Does such hunkering down betray resolution, simple stubbornness, or a home search as ambitious as any, housebound Hertzog searching in his own way?

He sleeps fitfully, the foreign object of the cast and the rising pain beneath an almost insuperable distraction. Strangely bright light assaults his eyes through the blinds next thing he knows. A later morning hour than he's used to rising, though it hardly matters. There is nowhere Hertzog needs to be. Flat on his back, he listens for his daughter, but can't hear a thing. Has she already fled? Arranged for Jude or someone else from the farm to pick her up at daybreak? He rises and pads down the stairs, elevating his injured arm.

The downstairs still exudes garlicky odors from their dinner. As soon as he enters the kitchen he sees her in the backyard through the window over the sink, hands on her hips, weed cords streaming from both fists, bare-footed below a faded pair of dungarees, her unkempt hair tied up in some sort of knot at the top. He marvels anew at Ellen's trim figure, the waistline of her dungarees cinched by a multi-colored piece of fabric serving as a belt. She seems to be appraising one of the garden beds beneath the red oak, overrun by weeds and the dense foliage, fat hips, and fewer pink blooms of rugosa shrubs. The morning light rips through the oak leaves, mottling Ellen's flesh and clothes with its shadows. Rebecca used to attend to the backyard beds with the same fastidiousness that she attended to all her affairs, but Hertzog has pretty much let these backyard plots go, outside the view of most neighbors, the Hinshaws excepted.

He slips on his pair of rubber gardening shoes over his socks in the mudroom and walks around back to join Ellen. Pale moths loiter within the thicket of neglected lawn, scatter in clouds upon each stride.

"Good morning," he says.

"Morning, Father," she replies. "Just figured I'd check out the gardens." She lifts her weedy fists for clarity. The fabric of her dungarees is frayed clear through at various locales to reveal olive flesh at her knees and thighs. The coeds at Emmenthaler by the end of his tenure had begun to wear designer dungarees frayed deliberately, and ludicrously, by the manufacturer. Ellen's dungarees seem to betray more honestly begotten wear.

"Your mother kept the yard tidier."

"I'll say. You could hire someone summertimes at this point, couldn't you? To help you keep up?"

"I suppose."

"I mean this rugosa's pretty and all, but it's taking over." A susurrus from the bees rises and falls from the randy shrubs. "The lupine too," she says. "It's an invasive you know. It's choking out the New Jersey tea over there." She lifts her nose across the lawn toward the embattled tea at the Hinshaw's fence-line, its fine white flowers struggling for light amidst the bigger purple cones of lupine. He notices goldfinches farther off mustarding the thistle feeder hanging from the Hinshaw's sugar maple, but he doesn't mention the birds or the bees as Ellen isn't finished speaking. "Did you plant all that lupine or did they just volunteer?"

"I can't remember," he lies, stupidly embarrassed to have invited the noxious specimen some time ago to disrupt Rebecca's well-organized beds populated by more mannerly plant citizens of Maine.

"And that row of cedars around the side. Those the same trees you and Mom planted like a gazillion years ago?"

He tells her yes, stunned that she remembers.

"Getting a bit crazy, don't you think? Surprised your neighbors haven't complained, that Stacey or whatever."

So she remembers Stacey's name.

She asks him if he has a pole-saw and he tells her yes, in the shed.

"We can at least thin them some, clear them off your roof and let some more light in the house."

She doesn't plan on running off this instant back to Cherryfield Farm, he realizes.

"So you can stay, Ellen?"

"Sure," she replies, crouching to cull a few more weeds, exposing the bony knobs at the base of her spine, the blue scrim of her underwear. "For a little while." He's not sure what this means, exactly—a few hours, a day, a week, a month?—but doesn't press. Instead, he retrieves a five-gallon bucket from the side of the house that she can use to deposit the weeds still streaming from her fists. She does so and suggests they take a trip to Meadowsweet after breakfast, get the yard squared away. "That's something we can do," she says.

He's happy that she plans on staying and that she wants to tend to the neglected garden. Yet it surprises him, this specific interest, and that she even remembers the name of Meadowsweet Nursery, just as her bravura cooking performance in the kitchen last night surprised him. Ellen never enjoyed gardening as a child, despite Rebecca's and

Hertzog's multiple attempts to entice her. They felt it would constitute a salutary outdoors activity for their daughter, who much preferred the indoors. She exhibited such difficulty forming and maintaining human friendships. Perhaps communing with the earth to help it express itself in shoot, leaf, flower, and fruit might constitute a less taxing relationship from which she might segue in due time toward the more challenging subject of other people.

When Ellen was a first or second grader, they bought seed trays from Gilbert Wisner at Meadowsweet and filled each cube with a plug of potting soil and a wildflower seed—rhodora, red clover, clasping harebell, forget-me-not, blue flag iris, and, yes, New Jersey tea. Unfortunately, Ellen could never accommodate herself to seed time. The cubes of dirt bored her long before the seeds nestled below the surface could germinate and sprout hopeful shoots. She refused to keep them moist with the mister attachment on the hose. Hertzog and Rebecca tried to encourage her and kept the seed trays moist on their own, even planted a bed they called Ellen's garden with more impressive seedlings, which also failed to inspire their child. They eventually let it go, like they let so many things go those days. Once Ellen was a bit older, however, Rebecca sometimes insisted that she come along with her to the nursery to buy plants, mulch, soil and whatnot for whatever landscaping project she had in mind, insisted that Ellen at least help out in this way to earn her keep.

"You're not our boarder, Ellen!" Rebecca would call through their daughter's shut bedroom door, while Ellen begged off the chore, successfully most of the time. It wasn't only, or even mostly, Hertzog who did all the hectoring.

That's why it was so strange that Ellen ever got mixed up with Jude and Cherryfield Farm the summer after she graduated from high school. Plants and pigs. Of all people. Of all places and things. He supposes she was desperate to escape the house, and him, though she couldn't imagine at the time going much farther than Cherryfield, and Jude.

Hertzog doesn't patronize Meadowsweet so often anymore, usually only for neem oil or Sevin dust (worst cases) to control whatever fungal or insect blight he can no longer ignore, Japanese beetles mostly. Last year he also had Gil sharpen the blades to the push mower he rarely uses. The nursery had mostly been Rebecca's haunt, her escape when she needed one, which was often. He wonders now from the passenger's seat, as Ellen wends her way up the highway outside town, what Gil will make of Ellen, if he'll even recognize her, thin and weathered, looking so not-Ellen.

They park in the pebbly dirt lot and make their way past the showy hydrangeas and azaleas, the hybridized irises and lilies out front, to the rows of hardier native grasses, wildflowers, and shrubs. Gil prefers the native plants, Hertzog knows, but most customers prefer the lustier greenhouse blooms cross-bred to endure their zone five environs, and a fellow must make a living. Both Hertzog and Ellen push one of the metal flat-bed carts. Hertzog's cart veers annoyingly to the left. Gil offers them his leathery upraised hand from behind his thicket of varied ferns a few rows down, his eyes lingering on Ellen before turning back to the elderly couple Hertzog doesn't recognize, likely peppering the proprietor with too many questions. The breeze carries confused aromas of enriched soil, mulch sourced from various trees, the pollen of manifold plants.

"The serviceberry shrubs look great," Ellen says, gaining his attention. "How about we plant three of these?" It's not lost on him that she chooses an odd number, remembering this lesson from Rebecca, maybe, who always clustered plants in odd numbers. He tells her sure, and guides her toward the larger five-gallon pots. He'd rather not wait so long to enjoy glimpsing waxwings and other birds feasting on the red berries, pollinators looping about the snowy blooms. He is suddenly excited about Ellen's plan to restore the backyard. They select a few additional hardy perennials that will hold their own against interlopers, attract furred and feathered wildlife and won't require too much care. Rhodora with its promise of blazing purple blooms. Arrowwood with its tough, shiny-dark foliage and fistfuls of small white flowers. Highbush cranberry, like Stacey's next door, with its maple-like leaves. Hertzog only hopes the deer won't prove a nuisance. Gil approaches them smelling of bug dope just as Ellen places a small elderberry shrub onto her wagon, advertising heady clusters of lace.

"Gosh sakes, what happened to your hand, David?"

"Oh, just a little accident." Gil nods and won't inquire further, just as most Mainers would know enough not to inquire further upon such a reply, one of the reasons Hertzog feels so well-placed in this frosty remove.

"Haven't seen you in a while, Ellen," Gil says, nonchalant, the muscles about his eyes twitching as he speaks, a neurological tic that seems to have grown more pronounced in the nursery owner over the years, like the flaky red islands of psoriasis on his forearms, exposed below the rolled sleeves of his ancient plaid shirt.

This is what happens as you age, Hertzog muses. You become more and more yourself. To change, as Claire had implied over coffee at the green, was a rarer thing.

"I've been away," Ellen explains.

"Well, good to see you back." He tells them if they need any help just give him a shout and off he goes.

They move on to rows of smaller plants, modest, multi-color flowers dancing on reed-like stems, vibrating with pollinators.

"Thoreau, you know, really liked clasping harebell," Hertzog says as he picks through the pots advertising these delicate purple bells. "He picked them for his sweetheart." He cannot suppress the comment; thankfully, Ellen doesn't seem annoyed.

"You mean the sweetheart you and Mom named me after?"

"Yes. His true love. Although he might have been intimate with Emerson's wife."

"Really?"

"No. Not really."

"Too bad," Ellen says.

While Hertzog has always secretly hoped that poor Thoreau enjoyed at least a night of carnal bliss with his mentor's neglected wife, he finds it difficult to imagine Thoreau carrying off something like this, given what he knows of his temperament from various sources, given that Lidian was either pregnant or recently pregnant for most of the months that he lived at The Bush. Yet, who knows? he thinks now, holding onto the possibility that his long-dead hero might have experienced physical love. He'd always found it at least somewhat suspect, the certainty with which most scholars referenced Thoreau's lifelong virginity, as if a scandalous tryst were something the bachelor would have committed to his journal. Then there was the famous falling out with his mentor, attributed casually (too casually?) to Thoreau's dour moods darkening his mentor's halls, his bitterness over his failure to secure an audience for his early essays and poems, the commercial failure of his first book. Might there have been a more pointed reason for the shadow that fell between these two most famous transcendentalists? What did we really know about the private lives of other people?

"But you never know," he tells his daughter now.

Back at home they each drink a glass of water from the tap and then get right to their outdoors business. Hertzog, one-armed, can't really do much, but he manages to make a contribution to their efforts, anyway, weeds the beds of the invasive grasses and lupine with his good hand, kneeling on a foam pad, careful to leave alone the white firecracker blooms of New Jersey tea. Ellen grubs out some of the rugosa, deploying loppers and a shovel. She plots out the design of the various new beds, seeking his approval, then digs the holes. It feels good to share this spot of time, in this place, with his daughter. The morning has broken cool and clear, as so many summer mornings do here after a rainy night. He straightens his back from his labors every so often and lifts his nose to the sky, savors the piney air in his lungs. He can hear the bite of Ellen's shovel tasting the loose earth, the wind she breathes through her throat to fuel her efforts, the high-pitched beeping of hummingbirds over the low fence in the Hinshaw's yard, maybe browsing their lilac or cranberry shrubs, both in bloom. He'd rather not ruin the moment, or the day, with unnecessary words. He recalls additional exaltations of silence by Thoreau. One early journal passage, in particular, rises to his consciousness. *The most important events make no stir on their first taking place—nor indeed in their effects directly. They seem hedged about by secrecy, produce no explosion, for they are gradual, and create no vacuum which requires to be suddenly filled with sound. As a birth takes place in silence and is whispered about the neighborhood. Corn grows in the night.*

He wonders, watching as Ellen drops doses of organic material with the shovel into the holes she dug, whether this moment with his daughter might be one of these most important events that he ought to honor with silence, whether speaking might impede this growing time for them both. Yet she seems to know so much about plants all of a sudden, handles the shovel with such élan over a bag of manure, piercing the yellow plastic sheath with jabs to effect a rainbow seam. He must make certain inquiries. He doesn't know how long Ellen plans on staying. Thoreau, for all his wisdom, never had a daughter.

"This time you've been away, Ellen," he punctures the silence, "did you work as a landscaper?"

"Nah," she replies, sprinkling manure into a hole.

"At a restaurant then? You sure know how to cook."

"For a while," she says. "While I was trying to go to college."

"College?"

"Don't act so surprised." She offers him her eyes for just a moment before returning to her labors.

"Which one?"

"A few. George Mason was one of them." Hertzog watches as she works the shovel about in the hole to mix the manure and peat moss with the existing soil.

"And what did you study?" He cannot suppress his pleasure, which puts Ellen off, as it ever put his daughter off, his displeasure somehow easier for her to truck.

"Can we just not talk about what I studied, Father? I shouldn't have said anything." She walks the few steps farther away from Hertzog to one of the five-gallon serviceberries, kneels beside it and pounds about the plastic sides of the pot with the heel of her fist with excessive vigor to free the rootball, then strains to pluck the whole plant by its base, shedding the pot, lumbering back toward the hole she has prepared.

"Why? Why shouldn't you have said anything, Ellen?"

"It's rootbound." She ignores his question. "Hand me the pruners over there, would you? We should snip some of these woody roots."

He leaves well enough alone, retrieves the red-handled Felcos and hands them to her. He watches as she roughs up the roots with a hand she's removed from canvas gloves. She then clips a few of the leggiest roots and sets the plant in the ground. A jay screams from somewhere high up in his red oak, as jays do. He returns to his weeding as Ellen labors to adjust the height of the new planting so its base lines up with the actual earth. He won't say another word for a while, he decides, hopes to recover their amicable silence, though Ellen's irritation somehow vibrates in the air between them. He hears her impatience with him in the buzzing of the bees on the rugosa, in the bickering of hummingbirds on their fly-bys, and in the jay still issuing its opinions from the oak. Someone, too, has fired up a lawnmower down the street, probably Tim Miller having detected a half-centimeter's growth. He peeks over at Ellen, scooping a mountain of dirt in a sphere about all the new plantings to create wells at the base. He wonders if she'll ask him to retrieve the hose, but she strides off after it herself, remembering where it must lay coiled.

He wipes sweat from his brow with his good hand. The sun has vaulted itself above the Hinshaw's pitched roof and sugar maple. He can feel the clammy perspiration forming beneath his cast. Food smells from Main rise to compete against the manure and peat moss.

He hears the Hinshaw's screen door creak open and slam shut just a few seconds before Stacey pokes her head over the hobblebush hedgeline, as he expected she would, eventually.

"Hey, what happened to you?" she asks. She seems to have just showered. Her blond outer portion of hair is damp and dark, hanging down over what Hertzog presumes is still the dyed black underlayer. He can see their tabby cat on its leash through the hobblebush other side of the short chain-link fence.

He tells her he just had a little accident and she tells him he'll have to think of a better story than that. Then she says hello to Ellen—having remembered her name—and Ellen (thankfully) says hello back, wiping the sweat from her face with the inside of her elbow. Her hair-knot has loosened, a cloud of dark tresses building about her head.

"Guess you won't be swimming for a while. Sucks. Sorry, David."

Hertzog tells her it's okay. He's pleased for the distraction of Stacey, who charges the very air with more positive energy.

"Love that belt," she's saying now to Ellen, who thanks her but keeps her attention on the shrub she waters with the hose, the integrity of the well holding up more or less. "So cool of you to help your dad with the garden," Stacey adds while walking her cat down the hedgeline. Hertzog wonders for the first time whether the creature is housetrained, whether the cat does all its business outdoors on a leash.

"Hey, I know something that'll keep you busy, David," his neighbor calls over the hobblebush on her way back. "I've been meaning to ask you. Taylor and I are taking the research vessel out high-tide week after next to collect data in the rockweed protection zone. Wondering if you wanted to come along. You too if you want, Ellen."

Here's where a well-adjusted person might accept the offer, or say *maybe*, or politely decline, offering up at least some vague competing obligations. But his daughter, never one of these people, ignores the offer altogether by trotting off to twist the spigot closed, leaving Hertzog's neighbor to wonder, her eyes trailing after Ellen, if she had even heard the proposal, Stacey's nose stud winking against the daybright.

Hertzog diverts Stacey's attention by thanking her and telling her that he'd love to go (*love to?*), but that he can't give a firm commitment just now, Ellen back home for who knows how long. This seems to satisfy her. She tells him she'll give him a heads-up the day before and if he or the both of them want to come along, great. She tucks a strand of damp hair behind her ear and follows her cat's lead to the other side of the yard. Hertzog watches after them above the short hedge. The creature seems to be hunting the moths that clouded Hertzog's feet, earlier, pouncing here and there on the Hinshaw's better-maintained lawn.

"That Stacey's just a little ball of energy now, isn't she?" Ellen says once she returns, dragging one of the bags of pine bark mulch over to the new shrubs, stumbling somewhat under the strain, ligament cords and veins testing the flesh about her biceps.

"Yes, she's...something else." He would chastise his daughter for her rudeness, or at least say something nice about Stacey—that she's finishing up her doctorate, that she's a good teacher and kind person, and that he's grown quite fond of her—yet won't drive a wedge between them now by criticizing Ellen or heaping praise upon Stacey.

"Can I ask you another question, Ellen?" he asks, instead. "It's not about what you've been doing these past ten years. Promise. It's not about Jude or Cherryfield."

"Okay. Sure. Shoot." Hertzog watches as Ellen dumps the whole bag of pine nuggets about the base of one of the new plantings, then drags over the next bag while Hertzog, on his knees, distributes the mulch with sweeps of his good arm. Some sort of weevil seems to have infiltrated Gil's mulch, but that's okay.

"What was it like for you to be our daughter? How did it really seem to you?"

She has settled a few paces down at a separate shrub she just planted, distributes the pine nuggets with the shovel. "You mean at the time? Or later?"

"At the time."

"At the time I thought you and Mother were perfect, which was infuriating, because you expected me to be perfect too. About everything. My table manners. School. Swimming. Even frickin' gardening." She gestures toward the small shrub before her with the shovel. "It wasn't fair."

"It didn't seem to me, Ellen, that we expected so very much of you."

Ellen huffs out her nostrils. "You asked me a question, Father, and I'm giving you an answer."

She's right, of course, to admonish him. He hears the Hinshaw's screen door slam shut. He lifts his eyes but doesn't see either of his neighbors. Stacey must have taken her cat inside.

"Okay. I understand. You're right. And later?"

"Huh?"

"How did you see things later?"

She stops spreading the mulch around, just leans her elbows against the tip of the shovel's handle. Pine bark flecks her sweaty brow and cheek. She must have tightened her hair-knot when he wasn't looking. "Later, after Mom was gone, while I was still in high school, I figured out that you weren't perfect at all. Neither of you. You were an English prof at a second-tier liberal arts college in the boondocks and Mom was a mid-level administrator who probably never would have made provost or president anywhere because she wasn't a brown-noser, or a man for that matter, so you were both stuck here at this place that would never be, like, Harvard, or even Bowdoin or Bates. You knew all this and so you hoped or expected I'd be brilliant or something. That I'd achieve what you both didn't or couldn't achieve, and when it didn't turn out that way, when I was just me, and maybe had certain problems that lots of girls have, or some girls, anyway, you just couldn't deal. So you both took out on me your frustrations or whatever because you didn't have anyone else to take it out on. I guess that's how I felt." She pierces a new bag of mulch with the tip of her shovel, the plastic sheath making a popping sound. Her hands tremble on the shovel's wooden handle. "That's how I felt later."

Hertzog feels his heart pounding in his chest, hears the goldfinches twittering at the Hinshaw's feeder. The fresh venom in Ellen's response stuns him. He must remind himself to breathe. He's tempted to protest on a variety of fronts. Rebecca, for starters, would surely have made provost or president here or elsewhere. She was already associate provost by the time of her accident. Plenty of schools, including Bowdoin as a matter of fact, had been courting her to apply for provost and other upper-level administrative positions. But she couldn't imagine putting herself on the market quite yet, their daughter the wreck that she was. If they were stuck at Emmenthaler, as Ellen put it, it was mostly because of Ellen herself. Yet it would be cruel for Hertzog to point this out now, and unfair. He had asked a question and his daughter had answered it. Plus, if her assessment of the way things ran wasn't spot-on, it wasn't totally wrong, either.

"And now, Ellen? This is how you still feel?"

"More or less."

He watches as his daughter heads over to the spigot to twist on the water again and maybe to escape the charged atmosphere. A new order of quiet obtains for the few moments it takes her to return with the streaming hose. The goldfinches seem to have sorted out their differences; the jay must have flown off a while ago. She sends ribbons of water from the hose to soak in the mulch. Hertzog watches the weevils scatter every which way under the assault as he considers his next words. But he doesn't know what to say. Ellen doesn't seem to know, either. She lifts her brown eyes from the torrent of water as if she's about to speak, but offers him only a glimpse of an unchecked expression, instead, conveying something close to sadness. It pierces him, summoning a memory he cannot deny, Ellen's high school graduation that he insisted she attend.

High school had been a near impossible challenge for his daughter, navigating endless assignments that failed to inspire, plus the few suspensions for smoking pot or for one of her screaming jags at a teacher or peer. It wasn't altogether clear that she would graduate at all. So when she did manage to pull her shit together and complete the requirements, Hertzog felt it was important to mark the occasion by attending the ceremony. Her mother would have wanted them to attend graduation, something of an unfair argument that he nonetheless deployed.

He regretted his decision from the moment he took his plastic seat on the football field lawn. Cassidy was her only pal he knew about in the actual world. As the seating was arranged alphabetically, however, they couldn't sit together up there on stage. While most of the kids chatted with the person beside them, Ellen wouldn't make the effort. Instead, she retreated somewhere very far away, or somewhere deep inside herself, which pretty much amounted to the same thing. He could see the blank look on her face quite clearly from his vantage. It was a heartbreaking thing to observe, his daughter's blank gaze as he sat there shrinking from the cloying smell of the field. Some ignoramus had applied cow manure too recently to the turf. The Hanson boy sitting next to Ellen had to nudge her to gain her attention when it was her turn to rise and receive her diploma from Principal Heller.

Immediately after Heller announced the class of graduates to the woops and wails of parents and other well-wishers in the crowd, the students scurried from their designated seats to retrieve the emerald caps they had tossed and formed clusters representing their various cliques. He watched as Ellen rose, having never shed her cap, looking sheepishly about, unsure of her next move. Hertzog rose too along with everyone else and tried making his way down the row to the aisle to reach Ellen, but it was difficult. Everyone was taking their time. He shoved his way past, which prompted a reprimand from someone, then lost his daughter in the crowd of green gowns. He wended his way through the various student clusters, issuing their boisterous cries, their aromas of perfume and cinnamon gum rising above the cow manure, and then he finally spotted her, adrift and alone, gazing this way and that across the lawn for him between the hostile thickets of peers. He raised his hand for her to see as he made his way over to her until she spotted him, whereupon her brown eyes, the musculature in her cheeks and brows, looked just the way they look now. Unchecked. Guileless.

As much as she resented him those days, claimed to hate him on any number of occasions—*I fucking hate you!*—he was all that she truly had in the world, as Ellen was all that Hertzog had.

"Here I am, Ellen," he had said, closing the space between them on the turf. "I'm right here." He gave her a brief hug, which she allowed, even if she didn't quite hug him back.

"Can we go home now?" she had asked.

"You can stay here, I want you to know," he says now. "Here at home." She doesn't say anything to this right away, but seems to ponder the offer as she plies the new plantings with too much water, filling each well several times and dispersing all that expensive manure and peat moss below. He doesn't want her to scurry off now to the spigot so he doesn't say anything about her watering. While he awaits her response, he gazes up over her shoulder at the Hinshaw's sugar maple, the foliage flashing two green tones in the breeze. He marvels at its deciduous brilliance, sending out these lusty sheets of chlorophyll summertimes to soak up sunlight and turn it into food, transferring these sugars and starches from leaf to trunk once the days grow shorter, shedding its leaves at just the right time to elude the perilous weight of snowfall on its branches and to offer its foliage foodstuff to the floor. He wonders at the invisible tree beneath the ground, the roots and fungal networks performing their vital communications across soil miles. The maple tree could not be more perfectly homed. This is not something that Hertzog usually does, contemplate the brilliance of trees, surrounded though he is by verdant woods, in the intellectual thrall of America's great champion of forest trees, no less. He wonders what his eyes have been doing all these years, whether he has seen at all the world so close at hand.

"Is that what you want, Father?" Ellen finally asks, still sending torrents of water to breach the well of one of the new serviceberries, but who fucking cares? "Is that why you haven't done anything with my room? I mean, my deodorant's still there on the frickin' dresser." He feels Ellen's tide, which had drawn so close, retreating once more. He has spooked her. She throws the hose down on the lawn and scurries off to close the valve. Hertzog watches as a goldfinch alights on the soil and mulch berm of the serviceberry well farthest from him, as it skitters into the bath that Ellen created at the shrub's base and that will take some time for the drenched soil to absorb. It takes so little, really, to attract dazzling creatures to your home. But the bird flits off in a blur of black and mustard upon Ellen's return.

"I'm not sure why I haven't futzed with your toiletries," he tells her. "Why I've instructed Magda to leave your things alone. I realize it's strange." He hasn't quite answered her original question, he realizes.

"Shit, Magda's still around?" She leans over a few of the smaller pots now, seems to contemplate what her next move should be, and finally plucks up a clasping harebell.

He tells her yes. Magda still lives in town. She still cleans a few houses. She is active in her church up in Machias, participated on a humanitarian trip to Puerto Rico a couple years back to help with relief efforts. She collects sea glass from the pebbly coast.

Ellen nods as she frees the harebell from its small pot, as she looks about at the progress of their labors. It'll take them two or three more trips to Meadowsweet for enough mulch to complete the job, she tells him.

"Okay," he says. He waits for her next words, hoping she'll veer back to his shore.

"So maybe I'll stay," she says, the harebell's purple blooms shimmying atop their long stems as she roughs up its roots. "For a few days, maybe."

23

March 26th, 1842
"Where is my heart gone—They say men cannot part with it and live."

"You must hurry home at once," Nathan Brooks beseeches after pounding on Mr. E.'s front door middle of break-fast, only the second Sunday of 1842. "Your brother," he declares from across the threshold, rheumy eyes trembling in their sockets. "He is most unwell."

H. bolts straight away across the frozen earth of Heywood Meadow to the family home, lingers not long enough to hear Mr. Brooks tell Lidian and Mr. E. that it's not the family illness that bedevils poor John. Rather, a terrific infection. Mother issues their family news to him in the foyer, the timbre of her notes quavering, H. still huffing winter-scorched breath past his throat. Father can barely lift his eyes from the burgundy rug and seems smaller than ever, his pallor ashen. The ladies Ward, of whom H. is distantly aware, sniffle and snuffle by the fireplace in the parlor, speaking into their hands. Sophia stands silent against the far wall, pinned there as if she were an Italian fresco.

His mother rehearses the unfortunate details of the story through tears, her face pinked and swollen. John had only sliced off a small morsel of skin on the tip of his thumb while stropping his razor the Saturday past beside the pencil sheds. He had replaced the dollop and fastened a rag about it to facilitate the healing. As it began to pain him on Tuesday, he visited Dr. Bartlett, who bandaged it afresh and sent him on his way. *Sent him on his way.* She utters the casual phrase as if to convince herself that Dr. Bartlett's nonchalance might still be credited, as if time were but a stream she goes a-fishing in, that she might travel its current back to blithe days.

"But the skin by Thursday," his father takes up the story, searching for the proper word, "the skin…"

"What, Father?"

"Has mortified. He has since been sapped of his strength and suffers sharp pains in curious locales beyond the injury, proper—his arm, his breast, and abdomen."

"His mouth, as well," his mother adds. "His mouth!"

"Yes, alas," his father says. "We fear the worst. We've summoned a doctor from Boston. He should be here—"

"Go to him," his mother interjects. "John has been asking for you. Wear your bravest face lest you frighten him."

H. bounds the stairs and dashes to his brother's upstairs bedroom. Aromas of camphor and turpentine assail him in the hall above the woodsmoke from bedroom fires. H. breathes the spirits and smoke deeply, summons his courage before crossing the threshold.

"Dearest brother!" H. cannot wear a false mask before John for even a second. His brother lies in his bed-shirt at a slight incline against the wooden headboard, perhaps to facilitate the breathing along with the aromatic spirits, strands of his thinning hair pasted against his forehead, the wet either from perspiration or the cooling cloth hanging from the lip of the wash basin, which their sister likely administers at intervals. His attention foursquare on John, he is only dimly aware of Helen's presence.

"David," John intones his former preferred name, which frightens H. Has delirium gripped his brother so soon? Why hadn't his parents summoned him earlier? John lifts his hand above the bedsheets, which H. grips, kneeling beside the bed. The hand is cold and damp, the grip weak.

"You can leave us now, Helen," H. commands, more sternly than he intended. She sits in a dining room chair that has been summoned to the room, her arms folded on her lap. She rises, obediently, silently. John will be his charge.

"It was only a small nick," John explains through labored breath, as if to apologize for his carelessness. "I thought nothing of it."

"Shh, dear brother. Save your strength. Mother and Father told me." John nods, and then his expression changes, the eyebrows knit in great concern as if he has gleaned the oncoming crisis. His chin lifts to the right as if on its own accord and he somehow throats a whistled groan from between clenched teeth. H. has never before glimpsed such a fearful grimace upon his brother's face, the teeth chattering at peculiar intervals as if from a chill.

"What is it? Where does it most pain you?"

John can only throat the same whistled groan, but jabs a finger at his stomach below the thin bed-sheet. H. strips the sheet to his waist and presses a palm against John's bed-shirt to feel the abdomen beneath. The muscles below his chest cavity—John carries not an ounce of fat—bulge hard as a cider barrel against his bedclothes. H. doesn't quite know how he might alleviate John's suffering. His whistled groans, the intermittent chattering of his teeth, continues. He kneads the distension with his fingers as if it were a dough, but stops upon the vigorous shake of his brother's head. Then, finally, John issues a forceful exhale and his stomach settles down into the grotto of his abdomen.

"So it goes these past hours, brother," John says, his forehead shellacked with wet. "Terrible fits seize me, blessed moments of repose in between. And it's no use trying to massage the seized muscles." He grips his left biceps with his right hand, clenches his eyes shut like clamshells. "Strange pains, too, between the spasms." He opens his eyes, the pain dissipating. "I'm sorry to have summoned you to see me in these throes. We've had such merry times, despite our recent troubles."

Ellen, H. thinks.

"Yes, John," he says. "I could not have asked for a more loving and charitable brother with whom to share life's adventures and guide me through its travails." H. rises from his brother's side, dips the wash cloth in the mild water in its porcelain basin, wrings the tepid fluid and plies the cloth against John's forehead.

H. has managed to summon his composure, but this is his fault entire. Had he not wished his brother dead on account of their mutual adoration of Ellen of Scituate? *If only John were dead,* he still remembers his recent plaint. And now, now, only months removed from such horrific fantasies, he witnesses the unmistakable symptoms of lockjaw in John.

And Ellen, in any wise, lost to them both.

"You will tend to me," John utters. "I will not have our parents and our sisters see me endure such agonies."

"Yes, dear brother. Here I am." He continues to stroke John's forehead with the cloth, strokes his temples and neck, the flesh curiously marbled white and red, the forces of death and life waging fierce battle in the dermas itself. H. rests a palm against John's forehead, which feels more cold than warm. Any fever that John may have suffered has since broken. "But let us hear what the doctor proposes," H. says. "He hastens from Boston."

John nods, resignedly.

H. retrieves the dining room chair from the wall and sets it beside the bed so that he might face John, who surrenders to sleep, his latest fit having depleted him. H. takes advantage of the moment to empty the basin outdoors. He does not mean to tarry, but pauses at the top of the stairs, the distinct frequency of his mother's voice freezing him in his tracks.

If the prodigal were home where he belonged, dear husband, none of this would have happened. Poor John wouldn't have been working so hard these past days in the pencil-sheds. Had he not been so tired, he never would have lanced his thumb. But we're not good enough—

Now now, Cynthia. Stop. Pray stop.

Off playing the lap-dog for his hero in the great white house, whittling popguns and toy whistles for the babes he wishes were his own. Mooning now after that Lidian.

Cynthia.

Mooning *after her! Everyone knows. It's a disgrace.*

Having heard enough, H. descends the stairs with the basin, the groans of the joinery silencing his parents.

H. leaves his brother's side only one more time during the balance of the morning to use the privy. John cannot swallow solid morsels of food, yet H. manages to spoon doses of bone broth at wide intervals. They talk about more cheerful days, or, rather, H. talks while John mostly listens to preserve his strength. Berry-picking in Hubbard's swamp. Melon-growing on the hill. Hunting for Indian relics at Nawshawtuct. The sturdy little boat they built, the *Musketaquid,* after H.'s trip to Maine. The fortnight spent on the Concord and Merrimack Rivers. The mischievous fox nosing their melons, he shares with John for the first time, having hoarded this memory up until now.

They do not talk about Ellen.

John's seizures intrude with increasing frequency and intensity, each onset signaled by the eerie stare John issues toward the corner of the ceiling, flashing scarlet veins across the undersides of his sclera. The involuntary stare precedes the rattle of John's teeth as his mandibles clench, balls of muscle rising beneath the thin foliage of his unkempt beard. There is nothing H. can do during these episodes but offer him ballast by gripping the knobs of his shoulders beneath his bedshirt and issue soothing notes by shaping the wind through his tongue and palate.

The doctor arrives before evening, having somehow employed a carriage on the Lord's day. H. hears the horses' hooves chuffing against the road, the whine of the wheels in want of fresh grease, and rushes downstairs to greet him.

"Dr. Phillips," the mutton-chopped doctor announces at the threshold, brandishing his behemoth Gladstone bag, surrendering his hat and great-coat to Helen. The great-coat smells of fires from other hearths. He does not pause for niceties such as shaking hands, but asks where he might find the patient. H. leads him upstairs, his parents making chase, Helen and Sophia lingering in the foyer.

Standing at the foot of the bed, Dr. Phillips asks John after his symptoms, John being just well enough between bouts to describe the seizures and the curious shooting pains that assail him. The doctor asks him additional questions. Can he swallow solid food? Can he drink liquids and hold them down? Can he swallow for him now? When has he last moved his bowels? How does it feel when he makes water? The doctor issues grave listening noises from his throat between John's terse responses, curious ridges rising from his exposed scalp as if it were his fierce brain, itself, exposed. "May I lay hands on you to continue my examination, sir?" he finally asks with a deference so gentle it frightens H. The good doctor massages John's throat between the pincers of his thumb and finger, then presses the fingers of both hands against John's abdomen above his bedshirt in various places, then taps at those same places, advising John to cry out if he causes pain. John does not cry out, though he may simply be too weary to cry. The doctor finally removes the bandage from John's thumb, releasing an unmistakable stench of rotten meat from which the doctor does not flinch. The wounded flesh has blued between the dried flecks of dark blood. "Well, well," he utters cryptically. He re-bandages the wound with fresh cotton and tape from his bag, taking his time about it, as if he were working out just now what he ought to say to his patient and his tribe. H. can hear the jays bickering outside, the wood floor groaning beneath the shifting weight of their bodies balancing themselves to remain upright, the bubbled complaints rising from Dr. Phillips' innards.

"Is there no hope?" their mother finally inquires. The doctor, seated on the mattress still, binding John's wound with great tenderness, does not turn to face their mother, but speaks the words to John.

"No *earthly* hope, I'm afraid, Master John. You must see to your affairs quickly."

John nods, having anticipated the judgment. H.'s mother dashes from the room, unable to contain her emotions. Their father makes chase to console her. H. feels the blood seep from his face, but he will maintain his composure for John's sake. He grips John's good hand from the bedside.

"There is little to bequeath at any rate," John says. "Some might consider that a blessing." His brother's heroic playfulness wrenches H.

"Your townspeople attest to your character with fondest words. Your cheerful comportment now, your very visage, affirms all that I have heard. It's a bitter cup you've been offered. I am most sorry."

"The cup that my Father gives me," John replies, "shall I not drink?"

Doctor Phillips manfully refuses remuneration at the door. He speaks soothing words to H.'s father and mother, his fire-stinking great-coat folded over his arms, having been fetched by Helen. He grips the rigid handle of his Gladstone bag with both hands beneath the fragrant coat, his hat set askew. He gazes at H. lingering at the foot of the stairs, shifts his gaze toward their shrunken father, then gazes back at H., his features inside the mutton chops settling into a new expression that smooths the curious ridges atop his scalp. He has settled something. He asks H. if he might accompany him to his carriage to assist him with his things, hands him his Gladstone bag at H.'s obedient approach, much heavier than H. anticipated. H. walks in stunned silence to the carriage, scarcely hears the jays screeching from the bare winter-battered branches of the maple across the road. The driver opens the side-door, whereupon the doctor tells H. to set down the bag on the carriage floor, chest-high to them both as they stand on the frozen earth. He opens the bag wider than before to reveal a hinged metal rack, the specifications of which H., even in his pained stupor, cannot help but admire. The rack holds narrow glass vials stoppered with cork on three separate levels.

"Your dear brother nears his end, as I have warned, but a most terrific and violent end, I tell only you now. The spasms and cramps to his extremities, his abdomen, his jaw, will increase in frequency and force." He reaches for one of the vials and lifts it from its compartment. The ochre glass conceals the color of the liquid it holds. "Laryngospasm of unremitting intensity will bring about the final struggle. I must prepare you." The doctor hands H. the ochre vial. "The muscles in his throat will contract utterly and unceasingly and he will be unable to summon his breath." He places a hand now on H.'s shoulder. The horses snort and snuff, eager to be on their way, soothed by the unintelligible glottals of the driver seated at his bench. "I am certain you will want to ease your dear brother's journey to his reward."

"Yes." H. is enough a man of the world that he knows the contents of the tincture the doctor has bequeathed to him. Laudanum, or perhaps an even stronger concentration of opium, as the simple black strip of tape wrapped about the middle of the glass seems to suggest.

"A drop or two upon the hour from this point forward. Ten drops within the span of an hour, or delivered in a single dose, will hasten his more peaceable journey."

H. thanks the good doctor, who climbs into the groaning carriage.

Entrusted by the good doctor, H. serves as constant nurse to his brother for the duration of his struggle. Prudence Ward as second witness, John assigns what portions of himself might be assignable, leaving H. his few volumes of poetry and prose and the green desk they had purchased for their short-lived experiment as schoolteachers. John exchanges bravest farewells to their friends, Channing, Brooks, and Hoar, during a brief visit. H. bars additional townspeople from the room. H. mostly bars the rest of the family from the room, too, per John's wishes, although he permits them entry during isolated moments of peaceable lucidity.

John loses control of his bowels shortly after nightfall, expelling the putrid ooze during one of his seizures. H. makes quick work of stripping his brother's night-shirt, cleansing John's mossy crotch and legs of the weirdly clear yet fragrant excrement, stripping the sheets, rolling his brother's spindly spent frame with great care to one side of his batchelor's bed, then to the other. He rifles through John's wardrobe to retrieve a clean nightshirt and then helps his brother to dress, rolling the shirt over his body as if it were an inverted sock. He repairs to the backyard with the soiled linens, his parents and sisters rising from the candle-lit table in the kitchen yet not interrupting his duties. He deposits the sheets in the barrel beside the pencil finishing shed, unsure what their mother will decide to do with them. The constellations seem to dim their lights through the poplar's bare scaffolding in deference to his human grief. His mother wordlessly hands him fresh linens inside the house.

As he stretches the fresh sheets over the horsehair mattress, rolling his brother once again like the most delicate dough, John asks him if he might play from his flute. It must be 'round midnight, yet H. accommodates him, of course. He retrieves the flute from the dresser top and summons the wind to play several verses of "Lightly Row" and "God Rest Ye Merry, Gentlemen." The notes reverberate with incongruous cheer throughout the house and up and down Concord's silent streets.

Night bleeds into day bleeds into night. H. administers two drops of the tincture beneath John's tongue every hour upon the hour. The drops take immediate soporific effect between John's horrific spasms. His brother's fixed stare at the onset of each crisis proves most terrifying, the involuntary manner with which he jerks his head against the constraints of the ligaments, his grey eyes bulging from their sockets. The bouts themselves grow more intense, as Dr. Phillips has warned, John's face flashing deeper shades of blue as he struggles for breath, emitting strange falsetto squeals through clamped teeth and throat.

"What demon possesses me, brother?" he cries just after a protracted seizure, the blood returning to prick his countenance. H. marvels at the strength John has summoned above the seizure and the opium to issue such a lament. He reaches to clutch his brother's good hand. Daybright invades the room. Tuesday morning, H. would guess, though he cannot be sure.

"Are you terribly frightened, John?"

His brother does not answer straight away. He gazes into his eyes instead, his chest rising and falling beneath the sheets.

"Yes, brother," John finally allows.

"Don't be frightened. Here I am with you. You are not alone."

His brother nods, though without conviction.

"Here," H. says, offering him two more drops of the tincture. John hungrily accepts the drops as a chick accepts its mother's nourishment. H. gauges the remaining contents of the ochre vial. He must choose his course wisely. He considers asking John for his permission to administer the additional medicine and put him at his ease, yet this does not seem to be his charge. "Open," he commands rather sternly, administers one drop, two, three, four, beneath his brother's tongue and instructs him to swallow. Then H. administers six more drops, nearly depleting the vial's contents, John's eyes widening at the audacious dose.

H. slips beneath the sheets in his clothes and wraps his arms about the shell of his brother. John rests his dewy head on H.'s chest. H. can feel his brother's heart beating quickly in his chest, or maybe it is his own heart that he feels.

"I'm so frightened," John utters once more. H. wonders whether John, in his delirium, realizes that he has already communicated his fright. The heart that H. feels has slowed.

"I know, dear brother. Do not be afraid. There is no man in this world more worthy of his reward than you."

The words, or the opium, or both, seem to pacify poor John. He turns on his side away from H., yet not in reproach. "Stay," he pleads the moment H. makes to slip from the horsehair mattress. And so H. nuzzles beside John, hips athwart hips. The two nestle like spoons. He hears John's thin breath as through a reed, slow, slowing. The breath smells faintly of almonds. His brother utters only a single additional word before fading, a word H. cannot help but hear.

Ellen.

24

Ellen stays for two days to help him about the house. Then she stays for two days more, which surprises him. Even so, Hertzog does not comment upon the length of her stay or inquire as to when she plans on leaving for Cherryfield and Jude as he fears that any such inquiry might hasten her departure. She stays long enough for them to fall into certain patterns negotiating each other's hereness in the old house they once again share. She rises before him each morning (to Hertzog's surprise), the mild complaint of the pine floorboards beneath her feet rousing him as she pads to the bathroom. He remains in bed while he listens to the whoosh and groan of the plumbing, offers her a wide berth.

Yet it's not only his wish to grant Ellen her space that keeps him quiet as a church mouse in bed as she mills about, morningtimes. There's an element of eavesdropping, too, he must confess. He listens and takes note of her footfalls in her bedroom before she treads down the hall to the bathroom, the dresser drawers she pulls open and shut an awful lot, the mysterious objects that clang against the floor, as if she were constantly (and sloppily) looking for something. And since when did she spend so much time in the bathroom? He doesn't rise until he hears her modest weight trouble the risers and joists of the stairs as she makes her way to the kitchen. Then he sees to his own morning business, taking care to brush his teeth and clear the sleep from his eyes before joining his daughter in the kitchen.

"I still haven't gotten used to these crazy-early Downeast sunrises," Ellen greets him one morning between slurps of her coffee at the maple table, scanning headlines in the *Bangor Daily News.* Any number of Thoreau's exaltations of the morning occurs to him, but he stifles his insufferable pedantic impulses.

"Thanks for making the coffee," he tells her instead, as he has told her the past few days. She wears the same sweatpants and one of three threadbare T-shirts before changing into her tattered jeans with the fabric belt cinched tight, her hair tamed askew with an elastic band. He has told her that she should sift through her old clothing in her dresser to see what fits, and she certainly seems to have done so by the noises emanating from her room, but she continues to wear these same clothes. Perhaps her old clothes are just too loose.

He prepares oatmeal portions for two now and does not neglect to slather the surface with honey and fresh berries. One morning he makes an omelet with tomatoes and goat cheese and sprigs of dill from herbs Stacey Hinshaw gifted to him over their hedgeline. When he sits with their food, Ellen slides the front page of the newspaper to him and then she sifts through less pressing headlines in the Homestead or Outdoor sections. The thin newspaper pages sometimes tremble in her hands as she holds the open paper between her elbows braced on the table, which must distract her as she typically proceeds to set the paper down flat against the table, clearing her throat. After their sunrise meals, he departs for his morning hike—though he won't be swimming the Bowl until his hand and wrist heal—and Ellen, well, he's not entirely sure what Ellen does the two or three morning hours before his return. He invites her along on his exercise the first morning, but doesn't protest when she declines, citing vague errands to keep her busy in town. Where does she go?

During the meaty middle of their day they tend to the garden (or Ellen does, mostly, while Hertzog looks on), making trips to Gil Wisner at Meadowsweet a couple times for more mulch and purple coneflowers to fill in some space beside the shed and neem oil for the newly blighted rugosa. Using the rusty pole saw, Ellen thins the dense copse of cedar branches crowding his roof and blotting the sunlight from both the Hinshaw's windows and their own, while Hertzog braces the ladder. He notes the supple way his daughter handles the saw and the rope that works the attached lopper for some of the smaller branches (no tremor here), though she does check her balance now and again. "Easy," he warns. Save for swimming, his daughter was never particularly coordinated. They discuss various topics during their chores. Ellen asks how his hand feels beneath the cast. She asks whether he needs more ibuprofen. They talk about global warming and the embattled lobster harvest so far this summer, the shedders that won't come shallow. They talk about the weather, the Red Sox and Yankees, and the salutary developments vis à vis health care policy in the state. They bemoan Maine's obstructionist, and just plain crazy, governor. They exchange pleasantries over the hedgeline with Stacey or Taylor when their neighbors tend to their own garden beds or walk their cat (the creature's name is Mason,

Hertzog learns). Stacey offers him fresh herbs. She reminds him about their upcoming research trip to the rockweed protection zone to gather data next week. She still hopes they can come along.

Claire stops by one day to check in on them (that's how she puts it after calling to them in the backyard from the side gate). She compliments them on the serviceberry shrubs and clasping harebell and asks after the names of some of the less popular shrubs and flowers they've planted. Dressed in her full uniform—pistol, stun-gun, mace, Billy-club and all—she at least takes off her hat to tour the yard. Her hair seems damp still from a recent shower. Claire stays just long enough to finish the iced tea Hertzog offers her, and ask, once Ellen makes herself scarce, if he's heard anything from Jude or a lawyer for Jude, about their altercation. He hasn't. That's good, Claire tells him. It's nice Ellen's staying with him, she adds, that they seem to be getting on. Hertzog agrees.

"You seem different," Claire says, handing him her empty glass. The glass feels cold against his good hand, the ice nested at the bottom not quite fully melted.

"It's just my arm." He raises the green fiberglass cast to punctuate his remark.

"No, it's not just that," Claire says, lifting her hat to her head.

After their backyard labors each day, Hertzog and Ellen take turns washing up in the stainless kitchen sink, then Hertzog retreats to his study for a few hours to work while Ellen reads downstairs or takes a walk. They seem, the both of them, wary of spooking the other through overexposure. Wariness defines their repartee, generally. They don't dare swim in each other's depths. They stick to the shallows. For now.

Certain passages from the early Journal pierce him upstairs as he reads and jots notes, passages he has overlooked all these years. *How insufficient is all wisdom without love—*" Hertzog's eyes alight upon these lines Thoreau writes in the spring of 1842, still mourning his significant dead. *There may be curtesy—there may be good will—there may be even temper there may be wit—and talent and sparkling conversation—and yet the soul pine for life. Just so sacred—and rich as my life is to myself—will it be to another. Ignorance and bungling with love is better than wisdom and skill without—Our life without love is like coke and ashes—like the cocoa nut in which the milk is dried up. I want to see the sweet sap of living wood in it.*

Hertzog has had little use for these sentiments in the past, hastily wrought and ungrammatical. He has homed in all these years, instead, on Thoreau's more eloquent passages from the Journal decrying the sickness of society and extolling the beneficence of nature and solitude. These passages (plenty from which to choose) reaffirmed certain notions about the transcendentalist that began to foment even while the tubercular townsman was still alive, conveniently promulgating a myth of an American archetype, that of the rugged male individualist pitted against the conventional European force of society and all that went along with it, a wife and children most principally. But Thoreau ever sought to collapse the distinction between supposed opposites: nature and culture, the individual and society, autonomy and love. Even as his romantic pursuits were quashed, and notwithstanding horrific tragedies in the households Thoreau and Emerson, he hadn't given up on love. He hadn't given up on his dear neighbors in Concord, human or animal. Were he truly the bitter recluse an increasing number of scholars seemed to take him for (one provocateur in *The New Yorker* recently cherry-picking episodes of his life to decry his general assholishness), he never would have bothered to perform his experiment and publish his results to the world. He never would have had so many lifelong friends and faithful correspondents. He was trying, ever trying, to do better by his fellow souls.

I never gave anyone the whole advantage of myself—Hertzog lingers over these lines of regret from the early journal, spring of 1842. *I never afforded him the culture of my love.*

Water rises to Hertzog's eyes and blurs his vision. He can hear his daughter downstairs puttering about the kitchen, the kiss of the refrigerator door opening. To stumble headlong into love—romantic or platonic—risk bungling the whole affair to offer someone the whole advantage of your *self.* Heroic sentiments. Claire was right. Something has shifted inside since Ellen's return, his very innards more susceptible to stimuli.

"We should think about supper," he tells Ellen each day once the light grows syrupy through the slats in the blinds, illuminating dust motes, departing his study to seek her out in the family room or kitchen downstairs, pleased that she spends so much time in the common rooms of the house now rather than hew to her former predilections by shutting herself away in her bedroom. She shops for their groceries at Hannaford and he lets her while he reads or simply rests in the family room. Ellen takes the lead in the kitchen as they prepare various meals through the week, eggplant parmigiana, chili crumbed through with some sort of alternative protein, and pasta primavera (all of which Hertzog enjoys), mushroom moussaka sauced over with something cheesy and white, which consigns him almost immediately to the upstairs bathroom. But that's okay.

After suppers they sit in the family room for a while and flip through inane network programming featuring bizarre athletic trials and talent competitions and communal living experiments, if only to exchange convivial commentary on the bizarre goings on. They've taken to preparing Jiffy Pop on the stove to enjoy in front of the TV, which Ellen had liked as a child. The bright popping noises of the kernels bursting their sheaths above the flame, the aluminum foil balloon rising from the wire-handled pan, summons smiles to their faces even now. He listens to his daughter crack the leftover kernels with her molars, just like she did as a girl, and must restrain himself from admonishing her. Hertzog says goodnight to his daughter early and falls asleep shortly after hearing the bathroom door in the hall whine closed, the click of the lock, the creak of the medicine cabinet, the whoosh and groan of the plumbing once again within the walls.

So this is what it's like, Hertzog marvels as he shuts his eyes the fifth night of Ellen's stay. To live in a home with another person. He had forgotten.

A sound from downstairs, however, compels him to open his eyes, the telltale whine from the basement door. Had he been asleep? Yes, he realizes, his tongue thick in his mouth now. Next, he hears the groan of wood as Ellen descends those creaky stairs, a mild *thunk* against a wall as (Hertzog can only guess) she checks her balance down the dark basement stairwell. What could she possibly be doing down there in the middle of the night? He can't dismiss his suspicions that Ellen has been surreptitiously looking for something all the while that she's been back, rifling through various drawers and whatnot, these suspicions connected to the more serious matter of the burglary at his house. The question remains: had Ellen sent Jude or someone else from the farm to search for whatever it was she was searching for now? He doesn't hear anything anymore, only the crickets sawing away outside. He rolls onto his back, exhales volubly as he stares at the ceiling and considers his crappy options. Shall he walk down to the basement now to ask his daughter what she thinks she's doing, middle of the night, tell her that she's woken him up with all her milling about, which is true? No. The thought of it brings back too many bad memories, the countless times he enacted pretty much the same ritual during Ellen's teenage years, confronting her at the foot of the stairs after she missed curfew. *What do you think you're doing, young lady?* He won't play the overbearing scold at this late date. Besides, he rationalizes, she's been alone in the house plenty of daylight hours, lately, when she can snoop around all she likes. Why would she be looking for something now? Probably just laundry she was doing. It feels good to think these thoughts as he rolls over and shuts his eyes. But then he remembers what Claire said back at the hospital about the burglary. She wasn't able to dismiss out of hand the possibility that Ellen might have been involved. *The timing's interesting,* she had said. *I'll give you that.*

Magda arrives to tidy up the house the next morning as Ellen (who still spares him most chores on account of his injury) rinses and dries their oatmeal dishes in the sink. He hears Magda shuffling about in the mudroom—hanging up her sweater, sitting on the bench to change her shoes—and smiles coyly at his daughter, who mouths "Magda?" over the fizzy sink water. Hertzog nods over the open leaves of the newspaper and watches as his longtime housekeeper enters the room. He's tired and somewhat cranky, he realizes, from having been stirred from his sleep last night. He'll have to guard his behavior. Magda freezes upon noticing the new human presence in the kitchen. Ellen turns off the water and turns to face her. Hertzog doesn't rush to clarify Ellen's identity, and Ellen, curiously, doesn't say hello, either. They both wait the few moments until Magda realizes that it's Ellen, the musculature relaxing on her face, her palms covering her mouth as if to keep a morsel inside.

"Hello, Magda," Ellen finally says, throwing her dish towel over her shoulder and reaching to embrace her elder.

"It's you!" Magda cries, folding Ellen into her arms. Next to his daughter, Magda seems much shorter and rounder than Hertzog is used to thinking of her. Magda holds Ellen close for quite some time, which surprises Hertzog. It must have been something of a relief for her, he always figured, when Ellen finally fled the house, his daughter never sparing Magda her histrionics when there was something to wail over, addressing Magda sometimes with lazily concealed hostility for breaching the bulwark of her privacy (for which Hertzog admonished Ellen, and which sometimes inspired another round of histrionics). Plus, Ellen's room was ever and always a pig-sty for Magda to negotiate. Hertzog has continued to pay her an exorbitant fee for her dwindling services these past years partly to compensate for the heavy duty of her earlier days with their household. But here's Magda now, all worked up over seeing Ellen again at home, lifting a tissue to her eyes that she seems to have brandished from thin air. He supposes that Ellen was a constant in Magda's life for quite some time, that Magda was present, or at least at the periphery, during his daughter's most formative events. She was one of the few people to watch his daughter's life unfold over time. This meant something.

Ellen offers Magda coffee, which pleases Hertzog, to see Ellen play the host, concerned over someone else's desires. But Magda doesn't drink coffee. She drinks tea, Earl Gray, specifically, as Hertzog announces. Magda, for her part, seems too flummoxed by Ellen's presence to disclose or even contemplate her preferences. So Hertzog invites Magda to take a seat while he tells Ellen where she might find the tea bags and the kettle.

"What happened, David, to your arm?" Magda finally inquires, having settled into her seat at the maple table. He ignores the question and Magda's too distracted by Ellen's presence to press.

They sit with her as she blows the steam over her tea mug and lobs various inquiries toward Ellen, whereupon Hertzog learns—despite Ellen's various deflections—that there was a man in the picture, someone other than Jude, up until a year or so ago. He was a programming director for a nonprofit involving animal welfare, apparently. His name was Travis. "Life happened," Ellen cryptically explains, when Magda asks what happened to the fellow. Hertzog wonders whether Magda might press for more details, but she decides to sip her tea, instead. *Life happened.*

Hertzog and his daughter take a short walk to the town green to get out of Magda's hair. Only a few vacationers loiter on the thin lawn now so early in the day. One father tosses a football to his two young sons. A young Indian couple sips coffee from Mainely Coffee paper cups on one of the benches while studying a map. Hertzog and his daughter wordlessly make their way to the bench seating beneath the empty gazebo, where the volunteer band plays pop standards Wednesday and Saturday evenings this time of year. Something is on Ellen's mind—he can tell by her sigh as she takes her seat.

"You know it's not like I planned on never calling or visiting, or letting you know what I was up to."

Magda's inquiries—ones Ellen had dodged—have prompted this disclosure, he somehow knows. Her interrogative presence seems to linger fruitfully in the atmosphere.

"So, what happened, then?" Hertzog feels his flesh rise beneath his cast as he awaits his daughter's response. He hears the horse chestnut foliage sigh upon a gust of wind, the falsetto complaint of one of the boys, the whine of truck hydraulics on Main.

"I don't know, Father. I just needed to get away, and so I got away, and then I started living my own life and I was going to call, but then it was just easier not to. And the next week, the next month, whatever, it was even easier than before, and so it was sort of a gradual thing, I guess is what I'm saying, until…" She sups the air through her nostrils audibly, as if searching the molecules for her next word.

"Until?"

"Until a few years after I left, I thought, Wow, I'm one of those kids estranged from her family, what was left of it anyway. You!" He doesn't like the way she says *You!* Something accusatory in it, he's pretty certain. He feels an irascible mood gaining traction.

"Well, you could have reached out at that point. You knew where to find me."

She huffs out her nostrils and folds her arms above her flat stomach, displeased with his admonishment, as he might have anticipated. He notices Barbara Miller, president of the botanical society and Tim's wife, waist deep in the middle of the flower bed, dead-heading the black-eyed Susans beneath her broad-billed visor.

"Yeah, Father, I guess," Ellen says. She crosses her ankles before her on the wooden deck, then crosses them the other way. "But you could have tried harder to find me too. It's not like it would have been so tough. But you never did."

"I suppose you're right about that."

"I sent you cards once in a while. They had postmarks, Father."

"Yes. I know."

Hertzog's not sure what else to say, realizes that anything he might say to further explain himself will likely come out wrong. He's not used to being put on the defensive like this. Ellen seems to resent his terse responses.

"It's like you get off on it, Father."

"What? What is it I get off on, Ellen?"

"Being on the outs with everyone and everything, as if the whole world and all the crummy people in it are just too much for you to bear. It started with Mom and me at home. You asked me before what it was like growing up with you. Well, you were always, I don't know, sort of lingering on the sidelines, maybe because you were the man or whatever. But still. You used it to your advantage. It got you out of stuff, leaving me for Mom to deal with most of the time. About your work, too, you were always complaining about the bratty students or some new chair or dean. Everyone but you was a sellout to the rich tradition of literature or academia or whatever."

He feels the blood rise to his face, concentrates on his breathing to control his growing anger. "It seems like you've given this a lot of thought."

"So it was probably the same with me, after," Ellen continues. "It was part of your whole thing to be on the outs with me. Having a grown daughter you talked to on the phone, emailed with, maybe visited once in a while didn't fit in with how you saw yourself in the world."

Now she's gone and done it, raised his hackles. *She* was the one who left, does he need to remind her? He focuses his eyes on Barbara, who seems to have moved on to the spirea shrubs. A hopeless attempt to keep his cool. He studies the orange-handled pruners working beneath her canvas gloves as he takes deep breaths, yet feels his eyes quivering in their sockets as he thinks again on his daughter's words. He should keep his big fat mouth closed, he knows enough to know, but since when was he ever capable of saying or doing the right thing in his daughter's presence?

"As long as we're getting down to brass tacks here, Ellen, do you really mean to sit here and pretend that you and Jude didn't have anything to do with the break-in at the house when you stopped by last time, when you lured me outside to take a stroll? I mean, honestly, since when did you ever enjoy hiking with me, or doing anything with me?" For some reason, he can't just let this go.

Ellen's eyes widen, he notices, her mouth draws open, the moment before she speaks.

"Oh my god, you're serious." Her tone conveys bewilderment, mostly, which gives way the next breath to something closer to his own angry temperature. "Jude told me you said something whacko like that after you lost your shit at the farm. I didn't believe him. But you actually said that. You actually *think* that!"

It's not quite a question, so he doesn't answer, knowing that anything he says at this point will only further inflame matters. Plus, he doesn't want to lie. He doesn't look Ellen straight in the face for fear of what he might see. He can somehow tell that she's not looking at him anymore, either. They both stare out at the lawn to summon their next thoughts. He sees the football's spiral rainbow across the green, disappear above the gazebo's roof for a moment before reappearing on its descent. He sees the Indian couple rise from the bench, the man folding the map and sliding it into his hip pocket, the woman gathering up their empty coffee cups and napkins and whatnot to discard. He sees Barbara fucking around still with those tight clusters of tiny pink flowers on the spirea shrubs. The pedestrian traffic seems to have picked up on Main, everyone off to enjoy what this halcyon summer day in Downeast Maine might bring.

"I'm outta here," Ellen finally says, slapping her hands down on her jeaned thighs as if to propel her from her seat. And just like that she's gone, striding off in the general direction of Main, probably to call Jude or someone else at the farm to pick her up, borrowing some tourist's cell phone for all Hertzog knows. He ought to get up and chase after his daughter before she escapes his sight, apologize for his rash accusation. Yet he doesn't rise to give chase or even call out to her. He lets her leave. He's good at that. It's an art, truly, his art, as she pretty much told him.

25

March 14th, 1842
The sad memory of departed friends is soon incrusted over with sublime & pleasing thoughts—as their monuments are overgrown with moss. Nature doth thus kindly heal every wound… By the mediation of a thousand little mosses and fungi, the most unsightly objects become radiant of beauty.

"I have come to retrieve my clothes," H. tells Lidian in the foyer of the great house the morn following John's death. Wednesday, he thinks. "I do not know when I shall return."

"Of course." She clears passage to the hall, her fingers interlocked before her. He advances down the dim corridor past the great man's study to his quarters, leaving Lidian in his wake. The coolness of his approach takes her aback, he realizes. A curious adamantine calm has descended upon H. in the hours since John's last breath.

He stuffs his few woolen items into the same bag he brought with him on that happier spring day many months ago. The children are nowhere to be seen or heard. Strange for Waldo, especially, not to assail him with his attentions. One of the Irish girls, Annabelle perhaps, must tend to the children now, having received her instructions. There has been a death in H.'s home. Should he return, he is not to be disturbed by the childrens' falsetto notes or deviltry of any ilk.

H. hears Mr. E.'s footfalls against the pine floor-planks as he gathers his last items from the small dresser. "A terrible sadness for us all, the death of dear John." The words launched at the threshold linger in the cold interior air. No one, of course, has started a fire in H.'s room. "Lidian and I, the both of us…" The great man's voice falters as he seeks additional words of consolation. "Bereavement fills our hearts."

H., troubling the threads of woolen socks with his thumbs, cannot quite face his mentor, but nods to acknowledge his thoughtful sentiments. Or he thinks that he nods. He cannot be sure that the muscles in his neck perform the actual movements. He does not care to speak at length, or at all. But Mr. E. presses on.

"His final moments? How did they pass? Was his soul at peace?"

Shall H. tell the master of John's terrific spasms, his terror as he struggled for breath, the final name on his lips—*Ellen*—the steady trickle of Lethe H. administered to blot all sense and hasten his brother's journey?

"He was perfectly calm," H. hears himself say, "even pleasant while reason lasted, and gleams of the same serenity and playfulness shone through his delirium to the last."

Young Waldo manages to escape the clutches of the Irish girl, distracted by the babe in her arms, before H. clears the grounds of the great white house. H. hears the chuff of the front door opening just as he bends left past the front gate toward Lexington. He somehow knows it's Waldo before he turns to face the child. He expects the boy to bound toward him and assail him with his attentions. Yet something about H.'s person must repel the advance, for the boy remains on the stoop, lifts his small palm to the sky to say farewell without the words and perhaps to convey a hundred other profound sentiments. H. lifts his palm toward Waldo, in kind. Farewell, dear boy.

The adamantine calm courses through H.'s blood straight through the Sunday funeral at the First Parish Church. He sits in strange repose in the front pew, Helen and Sophia either side of him, sobbing. H. would summon manful tears were he able, yet he cannot feel to feel. He finds it difficult to mind Reverend Frost's eulogy, though isolated snatches of description pierce whatever defenses he has thrown up. It occurs to H. that the good reverend describes a man very much like him, yet untainted by vain ambition, more pure and beloved. Poor John, cut down in his prime, the gentlest of souls, lover of all things good. The widow Lockhart regales them with a story of his brother's good-humored dispatch of the pesky squirrels that had infiltrated her attic through working a seam in the soffit beneath the roof, proper. His neighbors tell H. how highly John esteemed him, how his elder brother admired his facility with languages, his deep knowledge of natural philosophy, his skillfulness vis à vis carpentry and the mechanical arts. A blessing he bestowed on the family, serving as John's constant nurse during his final hours. If the town only knew the full truth, that his brotherly affection for John had cooled over their romantic rivalry, that they hadn't spoken as intimates for months prior to John's lethal infection, that he had wished John dead on more than one occasion so that he might pursue unfettered the object of their mutual adoration, and that he had scurried to Mr. E.'s family hearth mostly to escape his elder brother.

And more.

The realization only pricks him over their silent supper days after the funeral, the seventh pudding proffered to them by the good ladies of his mother's Antislavery Society. He had hastened his brother's demise with a tincture of opium not out of mercy, perhaps, but so he would not have to suffer the excoriation conveyed in John's utterance of that name. Ellen. For H. knew that John would speak her name as he met the final crisis. *Ellenelllenellenellenellen.* He collapses at the dining room table, tipping from the upholstered chair onto the Oriental rug, a cacophony of tumbled glass and cutlery punctuating his descent.

"Brother!" Helen kneels at his side, places her cold palm on his forehead. "He's burning with fever!" Her wide-set eyes seem to study him each on their own accord, after the fashion of certain reptiles. Pain shoots down his right arm. He grips the biceps with his left hand. The muscles in his abdomen contract beneath his elbow. His eyes roll to flash the veined sclera.

H. rides his father's shoulder to his narrow bed, the immediate crisis having abated. A stupor must command him, however, because a different quality of light colors the appointments of his batchelor quarters once his senses return. Father's flute on the cabinet-top, the poker beside the fire's grate, the volume by Chaucer on the nightstand, all yellowed by candle-light. The room smells of whale-oil from the lamps and wood-char from the oak-carcasses smoldering behind the grate.

"He returns to us," Helen says, just as stiffness seizes his jaw. The lower mandible juts upward of its own accord, gnashing his already tender teeth, forcing his eyes lidward, his bloody sclera exposed.

"Could John's affliction have been communicated somehow?" his father asks, holding the knobs of his son's shoulders.

"Impossible!" his mother cries. Then, "Impossible," once more to convince herself. Spasms seize H.'s stomach once again beneath his bed-shirt.

"Son?" His father issues this cryptic interrogative. His father's palms feel so small at his shoulders.

Dr. Bartlett arrives on Sophia's heels, the mousy tendrils of her hair having mostly escaped the top-bun she favors. The doctor smells of woodsmoke and bourbon, his face lashed by creases of concern.

He ushers the ladies from the room, employs H.'s father to help strip the patient of his clothes. H. glances down at his extremities, his navel and sex. His latest spasm having passed, his body seems utterly strange to him now, benumbed, the spindly muscles, pallid flesh and hirsute patches so wanting compared to certain primates. The doctor conducts a most thorough examination of H.'s person, using a flat switch of hickory to manipulate the scrotum and penis, and to encourage the lifting of one knee, then the other.

"Not a single laceration or puncture wound, and nary a creature—leech, ant, wasp, or spider—has assailed his flesh." He speaks to H.'s father rather than to H. himself. "Favorable news, indeed."

"But his symptoms. Spasms the same as poor John, rest his soul. Might he have contracted the disease through shared breath or simple touch? Or through contact with his brother's waste?"

Bartlett does not answer H.'s father straight away. Instead, he lifts the sheets over H.'s private business, bends to his knees and leans an ear against H.'s bare chest to perform his auscultation. H. and his father know to keep quiet during the procedure. The aroma of talcum from the doctor's battered nest of hair rises above the woodsmoke and bourbon-smells. "Breathe normally," he commands, issues a *mm-hmm,* then shifts his ear to a separate spot, scratching H.'s chest with his whiskers, issues another *mm-hmm.*

"The annals of medicine support no such theory of transmission," Bartlett finally avers, standing now. "His heart is strong. Whatever fever he might have suffered has broken." The doctor shifts his eyes toward H., the single hirsute brow rising. "You tended to your dear brother till the frightful end, did you not? That's the town scuttlebutt." H. affirms the veracity of the rumor.

"Rest now, my good man," the doctor advises, placing a hand on his arm. "A word with you outside," he says to his father in a stronger voice.

H. does not know what confidences Bartlett shares with his father. His father does not tell him once he returns to the room and H. does not ask.

"You must listen to Dr. Bartlett and rest, son," is all that his father says.

He sleeps fitfully through the night, dimly aware of candles bobbing across the room, someone stoking the fire-stove, dear Helen palming his forehead, her own labored breath betraying the family disease. Time tastes strange. His loved ones tend to him the best that they can, their faces ashen from this season of grief. Father remains more stoical as he forces warmed cider down H.'s throat and assists him with the bedpan. He hides something behind his visage, whatever grim prognosis Dr. Bartlett shared with him, likely. Mother says little to him, stands still during his father's and sisters' frenetic attentions, a sun to their planets in strange orbit. Days pass. The attentions of his father and sisters remain dutiful, though ever more silent and somber. They spoon him broths of beef and fowl, smear biscuits and breads with oleaginous fats to keep him from wasting away.

"You must cease carrying on so this instant, son!" his mother finally commands, several days—weeks?—into his infirmity. "It's self-indulgent and vainglorious, this aping of your poor brother's painful demise. A sacrilege to boot. To mock God's will so, forcing a fate not yours to claim. Buck up, son. Buck up now!'"

Her words pierce him.

"I'll try, Mother." He inches his back up against the headboard. And then, "I have always tried, if not in the manner that you would have me try."

"Do try. *Today* try. Rouse yourself from bed. Strengthen thyself, as God spaketh to Moses. There is so much sickness and suffering in this world. It won't do to court suffering, unbidden. It simply won't do!"

The expansiveness of her words and the tenor through which she speaks them suggests that she alludes to tragedies beyond dear John's passing—the scourge of slavery, the eradication of the Seminoles at home and the Tasmanian aborigines abroad, poverty and pestilence in their overstuffed cities, perhaps.

H. rises and dresses as soon as his mother takes her leave. He advances down the hall in deliberate steps, the bipedal workings of his legs newly strange. Prudence, standing beside his mother in the kitchen, wishes him good morning through glassed eyes. H. squints his eyes against the outdoors, the daybright filtered through a screen of cloud. He stands beneath the poplar in the grey cold for several seconds, unsure of what to do with his body and breath. He knows that it is cold but does not feel the cold. He gazes up at John's bluebird box. His eyes linger there, as if he might find his brother inside the vacant dwelling. Where else might he look for him? In moments his father, breathing smoke, brings him his great coat, wraps it around his shoulders not bothering with the sleeves, then tells him the news of Concord's latest tragedy that occurred hard upon John's passing, the separate tragedy that likely inspired his mother's chastisement, which has nothing to do with slavery or war or the rampant disease in their overstuffed cities.

"It's young Waldo," his father says. "We have been trying to decide when to tell you. And how. The poor lad passed eight days ago now. Scarlet fever. Snatched him quick."

The word-sounds travel slow and clear through the cold vapors between speaker and hearer. Yet H. cannot trust that his mind has conducted the proper translation, benumbed as he feels upon hearing the words.

"Did you hear what I said, son? Do you understand?" His father also doubts his senses.

"Yes, Father. How long have I been abed?"

"A month."

He returns to bed, shedding the great-coat, hides his eyes beneath the nest of his elbows. The span of a lifetime his heart has surely endured—how great a portion of human feeling can one organ filter? H. cannot be sure what portion of the paralytic sadness he now feels is for young Waldo. Or the extent to which Waldo's passing only heaps agony upon his original heartbreak (*dear brother!*). You attend, perhaps, only one funeral in your life.

H.'s vigor slowly returns. He cannot bring himself to write, or even to read the volume of Chaucer that lay on his nightstand. But he manages longer and longer daily walks with one of his sisters, or with both of them, or by himself. He does not feel wholly—what is the word?—*involved* in the world about him. Yet birdsong returns slowly to his ears. He traces the circuitry of squirrels through the bare branches. He finally appraises himself well enough to call upon Mr. E. and Lidian in their grief.

"How our circumstances have merged in the span of time between your visits," Lidian greets him at the door. H. detects the opprobrium in her observation and cannot fault her. How stingily he had received her condolences weeks ago—in Lidian's own time of need, how absent.

"Yes."

"My husband has been hoping you would be well enough to call upon us soon. And here you are." *My husband.* He cannot remember

Lidian ever uttering the phrase to him. She tells H. that he will find Mr. E. wandering the grounds. He has spent much of his time outdoors since Waldo's funeral.

H. retreats to seek out the sage rather than apologize for his cold behavior during his last visit, or for having missed Waldo's funeral, or for the manifold other ways in which he has surely failed dearest Lidian.

He locates the great man straight away in the orchard, troubling with his bare hand the scarred bark where they grafted a cherry scion just months ago to plum stock.

"Shall we walk?" Mr. E. suggests before H. can offer his condolences. H. follows his elder along the downslope of his orchard between the skeletons of fruit trees. They speak no words for several minutes, concentrating on their breath as they amble through the frozen woods past Mill Brook. H.'s stamina has increased in recent days thanks to his daily saunterings, yet he struggles, nonetheless, to match the great man's pace. Thankfully, Mr. E. halts at the clearing in Hubbard's shady swamp, forcing H. to stop short. His mentor directs his gaze up at the treeline of mixed evergreens and naked oaks as if he has seen something, or perhaps he only pauses to allow his protégé to catch his breath. H.'s family, and no doubt Dr. Bartlett, has reported to the town some version of their second son's complicated convalescence.

"I cannot imagine the pain you must feel upon losing dear Waldo," H. finally utters the words. Why hadn't he expressed these sentiments outright to Lidian?

"No," the great man says, breathing steam. He turns toward H. before continuing. His deep-set eyes below his formidable brow unnerve him. H. cannot hold the piercing gaze. "I marvel most at my inhuman resilience." H. lifts his eyes now to watch his companion's mouth form the words. "My firstborn son and namesake passes and I carry on, somehow. The apparatus of my breath and digestive processes continue apace. My mind summons words and phrases to exchange with my neighbors. Like now. With you." H. detects a modicum of shame in Mr. E.'s admission, which may be why he has waited until now, far from the family hearth, to express the sentiments. A flock of small birds flit across the clearing and disappear into the spruce foliage. H. glimpses the rusty flanks. He hears the rasp and wheeze of their calls. "These tits flit across my field of view and I see them," the sage continues, "and I hear them, and I think how spectacular to share a world with these brave birds."

"Yes," H. says. "A blessing that you can still see the birds and hear the birds and think the world good."

"While Waldo moulders in the ground?"

"You ought not to chastise yourself. The family relies upon your strength."

H. can tell even before he speaks that Mr. E. remains unconvinced.

"Try as I might, I cannot bring Waldo's death close to me. Or close enough. My strange fortitude only broadens the chasm between Lidian and me."

H. knows not what to say. Mr. E., too, remains silent for several moments. Only the throats of the titmouses remain unvalved as they continue to rasp and wheeze at one another, conducting their vital life business.

"But you suffer no want of human feeling, do you, friend?" the great man finally says.

"Sir?"

"Human kindness. It comes to you more readily."

The master is the first soul in all of creation to suggest such a thing.

"I'm afraid that people in the main would disagree. Most townspeople, as you know, even my students when John and I directed the Academy, find me aloof, if not ill-humored."

"Yes, that is how people in the main see you. But not your friends. Channing. Hoar. Richard. The town misconstrues your outward demeanor, as you may misconstrue your own behavior, I fear." He pauses, as if uncertain whether to complete the circuit of his thoughts, shifts his gaze from his protégé up toward the rasping, wheezing birds, invisible in the dense evergreen foliage. "I would speak frankly to you now," he finally says, still sparing H. his eyes.

"Of course."

"Your aloofness, your persnickety ways, betray not a lack of human feeling, but its overabundance. You maintain your impermeable exterior to shield yourself from the electric charge of emotion you feel only too readily before your fellows."

The master's words cut him to the quick. He no longer hears the birds.

"I can only imagine the contents of your proposal to that girl from Scituate, the elisions and circumlocutions. Did you manage one outright expression of your true ardor?"

It seems cruel of the master to recall the bitter episode. But he does not mean to be cruel, H. knows. Death having visited both their houses, time is too short for standing on ceremony before a friend. As H. himself has thought and written. *You must plant your feet firmly before your friend.* And the great man is not finished. He summons H.'s eyes with his own now.

"You cannot deny your Giant. Refuse him and he will stomp with ever greater ferocity through your person. To wit, the outsize grief of yours for poor John that followed hard upon your strangest stoicism. What else was such an outpouring of emotion than the stomping of your Giant?"

H. does not know how to respond to Mr. E.'s wise words, or if any response is required. The sage must recognize the gravity of what he has communicated for he proceeds across the clearing into the scrim of woods toward Brister's spring and the pond, leaving H. to his thoughts. He follows after the great man. The words have unloosed something in him. He hears the purposeful chatter of the titmouses again in the torn canopy overhead as they pass beneath. He hears the chuff of a woodchopper's ax. Within moments, the distant bark of his fox rises above the fading birdsong and the ax. H. waits for his elder to comment upon the strange canine peals, but he does not seem to hear the creature. H. sups the spruced air, cold and clean in his lungs. He feels the pleasant burn of his quadriceps as he labors to keep pace. Taking the measure of his leather footfalls, he notes curious fungi bursting from the winter-dead earth. A healing crust of fungi and moss beautifies even the woodland corpses of squirrel, bird, and beaver, does it not? All of nature conspires against gloom, it occurs to him, if one only welcomes the poetical sense. H. fumbles in vain for his missing daybook in his great-coat pocket, the first time in weeks he has thought to record his sentiments.

He must no longer deny his Giant. He shall follow his genius loveward as guilelessly as the maple leaf that flutters downstream. Willow leaf, rather. He will follow his genius as the willow leaf flutters over the brook. His journal, per the master's admonition, shall be the record of his love. He feels ripe once more, supping winter's sweet breath as he trots toward the pond. Having lain fallow so long, it is seed time with him.

26

The house feels curiously vacant and silent now that Ellen is gone, though she had been home for only a week. Hertzog tries to return to his former routine, but fidgets through his solitary meals and nighttime hours. He scarcely knows what to do with himself outside his morning walks. He can't swim on account of his hand and misses the morning exercise. He remains hopelessly distracted in his study, pondering Ellen instead of pondering Thoreau, and silence, and friendship, and love.

He imagines various possibilities for why she has returned to their little postage stamp of Maine. There's something he doesn't yet know, something she's deliberately withheld. He's sure of it. He considers what he does know. A more physically trim Ellen. A boyfriend, Travis, who had been in the picture but now was not in the picture, because "life happened," as Ellen put it to Magda. A stint at various colleges, including George Mason University. A course of study she preferred not to disclose. Landscape architecture? Horticulture? Something in the culinary arts or hospitality services? He must laugh at the last ludicrous possibility. Hospitality! Ellen! He considers the specific university once more. George Mason. Wasn't that one of those DC-area institutions popular among government types? Had she majored in criminal justice? Was it completely insane to imagine that his daughter might be an FBI agent, that she was undercover working a case against the local ne'er-do-well, Jude Winslow, exploiting her former relationship with the scumbag? He was up to something fishy out there, as the local police seemed to know. Who knew what Jude had gotten himself mixed up in? Rockweed poaching, the most obvious guess. All those blue tarps. The fresh-harvested seaweed hanging like bedsheets to dry across the clotheslines hidden behind the barn. He sold the morsels as a health food item (sea vegetables). Seaweed was the ingredient he touted in all those cosmetic products and healthcare supplements. But maybe he was supplying the Asian fertilizer companies and food manufacturers too. It was a good stabilizer, he had read in Stacey's literature, an unlikely ingredient in products ranging from ice creams to pet food. Or maybe Hertzog, a naïf in matters of malfeasance, was thinking altogether too small. Perhaps the whole Cherryfield Farm operation was now a ruse for a money laundering scheme, connected somehow with purveyors of heroin and other opioids. It seemed suspicious that it was still a cash-only farm store. A separate thought dawns. Hertzog considers all the young international types cycling through Jude's operation, comely young girls mostly. Maybe there was a human sex trafficking angle that Ellen had been assigned to pursue.

Hertzog considers all of these possibilities just long enough to dismiss them, at least the law enforcement role that he has conjured for Ellen. Pure fantasy, this notion—his daughter the high-functioning law-enforcement savior come back home to cleanse their backwater of the contaminant that was Jude. Wouldn't that be nice? He must smile at his folly, yet recognizes the impulse to conjure this life for Ellen as consistent with what most parents do, project fantasies upon their infant babes to realize, or not. Ellen figured out as much at some point and resented it. In her mind, he and Rebecca had expected that she be perfect to compensate for their shortcomings. It wasn't fair, Ellen had claimed just a few days ago over his new serviceberry shrubs. If this wasn't entirely, or even mostly, true, it *was* true that they had projected certain fantasies upon her. They had imagined Ellen as a mannerly girl, who ate her vegetables, did her homework, pursued certain passions (athletic, artistic, intellectual), appreciated the piney woods, formed a few lasting friendships, dated a few nice and maybe not so nice local boys her age, negotiated the heteronormative sex business best she could, went off to college, pursued a career of some sort (economically and spiritually sustaining) and maybe settled down with a husband to start a family of her own. They had imagined a life for her, in short, other than the life that she had mostly imagined for herself. To be a parent, Hertzog felt, was to conjure such fantasy worlds for your child. Across that yawning gap between the fantasy world and the child might best be described as the world that we are.

Just a few days after Ellen's abrupt departure (she's back at Cherryfield Farm, he imagines), Stacey reminds him over the hedgeline that they leave tomorrow at nine sharp for their research trip—given the tide's schedule—and it would be great if Hertzog and Ellen could join them. He says that Ellen won't be able to make it, that she "had to leave," but that he'll be happy to go along for the ride.

"Oh, wow, great," she replies, glancing down to untangle the leash connected to her cat's collar. Her gold piercing at the cartilaginous portion of her ear winks against the sun as she lifts her hand to clear her hair from her eyes. She doesn't try too hard to conceal her surprise, which makes him smile. He likes this about Stacey, the total absence of guile or subterfuge in her dealings with him. He remembers the way she looped her elbow inside his elbow beneath the copse of low trees just inside the granite shoreline after she broached his complicated relationship with Ellen. She had felt the comradely urge to express her human affection for her neighbor going through a rough patch and so she reached out to loop elbows. Simple. Stacey was one of those unguarded souls—unlike Thoreau, unlike Hertzog, unlike Ellen too—who didn't hesitate to offer a friend the whole advantage of herself.

It feels strange to sit in the back seat of the Hinshaw's late-model Toyota Corolla en route to the marina, his knees upraised and cramped against the seatback, the leafed-out deciduous foliage lining Main lashing his face with shadows. It reminds him of something unpleasant that he can't quite put his finger on until he does, his recent ride to the hospital in the back seat of the police cruiser while under arrest for assaulting Jude.

"You have enough room back there?" Stacey inquires. He says yes, even though he could use a bit more legroom. She slides her seat up, in any case, thankfully. Taylor at the wheel emits an odor that outmuscles the iron-smells from the still-slick road (it rained last night) and the coffee-smell from a mug at the console—emblazoned with a caricature of Darwin, unless Hertzog is mistaken—something musty and canine from his curly hair and dark beard if not quite malodorous. It's clear from the dent at the back of his neighbor's thick shock of curls that he hasn't showered this morning, and why should he have showered? He's about to splash into the frothy Atlantic, anyway, to collect some sort of data in the rockweed zone. Something about his brown eyes reflected in the rear-view mirror captivate Hertzog; the quiet and soulful way the eyes study the road ahead betray a mind prone to deep thoughts, mostly unexpressed.

"Too bad Ellen had to leave," Stacey says, turning sort of sideways to face him in the back seat, lifting her knees up to her chin and resting her feet on the upholstery, a coltish pose that quickens Hertzog's heart, despite himself.

"Yes, it's too bad." He won't encourage Stacey or her husband to linger on the topic of Ellen. "So how long have the two of you been married?"

"Jeez, what's it been, Stace, almost three years?" Taylor asks, lifting his coffee mug from the center console, sloshing some of the liquid onto his beard and T-shirt. The car swerves a bit over the double-yellow line before he corrects the drift with the wheel. Stacey admonishes him for his driving and for neglecting to bring a proper travel mug, and for *always* neglecting to use a travel mug in the car.

"Don't think it was easy, David, attracting a catch like Stacey here," Taylor jokes to defuse the scolding. "All the prettiest coeds are into amphipods these days. Only a special soul like my Stacey still gets fired up over macroalgae."

"Oh hush," Stacey says, flicking his shoulder with the back of her knuckles.

So Taylor has a sense of humor, Hertzog gathers. He hadn't detected it during their few exchanges over the hedgeline. He hadn't detected much of a personality at all behind the thick beard, realizing that Taylor had probably gleaned the same impressions about his reserved older neighbor.

They reach the woolly outskirts of town and Hertzog expects Taylor to pick up the pace. But he drives at the same slow speed, sipping his coffee now and again, in deference perhaps to the still-slick asphalt or to Stacey's scolding. Gazing out at the spruce and fir-lined road, Hertzog asks Taylor to tell him a bit more about his research.

"Uh-oh, here goes," Stacey says, knowing that her husband requires only the slightest encouragement to hold forth for hours on the subject of rockweed. She taps a dial to turn off the radio, which Hertzog hadn't realized was on until she had cut the sound.

"There's real urgency to the work now, especially given the growth of the local seaweed industry. Wasn't much of a problem until ten years ago or so, that's when Acadian Seaplants started in on rockweed and other seaweeds at an industrial scale, exporting most of the tonnage to Asia." Taylor takes several pulls of his coffee once again, the liquid frisking noisily through the baleen of his beard. "The Fukushima disaster and concerns over irradiated Japanese and Chinese seaweeds upped the demand for American seaweeds. Before that, the harvest hereabouts was just a niche thing, local long-hairs out in skiffs, scrabbling up on the rocks low-tide with their knives, filling up a few ash baskets to sell as a health food or as an organic fertilizer for local farmers."

"That doesn't seem so bad."

"No, it wasn't. But then Acadian Seaplants comes down from Canada—you know they're a Canadian outfit, right?"

Hertzog says that he didn't know just as some sort of winged insect erupts against the windshield, spewing sugary juices it had likely extracted moments ago from one of the forest maples. He wonders whether this is one of those invasive pests rusting broad swaths of red spruce, lately, whether Taylor will turn on the wipers and washer fluid to clear the mess, but Taylor is too preoccupied with his words. He decries the new harvesting boats outfitted with mechanical cutting heads and suction hoses at the bow, the lack of statewide regulations on the harvest, or any sort of management plan, and the mixed motives of the Seaweed Council. Taylor must finally recognize the bug's burst carcass in his line of sight, because he turns on the wipers, smearing the creature across the glass until several spurts of washer fluid mostly erase the stain.

"That's why the Rockweed Coalition started up," Stacey chimes in, "to advocate on behalf of the ecosystem, itself, while we conduct our studies to figure out harvesting impacts best we can and as fast as we can."

"So how much data do you still need? And what sort of data are you collecting?"

Ellen used to complain about this—Rebecca too—Hertzog's vaguely confrontational interrogative mode, as if he were some sort of federal prosecutor. But Taylor seems to appreciate Hertzog's interest.

"Lots," Taylor says. "And more types of data than Stacey and I can gather on our own. There haven't been so many phycologists like us studying harvesting impacts, or studying rockweed at all. At this point we hardly know dick is the truth of the matter."

"What we're studying now in the research grid we've set up," Stacey says, "is sort of just the first and most obvious place to start, the rate of regrowth of ascophyllum fronds upon cutting at various distances from the holdfasts."

There's something winning about the Hinshaw's repartee. Hertzog and Rebecca had once exchanged such easeful banter, finishing each other's sentences and all that, but then the bottom dropped out once they were a family of three. Or maybe all this blaming Ellen for the widening gulf between Rebecca and him was wrong. Fissures, if he were to be honest, had emerged between Hertzog and Rebecca even before their daughter's arrival. Then there was Rebecca's affair with Will Roberson. Hertzog liked to believe he didn't blame his wife so much given their difficulties at the time. But this wasn't quite the same thing as forgiving her. He had never truly forgiven her, he realizes. Hertzog wonders, but cannot know, whether he might have done so if they had the time, and whether Rebecca might have forgiven him for his emotional withholdings, his aloofness, during their difficulties, whether they might have retrieved the easeful camaraderie that Taylor and Stacey so clearly enjoy. But he can never truly know whether their marriage would have survived. This not knowing, it only now occurs to him, is what aches him so profoundly still, the sore tooth he can't resist troubling with his tongue, aches him as much as Rebecca's breathtaking not-hereness, itself, or maybe this is only the shape he gives to the hurt of her absence.

They soon reach the marina below the Dry Dock Café. Hertzog, stepping outside the car, glances up at the restaurant on its mild promontory and notices the few souls inside the broad windows enjoying their breakfasts, a waitress milling between the tables. Too far off to tell if it's that young woman with the Baltic accent, Katarina, who recently served him. He can't remember the last time he was down here at the water's edge rather than up there at the café. He can't remember the last time he had been on a boat, despite his proximity to the sea. He had never been prone to seasickness and hopes he won't embarrass himself today. The syrupy water seems lake calm, thankfully. Stacey and Taylor carry opposite ends of a cooler toward the dock, canvas backpacks hanging off each of their shoulders as well. He follows them, lifting his nose to take in the pleasant saline odors and survey the wide stretch of ocean beyond the protected harbor, small coniferous islands porcupining here and there, the meager final claims of the terrestrial realm. No cruise ship moored out in the channel today, thankfully, ferrying its multitudes ashore, the newlyweds and nearly-deads.

Although quiet now at mid-morning, it's typically a bustling marina, floating docks extending like branches from the raised concrete seawall to accommodate upwards of a hundred vessels, working-boats and pleasure-boats alike, plus mooring buoys just off the docks. The slips and mooring buoys seem about half-occupied by lobster boats and fewer recreational vessels—mostly sailboats at the buoys—bobbing against a mild wake. Seabirds make themselves comfortable on ship gunwales, masts, and dock lights here and there. Hertzog wonders whether fewer lobsterman than normal are out today setting and retrieving their pots given the difficulties with the soft-shells this season. One lobsterman in plain clothes stands on his aft-deck, repairing one of his pots by the look of things, an unlit cigarette dangling from between his lips.

Hertzog notices three young people in various elastic poses standing on the deck stretching their limbs upon their approach, student research assistants. Mesh bags that must contain their dive or snorkeling gear lay in clumps at their feet. He recognizes the young lady wearing dirty blond dreadlocks tamed by a blue bandana. She had been one of the students on Stacey's field trip, the one who made the joke about her boyfriend being a tubed weed, or something like that. The other two, a goateed young man and a petite young woman shrouded in plaid layers, he does not recognize. He measures up the vessel beside the students before reaching them. It's not a skiff, strictly speaking, but a large Boston Whaler center console with a T-top, likely donated by some benefactor as a tax write-off, the hull repainted in Emmenthaler blue and decorated with the college seal in white. LUX MENTIS SCIENTIA, he reads their Latin motto printed in a smile beneath a likeness of the sun. Knowledge is the Light of the Mind.

Stacey introduces him to their research assistants on deck while Taylor boards the vessel and starts running through his pre-launch checks at the console. Madeline, the name of the dreadlocked girl, though he can call her Maddy, she says. The small girl wrapped in plaid reminds him of Dorothy Hamill, sporting that pixie haircut that doesn't seem to be the current fashion. Good for her, he thinks. Her name is Kelsey. The fellow, Ross, claims to remember him from the field trip a few weeks ago. Then, in the next breath: "Dude, what happened to your arm?"

"You should see what the other guy looks like," Stacey says, not realizing the significance of her remark. He had finally told her it was only an accident and she let it go at that. Hertzog tries to wear an expression of mildly abashed amusement at her joke, the expression he would more naturally wear had he not actually broken his hand and wrist over Jude's thick skull.

"Permission to come aboard, captain?" Stacey asks Taylor and he tells them yes. Maddy and Kelsey load the cooler onto the deck as they hop aboard. They head toward the hatch at the bow and return with life jackets for everyone. Ross has remained on the dock, where he holds a black line he must have unfastened from the dock-cleat. It's clear from their silent choreography that the three students have been out on the research vessel before, probably several times. He watches as Kelsey dons her own life jacket, then follows suit, wraps it around his shoulders and clips it at the front. Compared to the bright orange Mae Wests that Hertzog associates with the term life jacket, this blue number seems suspiciously thin. Taylor, firing up the twin outboards, must notice his discomfiture, because he says, "The new PFDs automatically inflate once they hit the water. Else you can pull the cord. Nice, aren't they?" The odor of gasoline exhaust from the outboards displaces the more pleasant, if slightly fetid, marine aromas, while they sit there with the engine idling.

Hertzog tells him yes, that it's very comfortable.

"I don't think we'll be losing you over the side today, anyway," Stacey says. "I wouldn't have made you come if it was sporty out here."

Funny the way she puts this, that she feels she has pressured him to come. Taylor raises his nose up at Ross on the dock, a gesture that Ross must understand, because he throws the black rope onto the boat deck and hops after it on board. Taylor presses some sort of switch at the throttle that prompts the sound of hydraulics. "Just trimming the engines," he explains, nudging the throttles forward at the base of the levers. The marine smells regain primacy once Taylor starts motoring through the no-wake zone. It feels colder too as they pass the sailboats moored to their buoys, the water licking the bow. He's glad he wore jeans and a few layers, if he's not quite as wrapped up as Kelsey.

"Maybe stand on that side, David. It'll help distribute our weight more evenly."

Hertzog obeys and stands just beside the helm at the starboard side. Stacey stands opposite her husband on the port side, gripping for ballast the stainless scaffolding of the T-top. Taylor is taller than he realized, and bigger. He can smell his malty breath riding beneath the brine and fish-smells of the bay. The two female students sit at the bow, lifting shut eyes to the cold sun. Ross sits on the padded bench seat in front of the console facing the girls at the front. Hertzog takes deep draughts of air through his nostrils as they near the mouth of the protected bay, the cleaner cold salt of the open gulf outmuscling the warmer inshore currents trailing the aromas of dead and undead marine life. Taylor warns them all to hold on and punches the throttle to bring the vessel on plane, leaving the gulls in their wake, the bow settling flat against the sea. After reaching a certain depth (Hertzog notices Taylor scanning the Lowrance sonar on the console), he turns the wheel sharply to swing the boat northward. They follow the rough line of the coast, the spruce terraces pinked with granite between the trees, Taylor zig-zagging time to time to avoid the lobster trap buoys.

They motor up the jagged coastline for several minutes between a few spruced and unspruced granite islands, long enough for Hertzog to wonder how far away the research sector is located. But he doesn't ask, partly because he doesn't want to shout over the four-strokes, partly because it hardly matters, and partly because it feels impossibly good standing on the seaward side of the console with the boat on plane, checking his balance now and again, gripping the stainless scaffolding of the T-top with his good hand as Taylor negotiates the buoys, the cold ocean wind batting back the insignificant strands of his hair against his scalp, Hertzog's flesh rising at the mild chill beneath his layers. He sniffs at the salt air, sweetened some by the spruce. He savors the pleasant hum of the outboards, discouraging conversation and leaving him to his thoughts. He feels somehow fully inside his own body, alert and alive, yet simultaneously fully *involved* in the physical world all about. He lifts a finger on his good hand to wipe away the tear summoned by the fierce wind. Whitebait flashes time to time above the green surface in twos and threes, spooked maybe by the bow slicing through the dark water. He wonders what else lurks down there beneath the whitebait, organisms great and small carrying on their life business upon the pulse of the tides.

Before long, Taylor eases up on the throttle, causing the bow to dip then rise again as the boat finds its slower speed, and prompting the girls to sit up and gaze about. The bow sheds a greater expanse of white foam either side of the hull as it plows toward the research zone—Hertzog can see the special buoys now—and fragrant fuel exhaust washes over them once more.

"We've had to shoo away rockweed poachers from the research zone," Taylor tells him over the sputtering engines, just quiet enough at their slower speed to allow conversation.

"Some harvesters attach ropes to the rakes," Stacey says from the other side of the console, "then tie them to stern cleats and drag them through rockweed patches, ripping the seaweeds clear off their holdfasts."

"It's the lazy way to do it," Taylor adds. "As destructive to the intertidal ecology as bottom trawlers are to the sea floor."

Hertzog can't help but wonder if this is what Jude does. It's the sort of thing Jude would do, he thinks. The lazy thing. The girls at Cherryfield cleaning the seaweed had even mentioned the holdfasts they sometimes had to cull. To be fair, though, it didn't exactly seem like an industrial-scale operation Jude had going on, vis à vis seaweed, whatever lay moldering beneath those blue tarps. He wasn't Acadian Seaplants. Jude didn't even seem to be on the Hinshaw's radar, and surely they knew about the farm and its seaweed products. They likely saw him as one of those local long-hairs out in his skiff, filling up a few ash baskets at a time. This might be all that Jude was. The prospect should come as a relief to Hertzog, yet it only unsettles him further. It's done something for him, he realizes, projecting all of his animus onto Jude. Without Jude to blame for the matter of Ellen, where would he be?

They idle slowly inside the buoys until Taylor gives the okay—the Lowrance reads six feet, Hertzog notices—which prompts Maddy to lower the anchor to the sea floor from its pulpit at the bow. She feeds the chain, then the rope, through her fists rather than let it damage the live bottom. She's not the type to let Ross or anyone else do all the physical stuff, Hertzog gathers.

"We're holding, professor," she calls back to Taylor, tugs at the taut anchor-line over the bow to make sure.

Taylor cuts the engine and everyone except for Stacey and Hertzog begins preparing for their immersion, shedding their clothes to reveal swimsuits underneath, zipping themselves and one another into wetsuits retrieved from their mesh bags. It seems especially quiet, the outboards powered down, amplifying what little sound remains—the green water licking the bow, the piercing cries of an osprey working the shallows, the deck of the boat groaning beneath the disrobing and robing exercises of Taylor and his students.

"Should see our winter suits," Stacey says, noticing Hertzog noticing the wetsuits. She pulls a laptop out of her backpack. "Farmer Johns the winter suits are called. Quite a fashion statement. Water's in the sixties now so we hardly need wetsuits at all."

She turns on the laptop and walks him through his role for the day. She, or maybe Taylor, has prepared grids designating eight, twelve, sixteen, and twenty-inch zones, the length of the original cuts from the holdfasts. She shows him how to open and close each document, how to click the cursor on each square on the individual zones to enter the various growth measurements. All he has to do is enter the data. They'll tell him the zone they're reporting on, the grid identification number, and the numbers to the quarter-inch to enter on its square. After the brief tutorial, she reaches for her own gear, begins pulling on her wetsuit.

Hertzog spends the balance of the morning alone on the vessel looking after Stacey and the team as they flop about the rockweed patches in their wetsuits, wearing masks, snorkels, and short flippers too. Stacey buddies up with the girls while Ross has been assigned to Taylor. They carry buoyant, bright orange rubber ropes, jury-rigged as measuring devices. When their wetsuited backs rise to the surface, they look slick and black as seals. A pair of terns work the water's surface with black-tipped bills, popping in and out of Hertzog's field of view. The underwater forest across the no-cut research zone seems lush from Hertzog's vantage, green mats tipping toward yellow and orange in the sunbright, shadowed only infrequently by torn rags of cloud, the lolling seaweeds corrugating the otherwise smooth surface of the sea. He would estimate about an equal square footage of forested to unforested water across the zone, though who knows how much cut rockweed lingers below the surface, which he can't see? The thick mats capture flecks of rubbish from the human realm here and there, marring the vista: a crumpled aluminum can exploding against the sun like a camera flash, a piece of white cardboard or Styrofoam, maybe, slanting upwards from the weedy surface like a shark's fin, a tennis ball of all things propped dead-center of one of the mats like the yolk of an egg.

The team lingers for quite some time at each rockweed patch before making their way back toward the vessel, swimming quite a ways every twenty minutes or so to report their measurements for Hertzog to record on the laptop. The small girl, Kelsey, surprises him with her impressive freestyle stroke, all high elbows and strong pulls. Treading water, they read the numbers they've scribbled in black on some sort of white wristband they've slid over their wetsuit sleeves. A greater and greater density of green detritus clings to Taylor's black beard, he notices each time Taylor returns with Ross to report his data. He would look like some sort of Neptune of the sea were it not for the zinc oxide he's pasted across his nose.

Hertzog should be bored, but he's not bored. While the Hinshaws and their students perform their necessary work, he sits on one of the raised swivel seats at the console, his feet up on the gunwale, watching his companions work the patches with their orange measuring cords. He traces the flight of terns and gulls, along with the black skimmers, and the progress of the wispy clouds buffeted northward by the wind. He observes an enormous adult eider and four of its dark ducklings dabbing at a patch of sea vegetables a fair distance from the team. He thinks about Ellen and wonders what she's doing now. He concentrates on his breathing, pulls through his nostrils deep draughts of spruced air mineralized by the saltwater, and also smells the deeper vegetal notes of the seaweed and its associated creatures. He wonders why he never sought out the open ocean for its restorative powers. It seems a pity to receive this introduction so late.

After an hour or so the outcroppings inshore begin to show their shaggy heads. Sandpipers with their long thin bills and larger seabirds descend upon the rock islands, picking through the layered thickets. The funky vegetal and animal aromas edge out the cleaner salt and spruce smells. It finally occurs to Hertzog why the Hinshaws and their research assistants started their work so far inside. It's a race against the tide. They must collect their measurements while the tendrils sway freely in the water.

His gaze settles closer to his immediate circumference. He likes staring directly down from the gunwales into the green shallows. He can see individual flecks of algae in the pellucid water, the flash of whitebait now and again, the shadows of larger creatures lurking beneath. A rockweed patch corrugates the water's surface not ten feet from the stern, close enough that he can make out the inflated bladders beading the rusty tendrils at frequent intervals. He can't say that he's ever spent much time, or any time, observing seaweed, itself. His eyes have ever been drawn to the creatures associated with these patches higher on the great chain of being, like the eiders. But there's something about the way the seaweed lolls with the current, the seen and unseen architecture of the plant perfectly designed over millennia to sprawl just so at the ocean's incoming breath to claim its portion of the liquid estate, reap the solar and saline advantages of the intertidal zone. For whatever reason, he had always inferred something small and desperate about the rockweed's amphibious existence, clinging to the granite outcroppings for a tenuous hold. Yet the rockweed knows exactly what it's about, it occurs to him, in its own inscrutable rockweed way. He reaches down to brush the water with his hand, bothering the surface. The cold surprises him. Not for nothing Hertzog has preferred the freshwater Bowl for his daily exercise all these years. He squints up and away, beyond the closest patch of rockweed, to count the members of the research crew, sea froth spewing from their snorkels as if they were puny marine mammals.

The party finally returns to the vessel to board, first Stacey and the girls, then Taylor and Ross a few minutes later. They give each other fist-bumps on deck for their job well done and report their final measurements to Hertzog. They've been able to make faster work of it than usual, all of them in the water, Hertzog along as the safety on the vessel. They strip off their wetsuits and change into their dry clothes, doing so rather artfully beneath beach towels they secure about their waists and (in the case of the women) their tops too. Taylor, as soon as he changes, looks over the data Hertzog has entered into the laptop, issuing various words and grunts of affirmation upon reviewing and saving each document.

"Well, what do you think, David?" Stacey asks, reaching up to remove one of the elastic ties from her hair, then another, combing the freed blond and black strands with her splayed fingertips.

He tells her that he enjoyed helping out with the research and that it's pretty out here, except for the stray pieces of trash. He liked the eiders. The rockweed seems pretty healthy too. He's not sure why he adds this last bit, which Taylor seizes upon instantly.

"Yeah, if you don't know how to look, sure it looks healthy." He glances up from the laptop, then shuts it closed. "What's a little less biomass to the human eye? A few more yards of open water or so between blankets of protective weed? Or a patch of dense olive-brown fucus branches where more slender tendrils of ascophyllum used to be?"

"I take your point," Hertzog says. He was only making conversation. He hardly wishes to debate the matter of the intertidal region's health with Taylor, who suddenly seems a bit prickly.

"Even when it's not replaced by fucus"—Taylor won't be deterred—"the ascophyllum grows back differently once the apical tip is cut. It's more bushy with all these volunteer shoots, not unlike trees after they're pruned back."

"Less languorous and willowy," Stacey says. "You have to see it underwater to really appreciate the difference, how a regrown stand of rockweed functions in three-dimensions, underwater. Fronds. Bladders. Epiphytes attached here and there. It's quite amazing, really—how seaweed responds to the insult of harvest. We're just figuring this all out, which is why Taylor's a bit grumpy."

"Hey," Taylor protests mildly. Hertzog senses that Taylor and Stacey offer this lesson not merely for his own benefit but for their students' benefit. The kids have ceased stuffing gear into mesh bags and stand rapt at attention, bending their heads on their necks at canine angles to better aim their ears toward the sounds.

"Here's the thing, though," Stacey continues. "The response of an individual specie to our meddling, however impressive, isn't necessarily good for the biotic community as a whole. We haven't had time to set up any research controls and parameters to study the phenomenon of altered density to the regrown stands, post-harvest. But we need to. Because who knows the impacts to the ecosystem up and down the chain from a change like that in the biome? Periwinkles, scallops, crabs, urchins, mussels, tubeworms, isopods, whelks, scuds. Then all the fish and seabirds that feed on them, like the eiders. Biomass all by itself is just like the clunkiest way of all to measure impact."

"But it's not in the interest of the industry to use nuanced metrics," Taylor says. "The cod fishery seemed great to everyone for a long time too. Until it wasn't. They just came up with better and better technologies to clean the bottom of fewer and fewer fish. They didn't look at what they'd rather not see, how sick the fishery truly was."

Hertzog's insides register Taylor's words like something electric, though he can't quite put a thought to his feelings before Stacey begins speaking once more.

"Even the greenish color of the water itself isn't so great," she says. "Too many nutrients from our runoff. The salmon farms, paper mills and whatnot. Some think that's why the herring hasn't been as thick last couple years, why the shedders haven't come in this year like usual, why the lobsters have stayed deep."

"Oh," Hertzog says. He hadn't considered that the green color, the tiny algae catching the sun, might warrant concern.

Taylor fires up the twin-engines at the console, as if he's said his piece. "Pull up the anchor, Ross?" he asks, Ross bounding to the pulpit at the bow. The odor of gasoline exhaust overtakes the marine odors while Ross retrieves the anchor line, hand over fist.

"All made worse by global warming," Maddy says while they sit there idling, retrieving the thick cord of her dreadlocks from inside the back of her T-shirt. "Like Professor Hinshaw says, it's amazing what you don't see even if it's staring you right in the face."

The words pierce him. Again, he does not know precisely why. Perhaps because they echo Thoreau's sentiments expressed multiple times in his Journal, but most eloquently in one of his last essays, "Autumnal Tints." He can summon the lines from memory. *Objects are concealed from our view, not so much because they are out of the course of our visual ray as because we do not bring our minds and eyes to bear on them; for there is no power to see in the eye itself, any more than in any other jelly. We do not realize how far and widely, or how near and narrowly, we are to look. The greater part of the phenomena of Nature are for this reason concealed from us all our lives.*

Thoreau's words, and Maddy's words, and Taylor's words before her, cut close to the bone. And now he realizes why!

"Ellen."

He sounds his daughter's name the moment it arises to his consciousness, but not so loud, he thinks, that it can be heard above the idling engines and the rattle of the anchor's chain, which Ross stores now in the locker.

"You say something, David?" Taylor asks. So Hertzog's voice *had* been heard above the idling engines and the rattle of the anchor's chain.

Ellen. He hasn't seen his daughter at all, not at all! She has stood before him in full view, and he has refused to see her, to see her truly, that is. He sees her only now.

"No," Hertzog replies. "It's nothing."

27

Dec 24th, 1841
I want to go soon and live away by the pond where I shall hear only the wind whispering among the reeds—It will be success if I shall have left myself behind, But my friends ask what I will do when I get there? Will it not be employment enough to watch the progress of the seasons?

H. has returned for the time being to his cozy quarters in the great man's white house. He still nurses ambitions to dig his own burrow after his fox. He has even let slip his intentions to Margaret Fuller, who has taken to querying him from time to time on the status of his "lonely hut," her ostensible support spiced with mockery in the timbre of her delivery and choice of words. *Hut.* A house, albeit a modest one, he hopes to build. Not a mere hut. Margaret's dismissiveness only bolsters his resolve. He would begin housebuilding tout suite, but for various obstacles, most notably his still-sapped strength. He huffs for breath even now as he labors simply to turn the packed earth in the neglected field of the Old Manse, having decided to plant beans for the newly betrothed Hawthornes. The pair shall arrive any day now to their new home and village. His hands smart against the wooden handle of the hoe, blisters rising on both palms. The long weeks of his convalescence have stolen his wind and stripped his flesh of its sturdy shell. He stands upright to gather his breath and study the phrases of a tanager's song. His eyes sting from his sweat.

He bides his time this season of his recovery. He sets to repairing relations with dear Lidian, sews improved leather booties for her hens. The new shoes don't hobble the creatures quite so comically and protect Lidian's fair flesh from their scratching claws while she collects eggs for her custards. He courts young Ellen's monkeyshines and repairs the spring to her music box, though the tinkling notes summon tears to both their eyes in her bedroom. "Now now, dear sister," he says, bobbing her on his knee. *Poor Waldo.* He saunters westward farther and farther daily with pencil, daybook, and microscope, considers walking the breadth of Massachusetts soon, perhaps with Ellery Channing or Margaret's brother, Richard, or with Edward Hoar. Or perhaps alone. He looks and listens for John during his excursions into the wild. *Where shall I find thee, dear brother?* he writes in his journal, his poetic faculties stirring once more from their long slumber. He finally completes the review-essay of those Reports assigned to him by Fuller, his first full-throated piece on natural philosophy, "Natural History of Massachusetts," composes the final draft mostly by woodstove and candlelight in his bedroom beside the library. Completing this work bolsters his shaken faith in the resilience of Nature writ large. The wild realm outdoors, he ever more believes, merits and rewards the closest inspection, each and every natural fact. "The spruce, the hemlock, and the pine will not countenance despair," H. writes in the long piece. His dear sisters were wise and kind to have shepherded him through the outdoors cathedral to hasten his recovery. "Surely joy is the condition of life!" Professing his love of the world through words ever brings H. back to himself.

The colder months, once they arrive, are not without their entertainments. Soon as Walden Pond freezes, H. inveighs upon Nathaniel and Mr. E. and Ellery to join him for a skate. Ellery declines, claiming dyspepsia, but Nathaniel and the sage fasten their great-coats, strap their skates over their shoulders and the three take to the ice. Lidian and Nathaniel's wife, Sophia, join their merry band to cheer them on and laugh heartily at the vision of their earnest ineptitude, Nathaniel overbundled—albeit shivering still—and plodding along like a Greek statue, Mr. E. lashing the ice with choppy strides as if he were intent upon harvesting blocks for the icehouse, holding his arms stiffly before him. H. revels in his more fluid command of his extremities as he carves circles about his companions, hands clasped at his lower back.

"Here, take my hands, gentlemen of Concord," H. says, inserting himself between his friends. They place their mitten'd paws in his bare hands and H. leads them on a more upright and speedy glide. Lidian, from the spruced bank, commends him on his prowess. The next breath, H. notices, she takes pains to shout praise of a similar ilk after her husband and Nathaniel, then lowers her eyes.

Deeper in the woods, the woodchopper's ax *thunks* like the metronome. The fox barks.

This jovial excursion aside, tensions with Mr. E. build over the cold season as the weather draws them toward closer and closer contact indoors.

He wonders whether Mr. E. recognizes and resents the easeful banter exchanged between his protégé and wife, the tender glances Lidian once again directs toward him over the dining room table, the strangely gentle tenor of H.'s voice while he speaks to the lady of the house, and which he cannot seem to modulate. He also cannot wholly check the irascible moods that descend upon him time to time, particularly when he considers his recent losses, his meager literary renown, the dwindling of his prospects, financial and romantic. He intuits, somehow, that Ellen of Scituate has already given over her heart to another fellow, though this doesn't bother him so much. Rather, his position as second lieutenant here is what chafes as his yearnings toward Lidian only grow, as does his fondness for young Ellen. How many hours has he spent teaching her to read, or collaborating with the dear girl to invent great domestic dramas over her dollhouse that H. fashioned from the chest of drawers? "You're the poppa," Ellen ever insists, sliding to him the father doll H. fashioned from a corn husk after the Indians. "You're the poppa." Baby Edith, walking if not quite talking now, provides no dearth of entertainment and even instruction as H. observes her toddling about the house or the winter-defunct gardens and orchard with Lidian or with one of the Irish girls, laying her uncorrupted hands and eyes upon the glories on earth to behold. The sage was correct to note the *force* of the child, though Mr. E.—per Lidian's frequent asides—might spend more time with the little ones under his own roof.

All intercourse with the master seems laced with acrimony.

"Pass the butter after you use it, will you, H.?"

"I'll pass it to you *before* I use it, sir, of course."

"As you please."

"Gentlemen," says Lidian.

Poor Annabelle, the Irish servant, has resumed her custom of taking her meals with the cook.

Something of a relief, then, come spring when Mr. E. arranges with his brother, the Honorable William Emerson of Staten Island, for H. to tutor the judge's son, Willie. The change of scenery might excite his senses and prove an inspiring muse. He has heard tell of the giant tulip and sweetgum trees on Staten Island that grace not their New England latitude. Plus, New York City, the burgeoning literary capital of the nation, looms just a half-day's ferry ride from the island. Mr. E. has already written introductions to a half-dozen newspaper and magazine editors, and other learned men, whom it might profit H. to know. The sage advances him seventeen dollars for traveling expenses, a most generous gesture, albeit one that also reinforces the great man's wishes to be rid of his ward—and his rival for the affections of Lidian and the children—forthwith.

He reports on May 6th to the judge's Staten Island estate, "The Snuggery," tucked behind a wild grape arbor. The luxuriant wilds of the island do not disappoint. He ventures with Willie on daily saunterings to conduct lessons in natural philosophy, lingering amid the meadows, woodlots, and pastures. Painted cups and an unusual red-stamened honeysuckle blanket the meadows along with great thickets of wild garlic. The island cows feast on this pungent herb, which lends the most curious spice to the milk, tasting spoilt to some. He loves to listen to the lowing kine. Fortuitously enough, H.'s arrival on Staten Island coincides with the awakening of the seventeen-year locusts. The creatures sigh all summer from their invisible perches. The lady of the house, Susan, bemoans their monotonous song that fills the air, but H. admires their lusty cries and insatiable hunger as they set about nipping the edges of every green thing. *Life, life, evermore life!* he hears in their ceaseless din. He wishes he had thought to bring Father's flute to contribute his own music to the outdoors orchestra.

When time allows, H. walks either alone or with Willie to the sea. He savors the grand scale of everything about the sea-beach: the roaring white-capp'd water and the giant vessels transporting persons and goods from across the Atlantic, the teeming flocks of gulls and other seabirds issuing their strident oaths, the great thickets of green, orange, and brown seaweeds lolling in the shallows and washed up on shore. He peels back layers of the blankets atop the sand to upset the crabs, periwinkles, and insects, supping through his nostrils the rank, ripe aroma of dead and undead marine life. He strikes up conversations with the fishermen mending their nets on the decks of their beached vessels.

Nighttime in his batchelor's bedroom, he tends to his correspondence and jots musings in his journal by the odorous whale-oil candlelight. He tinkers with the poem to John he drafted some months ago in his journal and sends a copy in a letter to his sister Helen.

Brother where dost thou dwell?
What sun shines for thee now?

He is particularly proud of his fifth stanza, which fairly encapsulates the path of his genius these past months since his brother's death:

Where chiefly shall I look
To feel thy presence near?
Along the neighboring brook
May I thy voice still hear?

He misses John—mostly upon darksome night, having faithfully dispatched his household duties. When tiredness overtakes grief, he winds the music box Richard Fuller gave to him and listens to the plaintive notes above the sighing locusts as he surrenders to sleep.

He misses Lidian, too, he cannot deny.

Yet he dreams also of living a more Natural life.

It would be churlish of him to speak ill of the judge and Mrs. Susan E., who laud him for his mathematical expertise and offer him a wide berth. Yet only the dullest necessities of living seem to interest his harried hosts, who cannot be lured into conversation on the topics so dear to H. Nature. Books. Friendship. Love. Silence. They are not his kith or kin, he realizes even before the sweetgum foliage tips yellow-ward and the locusts fall silent, their scattered corpses consum'd by the island dogs, cats, chickens, and pigs.

As summer yields to autumn, he grows more prickly and impatient with his circumstances. Partly because his few forays up to the city repel him utterly. The mob sends him caroming between its brute shoulders and few editors seem interested in paying him for his essays on nature or social reform. And partly because his room contains no woodstove and he must dance around the judge for reading and writing hours in the heated library. Exacerbating matters, his health flags. A bout of bronchitis follows hard upon the first freeze and seizes his tired lungs. Then a baffling somnolence overtakes him, sometimes during the middle of his lessons with Willie in the library, as if H. had pledged allegiance to the god Hypnos. His hosts implore him to rest, but rest only intensifies his sluggishness. Outdoors exercise helps some, but the leafless trees wintertime oppress him. He searches in vain for stands of evergreen on the island that might house the chicadees and tits he holds so dear. He loves the whole race of pines, these sacred trees. He misses their mentholated odors that perfume all of Concord. Too, he comes to miss dear Lidian even more fiercely.

"You represent to me woman," he writes to her in tend'rest hand by candlelight in his cold room, a thick woolen blanket wrapped around his shoulders, breathing spirits of camphor from his handkerchief to free his clotted lungs. "I think I know your thoughts without seeing you, and as well here as in Concord. You are not at all strange to me." H. marvels at the electric circuit of his affections, unimpeded by the many miles between persons.

He arranges a visit home over the Thanksgiving holiday, assuring his hosts that he will return the second week of December. He pats Willie on the head and tells him that he has made fine progress—more or less true—and that he will see him anon. It may be that H. believes the words he speaks. But then his dear sisters, Helen and Sophia, greet him with chaste kisses soon as he steps off the coach. And the pines drench his senses above the horse dung on Main. And the phlegm clears from his throat and lungs upon his first winter walk with Ellery. And Prudence marvels over the tulip flowers he pressed and dried for her collection. And he delivers a well-received lyceum lecture his third night home on the waxy fruits of winter favored by Concord's hardiest year-round birds—butter-rumped warblers, chicadees and the like. And Lidian touches his sleev'd forearm in the bustling hall to congratulate him on his "commanding oratory." He has not yet called upon Mr. and Mrs. E. at The Bush, for reasons not altogether clear to him at first—then perfectly clear, upon a moment's reflection on his narrow bed in the family home that night. He fears the titanic power of his affections for Lidian. Had not his heart leapt to his throat just hours ago when she but touched his shirtsleeve?

Lidian calls for him at the Parkman House the next morn while he labors in the pencil sheds, earning his keep. Ever her obedient servant, he walks to The Bush after lunch, as requested, fully expecting that he might see the great man too. Mr. E., however, has departed to Boston by carriage to deliver one last lecture at Armory Hall before the holiday is full upon them. "The master of the house is always delivering one last lecture," Lidian complains in the parlor where she—not Annabelle or their other girl, H. notes—sets out tea and biscuits. Lidian knows that he prefers water to tea, but she is enough a woman of the world to consider it unthinkable to set out mere water for a caller.

"Where are the children?" he asks, taking a nervous sip from his cup. "And the Irish girls?"

"I sent them off on an excursion to Acton. I assure you we're alone." H. watches her as she sips at her tea, her downcast eyelashes, then the porcelain cup steady in her hand. He continues to watch her as she nestles the cup into its saucer on her lap almost soundlessly. Have they ever been alone together in this great house? Truly alone? He thinks not. "Come, my dearest H., I want to show you something."

She leads him out of the parlor, across the stairwell to his room beside the library, opens the door for his inspection. It seems untouched since his departure months ago. He notes the linens on the bed, Father's flute atop the chest of drawers, which he neglected to bring to Staten Island, the small chair and green writing desk in the corner he'd purchased with John for their fledgling school, his own daybook notes still strewn across its top. Yet he notes, especially, the fire she has started in the small stove, having planned in advance upon bringing him here, clearly.

"You've kept it just as I've left it." He won't remark upon the fire.

"Yes. It pleases me to spend some moments in your room each day, where I feel your presence most strongly." He feels Lidian's shoulder against his own shoulder, coughs into his hand, his lungs constricting his breath some on account of the family disease, and on account of his rising fear, alone in the house now with the object of his affections, in his very room with its cozy bed and warm fire. He knows now why she has called upon him, but such dalliances are surely the stuff of novels, and of legends, not of his own provincial life.

"Time is short," she says. She wraps both her hands about the insides of his arm, leans her cheek to his shoulder. She speaks, he knows, of their brief time as living, breathing beings on this green orb hurtling through the Kosmos, having noted his cough. Now she has taken him full into her arms, and what is H. to do but fold his own arms around Lidian.

"I've missed you so," she says, her cheek against his throat, tightening her hold. He feels the warmth of her body, the soft breasts against his torso. Never has he held a woman so. His body betrays him, as Lidian surely detects.

"We can't sin so in the master's own house, Lidian."

"Must we speak of sin—of him—now?"

Must he? H. has grown so tired of always—always!—deferring to others. To the wishes of his parents, to John, blessed be his memory, to the State (let's not forget), and to the great man too. Words he has committed to his own journal rise to his mind. *What demon possesses me that I behave so well?*

"I know nothing of such matters between men and women," he tells Lidian, warning her, holding her still in his arms. He feels her lungs expand and contract to catch and release great heaves of fire-warm'd air.

"Fear not, for *I* know something of such matters."

Their passions spent, and right quick, they rise from the bed stealthy as thieves, fumble awkwardly with their garments and their words. Dear Lidian steps toward the stove, opens the grate and jabs at the glowing logs with the poker. She clears her throat. He knows, by these mere gestures, that they will not carry on so in the days ahead afforded to them. The strange exercise of coitus leaves him feeling depleted (which he expected) yet even more alone (which he did not foresee). The physical union, that is, doesn't quite touch the part of him that ever hungers for contact. Sighing now, Lidian seems to sense his discomfiture, or perhaps she suffers from a similar malaise.

"I wanted only to offer you some comfort," he hears her say. She pokes a crusty log, as if to locate her next words hidden beneath. "And receive some comfort in return."

He takes to the ice of Walden alone on Thanksgiving morn but for his fox that slips from the scrim of woods to welcome him home. The creature canters half the distance toward him across the white expanse, sits on its haunches not ten rods off and slants his canine head as if to inquire where H. has been these long weeks. What a fine thing, to be so well known in the woods. What does it matter that he may never be known to a wife? He feels not the slightest bit sluggish these winter days in Concord, it only now occurs to him. He feels awake and alive here at home. H. will not again abandon his fox or these dear local woods. He returns to the Snuggery on Staten Island before the New Year only to retrieve his belongings and offer a more proper farewell to his kind hosts and to young William.

"I hope you feel better with Uncle Waldo and your family in Massachusetts," the lad says, which thickens H.'s throat.

H. sleeps in John's old room in the family home to wait out the winter and contemplate housebuilding. His flailing attempt at lovemaking with Lidian evermore convinces him that he ought to pursue a more spotless version of congress. He works long hours beside his father in the pencil sheds. Through tweaking the burs to his mill, he finally perfects the recipe to effect optimal viscosity of a cylindrical graphite capsule to insert into the drilled hole of a single cedar case. Mr. E. mails three pencils to his artist-friend, Mr. Cranch, who attests to its superiority over the more costly German models. The great man's overture of kindness assures H. of Lidian's discretion. He takes long walks to reacquaint himself with his winter woods, meadows, swamps, frozen ponds, and hillsides, and calls upon particular favorite trees spared the ax in his absence—pines, alders, and oaks—placing his palm upon their trunks, gazing up into their misted canopies. *Ah, Greybeard. Remember me?* He listens to the phoebe's piercing song in Walden's woods to hasten spring's arrival, watches it bob its tail from its perch as these perky phoebes do. He feels closest to John during these jaunts, his senses taking in the local phenomena so familiar to his brother. The ice whines most curiously as it thaws. He composes a new couplet for his elegy.

What bird wilt thou employ?
To bring me word of thee?

He secures an invitation, via Douglass, Garrison, and Ballou, to deliver a speech decrying slavery at Boston's Armory Hall, challenging (not without a modicum of guilt) the great man's more temperate recent remarks at said venue. "I know of few radicals as yet," he exhorts, "who are radical enough!" He repairs the shoe-leathers of a few townsmen to supplement his income as pencilmaker and sometime orator. Stitching sole to toe cap, throat, and vamp, he contemplates stitching together planks of pine with mortise and tenon. Surely, Mr. E. will permit him to take up housebuilding on his "Briars," as Ellery calls the great man's newly expanded holdings beside the pond. To stave off further incursions from the railroad, the great man has purchased several shoreside acres at Walden. H. fancies one cove, in particular, not far from the road, but a fair distance from the Concord & Fitchburg track that nears completion. H. ought to cut wood and collect stones for his foundation.

The ground is nearly unfrozen and might be broken, presently. In this way he shall dig to his own roots and change his life.

H. and Edward Hoar enjoy water privileges on the river the first warm day of the season. The day starts off splendidly. Perch and pickerel fairly leap over the gunwales of Edward's boat. It takes but an hour to secure their supper. The two row the better part of the morn with their mess of fish to Fairhaven Bay and set up camp by Well Meadow Brook. H. gathers kindling with Edward, who proposes to clean the fish with his jackknife if H. will start their cook-fire. The kindness of the offer does not escape him. Edward knows that his friend shrinks from the viscera of fish and fowl and would just as soon nourish himself on bread and potatoes and wild apples of sourest vintage. To spare his back, H. nurses their blaze atop a pine stump, having earlier begged a match from the nearest farmer ploughing his fields. It doesn't occur to H. to clear the blond grasses licking the stump. How many campfires has he manned over the years without incident? The flames mesmerize H.'s senses and usher tender thoughts of Lidian. And tender thoughts of John, too, roasting their paltry pigeon over a larger fire not so very long ago, and not so very far away. The dry southwest wind licks his new beard and rouses the flames. Stoking the fire absently with a stick he doesn't even notice that the blaze has leapt from the stump to the blond grasses other side, though he ought to have smelled the burning hay-smells.

"Gadzooks H.!" Edward rises from his fish-cleaning labors and stabs his bloody jackknife toward the calamity. "Fire! Fire!"

Edward's alarm finally returns H. to his senses. He sees now the dancing flames beyond the stump's circumference; he smells the burning hay-smells.

The two young men try to smother the spreading flames without burning themselves, ripping grasses with their bare hands and stamping their feet. But it's no use. Funneled by the cruel wind as if on a gunpowder trail, the purpling blazes crackle in a broad swath across the brush toward the young alders and spruce at the edge of the woods. "You're afire!" Edward warns, beating the flames from H.'s muslin shirt with scorched hands, both men retreating toward the river.

"It's no use!" H. cries, ripping his shirt over his head, casting it at his feet, stamping out the flames from the cloth. He dashes toward the boat for the board used as their seat. Edward follows and grabs an oar. They renew their efforts to smother the blaze, but these new weapons in their hands only fan the flames. A mint-smoke aroma of burning spruce fills the air. A chicken hawk screams overhead.

"Where will this demonic creature end?" Edward cries, dropping his oar.

"It'll jump the hill!" H. shouts. "It'll tear over the woods and devour the town!"

They split up to warn their neighbors and gather reinforcements. Edward takes the boat downriver while H. dashes toward town through the woods. The farmer who leant him the match now splits logs for the woodpile outside his barn, but seems little interested in H.'s breathless report.

"It's none of my stuff," he mutters stupidly, returning to his chore.

The next farmer down the road, however, sprints back to the scene of the struggle with H. to confirm the severity of his report. The two pass a woodchopper fleeing the fire in the opposite direction, gripping his ax with white-knuckles. "Great Scott!" the rustic fellow warns. "Turn about!"

"I'll run for help!" the farmer says, bolting back toward town on the woodchopper's heels. H. follows for several strides, until the farmer halts for a moment to protest. "You're too knackered to be of use, man! Stay!"

H. obeys. Panting from his exertions, he knows that he should do something while he awaits reinforcements with their shovels, axes, and hoes. Yet what can he do in the face of such a calamity, exhausted and alone and half-naked? He might as well gain a more proper perspective on the conflagration. He lumbers to the highest rock on Fairhaven Cliff and looks down upon the ginger waves lapping over the spruce, oak, and birch canopy, the whitest smoke pluming southwest. He ought to be horrified and ashamed by what he has wrought. And he does feel deepest regret. Yet not horror and shame, quite. A separate emotion stirs his innards, surprising him. Wonder. This awful spectacle before him prompted by his own hand. H. has never felt so—what's the word?—*involved* in nature. As if he were thunder and lightning made flesh. With this terrific fire H. has staked curious claim on these woods in a manner transcendent of Hubbard's and Wheeler's paltry paperwork.

H. faintly hears the rapid chime of alarm bells below the crash of a poor tree felled by the fire. Oh, what foolish blazes H. has set in Concord these last months! Townsmen, he knows, hasten now to the fight. He will join them all the day long to extinguish the fire, cut trenches to halt the flames' advance. Thereafter, he will throw himself upon the mercy of his elders, make recompense as the powers-that-be see fit. Neighbors, years hence, he somehow glimpses, will grouse behind his back: *Woods-burner. Burnt-woods. Fire-starter.* He will not acknowledge their wicked oaths. Nor will he speak or write of these curious insights that come to him unbidden. All that has transpired before this crisis—his foundering efforts as schoolteacher, his fraternal strife over lovely Ellen of Scituate, his quashed marriage proposal and piteous heartbreak, his cuckolding of Mr. E. and general covetise, the recent death of dear John and young Waldo and his own convalescence—he sees now as mere prelude to the heroic endeavors that lay before him. His shoulder smarts, finally, where the blaze pricked him in its ferocious infancy.

By H.'s estimate at the end of their travails, the fire has consumed just over 100 acres, maybe 150, but hardly the 300 acres a few persnickety townsmen report to the man from the *Concord Freeman*. He apologizes to his parents, shaken by the liquid blister on his shoulder the size of an egg yolk, and by the faint wheeze that accompanies his breath. They worry in the parlor over the repercussions and plan the family's response, while Helen and Sophia tend to him at the kitchen table, lance and dress his wound. They soak handkerchiefs with spirits that he breathes to restore his smoke-drench'd lungs. Sophia softly cries. Helen tells him he must rest, ushering him to his bedroom. He complies, worried over Helen's own embattled breaths, changes into his bedshirt and slips beneath the sheets. Sleep, however, eludes him.

H. escapes the family home round midnight and walks the darksome streets out of town, crickets sawing in the trees, then feels his way through the chill forest toward the charred acres. The rising carbon odors lead him true as the compass. The refulgent spring canopy vanishes once he reaches the blighted acres of blackened waste, exposing countless stars salted across the sky. The scorched earth crackles beneath his feet. He walks the entire way to the pine stump where he sparked the blaze just hours ago, though it seems days. The scattered silver carcasses of their fire-steam'd fish wink against the starbright on the ground of ashes. H. sits on the black stump and smells the broiled fish-smells above the carbonized forest; he listens to his noisome breath above the awful silence. Not even a single insect remains here to admonish H. with its complaints. Regret, once more, rises like bile in his throat. How many poor rabbits, chipmunks, and voles had breathed their last in their subterranean warrens? How many bird's nests had tumbled with their trees, nascent chicks boiling inside their encasements? How much wood-fuel for Concord's hearths had been wasted by H's profligate hand? He turns over these thoughts in his head as if they were a dough he was a-kneading, his nostrils drench'd with burnt dust and fish-smell. The next instant, through force of mind, he contemplates the regeneration of these scorched acres, the tender green shoots that will soon rise from these ashes. These woods he holds so dear he will set a-right. He will document the succession of forest trees and advertise to the world whatever truths he gleans. Sitting on this stump, his arched back glossed silver by the bared constellations, he once again glimpses his own rise. This terrific fire marks not so much his ignominy, but his liberation.

28

Hertzog worries about his daughter the whole sleepless night while he listens to the armored insects sawing away, the leaves of the trees sighing beneath the cacophony, casting their fingerprints across the moonlit walls of his bedroom. He has never truly seen Ellen. He knows this now. His visit to the intertidal zone of lolling seaweeds with the Hinshaws and their students reinforced what he has long known, if not quite fully owned, the limited scope of his vision. While Ellen lived under his roof as a child, he was too busy seeing all of Ellen's faults—many of them rather commonplace, in retrospect, as she recently noted. This season of her return, he has struggled to gain a clearer vantage on his daughter, partly on account of her own curious withholdings. She has been hiding her most salient circumstances. Perhaps she meant to test him. Or maybe she feared blinding him by too abrupt a disclosure and intended to reveal herself gradually. Maybe without words, in those very silences that Hertzog interpreted as her infuriating withholdings—while she huffed for breath and stumbled up the Randolph Trail toward the Bowl, while she grubbed out the overgrown rugosa in the backyard and deposited serviceberry shrubs, clasping harebell, and other wild flowers and grasses, spreading pine bark mulch beneath her trembling hands—she meant to show herself entire had he only been paying attention. He has been too slow to bring his mind to bear upon the actual Ellen before him from the moment he glimpsed her rising from the slate stoop of her onetime home to greet him.

He cannot exactly drive out to Cherryfield this morning to check on his daughter. Not after the fiasco of his last visit. He decides over his oatmeal that he will call the farm store's land line and see if Ellen will meet with him somewhere, Cassidy's restaurant maybe. It's too early to call now, he realizes, glancing at the analog display on the old GE oven. To kill time, he waters their new plantings in the backyard with the hose, listens to the rising calls of the juncos and chickadees and traces the complex circuit of their forage across the maples and pines in his yard and on the Hinshaw's property over the hedge. He listens to the buzz of dark pollinators looping between the new blooms and the remaining rugosa flowers as well. A hummingbird's scarlet gorget flashes against the sun and commands his attention as the creature flits between the purple bell-blossoms of their clasping harebell specimens. The sun seems unusually bright this morning, which reminds him that Ellen had trimmed some of the overgrown cedar foliage. He might have spared her this chore.

He dials up the farm store some minutes shy of eight a.m. While his fingers stab the buttons, he wonders who will answer the phone: the young man with the strange wooden piercings afflicting his earlobes or maybe one of the long-skirted young ladies he met sifting through the dried sheets of seaweed culling the detritus and holdfasts. He hopes one of the young ladies answers, each of whom he expects might be more receptive. But no one answers the phone. It doesn't even ring, nor does a discordant chime or recorded message from the phone company alert him to whatever might be wrong. Hertzog hears only a faint click followed by salty static each time he dials, at least seven or eight times, checking the number in the old phone book he has retained and waiting various intervals in between his attempts.

Something is wrong. He feels this simple truth in his bones. He'll drive out to Northridge and the farm, after all. What else more important does Hertzog have to do all day? His wrist aches beneath his cast as he drives between the dark woods toward Cherryfield. He steers with single-minded purpose, scarcely seeing the evergreens or the intermittent houses in various states of disrepair, or Teddy's diner, where Cassidy works, or the few cars and semis whizzing past in the opposite direction. He scarcely smells the ripe tree funk air out the open window or hears the Dopplered notes of the birds interrupted by the occasional bark of a country dog, the whirring blades of a helicopter somewhere overhead.

Yes, something is wrong up at the farm. Hertzog knows this even before the carbon and chemical aroma outmuscles the tree-funk and manure in the air, even before he rounds the last bend of spruce between neighboring fields, reaches Jude's street-side row of orchard trees and spies the narrow plume of dark smoke rising from somewhere on the Cherryfield property, then sees the police cruiser parked on the berm, its blue lights flashing silently from the roof, sees the two firetrucks that had plowed straight through a tilled field shaggy with greens to park just beside the scene of the struggle—that crappy wood and fiberglass outbuilding, where Jude's rotating assortment of farmworkers (and Ellen?) lived. Hertzog skids across the weed-choked berm to a stop behind the empty police cruiser and bursts out his door. He sees no flames about the half-sunken structure, only intersecting arcs of water from the firefighters' hoses and the gray smoke rising like steam now from the caved-in portion of the building, where they seem to concentrate their efforts.

An older woman in a bathrobe stands arms crossed just up the road a bit, a concerned neighbor, while a larger human cluster stands half the short distance to the catastrophe in the middle of the field. They watch as the firefighters douse what remains of the structure, five or six of them, most wrapped in blankets despite the rising heat of the day, hands covering their mouths, shoulders leaning against shoulders. Hertzog rushes toward the group, his sneakers sinking into the soft earth, nearly tripping over a plowed ridgeline, scanning faces for Ellen, whom he doesn't see. He recognizes one of the girls from the other day, though, her acne-blighted cheek and tangled nest of blond hair capturing his gaze.

"Where's Ellen? Ellen Hertzog!" he shouts, grasping the Dutch girl's blanketed shoulder with his good hand to summon her greater wakefulness. He can feel the thin girl's sharp bones riding beneath the blanket. She stares up at him, her eyes trembling in their sockets. She parts bloodless chapped lips but doesn't speak, discombobulated by the sight of him—half-recognizing him from the other day, maybe—or just traumatized by the fire from which she might have narrowly escaped by the look of things. Hertzog hears the whirring of the helicopter blades once more.

"She's gone," he thinks he hears a young man mutter over the chopping blades overhead.

"What? Huh?" He scans the cluster for the person attached to the voice.

"Ellen'll be okay, David!" the cry of a much clearer male voice resounds from somewhere across the field of shaggy lettuces. Hertzog releases the poor girl's shoulder and lifts his eyes over the blanketed cluster toward the voice. Jude. Barefooted and pajama-bottomed. He seems to have closed the gap from the general vicinity of the fire trucks closer to the doused blaze, having spied Hertzog's approach or hearing his voice, maybe. Hertzog barely recognizes Jude, his hair unrestrained and silvering past his shoulders, his stubbly face fissured with something close to fear, a bruise in its late color stage painting his neck, likely from one of Hertzog's flailing fists some days ago now. The helicopter's blades throb more distantly from the sky as he awaits Jude's next words. "They took her to the hospital at Emmenthaler just to make sure. Like fifteen minutes ago. She swallowed some smoke. She was the last to get out. But she's okay. Everyone's okay." The voice, stripped of its bluster, scarcely sounds like Jude.

"Thanks," Hertzog says, or thinks that he says. For he's already running back across the ridged field, then on the road in the car heading to Mercy, wondering how he failed to notice the ambulance that surely passed him heading the opposite direction on the small highway. He speeds the whole way back to town and the hospital, summoning higher notes from the overtaxed engine than he's used to hearing, his nostrils drenched with the rich fecal odors of Jude's field caked into the soles of his sneakers. He must swerve to evade a sluggish vulture bent over its roadkill just past Teddy's diner.

He reports both Ellen's name and his own name to the security guard at the kiosk just inside the glass doors of the hospital. "I'm her father," he says, to which the guard nods, glancing at his computer screen. The screen sprays the guard's dark face with blue light.

"She's been admitted," he announces. "Room 178." He hands Hertzog an adhesive Guest sticker. "Some sort of fire, huh?" Hertzog nods as he pastes the sticker to the breast pocket of his short-sleeve shirt. "Someone at intake'll buzz you in and show you the way once you get down there."

The door is propped open by the time he arrives at his daughter's room in the west wing, but he knocks in any case, partly to gain his breath so he doesn't frighten her. A muffled voice answers the knock, Ellen's voice, unless he's mistaken. "Come in," he thinks she says. He obeys. His eyes dart toward the far bed where Ellen lies at a slight incline. She lifts a palm above the bedsheets to ward off his concern, it seems, or just to say hello, or both. He notices some sort of clip on her fingernail attached to a cord. A clear plastic mask covers her mouth and nose, which explains her muffled voice. Weak white light leaks through the diaphanous curtain drawn closed on the window beyond her, competing poorly against the urine-hued light of the fluorescents.

"Ellen," he says, approaching her bedside, clutching with his good hand the metal rail, propped up for safety. Hertzog follows the tubing from her mask to a short stand holding a plastic pouch and nebulizer. The fluorescent light sprays those creases across her forehead and eyes, which betray a harsher life than either he or Rebecca planned for their daughter. She wears a sheer powder-blue hospital gown ticked with some sort of design rather than whatever nightclothes she might have been wearing when the fire broke out, nightclothes that might have been drenched with smoke or water, or charred by flames for all Hertzog knows, though his daughter appears uninjured. She lifts a hand to her mask and lowers it to her chin.

"Are you sure you should remove the mask, Ellen?" Tears seem to have streaked straight back from her eyes toward her ears, judging from her wet lashes, the trail of wet flesh past her crow's feet to the damp wisps of hair at her temples. The yellow air seems to vibrate between them. He hears a *click* every so often, which seems to come from the nebulizer. The room smells of strong antimicrobial cleanser perfumed with cloying woodsy notes, as if the floors and other hard surfaces here have been tended to more recently than the hallway outside.

"I'm fine, Father," she assures him, her voice graveled over by smoke or fatigue. "I think the breathing treatment's done, anyway. They're running fluids or something through me too." She raises her far hand, to which someone has taped an IV. He follows the line to the taller metal stand beside the nebulizer from which a bladder of clear fluid drips, drips, drips. He notices the monitor on the wall, broadcasting various numbers and scrolling graphs pertaining to his daughter's vitals, he intuits. "I'm not really crying if that's what you're wondering. I just can't stop tearing for some reason. The smoke, maybe."

Hertzog nods. She asks him to hand her another tissue from the small cardboard box on the complicated tray-table angled over her knees.

"We have to stop meeting here like this," he says as he hands her the fresh sheet he's plucked, hoping to leaven the atmosphere with humor.

"Yeah, how's your hand, anyway?" She dabs at both of her eyes with the dry tissue.

He tells her that his hand feels fine. She nods and then lets her head loll toward her far shoulder, as if it were very heavy.

"So what happened out there at the farm?" he asks, which prompts

Ellen to swivel her head back around, staring at him for a moment as if he were an amusing curiosity.

"There was a fire." Her laconic reply, the tenor rising through the sentence, makes Hertzog smile. She has never sounded more like a daughter of Maine.

"I've gathered that much, Ellen, but do you know how it started?"

She shrugs her shoulders.

"Electrical, I bet. That place—" Hertzog manages to check himself rather than decry Jude's half-assed ways. He always knew something bad would happen out there with one of those cheaply constructed outbuildings, though he tended to imagine wintertime catastrophes involving heavy snows, collapsed roofs, or carbon monoxide poisoning.

"Probably right," Ellen says. "There was a weird smell. I think that's what woke me."

"Thank God."

A crisp two-beat knock on the hollow door announces the nurse's visit the split-second before he glimpses the young woman's entrance on silent shoes. She introduces herself brightly to Hertzog, all high-ponied and purple-scrubbed, seems pleased to see that her patient has a visitor. Hertzog retreats to the periphery to let her do her job. He reads her name, Abigail, scrawled in purple marker on the whiteboard that he hadn't noticed before. There's nothing written on the line designating TODAY'S GOALS. He refrains from badgering Abigail—or Abby, as she introduced herself—with questions while she scans the numbers and graphs on the wall-mounted monitor, checks Ellen's IV drip, the nebulizer and its plastic pouch, while she listens to Ellen's heart through a stethoscope and issues directives on various breaths she instructs his daughter to take. Hertzog studies Ellen during the brief exam. He marvels at how nicely she accommodates Abby's requests, leaning forward now so that the nurse can place the stethoscope's diaphragm against her back. Hertzog holds his breath for whatever reason as Abby listens to her lungs. He hears the big hand of the clock on the wall take a half-step backward then a louder step forward.

It's a little thing, maybe, a grown woman following simple directions from a nurse. All the same, Hertzog isn't used to seeing his daughter negotiate these ordinary moments, working her way into the world of others. "Dr. Jaffrey might discharge you later today," the nurse says once she completes her exam, wrapping the earpieces of her stethoscope around her neck. "No promises, though." She replaces the plastic pouch connected to the nebulizer with a new one, explaining that the doctor has prescribed one more round of medicine. Steroids, Hertzog imagines, but doesn't ask. They can start up the nebulizer again soon as they like, Abby says, gesturing toward the switch on the machine, which she must have flicked off at some point. Hertzog hasn't heard any clicking in a while.

"So wait, Father," Ellen says as soon as Abby departs on her silent shoes, "how *did* you know there was a fire? How did you know I was in the hospital? Did Officer Libby call you or something?" The question must have occurred to Ellen during the nurse's exam.

Hertzog tells her no. Claire hadn't called him. He just needed to speak with her and tried calling first, but the line was dead so he drove out to Cherryfield this morning and saw what was what. Ellen nods as he speaks, staring past his shoulder, weighing his words.

"Why'd you need to talk with me so bad?" she asks, looking him straight in the eye now, which pierces him. He's not used to Ellen looking him, or anyone, in the eye.

And so he tells her: "I'm worried that you're sick, Ellen. Maybe very sick and that I've just been too blind to see."

He pauses here to let his words seep and gauge his daughter's response. He hears the clock on the wall take another half step backward then a louder step forward. But he doesn't lift his eyes from Ellen to look at the clock. His daughter can't hold his gaze any longer, which thickens his throat. He feels his flesh rise on his arm beneath his cast. She lifts the tissue, still in her hand, and dabs at her eyes.

"Is it cancer, Ellen? Is that what it is? We'll deal with it, whatever it is. Just tell me." Hertzog still fears the worst after all these years, having never fully recovered from Rebecca's tragedy, or from Ellen's cancer scare when she was a toddler, from the sure knowledge all parents carry that they might outlive their children.

"Jeez, I don't have cancer, Father. What makes you think I have cancer?"

"I don't know. You have something, though. Yes?"

Ellen's chest rises as she takes a deep breath. Hertzog waits for her words. He hears the climate-control air come rattling through the vent near the ceiling, the squeaking wheels as a gurney makes its way down the linoleum hall just outside the door.

"Yes. I have something."

"Won't you tell me what it is, Ellen?"

"It's MS, Dad. They say I have MS." She looks him straight in the eye again to tell him this. "It's not the biggest deal in the world."

"It's big enough, Ellen." She shrinks at his raised volume, shifts her gaze into the blank urine-lit air past the foot of the bed, and withdraws somewhere inside herself on the bed. He's taken too strident a tone, he realizes instantly. "I mean," he says in a softer voice, "I'm sorry, Ellen. I'm sorry that you're not well." The fresh knowledge sets Hertzog's mind to whirring. He doesn't know very much about MS, not nearly as much as an educated person ought to know about the illness. It's something neurological and progressive, he's pretty sure, something that impedes one's coordination and mobility, similar to Parkinson's, but maybe not quite so bad. Or is this only wishful thinking? He won't assail Ellen with a million questions now. There will be plenty of time for Hertzog to learn all there is to learn about the illness that plagues his daughter.

"How did you know I had something?" She presses the point.

He tells her that it wasn't any one thing that he noticed, but several smaller things: the tremor in her hand while she labored over the watering do-hickey at the pig-pen and while she sipped her coffee and read the newspaper in the kitchen, her unsure footing on the Randolph Trail and even that first time she visited him at the house, the strange way she fumbled for her words when she grew exercised, the way she seemed to know her way around the hospital, as if she had recently been treated, even her leaner frame, which seemed like a good thing at first (even Claire agreed) but maybe wasn't such a good thing. He doesn't tell her about his trip to the rockweed protection zone with the Hinshaws yesterday, Taylor's lecture on the ill-health of the biome despite outward appearances, which finally made something click in his mind about appearances and realities with regard to Ellen.

"This is why you came back, then, right? The MS?" How blithely the name of the condition slides off his tongue!

"Yes, Father." She dabs at her eyes again, flashing her spruce tattoo inside her arm. It may be the cloying woodsy cleanser gusting about in the ventilated air, it occurs to him, that irritates Ellen's eyes. Hertzog hands her a fresh tissue and takes the used one in her hand to discard. She lets him. He feels the warm wet of her tears in his palm. It seems this is all she has to say, but then something bright dances across her eyes once he returns from the trash bin near the door. "It's funny, Father. I didn't think I'd ever come back here. Like, ever. But then my eyes started wigging out on me and my right hand started shaking. The ER doctor ran some tests, ordered an MRI, and then after like a million hours some separate doctor came in and told me I had MS. She brought in some social services counselor to the exam room to help break the news, which only made it worse. I knew right then that I'd come home. Even before Travis bailed. He was my douche boyfriend I mentioned." Hertzog nods. "Funny, right? Because I wasn't even thinking of this place as home anymore before I found out I was sick."

"So you'll stay with me at the house now, I hope," he states more than asks. "It's not like you can go back to Jude's place anyway."

"Sure. Thanks." She lifts a tissue to her eyes once more, dabs at tears Hertzog hadn't noticed. "You sure it's okay, Father?"

"Of course it's okay. I asked you to stay with me the other day."

"Well, not exactly."

He frowns at Ellen's denial. But she's right, it occurs to him as he remembers his recent words over their new plantings in the backyard. He didn't ask her to move back into the house. Not exactly.

"I'm asking now, Ellen," he presses on. "I would very much like for you to move back into the house. We can even take in one or two of your friends for a time if they need somewhere to stay. There's plenty of room." His sudden enthusiasm seems to put her off. She exhales volubly, the breath escaping through fluttering lips. "It doesn't have to be forever if that's what you're worried about." He tries in this way to temper his mood, as if Ellen were a stray cat he fears spooking. "I know that we've never gotten along great," he says. "But here we are now, Ellen. It doesn't have to be like that anymore, does it? People can always change. *I* can change."

This wasn't what Claire thought, he reminds himself. She had said as much when they met on the green weeks ago, when he thought she might now take cream or sugar in her coffee and she had set him straight. People, Claire thought, didn't change. They just became more and more themselves. Yet Thoreau wrote often of the unique human capacity to turn over a new leaf. He can summon lines to this effect from his most famous book, verbatim. *I know of no more encouraging fact than the unquestionable ability of man to improve his life by conscious endeavor.*

Or, *What Champollion will decipher this hieroglyphic for us, that we may turn over a new leaf at last?* Or, writing at least half-symbolically (Hertzog believes now) in "Autumnal Tints," *I believe that all leaves, even grasses and mosses, acquire brighter colors just before their fall.*

"You really believe that, Father?"

"Yes. I do, Ellen. I do now."

He hears the unintelligible glottals of nurses or visitors carrying on in the hall, the whoosh of the plumbing through the far wall as he waits for Ellen to speak again. Her chapped lips twitch as she ponders her next words.

She dabs at her tears with the tissue using her other hand this time, the one with the nail-clip attached to a cord. Hertzog follows the hand as it travels back to the bedsheets above her lap, and then she does a funny thing with it, flicks her thumb against a finger and suddenly Hertzog sees the gold ring, two small sapphire hearts propped sideways, a slightly larger round diamond in the middle. She had finessed the jewels to the proper position on her finger the same way her mother used to do.

"Wait, that's your mother's ring, right?"

"Yeah. She gave it to me, but I never wore it. It was too girly for me back then."

Something clicks. Of course.

"*That's* what you've been looking for all over the house?"

Ellen nods her head against the pillow. "I totally forgot where I put it way back then. I thought about asking you if you knew where it was, but I didn't want you getting all weird about me losing it."

He asks his daughter where she finally found the ring. It comes as little surprise that it was in the basement, of course, on the ledge behind the oil-heater, where he'd heard her stirring about middle of the night. "I don't know why I didn't think about checking there first," Ellen tells him. "That's where I used to hide my weed that I didn't want you to find." She laughs, mildly, at the memory. "You were always snooping around my room for stuff like that."

"Can you blame me?" He says this with a smile, glad that he can summon a nostalgic mood for these difficult years in both their lives.

"I guess not," she says, smiling too, turning her head away from him toward the curtained window. He can tell that she's thinking about her next words so he waits for her to turn her head back toward him and speak, which she does. "I was going to tell you I found it that morning when Magda came over to clean. I just found it the night before. I was wearing it and everything but you didn't even notice. Then you lost your shit at me at the green."

"Yes, I'm sorry about that. I shouldn't have accused you of breaking into the house, even if—"

"Because I never broke into the house. I wouldn't do that. Jude wouldn't do that, either, by the way. I'm not even with him like that. I know you don't believe me, but it's true."

"I know, Ellen. I do believe you."

He does believe her.

"You're right that he's no prize or whatever. But Jude's never been as bad as you and Cassidy thought he was, either." Yes, Cassidy too had lobbied against Jude. Even before his business with Robin LaPointe, likely. Cassidy had mentioned to him that Ellen didn't have much use for her in the end, or something like that.

"I'm sure you're right, Ellen."

He tells his daughter that she ought to start her next breathing treatment now. She nods and places the mask over her nose and mouth, reaches with her hand to flick the switch on the nebulizer, then lolls her heavy head to the side again and half-shuts her eyes. Hertzog hears the machine clicking once more. There are more questions to ask, but for now he doesn't feel the need to speak another word. Instead, he reaches with his good hand for Ellen's hand above the sheets, which she allows without turning to face him. He savors their shared silence. Her hand feels dry and cold. His fingers brush against the ring, which also feels cold. It's cold in the room, he realizes only now. He stands there at her bedside and warms her cold hand in his warmer hand. He hears the slow progress of the clock against the wall. He smells the antiseptic, woods-spiced air. He watches his daughter breathe.

29

After Jan. 7th, 1844
What young experimentalists we are! There is not one here who lived ever a whole human life. And can say what that is.

The labor of housebuilding, at long last, H. undertakes alone. Upon Mr. E.'s blessing, he stakes out a prime patch of terra firma in a small clearing of woods at the north end of the pond. The parcel sits at a mild downslope between road and cove. His doorfront shall face southeast to greet the day's first light leaked across the chilled waters, visible through the wide-gapp'd teeth of spruce. Winter has only just loosed its grip these waning days of March, as evidenced by the few eruptions of darksome melt pockmarking the white sheet of pond ice.

Wielding an axe borrowed from Ellery, he sets to his task. He fells a few young white pines, tall and arrowy, pauses between blows to study the hopeful notes of Concord's early birds this season, the dusky pewee and the prettier lark decked out in its yellow and black courting plumage, their own minds set upon housebuilding. He knows no haste. Having recently scalded so many innocent trees yonder, he dispatches their brethren with utmost judiciousness and care. He savors the few flurries of snow that melt upon his lashes, his generous nose, and handbacks these first days, offering some refreshment to his exercised flesh. He concentrates upon his thoughts, the fine pungent aromas rising from his person to join the mushroomy earth odors, the hot breath in his throat. He takes not one bless'd breath for granted. He worries about his elder sister, Helen, who so bravely suffers the family disease. He walks around the pond to the opposite shore to spy his cove and beach from a new perspective and admires its gentle curvature. He saunters hither and thither when the mood strikes, offering his hale and hearties to the farmers and Irish laborers along his axis.

Working in this peripatetic manner, albeit determined in equal measure, he proceeds to fashion timber, stud, and rafter close to their stumps. Townsmen, and fewer women, heed the summons of his axe over the days to interrupt his labor with amicable queries pertaining to his experiment. *How long do you intend to live as a primitive? Are you not afright at the prospect of winter alone in your small hut? Do you intend to live on vegetable food and pond-water alone?* He is only too willing to chew the fat with country ramblers even as he hews the main timbers six inches square, as he chisels mortises and saws tenons (for by this time he has borrowed additional tools from various townsmen) on the gathering nest of woodchips spicing the air.

He lunches upon Mother's cold beans or buttered bread of his own baking and scans what passes for news in the days-old paper he uses for wrapping. The bread is made all the more delectable for the tangy pitch supped from his sticky, stained fingers, which most meddlesomely adhere to the paper. How on earth the squirrels pick apart the cones for the fruit without matting their fine fur in this gluey stuff he cannot fathom. A brave crow (or least a hungry one) hops across the leaf litter toward him during his lunch one day, cocking its head at a most curious angle. It takes H. but a low whistle at a rising pitch to prompt the bird to bound from the forest floor and nestle upon his shoulder, whereupon H. rewards the good crow's courage with a shard of bread scrounged from his coat pocket. Before long, H. surmises, this clever bird shall be picking his pockets.

He pays heed to the manifold events that transpire over a single day in the outdoors cathedral. He listens to the pond ice groan. He watches a goose lumber across the jigsaw shards, the pond sporting additional craters of dark water these lengthening days. He struggles to translate the creature's bugle-notes, betimes strident or doleful. He detects each ripe odor rising newly from the thawed earth. He marks a black snake lashed like a whip across the rocks in the pond's shallows and waits in vain for it to arise and sup the air. He wonders at the physiognomy that allows for such a protracted immersion. Certain neighbors, perhaps most, would judge him indolent for the manner in which he passes the days. He knows this.

The Irish, their work mostly done, have already begun to decamp from their rustic village beside the fresh-lain tracks. H.'s season of assembly thus coincides with this season of disassembly for these itinerant laborers. Between leisurely strokes of his axe, above the rising birdsong and earth-funk odors, H. hears the occasional strokes of a hammer as one of the men repairs his cart (as he later ascertains) to ready it for transporting his wife and children, and their possessions, up the line. He spies up the slope of his parcel whole families over consecutive days walking the road toward their next site of employ, wheeling in single carts all their essentials: beds of horsehair or feathers, a few pieces of clattering cookware, coffee mills, toolboxes, lamps, salvaged lumber, picture frames, sacks stuffed with coarse clothes and linens, three or four chairs, a hen or maybe two. Surely a lesson resides in such marvelous frugality.

Planing his own wood for floorboards looms as an insuperable task, so he cannot help but take advantage of propitious circumstances. He moseys the dogleg about the pond to the half-abandoned settlement to survey what resources he might scavenge or purchase for a modest sum. Wielding a lamp, a Mrs. Collins offers him a tour of her hillock shanty's dank, dirt-encrusted interior (whereupon H. immediately resolves to purchase two second-hand windows with glass in town for his own abode). He nonetheless admires the fine boards, nearly free of warp or wet from what he can gather in the flickering light. A surfeit of sturdy nails, staples, and spikes, too—Mr. Collins is nothing if not a conscientious carpenter—might be liberated and put to good use. He waits till the man of the house returns from his handyman's errand and purchases the whole shanty for four dollars and twenty-five cents, marking the transaction in his daybook. James Collins, cheered by his good fortune, promises to depart by daybreak next morn so that H. might take possession in whatever manner he intends.

Next day, H. returns with father's wheelbarrow, having resolved to return it loaded with fine sand from the pond for the family's sand paper and stove polish concern. He pries loose the shanty's boards, taking care to draw the stout nails as straight as possible. It takes four trips to haul his load to his plot. A thrush seems to follow the circuit of his ambles back and forth fluting its most cordant music from the lowest perches atop boulders, tree stumps, and fell'd branches, as thrushes do. He totes the boards down the slope to the pond and washes them in the frigid water, offering the raw stuff of his future home this baptismal of sorts. He lays the boards like bedfellows on the still-blond grass to dry in the sun, propping each end on cobblestones to aid the ventilation. It takes but two days to affect straight, sunbleach'd boards.

His sisters next morn mark his jovial mood over Mother's breakfast rolls and currant preserves they insist upon bringing to him. Poor Helen tries to hide her cough. Time at last to dig out his cellar, he relates. They watch on for a short while, then leave him to his business. The shovel bites through sumach and blackberry roots as he digs. The recent tutelage of Father's Texas Street carpenter serves him well. In scarcely two hours he carves out a subterranean warren six feet square by seven feet deep, which shall protect his future cache of potatoes, turnips, and carrots from frostbite. Although they had stoned the Texas Street house cellar, H. decides to leave the sides of his more modest abode un-stoned for shelving, the webbing of sturdy roots through the soil sufficient to hold the earth in place. The woodchuck or even his fox would not find his burrowing skills wanting. He must borrow Father's wheelbarrow once more to gather the cobblestones down at the pond suitable for the chimney's foundation, which takes but two trips.

The first day of May, H. summons friends to raise the frame should they be interested in his enterprise. Oh, what a merry band converges upon his homestead the next morn! Mr. E., Bronson, and Ellery enjoy the amble together from the great man's house, it seems, traversing the southern edge of the pond, then up the rise from H.'s cove. Nathaniel, he supposes, was too busily occupied to join the party. Shortly thereafter, the brothers Curtis descend the mild slope from the road above, while H.'s favorite farmer, Edmund Hosmer, along with his three strapping sons, their sleeves already rolled from their morning labors, shuffle off the road at last. They tote their ladder in a cart, as H. has requested, a squirrel screeching at the impertinence of their intrusion.

How marvelous to have friends in this world!

Upon Mr. Hosmer's wise counsel, and given the ample manpower on hand, they plant the branch-stripped trunk of a whole spruce into the middle of the cellar for a king post and then balance the ridge beam above. It takes but an hour, maybe half again, to raise and secure about the supports the sturdy frame H. has built. He allows Mr. Hosmer's boys to perform the bulk of the labor with square and hammer, mostly overseeing their efforts and rechecking their measurements to ensure his walls will stand straight and true. The modest proportions of his dwelling, framed now amid ground, woods, and sky, take him aback for a moment. He surveys the still-hollow structure from every angle. Once boarded and roofed, it will seem but an ink-stand perched a fair bit from the pond's edge. Yet it will do nicely as writer's garret and home.

H. has prepared at his family's new Texas house two loaves of his raisin bread to reward his companions for their morning labor. He slices the loaves into leaves and pastes them with salted butter, then distributes the bounty to his band. His fellows sit and sprawl in various states of repose upon the woodchips and rusty pine needles on the forest floor, though Mr. E. has deployed a fresh stump as a stool, which will surely stain the seat of his trowsers with its oozing pitch. They chew the strangely sweet bread in silence the first few bites, though a delighted moan emanates from Bronson—or is it Ellery?

Between swallows of their tasty victuals, H. finds himself fielding the few queries of his companions.

"I had thought you intended to devour yourself alive at a farther remove," says Ellery. "Why so close to the road, again?"

"Shall not my fellows profit from the example of my savage undertaking?"

"Might this prove a worthy site for an experimental school?" Bronson asks.

H. thinks not, considering the logistical difficulties.

"What shall you use for your privy?" Burrill Curtis asks next.

This seems a low concern, but he assures his fellows that he will not empty his bowels where he sups.

"Pray, are you certain we can't help with the boarding and plastering, the chimney and roof?" Mr. Hosmer proposes. "Our lot can make short work of it."

He is certain. He wishes to complete the task of housebuilding alone.

"Dost thou hope still to find a wife?" Mr. E. asks. "If so, methinks you ought not to remain too long in your lonely hut."

Mr. Hosmer clears his throat. One of his sons, Andrew, sniggers into his palm.

It smarts some to hear the great man refer to his house, a la Margaret, as a mere hut. It smarts more to hear him refer to the matter of wives. H. tells his landlord that he knows not how long he might remain in his house. He might stay for only a year or two, he says. Or five years. Or perchance a lifetime. He feels it best to remark not upon the great man's reference to marriage.

Mr. Hosmer, sensing the alter'd air, is the first to take his leave, rising and wiping the breadcrumbs from his lap. His boys follow his lead. "Fields won't plow themselves," he says.

Bronson bids farewell next, followed by the brothers Curtis.

Ellery then rises. He wets a finger and holds it to the air, a sardonic preamble to his query. "So, dear friend, when do you hope to take up residence in earnest?"

"Independence Day."

"Of course. A capital notion. Independence Day, indeed."

After clasping hands, Ellery is gone. Only Mr. E. remains, who rises from the sticky stump only after the last of Ellery's footfalls can be heard, prompting H. to rise as well.

"Lidian is with child," he hears the great man say. The words register in H.'s belly like a blow. "The babe shall be with us this summer, it appears."

"Congratulations," H. manages to reply, unsure over the full extent of what Mr. E. means to convey. Yet the great man holds his gaze now, silently, just long enough to clarify matters. H. must lower his eyes. Lidian, of course, was too heroic a soul to sustain their duplicity in light of such developments. He, too, must beg forgiveness.

"I don't—"

"He shall be my second son after Waldo, we feel quite certain." The great man's brave interjection drowns out the birdsong and the words from his protégé that he wishes not to hear. "We shall name him Edward." With this, Mr. E. extends his hand, which H. takes in his own. "I hope you find here"—the great man gazes about at the cabin, the woods, the pond at the downslope behind H.'s shoulder—"whatever it is that you long for, dear friend." H. watches as Mr. E. strides off in the direction of home, hands folded behind him, watches until he disappears behind a copse of trees.

H. stands still for some time after Mr. E. is gone, listening to his harried breath rise and fall in his throat, feeling his heartbeat begin to slow in his chest along with his breath, finally. *Edward*, he thinks, lifting a hand to his mouth, as if to keep something inside. He shifts his gaze toward his framed almost-home once more. He can hear squirrels scrabbling across the branches of a tree, the rising buzz of a katydid, but otherwise all is quiet. The renewed silence, and his sudden solitude, makes something shift inside H. The afternoon light spears through the spruce needles at a certain slant to strike a glancing blow. He wonders whether it is loneliness he feels the split-second before new birdsong pierces the quiet from somewhere high above in the scaffolding of spruce branches. *Here I am. There you are. Here I am. There you are.* This first vireo of the season bolsters H.'s resolve. And the sweet rhodora of the wood shall be a'blooming soon, he knows. And his fox shall come a'calling to greet him at his doorfront. And the chitter-chatter of bluebirds John so dearly loved will soon sound through the Concord skies. He will look for them in the field across the road where he hopes to set out seeds of the common small white bush bean. He has saved ample seeds from the Hawthorne's garden he planted last year as their housewarming gift.

Here I am. There you are. Here I am. There you are. He scans the treetops for the olive body and garnet-colored eyes of the vireo.

H. shall forgive himself all his trespasses. His burnt woods. His bitterest brotherly rivalry over dear Ellen of Scituate. His covetise and cuckoldry. His impulses reptile and sensual. A fate most mysterious rises to greet him. He shall love his fate to the core, swallow whole its fruit without paring—rind, flesh, seeds and all! This is all that he longs for now. The thawing water at this very moment issues the most curious sounds. What's this pond a'doing? These pines and birds, these foxes, woodchucks, and rabbits, these crickets and katydids? He must know more. He shall make his chart of this place and a corresponding chart of his soul, measure how both shores trend and broadcast the results. He shall know by life's end why just this circle of creation completes the world.

Epilogue

The three climb the Randolph Trail this morning toward the Bowl. Hertzog savors the early October woods as he hikes up the steps, several of them newly planked with blond wood. He conserves his breath by not speaking and sups the restorative mushroomy air crisped by fall. The woods seem healthy and fine to his senses, yet he knows enough to know that these wildest swatches of spruce, birch, beech, maple, aspen, and their associates struggle mightily in the altered air, that they aren't even quite wild, anymore, if wild means anything.

"Such a fine job the scout troop does with the trail," Claire says, contemplating the planks of still-blond wood. She plants her feet firmly with each step, Hertzog notices, her soles hardly scuffing the steps at all or skidding across the rocks, dirt, and leaf-litter. "Repainted the blazes this season too," she adds, lifting her nose to the smooth bark of a young birch and its freshly blued stripe painted above the snow-line.

"Yeah," Ellen agrees from the front, clutching the railing for ballast but getting along quite well, better than Hertzog huffing for breath at the rear. His fitness flagged during the long weeks his arm was in its cast. The pallid limb is still somewhat shrunken, but gaining strength by the day.

"Quiet today, ayuh?" Ellen says like a Mainer, maintaining her stride. She's right. The birds, like the summer people, have mostly finished their seasonal business and flitted off to warmer climes, ceding the town to the stalwart locals. The katydids, too, have ceased their whining from the overhead foliage. The maples here mingling with the darker conifers have just begun to tilt yellow-ward; their heavy leaves droop from the branches and seem anxious to join the moldering remains of last year's leaves crusting the forest floor. The low-bush blueberries sprawled across the rocky earth here and there have finished fruiting weeks ago.

"I'll take the quiet," Hertzog replies through his labored exhale, alluding none-too-subtly to the absent summer people, their recompense for the absent birds and blueberries, the slumbering katydids and the soon-to-be bare deciduous trees.

"Me too," Claire says. Shoulder-season now, they might enjoy the trail and Bowl entirely to themselves this morning. The fall-foliage tourists won't be arriving for a month's time and never quite come in droves to their backwater, given the conifer rule that mostly obtains.

They reach the switchbacks and follow the milder incline up the mountain. This allows Hertzog to regain his wind, but not so much that he still doesn't welcome the chance to rest when Ellen stops and leans down to pluck a glossy wintergreen leaf amid the more copious sweetfern and blueberry shrubs. She plops a morsel into her mouth.

"Yum," she says, just after flicking the spent shred from her lips to the ground.

"Good spotting," Hertzog says. The leaves overhead upon a brief gust offers Ellen their applause, as well, loud enough that he angles his head to identify the tree as a striped maple. He's always liked these particular maples and their audacious goose-footed leaves.

Ellen continues to lead the way, while Claire and Hertzog follow. The trail is wide enough here on the switchbacks that Claire and he can walk shoulder to shoulder behind their young leader. Ellen, perhaps to assure them of her vigor, sets an impressive pace that makes conversation impracticable. Hertzog focuses upon his breath, the beating of his heart, and his ruminations. How spectacular to have raised a child who knows wintergreen from sweetfern. She has done so well these past weeks since the Cherryfield fire. The new anti-inflammatory medication prescribed by Dr. Ramasamay has alleviated most of the stiffness in her limbs and joints, even the strange pain in her eyes that sometimes plagues her. She's finally called upon her old friend, Cassidy, who's visited them at the house a couple times with her boys, for whom Hertzog set up the old badminton net. His daughter has even begun working about twenty hours a week for Gilbert Wisner at Meadowsweet Nursery, who'd been looking to reduce his own hours for some time (although Hertzog cannot dismiss the possibility that Gil was mostly motivated by the chance to do something kind for the grown daughter of Rebecca Hertzog). Ellen could probably afford an apartment of her own in town, at least a nine-month off-season rental, but she has made no gesture in said direction. Hertzog hopes she won't leave their house anytime soon. He likes sharing his home with his grown-up girl. He had forgotten the simple solace of cohabitation with another soul. He savors especially the smallest daily evidence of Ellen's hereness in the small corner of the world they once again share: the creaking of the stair's joinery beneath her modest weight, the whoosh of the plumbing upon her command, the faint rosemary aroma of her shampoo that lingers in the humidified hallway after her evening shower, the slant of her small hiking boots nested beside his own on the wood floor of the mudroom, her fleece jacket hanging from its peg just above, the murmur of her voice outside through the thin window-panes of his study while she carries on over the hedge with Stacey or Taylor Hinshaw.

Ellen offers him a wide berth while he labors in his study—writing what has turned out to be a strange hybrid work imagining Thoreau's young life, his romantic travails, the loss of his brother and young Waldo, his search for a home and for love in the Cosmos, the consummation of his known affections for Lidian Emerson. He suspects the book, this fancy of his, will never see the light of day. But that's okay. Sometimes, rarely, Ellen will rouse him by shouting from the bottom of the stairs. *I'm heading up to Hannaford for oat milk, Father. Need anything?* People, Hertzog believes once more, were meant to be with people. He had forgotten. Not for nothing did Thoreau live nearly his entire life in the family home. People, those few who still thought about Thoreau at all, tended to lambaste him for his hypocrisy on this front. Some rugged individualist! (Others continue to assail him as a misanthropic crank, so it's not so easy being Thoreau these days.) Hertzog, for his part, used to feel sad that Thoreau never found a romantic life partner. But he doesn't feel this way, anymore. How wonderful a family home. How wonderful to enjoy any sort of family happiness, romantic or otherwise, in this world.

As Hertzog ambles up the trail, measuring his strides against Claire's strides beside him, he can't resist mulling over the possibilities for Ellen, and for himself, and for them all. What a season of change it has been for the family Hertzog. It takes his breath away.

Here I am. There you are. Here I am. There you are.

The piercing birdsong halts them in their tracks

"What type of bird is that again?" Claire asks. She stands so close to him that her shoulder brushes against his own shoulder as she gazes up at the maze of branches toward the hidden creature. He savors Claire's contact, this most ordinary intimacy he hadn't thought to pursue in years and never imagined he would once again realize.

"Red-eyed vireo," Ellen responds. "Right, Father?"

"Right." This bird that Thoreau also knew and loved. She knows red-eyed vireo just as she knows wintergreen and manifold other local phenomena—animal, vegetable, and mineral. It isn't such a little thing. They continue to look up into the forest canopy for the creature, but it's hidden pretty well behind the riot of leaves.

Here I am. There you are. Here I am. There you are.

"Wow," Ellen says, "shouldn't they all be gone by now?"

Hertzog tells her yes, that most of them have probably already migrated and the rest will be off any day now for the tropics. "But they'll be back," he says.

They soon reach the trail's crest and follow the descent. This is farther than he had hiked with Ellen on the trail the last time they were here, while small-time burglars milled through his house for opioids and cash. He's not altogether convinced that Ellen will make it all the way to the pond, even though they've packed their swimsuits, even though this was Ellen's idea.

He smells the iron and algal aromas of the water the instant before he glimpses the liquid eye through the foliage. He wonders whether Ellen sees and smells the water too. Then he hears his daughter's audible exhale and knows that she does, though she doesn't break stride. The trail dips below the lip of the pond, which disappears for several yards until the rocky path rises once again to its level. Ellen finally halts in her tracks and places her hands on her hips, the greater part of the Bowl's circumference visible behind the prison-bar trunks of tall spruce stripped of their lowermost foliage. Claire and he advance to Ellen's side. He can hear his daughter breathing as he admires her healthy shock of hair, barely restrained by its elastic band, curly tendrils adhering to her perspired forehead and cheeks.

"It looks so small."

She seems vaguely disappointed.

"It's never been very big, Ellen. It's just a pond. That's all it's ever been."

A kingfisher's rattle echoes from somewhere over the water and pierces Hertzog, more so than usual. The bird's call doesn't seem to register with Ellen, thankfully.

"Pretty, though," she says. "It's still pretty."

"Is this the first time you've seen the Bowl since you've been back?"

Claire asks, neutrally. She's been awfully good with Ellen these past weeks. Interested in her, but not too interested.

"Yeah," Ellen replies, her glazed eyes still fixed on the pond through the bars of spruce. "I was planning to come here that time I hiked the Spring Trail soon after I got back. That time you said you heard me?" Hertzog had recently told Ellen that he thought he heard her on the trail before she surprised him on his stoop months ago. "I just couldn't do it. I didn't want to see it."

"Shall we head back?" Claire proposes. "There's no reason you should have to visit the Bowl if it bothers you." She turns toward Hertzog, summoning his opinion.

"Yes, Ellen, we can head back now if you want," he says, though he doesn't feel they should head back now.

Ellen doesn't say anything right away, just weighs the proposition with an almost imperceptible nod of her head. The green aromas of the water fairly drench Hertzog's nostrils now along with new minty odors of the woods. He hears a small animal, a squirrel or chipmunk, rustling across the ground confettied with the earth's crisp detritus. The tender skin on his weak arm rises to court the fragrant breeze filtered by the forest. He feels his hot breath travel the length of his throat and tastes the spearmint currents upon each inhale. All his senses are on high-alert as he awaits Ellen's words.

"I always thought it was my fault," she finally says, staring dazedly at the water through the spruce. Hertzog glances at his daughter and then follows her eyes back toward the Bowl. A ripple from the cool wind blurs its dark surface, or does the blur originate in his own eye?

"I know you did, Ellen. I should have tried harder, much harder, to let you know that it wasn't your fault. That it wasn't your fault at all. That it was my fault if it was anyone's."

He hadn't fully realized until just now that he had withheld from his daughter such outright assurance. For part of him had blamed Ellen—Jude wasn't entirely wrong about this—the small part left over after blaming himself and blaming Rebecca and blaming the universe.

"It was just a freak accident," Claire says. "No use doling out blame."

Hertzog watches his daughter's slow nod.

"She loved you an awful lot," he tells Ellen, who takes an audible intake of oxygen, as if breathing in these words.

"I know," she says. "I know she did."

His eyes alight upon Rebecca's girlish gold ring on his daughter's finger, accented by those small sapphire hearts propped sideways, the one that Rebecca had given to Ellen years ago and that Ellen had found in her little hiding place in the basement. Rebecca would be so happy to see their daughter back in town now and living at home, neither Hertzog nor Ellen quite so alone, anymore. He feels closer to his wife than he's felt in a very long time, thinking these thoughts.

They wend their way the few remaining yards along the trail to the pond's beveled edge and follow the narrower trail single-file the short way south, scaling small boulders from time to time and bracing their hands against the roughened bark of spruce and smoother birch for ballast. They drop their backpacks on the flat surface of the pink granite ledge at the southern shore. Hertzog plops down on the sun-baked rock, expelling a groan that connotes equal portions fatigue and relief. The warm rock feels good against his back as he savors the sudden view of blue sky unimpeded by the forest's canopy. He props himself up on his good elbow to look about the Bowl, his eyes lingering upon the white eyebrow of sand at the northwestern shore. They seem to be the only human souls here, as Hertzog expected. Soon as Labor Day passed, the folding chairs at the public beach were locked in their shed along with the disassembled lifeguard stand and aluminum rescue boat. He returns his gaze to their immediate sphere. A few bugs breaststroke across the tea-stained surface of the water just over the ledge beyond his hiking shoes. Reeds he hadn't noticed before puncture the water's skin along the shallows, fluttering in the breeze like a sparse, foot-tall lawn. He wonders what the Hinshaws would say about these new reeds. A worrisome development, likely. Too many nutrients in the water from the rising temps and the gaggle of summer people, their litter and urine.

"It's frickin' freezing!" Ellen says. She's wasted no time, having already stripped to her swimsuit and waded out to her knees. Hertzog smiles at the starkness of her tan lines, the rosy skin at the scoop of her neckline, her browned forearms and knees below pallid biceps and upper thighs. "Come on, Father, get in already."

Hertzog strips to his bathing trunks and eases himself into the night-cooled water from a seated position at the ledge, keeping only his thinning scalp dry. Ellen, standing a bit deeper, bobs up and down a few times to dunk her head and acclimate to the cold. He sees the kingfisher beyond her hawking its wings above the water closer to the pond's middle, sparing them its rattle while it hunts. They won't attempt to swim across the lake or any such foolishness today, Ellen's condition to consider, those unpredictable muscles. And heck if he'll act the scofflaw while in the presence of his law enforcement companion. He takes his exercise at the Y or the Emmenthaler aquatic center now. Former colleagues greet him with a warmth he hadn't expected and commend him on his stroke. He turns toward Claire, still folding her clothes into her backpack in that fastidious manner of hers, not so different from his own fastidious ways. "The water's fine, Claire," he assures her, as if she needed assuring.

"Yeah, you get used to it," Ellen says, spreading her arms for a few breaststroke pulls into deeper water. She doesn't wear goggles and Hertzog can't tell what she does with her eyes underwater, but her stroke looks good, confident. Cunning Claire finally makes her way to the edge of the granite and scoots herself into the cold water without cringing at all. She takes a few freestyle strokes toward him, then drops her feet and lifts her face, the mossy water pearling on her fine cheekbones marbled with blood. The water comes up nearly to her chin but she can stand. He compliments her on her stroke and then turns back toward Ellen, several yards off now toward the pond's deep middle, where the kingfisher still hawks its wings. Her stroke leaves a small wake.

"Come back now, Ellen!" he cries just as his daughter lowers her head into her glide. His words ricochet off the pond's spruce walls but she can't hear them. "Come back!" he shouts again. Then, louder: "Ellen!"

How can she do this to him? Primordial panic seizes his gut. He hears the kingfisher's rattle now in the sky, but won't take his eyes off Ellen. He must swim out to retrieve her, he thinks, just a split-second before he notices her head bobbing higher from the water's surface as she pauses to tread water. He waves both arms above his head. Claire, too, waves an arm toward Ellen, yet without much urgency.

"Come back!" he shouts.

A bullfrog burps from the reeds, which Hertzog doesn't hear. A coppery fish leaps from the syrupy water, which he doesn't see. "She's fine, David. Don't holler at her. She'll come back."

She'll come back, Hertzog hopes. He watches in silence as his daughter continues to tread water, not so very far off, truly. Ellen's eyes flash against the sun as she shifts her gaze toward his shore. He glimpses in them, or thinks that he glimpses, a perfect reflection of the world that

Ellen sees. The brown pond water beneath her chin. Claire's contours and his own contours. The pinked granite outcroppings amid the foliage. The serrated spruceline below blue sky.

AUTHOR'S NOTE

Direct quotations from Henry D. Thoreau's Journal, specifically from the authoritative edition published by Princeton University Press, *Journal I: 1837-1844,* ed. Elizabeth Hall Witherell et al. (1981), appear as the italicized entries that open half of the preceding chapters. In addition to Thoreau's Journal, I consulted a number of primary and secondary sources by and about Thoreau to imagine, in the rather third-hand way that the terms of my novel demanded, the early years of Thoreau's life. The most significant of these sources include Thoreau's *The Correspondence: Volume I: 1843-1848,* ed. Elizabeth Hall Witherell et al. (Princeton University Press 2013), *A Week on the Concord and Merrimack Rivers* (James Munroe & Co. 1849), and *Walden* (Ticknor and Fields 1854), Stanley Cavell's *The Senses of Walden* (Penguin 1972), Walter Harding's *The Days of Henry Thoreau: A Biography* (Knopf 1965), Robert D. Richardson Jr.'s *Henry Thoreau: A Life of the Mind* (University of California Press 1986), Laura Dassow Walls' *Henry David Thoreau: A Life* (University of Chicago Press 2017), Richard Lebeaux's *Young Man Thoreau* (University of Massachusetts 1977), *Thoreau's Wildflowers,* ed. Geoff Wisner (Yale University Press 2016), and H. Daniel Peck's *Thoreau's Morning Work* (Yale University Press 1990). I encourage readers interested in more fact-based accounts of Thoreau's life and work to start with these fine texts.

I consulted a variety of sources to familiarize myself with the unique flora and fauna of the beautiful state of Maine, but I am particularly indebted to Jim Krosschell's *One Man's Maine: Essays on a Love Affair* (Green Writers Press 2017), Christopher White's *The Last Lobster: Boom or Bust for Maine's Greatest Fishery?* (St. Martin's Press 2018), Maureen Heffernan's *Native Plants for Your Maine Garden* (Down East Books 2010), Russell D. Butcher's *Field Guide to Acadia National Park, Maine* (Taylor Trade Publishing 2005), Susan Hand Shetterly's *Seaweed Chronicles: A World at the Water's Edge* (Algonquin Books 2018), and Rachel Carson's classic, *The Edge of the Sea* (Houghton Mifflin 1955), for its inspired prose and ecological insight, both of which endure.

Acknowledgments

Heartfelt thanks to:

Laura Strachan, peerless agent and friend.

Jaynie Royal, Regal House Publishing Editor-in-Chief, for believing in this book.

The literary magazine editors, who have supported my recent shorter works of fiction and creative nonfiction, giving me the crucial confidence to persevere with this longer work, and who include: Simmons Buntin and Elizabeth Dodd (*Terrain.org*), Kwame Dawes and Siwar Masannat (*Prairie Schooner*), Caleb Berer and Albert Kapikian (*Potomac Review*), Sarah Harshbarger (*Grist*), Polly Buckingham (*Willow Springs*), Ron Mitchell and Casey Pycior (*Southern Indiana Review*), Mark Powell (*Cold Mountain Review*), Lauren Westerfield, Grant Maierhofer and Julian Ankney (*Blood Orange Review*), Lee Hope and Anjali Mitter Duva (*Solstice*), Andrew Tonkovich (*Santa Monica Review*), Tom Jeffreys (*The Learned Pig*), Jonathan Freeman-Coppadge and Carolyn Wilson-Scott (*Oyster River Pages*), Brendan Curtin and Debra Marquart (*Flyway*), and Scott Slovic (*ISLE*).

Fellow writer-friends, for the inspiration of their work and their support of mine, who include: Mike Branch, Joni Tevis, C. B. Bernard, David Keplinger, Janisse Ray, Susan Fox Rogers, Susan Cerulean, Erika Dreifus, Pearl Abraham, Margot Singer, Brittany Ackerman, Jenna Gersie, Rachel Kadish, Toni Jensen, Anna Solomon, Jonathan Rosen, Nicole Walker, JoeAnn Hart, Leigh Newman, Yael Goldstein-Love, Tova Mirvis, Emily Nemens, Emily Strelow and, of course, my writer-colleagues in the Department of English at FAU, Stephanie Anderson, Papatya Bucak, Becka McKay, Romeo Oriogun, and Jason Schwartz.

Professor Bob Burkholder of The Pennsylvania State University, for introducing me in inspired fashion to the work of Henry David Thoreau.

Vanessa Bonebrake, John Potts, Kathy Potts, Rachel Sexton, Rachel Bobich, Lisa Childers, Mike Kohner, Ricardo Costabal, Igor Galati, Brian Pawlowski, Rhiannon Wilson, Alexa Gustin, and the entire AVA Aquatics Swim Group, for the daily training and friendship.

Puranjot Kaur, Heidi Turner, and all the members of the Cold Tits,

Warm Hearts open water swim group on Mount Desert Island, Maine, for sharing beautiful Echo Lake with me and other swimmers "from away."

My colleagues at FAU in the Department of English and the Dorothy F. Schmidt College of Arts and Letters.

Margot Bucak, for reading an early version of this novel and offering useful feedback and encouragement.

My students.

My parents, Stephen and Nancy Furman.

My siblings, Richard Furman and Dana Friedfeld, to whom this book is dedicated.

And to my wife, Wendy, and our children, Henry, Sophia, and Eva.